Daisy Goodwin's work as a TV producer and presenter includes *Reader, I Married Him, Bookworm* and *The Nation's Favourite Poems;* she is also the creator of *Grand Designs* and wrote the script for ITV's *Victoria*. She has edited numerous poetry anthologies, including the bestselling *101 Poems That Could Save Your Life*, and is the author of *Silver River*, a memoir, as well as two novels, *My Last Duchess* and *The Fortune Hunter*. Goodwin reviews regularly for *The Times* and *The Sunday Times* and writes a bibliotherapy column for the *Daily Mail*.

Praise for Daisy Goodwin:

'Sparkling and thoroughly engaging . . . a highly enjoyable and intelligent read'   *The Sunday Times*

'A hugely enjoyable historical romp and a major new talent'
                                                                                          Sunday Express

'Daisy Goodwin's debut novel is a delightful confection – a clash of cultures set in late 19th-century England, embellished with the glittering lavishness that the period implies'   *Marie Claire*

'Delicious and clever and addictive'   Elizabeth Buchan

'Daisy Goodwin has triumphed again. In *The Fortune Hunter* she weaves a rich and textured tale of desire and ambition'   Amanda Foreman

'A sumptuous, scrumptious confection, with country houses, Austrian Empresses and Victorian glamour galore'   Lucy Worsley

'Richly evocative of the period and genuinely involving' *Woman & Home*

'An intelligent and entertaining romp'   *Good Housekeeping*

'Expertly drawn characters, exquisite period detail . . . a sparkling read'
                                                                                                    Lady

By Daisy Goodwin

Fiction
My Last Duchess
The Fortune Hunter

Non-fiction
Silver River

VICTORIA

DAISY
GOODWIN

REVIEW

First published in Great Britain in paperback in 2016 by Headline Review
An imprint of HEADLINE PUBLISHING GROUP

1

Cataloguing in Publication Data is available from the British Library

ISBN (Trade paperback) 978 0 7553 9610 8
ISBN (Paperback) 978 0 7553 9611 5

Typeset in Adobe Caslon by Palimpsest Book Production Limited, Falkirk, Stirlingshire

Printed and bound in Great Britain by
Clays Ltd, St Ives plc

HEADLINE PUBLISHING GROUP
An Hachette UK Company
Carmelite House
50 Victoria Embankment
London EC4Y 0DZ

www.headline.co.uk
www.hachette.co.uk

For Ottilie and Lydia
Mentor and Muse

Prologue

Kensington Palace, September 1835

A SHAFT OF DAWN LIGHT FELL ON THE CRACK IN THE corner of the ceiling. Yesterday it had looked like a pair of spectacles, but overnight a spider had embroidered the fissure, filling in the gaps, so that now it looked, she thought, like a crown. Not the crown that her uncle wore, which had looked heavy and uncomfortable, but the sort that a Queen might wear – lacy, delicate but still strong. After all, her head, as Mama and Sir John never ceased to point out, was extremely small; when the time came, and there could be no doubt now that it would, she would need a crown that fitted.

There was a snore from the big bed. '*Nein, nein,*' cried her mother, wrestling with her sleep demons. When she became Queen, she would insist on having a room of her own. Mama would cry, of course, and say that she was only trying to protect her precious Drina, but she would be firm. She imagined saying, 'As the Queen, I have the Household Cavalry to protect me, Mama. I imagine I will be quite safe in my own room.'

She would one day be Queen; she knew that now. Her Uncle

King was old and not in good health, and it was clearly too late for his wife, Queen Adelaide, to produce an heir to the throne. But Victoria – as she called herself although her mother and everyone else called her Alexandrina, or even worse Drina, a nickname she found demeaning rather than endearing – did not know when that time would come. If the King were to die before she attained her majority in two years' time, it was highly likely that her mother, the Duchess of Kent, would be appointed Regent, and Sir John Conroy, her special friend, would be at her side. Victoria looked at the ceiling; Conroy was like the spider – he had spun his web over the Palace – her mother was caught fast, but, thought Victoria, she would never allow herself to be trapped.

Victoria shivered, even though it was a warm June morning. Every week in church she prayed for the health of her Uncle King, and in her head she always added a little note to the Almighty, that if He did decide to take His Majesty William IV to His bosom, please could He wait until after her eighteenth birthday?

Victoria did not have a clear idea of what being Queen would mean. She had history lessons from her governess Lehzen, and tutorials on the constitution from the Dean of Westminster, but no one could tell her what a Queen actually did all day. Her Uncle King seemed to spend most of his time taking snuff and complaining about what he called the 'Damned Whigs'. Victoria had only seen him wearing his crown once, and that was because she had asked him to put it on for her. He told her he wore it when he opened Parliament, and asked if she would like to come with him. Victoria had answered that she would like to very much, but then her mother had said that she was too young. Victoria had heard Mama talking about it afterwards with Sir John; she had been looking at an album of watercolours behind the sofa and they had not seen her.

'As if I would allow Drina to be seen in public with that awful old man,' her mother had said crossly.

'The sooner he drinks himself to death, the better,' Sir John had replied. 'This country needs a monarch, not a buffoon.'

The Duchess had sighed. 'Poor little Drina. She is so young for such responsibility.'

Sir John had put his hand on her mother's arm and said, 'But she will not be ruling alone. You and I will make sure that she does not do anything foolish. She will be in safe hands.'

Her mother had simpered, as she always did when Sir John touched her. 'My poor little fatherless girl, how lucky she is to have you, a man who will support her in everything.'

Victoria heard a step in the hall. Normally she had to stay in bed until her mother woke up, but today they were going to Ramsgate for the sea air, and they were to leave at nine o'clock. She was so looking forward to going away. At least in Ramsgate she would be able to look out of the window and see real people. Here in Kensington she never saw anyone. Most girls of her age would be going into society by now, but her mother and Sir John said that it was too dangerous for her to be with people of her own age. 'Your reputation is precious,' Sir John always said. 'Once lost, it is gone for ever. A young girl like you is bound to make mistakes. It is better that you don't have the opportunity.' Victoria had said nothing; she had learnt a long time ago that to protest was useless. Conroy's voice was always louder than hers, and her mother always supported him. All she could do was wait.

The Duchess, as usual, took a very long time to dress. Victoria and Lehzen were already sitting in the carriage by the time that her mother emerged with Conroy and her lady-in-waiting, Lady Flora Hastings. Victoria saw the three of them together on the steps, laughing at something. From the way that they glanced over to the carriage, Victoria knew that they were talking about her. Then the Duchess spoke to Lady Flora, who came down the steps towards the carriage.

'Good morning, Your Royal Highness, Baroness.' Lady Flora, a sandy-haired woman in her late twenties who always carried a Bible in her pocket, got into the carriage. 'The Duchess has asked me to accompany you and the Baroness to Ramsgate.' Lady Flora smiled, showing her gums. 'And I thought it might be an opportunity for us to go through some points of protocol. When my brother came to visit the other day, I noticed you referred to him as His Grace. But you should know that only Dukes are called Your Grace. A mere Marquess like my brother,' here the gums became even more prominent, 'is not entitled to such an honorific. He was delighted, of course – every Marquess wants to be a Duke – but I thought it was my duty to inform you of the mistake. It is a small thing, I know, but these details are so important, as I am sure you will agree.'

Victoria said nothing, but glanced at Lehzen, who was clearly resenting Lady Flora's intrusion as much as she was. Lady Flora leant forward. 'Of course, Baroness, you have been an exemplary governess, but there are nuances that, being German, you cannot expect to understand.'

Seeing a little flicker in Lehzen's jaw, Victoria said, 'I believe I have a headache. I think I shall try and sleep in the carriage.'

Flora nodded, though clearly irked not to be given further chances to point out Victoria and Lehzen's shortcomings. Looking at her sallow, disappointed face, Victoria closed her eyes with relief. As she dozed off, she wondered, not for the first time, why her mother always chose to share a carriage with Sir John Conroy and never with her.

Although her headache in the carriage was a ruse to avoid the insufferable Lady Flora's lectures, Victoria began to feel genuinely unwell on the second day of her visit to Ramsgate. When she woke up, her throat was so sore she could barely swallow.

She went over to her mother's bed. The Duchess was fast asleep, and Victoria had to push at her shoulder quite hard before she opened her eyes. '*Was ist los*, Drina?' she said, annoyed. 'Why are you waking me up? It is still so early.'

'I have a sore throat, Mama, and such a headache. I think perhaps I need to see the doctor.'

The Duchess sighed and, raising herself up in the bed, put her hand to Victoria's forehead. The hand felt cool and soft against her skin. Victoria leant against it, suddenly longing to lie down and put her head on her mother's shoulder. Perhaps her mother would allow her to get into her bed.

'*Ach*, it is just as normal. You are always exaggerating, Drina.' The Duchess put her curl-papered head on the pillows and went back to sleep.

When Lehzen saw Victoria grimace as she tried to swallow her tea at the breakfast table, she came over at once. 'What is the matter, Highness, are you not feeling well?'

'It hurts to swallow, Lehzen.' Although the great pleasure of her days at Ramsgate was to walk along the front looking at the sea and at the dresses of the other ladies, with her spaniel, Dash, running around at her feet, today all Victoria wanted to do was to lie down in a cool, dark room.

This time it was Lehzen who put her hand on Victoria's

forehead. It was warmer than her mother's hand and not so soft, but comforting. Wincing and giving Victoria's cheek a stroke, the governess went over to the Duchess, who was drinking coffee at a table in the window with Sir John and Lady Flora.

'I think, Ma'am, that we should call Dr Clark down from London. I am afraid that the Princess is unwell.'

'Oh, Lehzen, you are always fussing. I felt Drina's head this morning myself, and it was fine.'

'To summon the royal doctor from London,' said Conroy, 'would occasion much alarm. We do not want the people to think that the Princess is delicate. If indeed she is unwell, and I have to say she looks quite healthy to me, then we should consult a local man.'

Lehzen took a step towards Conroy and said, 'I am telling you, Sir John, that the Princess must see a doctor, a good one. What does it matter what people think when her health is in danger?'

The Duchess threw up her hands, and said in her strong German accent, 'Oh, Baroness, you always exaggerate so. It is just a summer cold, and there is no need for having all this fuss.'

Lehzen was about to protest again when the Duchess put up a hand to stop her. 'I think, Baroness, that I know what is best for my daughter.'

Conroy nodded and said in his confident baritone, 'The Duchess is right. The Princess has a tendency to malinger, as we know.'

Victoria did not hear Lehzen's reply, as dizziness over-whelmed her and she found herself falling to the floor.

She woke up in a darkened room. But it was not cool; indeed, she felt so hot she thought she must melt. She must have made a noise because Lehzen was at her side, putting a cold cloth on her cheeks and forehead.

'I am so hot, Lehzen.'

'It is the fever, but it will pass.'

'Where is Mama?'

Lehzen sighed. 'She will be here soon, *Liebes,* I am sure.'

Victoria closed her eyes and fell back into the hot fitful sleep of fever.

At some point in that long day, Victoria surfaced and could smell the lavender water her mother always wore. She tried to call to her, but her voice was just a dry croak. When she opened her eyes, the room was still dark and she could see nothing. Then she heard her mother speak. 'Poor little Drina, she has been so ill. I hope it will not affect her looks.'

'Dr Clark says that she is strong and will pull through,' Conroy answered.

'If anything were to happen to her, my life would be over! I would have to go back to Coburg.'

'When the fever passes, I think we should make some arrangements as to the future. If I were to become her Private Secretary, it would mean there could be no . . . foolishness.'

Victoria heard her mother say, 'Dear Sir John. You will guide Victoria as you have always guided me.' Victoria heard a sigh and then some rustling, and then Conroy said in a lower voice, 'We will guide her together.'

'Always.'

Victoria turned her face to find a cool place on the pillow and disappeared into her feverish dreams.

The next time she opened her eyes, there was light coming in through the windows and Lehzen's anxious face bending over her. 'How are you feeling, Highness?'

Victoria smiled. 'Better, I think.'

She felt a hand take her wrist, and saw Dr Clark standing by her bedside. 'The pulse is much stronger today. I think the Princess might have some nourishment, a little broth or beef tea.'

'Certainly, Doctor, I will attend to it immediately.' Lehzen was going to the door when the Duchess rushed in, her hair in an elaborate confection of ringlets on either side of her head.

'Drina! I have been so worried.' She looked at Dr Clark. 'May I touch her, Doctor?'

The doctor bowed. 'Now that the fever has passed, there is no danger of contagion, Ma'am.'

The Duchess sat on the bed and started to stroke Victoria's cheek. 'You look so pale and thin, but your looks will return. We will take such good care of you.'

Victoria tried to smile, but found it too much effort. She thought her mother looked very fine that morning. She was wearing a dress in striped silk that Victoria had not seen before and new diamond drops dangling from her ears.

'Thank goodness I sent to London for you, Dr Clark,' said the Duchess. 'Who knows what might have happened otherwise?'

'I believe the Princess has contracted typhus, which can be fatal, but I feel sure that with the right care Her Royal Highness will make a full recovery.'

Lehzen returned carrying a bowl of broth. She sat down on the other side of the bed, and started to spoon it into Victoria's mouth.

'Thank you, Lehzen, but I will be feeding my daughter.' The Duchess took the spoon and the bowl out of the Baroness's hands. Victoria watched as Lehzen went to stand at the back of the room.

Her mother pushed the spoon against her lips and Victoria let the broth trickle down her throat. 'And now another one, *Liebes.*'

Victoria opened her mouth obediently.

A floorboard creaked loudly as Conroy came into the room. 'What a touching scene! The devoted mother nursing her daughter back to health.'

Victoria closed her mouth. 'Just a little more, *Liebes,*' said the Duchess, but Victoria shook her head.

Conroy loomed over her, standing behind her mother. 'I must congratulate you on your recovery, Your Royal Highness. Thank goodness you have inherited your mother's robust constitution.'

The Duchess smiled. 'Drina is a true Coburg.'

Conroy bared his teeth at Victoria in a smile. 'But now you are on the road to recovery, there is a matter that we must attend to. Unlike you, the King is not so robust, and it is vital that we are prepared for what comes next.'

He reached inside his coat and pulled out a piece of paper covered in script. 'I have prepared a document appointing me as your Private Secretary. Your mother and I think that is the best way to ensure that you will be protected when you come to the throne.'

'Yes, Drina, you are so young and so frail. Sir John will be your rock.'

From where she lay, Victoria could see Conroy's hand resting on her mother's shoulder and the flush that was spreading across her mother's cheek.

Conroy put the paper on the bed next to her hand and picked up a quill and an inkwell from the writing desk next to the window. 'It is all very easy.' Conroy stood by the bed with the pen and ink. 'When you have signed the paper, I will make all the arrangements.'

'You are so lucky, Drina, to have someone who will always protect your interests,' said the Duchess.

Conroy bent down with the quill, and Victoria could smell the ambition on his breath. She looked into his dark eyes, and shook her head.

Conroy stared at her, a tiny muscle quivering at the corner of his mouth. 'I look forward to serving you as faithfully as I have your mother.'

Victoria shook her head again. Conroy looked at the Duchess, who put her hand on her daughter's. 'We just want to do what is best for you, *Liebes*. To protect you from your so wicked uncles. That awful Cumberland will do everything to stop you from being Queen.'

Victoria tried to sit up, but her body betrayed her and she felt tears of frustration coming to her eyes. She saw that Lehzen was leaning forward, her hands clenched, her eyes blazing with fury at Conroy. Her governess's anger gave Victoria heart. She turned her head to her mother and said as loudly as she could, 'No, Mama.'

Her mother's ringlets quivered. 'Oh, Drina, you are still weak from the fever. We will talk about this later.'

She felt Conroy press the quill into her hand and put it on the paper. 'We can talk about the details certainly, but first you must sign this.'

Victoria turned to Conroy and said with great effort, 'I . . . will . . . never . . . sign.'

Conroy's hand tightened around her wrist as he bent down and whispered in her ear, 'But you must.'

Somehow she found the strength to pull her hand away. In

doing so she upset the inkwell, whose contents poured in a great black stain across the bedclothes. Her mother shrieked in alarm, as she stood up to protect her new dress. 'Oh, Drina, what have you done!'

Conroy stared at her in fury. 'I cannot allow this . . . this behaviour. I will not have it.'

He raised his hand, and for a moment Victoria thought he might strike her, but Lehzen stepped in front of him. 'I think the Princess is looking flushed, don't you agree, Doctor? Perhaps you should check her pulse in case the fever is returning.'

Dr Clark hesitated, not wanting to upset his patron, the Duchess. Reflecting, however, that it would be even worse to antagonise the heir to the throne, he stepped forward and took Victoria's wrist. 'Indeed the pulse appears to be somewhat elevated. I think the Princess should rest now – it would be most unfortunate if the fever should return.'

The Duchess looked at Conroy, who was standing quite still, his face white with anger. 'Come, Sir John, we will talk to Drina again when she is more herself. She is too ill to know what she is doing.' Taking him by the arm, she guided him out of the room, Dr Clark following in their wake.

When they were alone, Victoria looked up at Lehzen, who was trying to contain the ink stain on the bedding, and whispered, 'Thank you.'

The Baroness bent down and kissed her on the forehead. 'You were so brave, Highness.' She squeezed Victoria's hand. 'I know that you will be a great Queen.'

Victoria smiled before closing her eyes in exhaustion. She could still make out the faint scent of lavender. She would never forgive her mother for allowing Conroy to bully her like this. How could Mama not see that her own daughter was more important than that awful man? They would come back again, she knew, with their paper. But she would never sign it. They would all be sorry – Mama, Conroy, Lady Flora – for being so hateful. They thought she was nothing, a pawn to be moved about, but one day she would be Queen. Then everything would be different. If only her Uncle King would live until she was eighteen.

Book One

Chapter One

Kensington Palace, June 20th 1837

WHEN SHE OPENED HER EYES, VICTORIA SAW A FAINT sliver of light coming through the shutters. She could hear her mother breathing in the big bed on the other side of the room. But not for much longer. Soon, Victoria thought, she would have her own bedroom. Soon she would be able to walk down the stairs without holding Lehzen's hand; soon she would be able to do whatever she pleased. She had celebrated her eighteenth birthday last month, so when the moment came, she would reign alone.

Dash lifted his head and then Victoria heard her governess's quick footsteps. If Lehzen was coming now, it could only mean one thing. She got out of bed and went to the door, opening it just as Lehzen was putting out her hand to knock. The Baroness looked so comical standing there with her hand outstretched that Victoria started to giggle, but checked herself as she saw the expression on her governess's face.

'The messenger from Windsor is downstairs. He is wearing a black armband.' Lehzen lowered herself into a deep curtsey. 'Your Majesty.'

She felt the smile spread across her face before she could stop herself. Reaching out her hand, Victoria pulled Lehzen up to face her, and was touched by the devotion she saw in the older woman's worried brown eyes.

'Dearest Lehzen, I am so glad that you are the first person to call me that.'

The governess looked over towards the sleeping figure in the bed, but Victoria shook her head. 'I don't want to wake Mama just yet. The first thing she will do is to call Sir John and then they will start telling me what to do.'

Lehzen's lips twitched. 'But you are the Queen, Drina.' She stopped, realising her blunder. 'I mean, "Majesty". There is no one who can tell you what to do now.'

Victoria smiled.

A door opened at the end of the corridor, and Brodie the hall boy hurtled through it, slowing himself down to a more respectable pace when he saw the two women. As he drew near, Victoria noticed him hesitate and then commit himself to a deep bow. She felt herself wanting to smile; he was almost as small as she was, so the gesture seemed droll, but she knew that it was her duty now to keep a straight face. A Queen could laugh, but not at her subjects.

'The Archbishop is here,' he announced, then hastily added, 'Your Majesty.' Brodie's small freckled face was suffused with relief at having addressed her correctly.

Lehzen looked at him sharply. 'And you have told no one else?'

The boy looked affronted. 'I came straight to you, Baroness, as instructed.' There was a slight pause until Lehzen took a coin out of her reticule and gave it to the boy, who scampered away, all pretence at dignity obliterated by his delight with his prize.

'You should go now, Majesty, before . . .' Lehzen glanced over Victoria's shoulder at the figure in the bed.

Victoria pulled her shawl down over her nightdress. Although she would prefer to get dressed first, she knew that by the time she had arranged herself, the rest of the household would be awake and her mother and Sir John would start to interfere. No, she would go now; she would start as she meant to go on.

Victoria followed Lehzen through the Picture Gallery, past the portrait of Queen Anne, who as Lehzen never ceased to remind her, was the last woman to sit on the English throne. Passing Anne's sulky, disappointed face, Victoria hoped that she would never look so unfortunate. She caught a glimpse of herself in the looking glass. Her cheeks were pink, and her blue eyes were sparkling with excitement. She was not dressed like a Queen, in a nightdress with her hair loose across her shoulders, but she thought that today she looked like one.

When they reached the top of the great staircase, Lehzen put out her hand, as she always did.

Victoria took a deep breath. 'Thank you, Lehzen, but I can manage unaided.'

Surprise and worry flickered in succession across the other woman's face.

'You know that your mother told me that I must always be there in case you are falling.'

Victoria looked up at her. 'I am quite capable of walking down the stairs without mishap.'

Lehzen wanted to protest, but seeing the look in Victoria's eye, she subsided.

Victoria started down the steps and said, looking over her shoulder, 'Things cannot be as they were, Lehzen. Now that I am Queen.'

Lehzen stopped moving, her foot poised over the step, as if frozen in mid-air. Her words were slow and painful. 'You will no longer be needing a governess, I suppose. Perhaps it is time that I went home to Hanover.'

Victoria stretched out her hand, and her face softened. 'Oh, Lehzen, I didn't mean that. I don't want you to go anywhere. Just because I choose to walk down the stairs by myself, that doesn't mean I don't want you by my side.'

Lehzen took Victoria's hand, and the colour began to return to her face. 'I never wish to leave you, Majesty. My only wish is to serve you.'

'And you will, Lehzen. But I don't need you to help me down the stairs any more.' Victoria looked upstairs to where her mother slept on. 'That part of my life is over.'

Lehzen nodded her understanding.

'And you can tell the servants that I will be moving into Queen Mary's bedroom tonight. I think it is time that I had a room of my own, don't you agree?'

Lehzen smiled. 'Yes, Majesty. I think a Queen does not sleep on a cot next to her mother's bed.'

At the foot of the stairs, she paused. The Archbishop and the Lord Chamberlain were behind the library door. She had been waiting for this moment for so long, and yet now it was upon her, she had to fight a sudden impulse to flee to the comfort of her schoolroom.

She had never been in a room alone with a man before, let alone an Archbishop. Then she heard the clatter of Dash's paws as he came down the wooden staircase. He sat at her feet looking up at her expectantly. He, at least, was ready for the adventure that lay ahead. Victoria swallowed her fear and walked towards the door. She was the Queen now.

The two grey-haired old men bowed as she entered the library, and Victoria heard the sound of the Archbishop's knee cracking as he knelt to kiss her hand.

'I regret to inform you that your uncle, the King, passed away at 2.34 this morning,' the Archbishop said. 'Queen Adelaide was at his side.'

Victoria looked up at the two whiskery faces looming above her. 'My poor dear uncle. May God have mercy on his soul.'

Both men bent their heads. Victoria wondered what she should say next, but her thoughts were interrupted by the feeling of a small rough tongue licking her foot. Dash was trying to get her attention. She bit her lip.

'The King's last wish was to commend Queen Adelaide to your care.' The Lord Chamberlain looked down at Dash, and his eyelids flickered. Victoria knew that look, which she had seen many times before; it was the expression worn by a man who felt that what he was doing was beneath his dignity. His proper place, it said, was dealing with the mighty affairs of state, not pandering to a young girl and her dog.

Victoria pulled her shoulders back and stuck her chin in the air, trying to lift herself from four foot eleven inches to a full five feet – if only she had a few more inches. It was uncommonly hard to be regal when everyone could see the top of your head. But, she reminded herself, it didn't matter how tall she was. She thought for a moment and decided to use the phrase she had once heard her Uncle King utter, and had longed to use ever since.

'Thank you, Archbishop, Lord Chamberlain. You have my permission to withdraw.'

She kept her face as still as she could as the two men bowed and proceeded to walk backwards out of the room. There was something irresistibly comic about the sight of these two old men retreating as if pulled by invisible strings, but she knew that she must not laugh. Being the Queen gave her the right to dismiss but not to ridicule. The thing every monarch needed was dignity. She remembered how embarrassed she had been when her uncle had started to sing a song about a drunken sailor in the middle of a state banquet. He had, she thought, been quite drunk, and as he sang little strings of saliva had formed at the side of his mouth. She had looked down the table at the faces of the courtiers to see how they would react, but to a man they had kept their faces smooth and impassive as if nothing untoward was going on. The only sign that anyone had noticed the King's drunken antics was a young footman whose shoulders were shaking with laughter until an older colleague nudged him to stop. She had resolved then that she would never let this happen when she was Queen. The idea that her courtiers might be laughing at her behind those smooth faces was not to be borne.

Victoria looked about her, but as there was no one in sight she picked up the hem of her nightdress and started to run up the stairs, Dash barking at her heels. Running was forbidden under the Kensington System, the system of rules set up by her mother and Conroy to govern every aspect of her existence. Running upstairs would have been unthinkable only yesterday, but today she could do whatever she liked.

Jenkins, her dresser, was waiting for her. The black silk dress, the one that had been ordered last week when it had become clear that the King would not recover from his illness, was laid out on the chaise longue. Jenkins had wanted to order several dresses, but Sir John had said that it was a needless expense. That was another thing that would have to change now she was Queen.

Jenkins was looking at her curiously. Victoria realised that she was clenching her fists.

'You must order the rest of my mourning clothes now, Jenkins. I see no reason for further delay.'

'Yes, Ma'am.' Jenkins's round face was split by the width of her smile.

Victoria put her arms up, and the dresser pulled the black dress over her head. She turned to face herself in the cheval glass. The black silk dress with its caterpillar sleeves was quite different from the simple muslin dresses in pastel colours that her mother deemed suitable. The mourning dress made her look older, and the crenellated sleeves gave her outline a sharpness that she found pleasing. She smoothed the folds of silk at her waist.

Hearing a sound somewhere between a sigh and a gasp, Victoria turned to see Lehzen standing behind her.

'Oh . . . forgive me . . . Majesty. I am not used to seeing you in black, you look so . . . grown up.'

Victoria smiled at Lehzen. 'I am glad. It is time that people stopped seeing me as a little girl.'

The door from the bedroom burst open. The Duchess of Kent rushed in, her hair still in curling papers, her Paisley shawl flapping around her.

'*Mein Kind*, where did you go?' The Duchess's voice was, as always, reproachful. But then Victoria saw her mother register the black dress, and watched as her expression changed from injury to shock.

'*Der König?*'

Victoria nodded. Her mother put her arms around her, and she allowed herself to relax into that lavender-scented embrace. '*Mein kleines Mädchen ist die Kaiserin.*'

Victoria pulled herself away. 'No more German, Mama. You are the mother of the Queen of England now.'

The Duchess nodded, her curl papers shaking. She put a trembling hand to Victoria's cheek. Her pale blue eyes were wet.

'Oh, my little Drina, have I ever told you about my journey from Amorbach across France when I was carrying you in my belly?' She mimed the bulk of an eight-month pregnancy.

Victoria nodded. 'Many times, Mama.' But the Duchess was not to be forestalled.

'It was just a hired carriage, and so uncomfortable. But I was crossing my legs the whole time, so that you, *Liebes*, could be born in England. I knew that if you were born anywhere else, then those awful uncles of yours would say that you were not English and then you could not be Queen. But I held on.'

The Duchess smiled at her own obstetrical feat. She was right, of course, Victoria knew that. There were enough people already who doubted whether an eighteen-year-old girl would make a suitable monarch, but the idea of an eighteen-year-old girl who had been born in Germany would never be countenanced.

'If only your poor father could have lived to see this day.' The Duchess looked up at the life-sized picture of the late Duke of Kent, standing with his hand resting on a cannon, that hung behind them.

'But Mama, even if he hadn't died when I was a baby, he

would never have seen me become Queen now, would he? The only reason I am Queen is that he is dead.'

The Duchess shook her head, impatient with Victoria's pedantic insistence on the facts of the succession. 'Yes, I know, but you know what I mean, Drina. He would be so happy to think that out of all his brothers, it was *his* child who was becoming the Queen. Just think, if I had not been what your father was always calling a Coburg brood mare, then that monster, your Uncle Cumberland, would be the King.' The Duchess shuddered theatrically and crossed herself.

'Well, he isn't. Not of England, anyway. But of course he is the King of Hanover now,' said Victoria. It was a wrinkle in the laws of succession that while she could inherit the British throne, as a woman she was barred from reigning over the German state that had been ruled jointly since the Elector of Hanover had become George I in 1713. Her Uncle Cumberland as the next male heir had inherited the German duchy.

'Hanover! It is, how do you call it, a pimple, in the middle of Germany. Let him go and be King there, and leave us alone.'

Victoria tugged at the bodice of her dress so that it lay straight. Her mother had tried to frighten her with the man she called 'your wicked Uncle Cumberland' ever since she could remember. He was the reason that Victoria had always slept in her mother's bedroom, the Duchess believing that if Cumberland were to come for Victoria in the night then she would at least be able interpose her body between the assassin and her child.

Victoria had no difficulty in believing her uncle capable of murder; he was almost comically villainous in appearance – tall and cadaverous with a livid duelling scar down one cheek. When Cumberland's valet had been found with his throat cut, it had been generally assumed that Cumberland had been responsible. She had less confidence in her mother's ability to defend her. Determined as the Duchess was, Victoria did not think even she would be able to fend off a six-foot man with a cutthroat razor.

Her mother was fussing now. 'Why didn't you wake me up at once?' She looked reproachfully at Lehzen. 'You should have told me, Baroness.'

The Baroness bowed her head, but said nothing. She could hardly say she had been acting on the explicit instructions of the daughter. Before the Duchess could remonstrate further, the door opened and Sir John Conroy walked in, planting himself, as he always did, in the middle of the room as if taking possession of a newly conquered territory.

The Duchess turned immediately and fluttered towards him. 'Oh, Sir John, have you heard? That awful old man is dead, and our little Drina is Queen.'

Watching the Duchess lay a hand on his arm, Victoria felt a shiver of revulsion run through her. Why couldn't her mother see that it was beneath her dignity as a royal Duchess and now the mother of a Queen to be always fawning on this odious fellow as if he were the man of rank and fortune instead of her paid advisor?

Conroy spoke in his deep booming voice with its slight Irish inflection, his words, as ever, uttered with total conviction. 'The first thing to decide is how you will style yourself. Alexandrina is too foreign, and Victoria is hardly the name for a Queen. You could adopt Elizabeth, perhaps, or Anne. Yes,' Conroy's long handsome face was flushed with his proximity to power, 'Elizabeth II sounds very well. Very well indeed.'

He turned to the woman who had followed him into the room. 'Don't you think so, Lady Flora?'

Victoria stared straight ahead. She thought that if she did not look at Conroy and Flora Hastings, they might realise that they were not welcome.

But she heard the rustle of Lady Flora's curtsey, and her murmur, 'To be called Elizabeth would be a reminder of a great Queen.' The implication could not have been clearer. It would take more than a name to turn a little girl into a monarch.

The Duchess turned back to Victoria. 'Has the Archbishop come? I will just be getting dressed and then we can go and see him together.'

Victoria turned to face her. She could feel her heart pounding as she said in a voice that was braver than she felt, 'Thank you, Mama, but that won't be necessary. The Archbishop and the Lord Chamberlain were here earlier. They have already kissed hands.'

The Duchess looked at her in horror. 'You saw them alone! But Drina! What were you thinking?'

Victoria paused before replying as evenly as she could, 'A month ago, on my eighteenth birthday, I became old enough to be Queen, and therefore quite capable of seeing my ministers alone.'

The Duchess looked, as she always did in times of difficulty, to Conroy. Victoria was pleased to note he was developing a slight twitch in his left eye.

There was a crash as Conroy banged his silver-topped cane on the wooden floor. 'This is not a game! In the future,' he hesitated, but managed to form his lips around her new title, 'Ma'am, you will always be accompanied by your mother or me. You cannot do this alone.'

Victoria could not help but take a step backwards as he loomed towards her. But she told herself there was no reason to be frightened; there was nothing he could do to her any more. At her feet she heard Dash growling.

Bending down, she picked up the spaniel. 'Oh, don't worry, Sir John, I have no intention of being alone.' Ignoring her mother's imploring face, she turned her head to look straight at him. 'You see, I have Dash.'

And, discretion being the better part of valour, she walked out of the room, holding Dash tightly in her arms. She ran down the corridor and then stopped, her head still throbbing with the sound of Conroy's cane as it struck the floor. She knew that there was nothing to be frightened of any more, but still the act of defying him had left her breathless.

Chapter Two

THE CURTAINS ON THE BED WERE MADE OF DARK brocade shot with silver; they were heavy with dust that looked as though it had lain undisturbed since the death of the bed's last occupant, Queen Mary, of smallpox sometime in the late seventeenth century. The Stuart Queen had always been a favourite of Victoria's. She was the only Queen in her own right to live here at Kensington, although of course she had not reigned alone, but in a dual monarchy with her husband William of Orange.

As Victoria sat on the bed in the room that had once belonged to Queen Mary, she wondered if that long-dead Queen had felt as nervous as she did now. She had waited for this moment for so long. She had imagined in great detail the satisfaction she would feel in at last being able to put Conroy in his place. But instead of triumph, she felt unstable, as if by defying Conroy she had somehow undermined her own foundations. But then she remembered that moment in Ramsgate when Conroy had tried to force her to sign that paper making him her Private Secretary.

Victoria lay back on Queen Mary's bed, and her movement unsettled a huge cloud of dust. She sat up again immediately;

she could feel a sneeze pending, a prickling against her eyeballs. Everything about Kensington was dusty and irritating. The room would have to be thoroughly cleaned and aired before she could sleep there.

She looked over to the corner of the room, where Dash was sniffing suspiciously at something. She stood up and called for Lehzen, who appeared so quickly that she must have been lurking outside. 'Will you make sure that this room is thoroughly aired? I don't think it's been cleaned since the seventeenth century.'

Lehzen hesitated. 'Of course, Majesty, but the running of the household here is not my responsibility.'

Victoria replied, 'You forget, Lehzen, that Kensington Palace is now mine, and I have decided that you should take charge. Look at this room! There are mice droppings everywhere. That would not happen in a properly run household.'

Lehzen nodded her agreement. 'I am afraid that Sir John is not interested in cleanliness. The servants here know that and they do not perform their duties with diligence.'

'Well, I am sure you will change all that, Lehzen, when you are in charge of the household. You are a very good teacher, after all.'

Lehzen folded her hands in satisfaction. 'I believe Sir John will not be happy about this change of government.'

Victoria smiled back at her. 'No, I don't suppose he will. But I am no longer under any obligation to please Sir John. He is the comptroller of my mother's household, not mine.'

'Yes, Majesty.'

'Everything is going to be different now.'

The two women smiled at each other.

Victoria walked over to the window and looked out at the

green canopy of trees in the Park beyond the formal gardens.

'For a start, I do not intend to stay here at Kensington. It is miles away from anything, and quite unsuitable as a royal residence.'

Lehzen looked at her in surprise. Victoria continued, 'I think I shall look over Buckingham House. It is in the centre of town, at least, and I believe it has a throne room.'

Lehzen nodded. 'I have heard that your uncle, King George, had it decorated most extravagantly.'

'Better a little extravagance than living in a dusty mouse nest in the middle of the country!' Victoria pulled at one of the ancient curtains to emphasise her point, and it came away in tatters. She started to laugh, and after a moment Lehzen joined in.

They were still laughing when the Duchess found them. She was now clothed in black, as the court was in the official mourning period for the King, but her dress was made of a richly figured black silk. There were diamonds in her elaborately arranged hair. At forty-seven, the Duchess was an attractive woman, her face with its large blue eyes and rosy colouring only marred by the sulky set of her mouth.

'*Warum lachst du?* What is so amusing?'

Victoria held out the fistful of disintegrating curtain. The Duchess frowned. 'But why is this making you laugh, Drina? It is not so funny, I think.'

'I put my hand out and the curtain just fell to bits. It was very droll.' Victoria saw the incomprehension in her mother's eyes.

'But why are you in here, anyway, Drina? Surely you have more pressing matters to attend to than exploring the Palace.'

Victoria took a deep breath. 'I have decided to make this

my bedroom, Mama. It belonged to a Queen Regnant, like me, so I think it is suitable.'

The Duchess's hand fluttered to her mouth. 'But Drina, my *Liebes*, you have slept beside me since you were a tiny baby. I wonder how you will manage if I am not there to comfort you in the night when you are having an *Alptraum*.' The Duchess looked so distressed that Victoria felt almost sorry for her.

'You have taken great care of me, Mama. I know that. But things are different now.'

'But if your Uncle Cumberland comes for you in the night, how will I protect you?'

Victoria laughed, and she saw Lehzen smiling, out of the corner of her eye. 'I think protecting me is now the job of the Household Cavalry. You can stop worrying, Mama. There is nothing that Uncle Cumberland can do to me, unless he wants to be arrested for treason.'

The Duchess shook her head and, putting it on one side, she tried another tack. 'Did you know that Queen Mary died in this room, lying in this bed? I would not be happy sleeping here, knowing such a story.' She shrugged, and the corners of her mouth turned down.

Victoria had not known that her ancestor had died as well as lived in this room, but then, she thought, neither did her mother. The Duchess was quite capable of inventing a story if it suited her requirements.

'I think, Mama, that once this room has been properly cleaned and aired, I will not be troubled by its history.'

The Duchess threw up her hands.

'And besides, Mama, I will not be sleeping here for long. I intend to move to Buckingham House as soon as is possible.'

The Duchess looked startled. 'You must talk to Sir John

before you do anything. To move the household, that is not a decision that you can take alone.'

'Really, Mama? I think that as the Sovereign I am the only person who can decide where I live. And really it is no business of Sir John's, as it is my household that will be moving, not yours.'

To Victoria's intense surprise and annoyance, her mother laughed. 'Oh, Drina, this is showing how little you know about how the world works. Do you really think that you, an unmarried girl of eighteen, can set up an establishment on her own, even if you are the Queen?'

Victoria said nothing. She knew what she intended.

'And do you really think that you can manage all this with only the Baroness to help you?' The Duchess looked at Lehzen with dislike.

'I am not a child any more, Mama.'

'And yet you act like one, Drina. But I understand that this is all a shock for you. When you have come to your senses, we will talk sensibly with Sir John about the future.'

Before Victoria could reply, the Duchess left the room. To express her feelings, Victoria gave the post of the bed a sharp kick, causing a cloud of moth-eaten hangings to collapse.

Victoria turned to Lehzen. 'Please have this room made habitable at once. I cannot spend another night in the same room as Mama.'

Chapter Three

VICTORIA LOOKED UP AT THE PORTRAIT OF HER FATHER wearing his uniform and standing beside a cannon. She could not forget, even if she wanted to, that she was a soldier's daughter.

She turned round and opened one of the red boxes on her desk. They had come that morning as soon as the death of her uncle had been officially announced. Evidently the business of government, whatever that was exactly, must go on.

Victoria picked up the document at the top of the pile and began to read. It appeared to be about the appointment of a new bishop in Lincoln, but it was written in such convoluted language that Victoria could not be sure. How was she meant to choose between the various candidates – she had never heard of any of them. As she flicked through the other documents she began to feel anxious: there were endless lists of officers waiting for commissions, a paper from the Foreign Office about the movement of troops in Afghanistan, a memorandum from the Lord Chamberlain about Queen Adelaide's widow's pension.

Victoria sat down, trying not to panic. She picked up one of the dolls that sat on their own chairs nearby. This doll was wearing the tinsel crown she made for it all those years ago in

Lehzen's schoolroom. Talking to dolls was hardly the behaviour of a Queen, but Mama and Conroy had not liked her to play with other children, apart from Conroy's awful daughter Jane, so in the long lonely hours of her childhood, Victoria had had to invent her own companions. No. 123 she felt was a little older than her, the kind of friend that one would go to for advice and counsel. She looked at the doll's button black eyes and said, 'How does a Queen deal with her correspondence, do you think, No. 123?'

'Still playing with dolls, Your Royal Highness?' Conroy's voice made her start. 'Oh, forgive me, still playing with dolls, Your Majesty?' Conroy repeated, and smiled with malicious pleasure.

The Duchess bustled in after him. 'Really, you must put such childish things away now you are Queen, Drina.'

Victoria put No. 123 down on the desk. Instinctively she took a step back from Conroy.

'I see your boxes have arrived . . . Ma'am,' said Conroy. 'You will have so many pressing matters to attend to.'

He picked up the document that Victoria had been looking at. 'Ah, the bishopric of Lincoln. Quite a thorny decision. I hardly think that the Dean of Wells is suitable; I hear that he is quite evangelical in his views. I think you must appoint someone who is more in sympathy with. . .'

Victoria snatched the paper away from him. 'I don't think I gave you permission to look at my papers, Sir John.'

The Duchess gasped, but Conroy merely raised an eyebrow. 'I was simply trying to help you, Ma'am, with your official duties. I thought, given that you seemed to be otherwise engaged,' he glanced at No. 123, 'you might profit from some assistance.'

Victoria looked up at the plump, bellicose face of her father and with all the courage she could summon took a step towards Conroy. 'I think, Sir John, that when I need your help, I will ask for it!'

The silence in the room was complete, and then Conroy laughed. 'Do you really think that a girl like you, ignorant and unformed, can serve her country without advice? Can you possibly imagine that you can step straight from the schoolroom onto the throne?' His voice was light, and he turned to the Duchess, who smiled back at him.

Her mother's smile made Victoria dig her fingernails into her palms, but she would not give way. 'I would have been better prepared, if you and Mama had allowed me to come out into society instead of keeping me shut up here in Kensington.'

'We had to protect you, Drina,' her mother said, shaking her head.

'We have always done what is best for you, Ma'am. And that is why we are here now, to prevent you from making any childish mistakes.' Conroy allowed his eyes to flick over to the dolls sitting on their tiny thrones.

Victoria took a deep breath. 'I think you forget, Sir John, that I am my father's daughter and the granddaughter of a King. I am determined to serve my country to the best of my ability.' She looked over to her mother. 'You know I am ready, Mama. You understand how much I want to make you and poor dear Papa proud.'

Her mother looked at her for a moment with the tenderness that Victoria craved, but then, as if frightened by an independent feeling, she turned towards Sir John, whose smile had remained fixed throughout.

'Your sentiments are admirable, Ma'am. But might I suggest

that an eighteen-year-old girl would serve her country most successfully if she accepts help and guidance? Your mother wants nothing more than to serve you, and I suggest that as your Private Secretary I will be able to guide you to the greater glory of the country you now reign over.'

Conroy kept his voice light, but Victoria could see the give-away twitch at the corner of his left eye. This gave her courage.

'I thank you for your observations, but I must tell you I don't remember appointing you as my Private Secretary, Sir John. And now, since, as you say, I have a great deal of government business to attend to, you have my permission to withdraw.'

Conroy flinched. She saw his hand move, as if he were about to strike her, but although she knew him quite capable of it, Victoria stood firm. She kept her eyes on him, clenching her hands together so that he should not see them trembling.

Conroy loomed over her, but Victoria did not waver. At last, he bowed his head with great deliberation. Still facing her, he walked backwards out of the room.

As soon as he was out of sight, Victoria let out the breath she had been holding in a great rush.

'How rude you are being to Sir John, Drina,' the Duchess was tearfully indignant, 'when all he is being is your friend.'

Victoria turned to face her mother. 'Oh no, Mama, you are mistaken. He is your friend, not mine.'

And before her mother could answer, or indeed see the tears that were threatening, Victoria ran out of the room.

Chapter Four

WILLIAM LAMB, THE SECOND VISCOUNT MELBOURNE
and Prime Minister of Great Britain and Ireland,
opened his eyes with reluctance. His servants had strict instructions not to wake him unless there was an emergency. He
looked at his butler's grave face, and then saw the King's
Messenger standing behind him. Seeing the black armband on
the man's right arm, he sat up immediately.

'The King?'

The messenger nodded and handed him the dispatch.

Melbourne looked at the butler. 'Coffee.'

An hour or so later, Melbourne was riding along Rotten
Row to Kensington Palace. It would have been more fitting to
go in his carriage, but he had eaten and drunk too freely last
night and the ride would do him good. He had got into the
habit of falling asleep in his study after the second bottle of
claret, which did not help his temper the next day. He wished
that he could fall asleep, as he used to, as soon as his head
touched the pillow, but that knack had eluded him along with
marital happiness.

'William!' a woman called to him from a carriage going the
other way. He saw Emma Portman sitting in her brougham

alongside her husband, who looked, as he always did, rather surprised that he could sit up unaided.

He nodded to them both, but Emma was not to be dismissed so easily. 'Is it true the King is dead?'

'Yes. I am just on my way to Kensington to kiss hands with our new Queen.'

Emma put her head on one side. 'Then why the long face, William? Surely anyone is better than that old buffoon, God rest his soul.'

Lord Portman lifted his head and said in his querulous lisp, 'Ith it true that the Queen's head ith too big for her body? I heard that ith why they keep her shut away in Kensington.'

Emma shook her head impatiently. 'Nonsense, Portman, I have seen the Queen, and she is perfectly formed. I think you will like her, William.'

Melbourne shrugged, said, 'Perhaps, but the truth is, Emma, after eight years I am tired of governing. I would much rather consult the rooks at Brocket Hall.'

Emma tapped her fan on the side of the carriage sharply. 'The rooks must wait. Your Queen needs you, your country needs you, and it must be said I would very much like a place at court.'

Melbourne could not help but smile. He had known Emma all his life and had never known her fail to get her own way. Only a woman of her ability could have manoeuvred her dolt of a husband into a cabinet post, even if he was only Under-Secretary for the Colonies. If Emma Portman wanted to join the royal household, then nothing would stop her.

'In that case, Emma, I see that I have no choice but to shoulder my burden.' He tipped his hat to her and rode on.

It was a pleasant ride, the sun reflecting on the Serpentine

lake as he rode over the bridge. As he approached the gardens
of the Palace, the trees grew thicker, and he fancied himself
momentarily as the Prince in the Perrault tale of the Sleeping
Beauty going to rouse a princess who had been asleep for a
hundred years. Of course, the princess, who he must now think
of as the Queen, would be wide-awake now. The Duchess, he
knew, had been making daily enquiries as to the state of the
King's health; she and Conroy had no doubt been planning
for this moment for years.

Melbourne wondered how the Queen, whose small figure
and doll-like features he had only glimpsed at one of the late
King's Drawing Rooms, would cope with her new responsibilities. She had seemed so very young. But as Emma had said,
anything would be better than the last occupants of the throne.
The wits at Brooks's had pronounced the last three kings 'an
imbecile, a profligate and a buffoon'. The new Queen had to
be preferable to the late King, with his intemperate swearing
and those bulging Hanoverian eyes that looked, when he was
in a temper, as if they would pop out of his head. No, a young
woman would make a pleasant change, just so long as she did
not get the vapours when asked to do something unpleasant.
Melbourne wondered if he would be required to carry smelling
salts in his pocket along with his watch.

He reached the gates of Kensington Palace and noticed that
the paint was peeling from the iron scrollwork. It did not feel
like a Palace, more like a place where the odds and ends of
the royal family could be tidied away out of harm's reach. The
Duchess of Kent had lived there since she had been the obscure
German widow of one of George III's many sons. Now she
was the mother of the Queen.

No one could have foreseen it. The Duke of Kent had been

one of four royal Dukes to discard their mistresses and hurry
to Germany in search of a royal bride after the death of Princess
Charlotte, George III's only legitimate grandchild, in childbirth.
The betting had been on the Duke of Clarence, the late King
as he then was, who had after all fathered ten children on Mrs
Jordan. But he did not enjoy the same luck with his scrawny
German bride, Adelaide of Saxe-Meiningen. Their two daugh-
ters had not lived long enough to be christened.

Kent, however, the next brother down, had picked himself
a widow who had already given birth to two children. She was
a Coburg, commonly known as the brood mares of Europe.
Their daughter, Alexandrina Victoria, had arrived a year after
the wedding, promptly followed by the death of the Duke from
a chill. Of course at the time no one had thought that Kent's
baby daughter would inherit the throne, but while George IV
showed no sign of remarrying, and the Clarences failed to
produce a child that survived, the little Princess of Kent had
been growing up in the nursery at Kensington.

Melbourne wondered what kind of education she had
received. A boy would have had a governor and a course of
formal instruction. But a girl, how should a future Queen be
educated? Melbourne hoped that she had received instruction
in more than watercolours and the pianoforte, or whatever were
considered the indispensable accomplishments of a lady of rank.

There was a man standing at the entrance of the Palace. A
tall thin figure with dark hair who could only be Sir John
Conroy, Melbourne thought. He had met him once years ago,
and had been surprised by how much he had disliked him.
There had been something overweening about him that
Melbourne had not cared for.

As he handed his horse to the groom, Conroy came down

the steps to greet him, a smile of welcome etched onto his long face. 'Lord Melbourne.' Conroy bent his head in greeting. 'Might I have a word with you?'

Melbourne saw that he could not escape. 'I am on my way to see the Queen.'

'Yes. It is of the . . . Queen that I wish to speak. You know, of course, that she has led the most sheltered life until now.'

Melbourne noticed two patches of red on the other man's cheeks. He was clearly in a state of some excitement.

'I know very little about the Queen, as she has not, as you say, been seen much in society.'

'As equerry to the late Duke and then as the Duchess's most trusted advisor, I have watched over the Queen's upbringing since she was a baby. I have done everything in my power to prepare her for the responsibilities that lay before her.'

'Indeed, Sir John. Then it perhaps is a pity that you did not introduce her more into the world that she is to rule.'

Sir John lifted his head up and looked Melbourne in the eye. 'The Queen is very young and impressionable. The Duchess did not want her to be . . . distracted.'

Melbourne did not reply. He thought it much more likely that the Duchess and Conroy had kept their charge out of the public eye in order to have her completely in their control. How unfortunate for them that the Queen was now eighteen and there was no need to appoint a Regent.

'I think there is no one more suitable than me to act as the Queen's Private Secretary,' Conroy went on. 'No one knows better where her strengths and weaknesses lie.'

Melbourne nodded. 'No doubt. But I believe that to be the Queen's decision, not mine.'

Sir John smiled his mirthless smile. 'The Queen does not

always understand what is in her best interests, but I am sure that with some guidance from you, she will make the right appointment.'

'I am sure she will, Sir John. And now if you will excuse me.' Before Sir John could say anything more, Melbourne was up the steps and walking into the Palace.

Chapter Five

FROM THE WINDOW OF HER SITTING ROOM, VICTORIA could see Conroy talking to a tall man she thought was Lord Melbourne. Conroy, she could see, was bathing the Prime Minister in all the charm of which he was capable. Since Melbourne's back was to her, however, she could not tell how he was taking it.

Lehzen came to the door. She had an expression on her face that Victoria could not quite determine. 'The Prime Minister, Lord Melbourne, is here, Majesty.'

'I am ready to see him.'

Lehzen did not move. Victoria looked at her, surprised. 'I do not want to keep him waiting, Lehzen.'

Still the Baroness hesitated, then, 'I think I should stay with you, as a chaperone.'

Victoria laughed. 'The Queen of England and her Prime Minister do not need a chaperone, Lehzen. I will see him alone, as I intend to see all my ministers. Now please go and fetch him.'

Lehzen stood her ground. 'Drina . . . Majesty, I have always tried to shield you from these things, but really I must not leave you alone with him. Lord Melbourne is . . .' she searched for the right English word, 'disreputable. His wife, Lady Caroline, ran away with Lord Byron and he has been involved with many women. Only last year he was taken to the court for having criminal conversation with a Mrs Norton. You must have protection.'

Victoria, who had had no idea that her Prime Minister had such a reputation, found she was more intrigued than alarmed. 'What is a criminal conversation?'

The Baroness mumbled, 'It is an . . . immoral encounter, Majesty. That is why you should not be alone with him.'

Lehzen's face was so crumpled with anxiety that Victoria wanted to reach out and smooth the lines away from her forehead. But the idea that she was somehow at risk was absurd. There was only one man she was frightened of, and that was not Lord Melbourne. The thing worrying her now was not her Prime Minister's reputation but how close he was to Conroy. What had they been talking about outside?

'Don't worry, Lehzen, I will be quite safe. And if he does anything disreputable,' she looked down at the spaniel, 'I am sure Dash will intervene.'

Lehzen bowed her head and retreated.

Victoria glanced at herself in the mirror. She wished that she did not look quite so young. Although her hair was up, the chignon at the back of her head only emphasized how small her face was, and the black dress made her look pale. She gave her cheeks a pinch.

'The Viscount Melbourne,' the footman announced. Victoria's first impression was of a man who seemed pleased to see her. He was tall, and while his hair was streaked with grey and he must be about the same age as Conroy, the expression in his green eyes made him look much younger.

Melbourne knelt and kissed her outstretched hand. 'May I offer my condolences on the death of your uncle the King, Your Majesty.'

Victoria nodded. 'Poor Uncle King, he was always kind to me. Even if he did have some strange ideas about whom I should marry.'

Clearly smelling salts would not be needed, Melbourne thought to himself.

'Indeed, Ma'am? I believe he favoured the Prince of Orange.'

'A prince with a head the size of a pumpkin.'

Melbourne's lips twitched. 'I see you have a keen eye for detail, Ma'am.'

Victoria looked at him sharply: was he making fun of her?

Melbourne cast an eye around the room, noticing the picture of the Duke of Kent standing next to an unfeasibly large cannon. He had never met the Duke but was well acquainted with the stories of the savage punishments he had inflicted on his troops. He hoped that the little woman before him had not inherited her father's passion for discipline. He looked away quickly and saw a doll sitting on a miniature chair wearing a tattered tinsel crown. He glanced at the Queen. 'What a charming doll. Does she have a name?'

Victoria shook her head. 'She is No. 123. Mama gave her to me on my eleventh birthday.'

'With the crown?'

'No, that came later. I made it on the day I realised that, if I lived, I would be Queen.'

'And when was that, Ma'am?' Melbourne asked.

'I was thirteen. I was having a lesson with Lehzen and she showed me the family tree. I looked at it for a long time and then I saw that I was next.'

Her voice was her great feature, Melbourne thought, light and cool without a trace of shrillness. She might be small and without particular beauty, but her voice was unmistakably regal.

'Was it a shock, Ma'am?'

She returned his gaze with great seriousness. 'I remember thinking that my uncle's crown would be too big for me.'

Melbourne felt disconcerted. He had been talking to her as if to a child, but seeing the tilt of her head and the spark in her pale blue eyes, he knew he had underestimated her.

Looking out of the window, the Queen said, 'I believe you know Sir John Conroy?'

Melbourne heard the tension in her voice and saw the defiant set of the shoulders.

'I have certainly met him, Ma'am, but we are no more than acquaintances. I believe he would like to be your Private Secretary.'

Victoria turned round to face him, her small face pink with indignation. 'That is out of the question. He means to run me as he runs my mother.'

Melbourne hesitated; he was beginning to understand what the Queen's upbringing had been. 'Then you must have someone else.'

Victoria nodded, relieved; this man seemed actually to listen to her, instead of telling her what to do. Melbourne continued. 'If I might make a suggestion, perhaps I could act as your Secretary for the moment. I see that the boxes have already started arriving, and I am afraid that the business of government will not wait. I can imagine that it must seem rather over-whelming when you have so little experience, but I assure you that with some guidance you will soon be the master or rather the mistress of it all.'

At the word guidance, Victoria began to tremble with indignation. She had almost been deceived by Melbourne's ease of manner, but it was clear that he wanted to control her just as Conroy did. She lifted her chin and drew herself as erect as possible. 'Thank you, Lord Melbourne, but I believe I can manage.'

Melbourne bowed. 'I shall disturb you no longer then, Ma'am. I shall only remind you that the Privy Council meets tomorrow, and it is customary for the monarch to say a few words at the beginning of the meeting.'

'I am quite aware of my responsibilities, Lord Melbourne.'

To her surprise Melbourne appeared to be smiling. 'I am delighted to hear it, Ma'am. Good day to you,' and with that he gave her a bow and left the room, that easy smile still lingering.

Victoria's knees felt weak, and she sat down rather suddenly. Melbourne's remark about the speech to the Privy Council had come as a shock. She knew that presiding over the Council was one of her constitutional duties, but had not realised she would have to give a formal address.

There were so many things she didn't know. Lehzen had done her best, but a German governess alone could hardly be expected to educate the future Queen of England in her constitutional responsibilities. Victoria should have had other tutors, but Conroy had persuaded her mother that anyone from outside the household might exert too great an influence – an influence that he wanted to reserve to himself. But she would not ask for help now. However hard it was, she would do this alone.

Through the window came the sound of a bell tolling to announce the death of the King to passersby. She stood up and went to the window. A small group of people had gathered by the gates, which were now guarded by men from the Household Cavalry, as befitted her new status. A small girl who was standing holding her mother's skirts had a doll quite like No. 123. Victoria was possessed by a sudden impulse to run outside and show the little girl her own doll, to make her solemn face light up with surprise and pleasure. But she did not move. A Queen, she knew, did not act on impulse.

Chapter Six

ENGE, THE STEWARD, BROUGHT THE LETTER IN ON A
silver salver. Victoria looked up from her desk, where
she had been trying, unsuccessfully, for the last two hours to
compose a speech for the Privy Council. 'With Lord Melbourne's
compliments, Ma'am.'

Victoria took the letter and laid it beside her own sheet of
paper. She had got as far as writing, 'My lords.' This much she
knew was correct, but did that include the Archbishop, who
was a Privy Councillor, or Sir Robert Peel, who was not a lord?
It was all so complicated. She could ask Lehzen, but she
suspected that she would not have the answer. Conroy would
know, of course, but she would rather make a public mistake
than ask for his assistance.

She picked up Melbourne's letter and broke the seal. There
was an enclosure with the letter:

Your Majesty,

 *It occurred to me yesterday that you may not yet be familiar
with all the protocol surrounding the Privy Council. It would
be impossible for you to anticipate all the procedures of a body
you have never had the pleasure, a word I use with some*

hesitation, of meeting. Therefore, I have taken the great, but I hope not altogether unwelcome, liberty of drafting a speech for you. I do not presume to tell you what to say, only to give you the most correct form with which to say it. I do not have to remind you that the Duke of Cumberland, soon to be the King of Hanover, will be present, and he is, as you know, a stickler for protocol.

Believe me to be your obedient servant, etc etc, Melbourne

She picked up the paper that had come with the letter. As promised, it was a draft of a speech that gave her the outline of how she should address the council. 'My Lords spiritual and temporal' was the correct address apparently, but he only made suggestions as to what she might say:

an allusion to the virtues of your uncle the late King, would be customary here. In case you struggle to think of any, I suggest that you mention his excellent timekeeping. The King may never have had a sensible thought but at least he was always prompt.

Melbourne's tone was rather disrespectful to her uncle, but Victoria could not help smiling. King William had indeed been obsessed with punctuality. At Windsor his favourite thing was to follow the man who wound up the clocks, his round face beaming with pleasure when all the timepieces chimed together.

She had almost finished copying out her speech when Lehzen came in, carrying a long box. 'The Lord Chamberlain sent this, Majesty.'

Victoria opened the box and saw the star-shaped Order of

the Garter on its blue ribbon. Knights of the Garter, the oldest order of chivalry in Europe, wore an actual garter round their left leg, but for a woman that was not possible.

She bent her head as Lehzen put the sash over her head. It seemed strange to be putting it on without ceremony; normally the heir to the throne would have been made a Knight of the Garter by his predecessor. In her case, of course, her sex precluded this. But now she was Sovereign of the Garter, and she alone could make new appointments to the Order.

She went over to the looking glass and tried to adjust the sash. The Order, a bejewelled star with the legend *Honi soit qui mal y pense* (*Shame on him who thinks evil of it*), was perched rather unfortunately on her corseted bosom.

Victoria caught Lehzen's eye in the looking glass. 'This has not, I believe, been designed for a woman to wear, Baroness.'

Lehzen allowed herself a small smile. 'Indeed, Majesty. Might I suggest?' She came forward and tried to adjust the sash so the Order lay flat against her waist. But the Order was too big to lie comfortably – either it was perched ludicrously on her chest or it dug into her waist.

Victoria took it off and turned back to Melbourne's letter. She had noticed a postscript on the other side:

You will, of course, as Sovereign, be wearing the Order of the Garter. It is rather an unwieldy thing, so might I suggest that you follow the example of your predecessor as Queen Regnant, Queen Anne, and wear it on your right arm. It is important to be comfortable, as I am sure you will agree.

'I think I will wear it on my arm, Lehzen. I am not a man, and there is no reason for me to dress like one.'

Chapter Seven

*I*T WOULD BE STANDING ROOM ONLY, THOUGHT
Melbourne, as he watched the Privy Councillors crowd
into the Red Saloon at Kensington Palace. He saw the tall,
hook-nosed figure of the Duke of Wellington and his burly
companion Robert Peel, the leader of the Tories in the
Commons, jostling for space with the Archbishop of Canterbury.
Only the Duke of Cumberland could cause his fellow
Councillors to make room for him. The scar on the Duke's
right cheek looked particularly livid this morning, perhaps
inflamed by the disappointment that must surely be his.
Melbourne had no doubt that Cumberland was not happy with
the laws of succession that put his eighteen-year-old niece on
the throne instead of him. Hanover, by all accounts a dreary
place, was not much of a consolation prize.

He wondered if the Queen would use the speech he had
drafted for her. She had been so vehement about not needing
assistance during their meeting, but on his way home he had
decided that even if she did not ask for his help, it was still his
duty to offer it. There was something admirable about her spirit;
he had not expected to find her so remarkably distinct. That
almost tangible outline to her reminded him of his late wife,

Caro. She too had been eighteen when he had first seen her.

There was a change in the rhythm of the murmurs around him, the rumble of self-congratulation replaced by an expectant whisper. Melbourne turned and saw the doors at the other end of the saloon being opened by the footmen. There, framed by the doorway, stood the diminutive figure of the Queen. A collective gasp filled the room. Even though everyone present had come to meet their new monarch, it was still somehow unnatural to see a woman, and such a young, slight one, in the place hitherto taken by a succession of old and increasingly portly men.

Victoria heard that gasp and put her hand to the pocket in her skirt to check that the speech was still there. Looking out at the sea of faces in front of her, she realised she had never been in a room with so many men. It was quite peculiar, but she supposed she would have to get used to it. Still, it felt as if she was walking into a forest, full of trees with black trunks and silver leaves.

She walked slowly up to the small dais that had been prepared for her. It was not very high, but would at least bring her up to the eye level of the other people in the room.

Victoria glanced around from the dais. Most of the group were strangers, but she recognised the gloomy face of the Archbishop, then the twisted snarl of her uncle. Quickly she looked down at the floor.

After a deep breath, Victoria pulled out the speech from her pocket and began to read. 'My Lords spiritual and temporal, it is with a great sense of the honour that has been conferred upon me that I stand before you –'

'Speak up, Ma'am, I can't hear you.' Her Uncle Cumberland had his hand to his ear in a pantomime of deafness. Looking at his malevolent face, Victoria felt her stomach clench. She tried to speak again and found she could make no sound, but swallowed and closed her eyes. When she opened them, she looked up and saw Lord Melbourne giving her a little nod of encouragement as if to say, *Go on.*

Victoria looked back at the paper in front of her – she had the speech by heart, but it felt reassuring to have something to hold – and continued. 'I know that some would say my sex makes me unsuited for the responsibilities that lie before me, but I am here before you to pledge my life to the service of my country.'

She glanced again at Melbourne, who smiled as he recognised the words he had written for her. Emboldened by that smile, she went on, and felt the atmosphere in the room subside from angry turmoil to something more docile. They were not resisting; they actually seemed to be listening.

'And may God have mercy on me and my people.' As she finished, Victoria sat down on the temporary throne, which was actually a rather uncomfortable chair from her mother's apartments. The Privy Councillors formed a line as they came before her to swear allegiance.

To her relief, Melbourne was first, and as he knelt before her in a formal obeisance she whispered, 'Thank you for your letter, Lord Melbourne.'

He looked up at her, and she thought that he was remarkably handsome for a man old enough to be her father. 'I am glad you found it useful, Ma'am.'

He moved away behind her and was replaced by an old man with a port-wine stain on his face whom she had never seen before. He heaved himself onto one knee and kissed her hand with rather unpleasant gusto. She expected him to move on, but he remained there, swaying slightly with the effort of being in this unfamiliar and uncomfortable position.

Victoria wondered why he didn't get up, and then realised to her dismay that he was waiting for her to greet him by name. Clearly he felt that he was an important enough figure to be personally acknowledged by his new Sovereign. The murmurs in the room began to reverberate. Victoria felt the blood rushing to her cheeks; she couldn't very well ask the man who he was, which would add insult to injury. Then, to her surprise and intense relief, she heard a voice in her ear whisper, 'Viscount Falkland, Ma'am.'

'Viscount Falkland,' she said, and at last the man staggered to his feet and retreated to join the others. Victoria glanced at Melbourne, who was standing beside her now. How fortunate that he had seen her dilemma. To fail so visibly on her first public engagement was unthinkable.

The Councillors continued to file in front of her to kiss her hand, Melbourne bending to murmur the name in her ear when it was clear she had no recollection. She wondered how her Uncle William, who could barely remember the name of his own wife, had managed such a feat of memory. Maybe, she thought, it would be no disgrace for him to forget a name, but she knew that the same tolerance did not apply to her.

'I think this Councillor needs no introduction, Ma'am.'

The line came to an end and she found herself confronted by her Uncle Cumberland. At first he made no attempt to disguise his contempt, but then with much deliberation he lowered himself on one knee and took her outstretched hand as if it were red hot. He murmured as if he could barely bring himself to say the words, 'Your Majesty.'

Victoria dropped his hand and forced herself to look her

uncle in the eye. 'I must congratulate you, Uncle. When will you be going to your new kingdom?'

Cumberland waved his hand in dismissal. 'I am in no hurry. My first duty is to the British throne.'

The threat in his tone was unmistakable. She heard Melbourne shifting behind her.

'I am sure the people of Hanover will be sorry to hear that,' she said with as much tartness as she could muster.

Cumberland's damaged eyelid did not close completely. 'I think they should be prepared to wait. There is so much to be attended to here.'

Victoria was thinking of how best she could retort when she heard Melbourne's voice behind her, cool and encouraging. 'The crowds have been gathering all day, Ma'am, despite the inclement weather. I believe that now might be the time to read the proclamation.'

Looking at Cumberland, Victoria got to her feet. 'Yes, indeed. I don't want to keep *my* people waiting.' She had the satisfaction of seeing Cumberland look away first.

The swarm of Privy Councillors parted before her as she followed Melbourne out onto the balcony in front of the Palace. The roar from the crowd as she approached the window almost pushed her back inside. The Lord Chamberlain was standing beside her with the scroll in his hand that would declare her to be Queen in front of her people. Melbourne was just behind her.

As the Lord Chamberlain readied himself to make the official announcement, she turned to Melbourne. She needed to attend to something most important, and she thought he might understand. 'I am called Alexandrina Victoria in the proclamation, I believe?'

'Yes, Ma'am.'

'Yet I do not like the name Alexandrina. From now on I wish to be known only by my second name, Victoria.'

Melbourne nodded.

'Victoria,' he said, rolling the name around his mouth as if tasting it for the first time. 'Queen Victoria,' and he smiled.

Stepping out onto the balcony, Victoria heard the noise of the crowd swell until finally a woman shouted, 'God Save the Queen.'

Victoria looked out over the upturned faces, and she waved to her people.

Chapter Eight

THE CARRIAGE TURNED IN THROUGH THE MARBLE Arch, the great ceremonial entrance to Buckingham House. Although it had been described as a royal wedding cake at the time it was built, thanks to the London fogs the icing was now more yellow in hue than white.

Victoria had been to Buckingham House once before as a little girl. She remembered being amazed by the size of her Uncle George's calves straining against their silk stockings. He had pinched her cheek hard enough to make her wince, but made up for it by offering her a sweetmeat from the silver box beside him. She had accepted gratefully, as there was nothing she liked better, but to her mortification Mama had snatched the Turkish Delight out of her hand, claiming it would ruin her appetite. The King had looked offended, and Victoria had been furious. Later the Duchess had told her that she should never accept any food offered by her uncles, in case it had been 'tampered with'. Victoria, who had not really understood her mother's meaning, had asked Lehzen, but her governess had shrugged and said that the Duchess had her own ideas.

As her carriage came through the arch, Victoria gasped as she saw the façade of the house. 'So many windows.'

'Indeed, Ma'am. This house almost bankrupted your Uncle George,' said Lord Melbourne. The other occupant of the carriage, Baroness Lehzen, said nothing.

'It will be so light after Kensington,' said Victoria.

'Was it so very dark there, Ma'am?'

Victoria glanced at him. 'It was hard, sometimes, to see things clearly.'

Melbourne inclined his head, acknowledging the unspoken meaning.

Victoria had not quite known how to go about the business of moving from Kensington. Her mother had been baffled by the suggestion, failing to understand why anyone would want to live in the middle of the city, with all its noxious fumes, when they could enjoy the sweet air of Kensington, surrounded by parkland. In the end, Victoria had mentioned her wish to Lord Melbourne, who had agreed that a monarch should be seen by her public on a regular basis and she would be much closer to her people at Buckingham House.

Victoria had been pleasantly surprised at the speed with which Melbourne had arranged matters. In the week since she had become Queen, she had found that her courtiers seemed to take more pleasure in denying her wishes than in fulfilling them. On the previous day, the sun had shone, but Victoria could barely see the trees through the windows of the Long Gallery, which were mired in grime. When she mentioned her displeasure to the Lord Chamberlain, Lord Uxbridge, a man with hair growing out of his ears and a strong smell of madeira about his person, she had heard a sharp intake of breath. This was followed by a long and largely incomprehensible speech about precedent, from which she gathered that he was responsible for cleaning only the *inside* of the windows; the outside were the bailiwick of the Master of the Horse or some such. Victoria's evident irritation at this answer had not seemed to make any difference. This was the way things were done, and it appeared that this was the way things would always be done.

But Lord Melbourne, today at least, seemed to be a man of his word. He and Victoria had had their weekly audience in the morning, and this afternoon they were about to look around Buckingham House.

They were met on the steps by Lord Uxbridge, whose nose seemed to have swollen to twice its natural size. 'I had hoped, Ma'am, for a little more notice. The house has been shut up for some time, and the dust, I am afraid, has been allowed to accumulate. If I might suggest that you return next week when there has been time to arrange things properly?'

'I am not afraid of dust, Lord Uxbridge. There is enough of it at Kensington.'

Lord Uxbridge was about to protest when Melbourne spoke. 'I am surprised, Uxbridge, that the house should not be in a state of readiness. Have the servants been dismissed?'

'I am afraid that when a house is not used regularly, some attention to detail is lost.'

Melbourne laughed. 'What you mean, Uxbridge, is that the servants here are good-for-nothings who have been eating and drinking at Her Majesty's expense while doing no work. A situation that has developed even though the housekeeper here is, I believe, a particular friend of yours?'

Victoria saw the Lord Chamberlain's face, already flushed, swell with such emotion that his nose looked as though it might actually burst. She did not fully understand why Melbourne's mention of the housekeeper should have brought him to a state of near apoplexy, but she was glad to see him turn and gesture to the footmen, whose wigs she had already noted were rather grubby, to open the doors.

Walking into the entrance hall and gazing at the gilded cornices of the distant ceiling, Victoria felt quite giddy. Even with all the furniture shrouded in dustsheets, the rooms felt so much more magnificent than her apartments at Kensington.

They walked down the long corridor, with the footmen running ahead of them to pull away the covers. The room seemed to blossom in front of them as gilt chairs, malachite side tables, and marble torchères were revealed.

They came to a set of double doors, which opened onto a vast expanse of red, white and gold. At the end, on a red dais, was the throne, upholstered in red velvet with her uncle's monogram GR embroidered on the hangings in gold thread.

Victoria hesitated for a second, then walked across the room and sat down on the throne. As she settled herself, she disturbed a cloud of dust from the cushions.

'I find it hard to credit, Uxbridge, that the Queen appears to be sitting on a dusty throne.' Lord Melbourne's voice was light as always, but no one could mistake his disapproval. The other man's shoulders were slumped, all his earlier bluster gone.

Victoria realised that while the throne was comfortable, her feet did not touch the floor. Melbourne noticing this said, 'I think, Ma'am, that before you hold your first official Drawing Room, we must find you a throne that fits.'

She looked down at her feet dangling in the air. 'It is hard to be dignified when your feet are six inches off the ground, that is true.'

She glanced up to see Melbourne smiling at her. 'Indeed, Ma'am, and I believe the monogram needs changing too.'

Victoria laughed. 'Yes, I believe you are right.'

Lehzen stepped forward. 'Perhaps, Majesty, we should look over your private apartments. Lord Uxbridge, would you be showing us the way?' Lehzen nodded towards the Lord Chamberlain.

There was a sharpness to her voice that made Victoria look at her governess. There were two red spots on Lehzen's cheeks. She remembered her governess's warning about Melbourne; surely she didn't still think he was unsuitable company? But then she saw Lehzen look at Melbourne and realised that her governess was jealous. The Baroness was used to having Victoria all to herself.

They followed Lord Uxbridge through a picture gallery lit by a glass skylight. Melbourne stopped in front of a painting depicting a woman holding a small dog.

'He had good taste, your uncle, even if he had no judgement.'

'Is that possible, Lord Melbourne?'

'Most likely, Ma'am. In my experience an exquisite appreciation for the finer things in life can run alongside the most terrible folly. Your uncle never bought a bad picture or fell in love with a tiresome woman, but he had no common sense at all.'

'I see,' said Victoria.

'But he left some very fine buildings. The Pavilion at Brighton is quite remarkable, and he has turned this place into something fit for a King. Perhaps that's legacy enough for him. There isn't much else, God knows.'

'I hope, Lord Melbourne, that when I am dead, people don't talk about me with so little respect.'

'You are shocked, Ma'am, by my *lèse-majesté*. And maybe you are right, but I took you for someone who appreciates frankness.'

'It is something that no doubt I shall learn to appreciate.'

There was a cough from Lord Uxbridge, who gestured towards a set of double doors. 'This is the way to the private apartments, Ma'am.'

The private apartments were as resplendent as the rest of the Palace. Every surface was gilded, and the rooms were made to look even larger by the profusion of mirrors. Only the bedroom, with its bed topped by a canopy hung with red brocade, was without a looking glass.

'I think these apartments, with some alterations, might prove suitable for your use, Ma'am,' said Lord Uxbridge.

Melbourne looked around and raised an eyebrow. 'You might want to change the furniture for something more feminine.'

'I wonder why, in a place with so many mirrors, there are none in the bedroom? Surely my uncle must have wanted to check his appearance before facing the world,' said Victoria.

The Lord Chamberlain looked at Melbourne, who, with a slight grimace, began, 'At the risk of again offending the shade of the late King, I suspect that at the time when he was living here, he was not altogether happy with his reflection, Ma'am. He had been much admired for his figure in his youth, but I am afraid that as time went on he became altogether too fond of the pleasures of the table and his waistline suffered as a consequence. Indeed, at the end of his life he found it impossible to walk unaided on account of his girth. I believe that this room was a place where he could retreat and not have to be reminded of his ungainliness every time he turned his head.'

'You sound as if you feel sorry for him.'

'I can't deny it. He may have been foolish, but his life was not a happy one.'

Victoria looked around the vast chamber. 'I think I shall

find it difficult to sleep here all alone. Lehzen, I shall need to have you near me.'

Lehzen smiled with something like relief, and Victoria turned to Uxbridge. 'Is there somewhere suitable for the Baroness to have a room?'

'Indeed, Ma'am. There is a bedroom just here, through this interconnecting door.'

The small antechamber was decorated with painted Chinese silk panels and had a delicate faux bamboo bed.

'But this room is charming! Much more intimate than the other room. I wonder who slept here?'

Lehzen made one of her noises, and Victoria saw Melbourne and Uxbridge exchange looks.

'Is there some mystery, Lord Uxbridge?'

Uxbridge looked at his shoes. There was a pause, and then Melbourne spoke. 'This room, I believe, belonged to Mrs Fitzherbert, your late uncle's wife.'

'His wife? But I thought he married a German princess.'

'Caroline of Brunswick did indeed marry the King, but before that, Ma'am, he married a Maria Fitzherbert.'

Victoria was puzzled. 'I don't understand. Did Mrs Fitzherbert die?'

'No, Ma'am.'

'So can my uncle have been married to two women at once? Isn't that what they call bigamy? I thought that was a crime.' Victoria was shocked; her mother had always talked about her uncles being wicked, but she had assumed that Mama was, as usual, exaggerating.

'Indeed it is, Ma'am, but the rules are a little different if you are Prince of the Blood Royal. The Prince of Wales, as he then was, went through a marriage ceremony with Mrs

Fitzherbert, but because he did not have his father's consent, the marriage was illegal. The Prince and the lady both knew this, but as Mrs Fitzherbert was a Catholic she was most determined to have the sanction of the Church before surrendering her virtue.'

Lehzen gasped and said urgently, 'I think, Majesty, that we should return to Kensington. The armourer is coming this afternoon.'

Victoria turned to Melbourne. 'Thank you for explaining things to me, Lord Melbourne. There is so much, I realise, that I don't know. Even about my own family.'

'All families have their secrets, Ma'am. But I am glad to have been of service.'

Victoria moved towards the door.

'Perhaps, Ma'am, you might care to look at the Duchess's rooms, before you go,' said Lord Uxbridge.

Victoria stopped. 'Oh, I am not sure that will be necessary. I believe the Duchess is quite comfortable at Kensington. It seems a pity to disturb her.'

Melbourne, who had been looking out of the window, turned to look at her. 'Forgive me, Ma'am, but I think it would be a mistake if the Duchess were to remain at Kensington.'

'A mistake, Lord Melbourne? Surely that is a matter for my mother and me?'

Could it be that Melbourne was actually agreeing with her mother?

Melbourne walked towards her and said in a lower voice, so that Lehzen and Uxbridge could not hear, 'I do not presume to interfere in a family matter, Ma'am. But I should tell you that if you, an unmarried girl of eighteen, were to live apart from your mother, it would cause adverse comment. Your uncles were not models of virtue, but I think, Ma'am, that you do not want to make your people think that you follow in their footsteps.'

'But I am nothing like my uncles,' Victoria argued. 'I have no intention of behaving in an immoral way.'

'I am glad to hear it, Ma'am. But if you leave your mother behind at Kensington, there will be talk of an unpleasant kind, and that would be a shame so early in your reign.'

'I see.' Victoria pressed her lips together. She knew deep down that Melbourne was right, but that did not make it any less infuriating.

'You are annoyed with me for saying this, Ma'am, but I feel it is my duty. You are, of course, quite at liberty to ignore me.' Melbourne smiled at her. 'I shall not be offended. I know very well that it is much easier to give advice than to take it.'

Victoria paused. 'Perhaps it would be . . . inconvenient to have Mama as far away as Kensington. There are sometimes things I need to ask her, and it would be tiresome to be sending messengers all the time.'

Lord Uxbridge showed them a suite of rooms adjacent to the monarch's apartments. Victoria walked through them and then turned to Lord Uxbridge. 'These rooms are quite suitable, but I am afraid they are in the wrong place.'

'The wrong place, Ma'am?'

'Yes. I am not happy with their location.'

Uxbridge looked puzzled. Melbourne cleared his throat. 'I am sure that there is a similar suite of rooms in the north wing, Uxbridge.'

'Yes, indeed, but there would be no easy access to your apartments, Ma'am, as the only communication is through the central block.'

'Oh, I think that would suit very well. Mama would not like

to be disturbed all the time by my comings and goings, don't you agree, Lord Melbourne?'

'Most considerate, Ma'am.'

'Well, now that has been arranged, I should like to move in without delay, Lord Uxbridge.'

Uxbridge picked at one of the buttons on his waistcoat. 'When you say without delay, Ma'am, you are of course, aware that it will take some time to arrange things to your liking.'

'Very well. I can wait until Monday.'

'Monday, Ma'am? But that is only four days away! I am afraid it is quite impossible.'

'Impossible, Lord Uxbridge?' said Victoria in her most regal tone

Uxbridge's waistcoat button finally succumbed to its owner's fidgeting. It sprang from his hands across the room and landed with a little clatter on the parquet floor at Melbourne's feet.

Melbourne picked it up and handed it back to his owner. 'I am sure, Uxbridge, that when you consider the situation you will discover that it will be quite possible for the Queen and her household to move in on Monday. And I think that you might want to make some changes among the servants. A dusty throne does not set a good example.'

Uxbridge made a gesture somewhere between a bow and gesture of defeat. 'I shall make the necessary arrangements, Ma'am.'

Victoria smiled. 'And now I would like to see the gardens. I hear they are most splendid.'

They walked down the gravel paths towards the lake, Lehzen and Uxbridge in front, the Queen and Melbourne behind them. Victoria turned to Melbourne. 'Why did Lord Uxbridge go such a violent shade of red when you mentioned the house-keeper here, Lord Melbourne?'

'She is his mistress, Ma'am. And while she may very well perform her duties in that regard in the most exemplary fashion, as a housekeeper I believe she is not satisfactory.'

Victoria paused; no one had spoken to her so openly about such things before. She knew she should be scandalised, but found to her surprise that she felt flattered. Her mother, Conroy, even Lehzen might have tried to conceal the truth, but Melbourne did not think it necessary.

'You speak very frankly, Lord Melbourne.'

'I hope I do not offend you, Ma'am. I speak not to a young lady of delicate sensibilities but to a Sovereign.'

Victoria smiled. 'I cannot object to that. Indeed, I think I prefer it. I am tired of being treated as young lady without a thought in her head.'

'No one can do that now, Ma'am.'

'You would be surprised, Lord Melbourne. Only this morning Sir John Conroy and Flora Hastings came to my sitting room unannounced with a list of ladies they deem suitable for my household. Flora Hastings told me that she had picked girls who were not above average height!'

'That was thoughtful of her, perhaps, but hardly tactful to mention it.'

'They are always teasing me for being small. They think that just because I have not grown in stature I have not matured in mind. Conroy, Lady Flora, even Mama still think of me as a child, not as a Queen. Indeed, they don't believe me capable of ruling.'

Melbourne stopped on the gravel path and turned to look at Victoria. 'Then they are mistaken, Ma'am. I have not known you long, it is true, but I observed in you a natural dignity that cannot be learnt.'

'You don't think, then, that I am too small?'

'To me, Ma'am, you are every inch a Queen. And anyone who says otherwise should be sent straight to the Tower.'

'Oh, is that still allowed?' said Victoria.

'I don't know if the Traitor's Gate is still open, but I am sure there are modern equivalents.'

Victoria laughed. 'I believe you are teasing me.'

'Not at all. I merely point out the truth, which anyone would be foolish to ignore.'

Victoria saw Lehzen looking at her from the other side of the lake. From the reproachful tilt of her governess's head, Victoria could tell she was feeling left out.

She said 'When we first met, Lord Melbourne, you offered to act as my Private Secretary.'

'And you refused my offer, Ma'am.'

Victoria hesitated and then, 'Would you still be prepared to act in that capacity? I find I do need some assistance, and I believe that you would be the most suitable person to help me.'

Melbourne made a little bow. 'It would be a privilege and a pleasure to serve you in any way I can, Ma'am.'

Victoria saw Lehzen coming back round the lake towards them. 'I think we are very well suited,' she paused and then, smiling at her own daring, 'Lord M.' Melbourne smiled back at her. 'There is one thing that puzzles me.' Victoria gestured across the sweeping lawns to the great curved façade of the house.

'Why is this called Buckingham House? It looks more like a Palace to me.'

'Well, Ma'am, I believe you can call it whatever you like.'

Chapter Nine

VICTORIA HAD GIVEN LEHZEN THE TASK OF SHOWING her mother, the Duchess of Kent, to her new apartments in Buckingham Palace. As the two women climbed the grand double-pronged staircase, turning left towards the north wing of the house, Lady Flora Hastings and Sir John Conroy following behind, they saw a cluster of footmen carrying the portrait of the Duke of Kent up the opposite staircase.

Seeing this, the Duchess stopped and turned to Lehzen. 'Where is the painting of my poor dead husband going? I hope it will be in a place of respect.'

'Oh yes, Ma'am. The Queen has asked for it to be placed in her own sitting room.'

'I see.'

They continued to walk up the stairs until they reached the suite of rooms that Victoria had chosen for her mother. The walls were hung with yellow silk and the furniture had been made by Chippendale in walnut.

'The Queen hopes that you will be happy with these apartments, Ma'am. As you can see, they have a fine view of the gardens and the lake.' Lehzen gestured towards the window, but the Duchess ignored her and stood in the middle of the room and sniffed.

'The rooms are tolerable, I suppose, but I do not care for the colour yellow, as my daughter is aware.' Lehzen bowed her head. 'And where are Drina's rooms, Baroness?'

'The Queen's rooms are in the south wing, Ma'am, adjacent to the State rooms.'

Something about Lehzen's tone made the Duchess look at her sharply. 'And where do you sleep, Baroness?'

'I have a room next to the Queen's.' Lehzen paused and then added with a little smile, 'With an interconnecting door.' The Duchess turned away. 'And now if you will excuse me, Ma'am, I must go and check on the arrangement of Her Majesty's apartments. She has, as you know,' Lehzen looked at Sir John Conroy, 'put me in charge of her household.'

Lehzen left the room without looking back.

Crossing over to the other wing, she found Victoria waiting for her.

'How does Mama like her new rooms?'

'I think, Majesty, that perhaps you might want to ask the Duchess yourself.'

Victoria sighed. 'Very well. Are they all there?'

'If you mean Sir John Conroy and Lady Flora Hastings, then yes, they were with the Duchess when I left.'

'I see.'

Victoria looked at Lehzen, who shook her head. 'I don't think, Ma'am, that the Duchess would want to see *me* again so soon.'

'I don't see what she has to complain about. The rooms are furnished most elegantly, don't you think?'

'Yes, Majesty, but you know that the Duchess has most particular tastes.'

Victoria picked up her skirts with both hands and, turning, ran up the north staircase two steps at a time. There was still a delicious thrill in being able to do exactly as she pleased, after all those years of having to wait and hold Lehzen's hand. When she reached the top, she saw a footman looking at her in amazement and regretted her impulsiveness. She pulled herself up short.

'Please announce me to the Duchess.'

The footman nodded. Victoria thought that if she was going to have to visit her mother with Conroy and Flora in attendance, she would make her entrance as a Queen.

'Her Majesty the Queen,' the footman announced.

Victoria walked into the room, and from the corner of her eye she registered Conroy's grudging head bow and Flora Hastings's exaggerated curtsey. Her mother remained seated. Victoria could see that the corners of her mouth were turned down.

'I came to see how you were getting on in your new rooms, Mama.'

'So kind of you,' the Duchess glared at her, 'to come all this way.'

Victoria walked over to the window. 'What a charming view you have. Look how the summer house is reflected in the lake. I find the gardens here so pretty.'

'You are so easily pleased, Drina.'

Sir John cleared his throat. 'I believe, Ma'am, now that the household is installed here at Buckingham House –'

Victoria interrupted him. 'Palace, Sir John. Buckingham Palace.'

Conroy inclined his head a fraction. 'Now that you are established at Buckingham Palace, it is time that you gave your first
official Drawing Room. It will require careful planning, of course,
but I have already started the list of invitations. All the ambassadors, the other members of the royal family, and then you
will want to have politicians from both sides of the –'

Feeling a little surprised at her own boldness, Victoria put
up her hand to stop him. 'I have already made the list, thank
you, Sir John.'

'You drew up the list alone, Ma'am? Do you think that's
wise? The protocol around these occasions is treacherous.'

'I am aware of that, Sir John. That is why I asked Lord
Melbourne to make the arrangements. I believe he is quite
experienced in these matters.'

'Yes, indeed, but I am surprised that as Prime Minister he
has the time to attend to such things.'

'I believe Lord Melbourne must be the judge of that. He
has offered to act as my Private Secretary, and I have accepted
him in that position.'

Conroy picked up his cane, and Victoria thought for a
moment that he was about to strike the floor. A glance from
Lady Flora seemed to check his impulse.

'I see. You have your reasons, no doubt, although I think it
ill-advised to spend quite so much time with the Prime
Minister.'

Victoria's mother nodded her head vigorously in accord. 'You
haff to be impartial, Drina. Your father was a Whig, but he
was always being polite to the Tories.' Her German accent was
always more pronounced when she was agitated.

'Which brings me to the matter of your ladies-in-waiting,
Ma'am,' said Conroy. 'These appointments are so crucial for

setting the tone of your court. You will need at least eight – a Mistress of the Robes, Ladies of the Bedchamber, and then a number of maids-of-honour.'

Victoria looked at him impassively, then turned towards the door. 'I really must be going, Sir John. Good day, Lady Flora. Mama.'

She walked out of the room before her mother or Conroy could say anything more, but as she reached the landing, she heard footsteps behind her.

'One moment, Ma'am.'

Turning, Victoria was accosted by the angular figure of Lady Flora clutching a piece of paper. 'I have some suggestions here, Ma'am, for your maids-of-honour. These appointments are always unmarried. I have chosen those who are discreet and sensible, as young girls can be so flighty.' She looked as though she included Victoria among that category.

Flora held out the paper toward Victoria. 'And if there is anything else I can do to assist you, Ma'am, please don't hesitate to ask. The Baroness, being German, may not have been able to prepare you fully for your new responsibilities and the protocol of the court, but my family have been courtiers for generations.'

Victoria knew that in order to be rid of Lady Flora she had to take the proffered piece of paper. She plucked it out of the woman's hand and, giving her the briefest nod, proceeded down the staircase. She did her mother's lady-in-waiting the courtesy of pausing until she had reached the foot of the stairs before crumpling the paper up and dropping it on the floor.

Chapter Ten

IN THE THREE MONTHS SINCE SHE HAD MOVED INTO Buckingham Palace, Victoria had begun to understand the question that had puzzled her as a child: what did a Queen do all day? Apart from the hour she spent having her hair put up and getting dressed, her mornings were spent going through her official boxes with her Prime Minister. At first she had been overwhelmed by the sheer volume of the documents they contained, but then as Lord M had explained to her about the importance of checks and balances – an evangelical bishop should always be paired with a more traditional dean, for example, and for every professional soldier allowed into the household regiments there should be an officer of aristocratic lineage permitted to buy his way in – she began to see her way through the sheaves of paper. As she grew to understand the nuances, the daily exercise of power had delighted her; and there was nothing she liked more than to discuss the way that the world worked with her Prime Minister.

But this practical work, this exercise of patronage, was only one part of her duties. As Lord M always reminded her, a Queen also had a duty to show herself to her public. Every afternoon she would ride out in the Park, usually with her

Prime Minister, and once or twice a month she would make a visit to a charitable institution such as an almshouse or a hospital. These visits were always brief, but Victoria enjoyed riding through the streets waving to the crowds. And then, as Melbourne explained, there were her ceremonial duties: Opening Parliament, officiating at the Garter ceremonies, and of course the Drawing Rooms, where the diplomatic world would come to present their credentials to the Sovereign.

Today was Victoria's first Drawing Room, and the carriages stretched right to the end of the Mall. Everybody who had received a card had decided to attend. This had not been the case with the last King, whose Drawing Rooms at the end of his reign had consisted of little more than the King and a dozen stalwart courtiers.

But everyone wanted to see the new Queen. So many rumours were circulating as to her size (could it really be true that she was a dwarf?), her intellect (doubts had been expressed in the Pall Mall clubs as to her ability to read and write), and her command of English (there was speculation in the gutter press that, owing to her upbringing among Germans, the new Queen spoke with a pronounced accent).

Melbourne, who had heard all these stories, had long decided not to dignify them with a rebuttal. He knew from painful experience that to deny a rumour only served to give it currency. Much better to let the gossips find out for themselves how far off the mark they were.

He hoped that the Queen would not collapse under the weight of so much scrutiny. And then he smiled at his own folly.

'I rather think the silver brocade today, Jenkins.' Victoria pointed at one of the two dresses that her dresser was holding up. 'The figured silk is pretty, though.' Although the period of strict mourning for the King had only just ended, Victoria had spent the first month of her reign ordering a resplendent new wardrobe so that she would be ready to dazzle the court at her first Drawing Room. Her mother had always made her wear plain muslins, so Victoria had taken great pleasure in ordering dresses made from the richest materials: silks, velvets and brocades.

She turned from one to the other in a fever of indecision. 'What do you think, Lehzen?'

'I think the colour of the silk is matching your eyes, Majesty. It is most becoming.'

'I know, but Lord M says that he hates to see a woman in blue. He says it is not an elegant colour.'

Lehzen sniffed.

'Yes, I shall wear the brocade. I think it is more fashionable.'

Lehzen sniffed again.

'Do you have a cold, Baroness? Or do you disapprove of my choice?'

'I would never disagree with *your* choice, Majesty.'

Victoria saw the downward droop of her governess's mouth in the mirror, but decided to ignore it.

'Diamonds or pearls?' she said, pointing at her jewellery box.

Melbourne was waiting for her in the antechamber that led from the private to the State apartments. 'How splendid you look, Ma'am.'

'Do you like this brocade? It comes from Venice, I believe.

Mama does not like it; she says I am not old enough to wear it.'

'I think a Queen can wear anything she wants.'

'Except blue, you told me that you never liked to see a woman in blue.'

'Did I, Ma'am?' Melbourne smiled. 'Are you ready to go in?'

'Quite ready, Lord M.'

The buzz and chatter of the three hundred guests went quiet as the double doors opened, and every head turned to catch sight of the new Queen. The silence gradually evaporated into a hum of excitement as people turned to each other to confirm their impressions of their new monarch.

'Small, certainly, but not a midget.'

'Everything is quite in proportion.'

'Of course she has the Hanoverian chin.'

'You mean the lack of one.'

'Nonsense. She is quite charming. What a change to have a pretty young Queen.'

'An eighteen-year-old girl who is barely out of the schoolroom, with a made-up name. I have never heard of anyone called Victoria. It's preposterous.'

'I would rather have a Queen Victoria than a King Ernest.'

'I think Melbourne agrees. I have never seen him so attentive to a woman who wasn't someone else's wife.'

'I hear they are calling him the royal nursemaid in White's.'

'Well, he has the experience – think of his wife.'

'Little Vicky must seem easy after Caro.'

'She needs a husband, of course.'

'Some German prince with side whiskers and onions in his pockets.'

'Heavens preserve us. There are enough Germans in the Palace.'

'Pumpernickel Palace.'

But Victoria could hear none of the swirl of chatter and gossip that surrounded her. The only voice she attended to was that of Lord Melbourne whispering in her ear the names and attributes of the guests as they ascended the dais to be presented.

'This is the Duchess of Sutherland, Ma'am. I think she would be an excellent candidate for Mistress of the Robes.'

Victoria looked at the tall, elegant brunette in front of her, whose hair was arranged *à l'anglaise* with cascades of ringlets on either side of her face. It was a style that Victoria admired very much but had never dared attempt.

She smiled as the Duchess raised herself from her curtsey. 'I look forward to making your acquaintance, Duchess.'

As the Duchess retreated with great dignity towards the throng, Victoria remarked to Melbourne, 'She is most elegant, certainly, but is she respectable?'

Melbourne hardly missed a beat. 'As respectable as a great lady can be, Ma'am.'

'Lehzen says that the morals of the women in the highest ranks of society are deplorable. The Duchesses, she says, are the worst.'

'Is the Baroness speaking from first-hand experience, I wonder, or has she perhaps been listening to gossip?'

'That is possible. Do you know that before our first audience she warned me about your reputation? She said you were disreputable.'

'Well, the Baroness is quite right there, of course.' Melbourne smiled at her. 'If I were not your Prime Minister, there could be no excuse for you being alone with someone like me.'

'Now you are teasing me, Lord M.'

'On the contrary. Now, Ma'am, I would like to present Lady Portman. Her husband is the Under-Secretary for the Colonies and something of a booby, but Emma Portman knows every-body and everything and I think would make an excellent member of your household.'

Lady Portman, a well presented woman in middle age whose grey eyes glittered with intelligence, curtseyed before her.

'Lady Portman knew your father, Ma'am.'

Emma Portman smiled. 'I had the pleasure of dancing the polka with him, Your Majesty. The late Duke was an excellent dancer.'

Victoria looked delighted. 'Really. I did not know that. I suppose that is why I love dancing so much, but I have not had much chance to practise.'

Emma smiled. 'But surely there is to be a Coronation Ball, Ma'am? I believe it is customary.'

'Oh I do hope so.' She turned to Melbourne, suddenly concerned. 'That is, if you think we can afford it, Lord M?'

Melbourne smiled. 'As I trust you will only be having one Coronation, Ma'am, I think we can afford a little celebration.'

Victoria beamed. 'I shall open the ball with you, Lord M.'

'Oh, I think you will find there will be more promising dancing partners, Ma'am, but perhaps you will save me a dance further down your card.'

It was fortunate perhaps that only Lady Portman overheard this exchange; but others in the ballroom could not fail to observe the entente between the monarch and her Prime Minister. Sir John Conroy, who stood behind the sofa where the Duchess of Kent and Lady Flora sat, watched the conver-sation between the pair with a face that seemed frozen in disapproval.

'It seems, Ma'am, that Melbourne means to fill your daugh-ter's household with the wives of his ministers. Do you see how he is introducing her only to ladies of the Whig faction?'

'But it is customary, I think, Sir John, for the ladies to come from the same party as the Prime Minister.'

'Perhaps, but they are all the wives of Melbourne's particular friends. There is no one to check his influence on her.'

'I think she is a young girl who is enjoying the attentions of a man very much older than herself. It will all change when she marries.' The Duchess shrugged. 'I shall write to Leopold and suggest that Albert and Ernst come and visit soon. Her cousins will distract her from Lord Melbourne.'

'I wish I could share your confidence, Ma'am,' said Conroy.

Lady Flora leant towards the Duchess. 'Her partiality for Melbourne has been much remarked. My brother says that it is the cause of gossip in the clubs. I wonder if the Queen is aware of how much interest her behaviour is provoking.'

The Duchess looked over to where her daughter was whispering to Melbourne behind her fan. 'I am thinking that my daughter is aware of the dignity of her position, but there can be no harm in giving her some guidance,' she sighed, 'although it is not as easy for me to see her as it was at Kensington. We used to be so close; every night I would listen to her breathing and thank God that she was still alive. But now if I want to talk to her, I have to make an appointment.'

The line of guests to be presented to the Queen had finally dwindled to nothing. Seeing the Queen fighting to suppress a yawn, Melbourne leant over and asked her if she would like to bring the ceremony to a close.

'Oh, I have enjoyed it tremendously. But I confess that talking to so many new people has made me a trifle fatigued. I did not know there were so many ambassadors to the Court of St James. The world is a much bigger place than I imagined.'

'You are a long way from Kensington today, Ma'am.'

'I wish sometimes that I had been better prepared. I know that people expect me to talk to them, but I can never think of anything interesting to say.'

'You mustn't worry on that score, Ma'am. Everything a Queen says is interesting.'

Seeing her mother making her way towards her, and having no desire to talk to her, Victoria stood up. At her movement the assembled company also stood and parted before their Queen like the Red Sea before Moses. As she left the room, the hum of conversation rose. If anyone noticed that the Queen had seemed anxious to avoid her mother, they did not mention it, or at least not until the men in their silk stockings and the women in their ostrich plumes were waiting outside for their carriages.

'Did you see how the Queen scurried away as the Duchess of Kent approached? It looked as though she would rather put an end to the Drawing Room than talk to her.'

'Sir John Conroy had a face like thunder. I suppose the Queen is not as susceptible to his charms as the Duchess.'

'The star of the Conroyals seems to be in decline.'

'Conroyals! That's droll.'

'But apt, don't you think?'

'Undoubtedly.'

Chapter Eleven

THE GREEN DRAWING ROOM IN BUCKINGHAM PALACE was the place where Victoria liked to sit with her ladies. It had the advantage of only having one entrance, so that if she gave orders that she did not want to be disturbed, it was impossible for the Duchess or anyone else to come in through a back door.

Victoria had been a little nervous at first about appointing the Duchess of Sutherland and Lady Portman to her household. Lady Portman was only a little younger than her mother and famous as a wit. Lord M had told her that he had only made Lord Portman a minister so that he could benefit from Emma's experience.

Harriet Sutherland, who was much closer to Victoria in age, was known as a leader of fashion. Engravings of her latest hairstyle or the ingenious way in which she knotted her fichu were much in demand. Her penchant for wearing a thin gold chain across her brow had set a fashion in the drawing rooms of Mayfair and indeed in the Palace, where Victoria herself was now wearing gold links threaded through her chignon with a small pendant lying in the middle of her forehead.

For all her elegance, however, Harriet was not in the least intimidating and was always ready to advise on the niceties of fashion, although Victoria did not agree with the Duchess's reluctance to wear diamonds in the daytime. One of the great pleasures of her new position were the jewels that were now in her possession. But in deference to the Duchess, she had only put a couple of diamond clips in her hair.

Today they were looking at one of the illustrated fashion magazines that Victoria had had sent over from Paris. The current fashion for leg of mutton sleeves had reached its zenith, and Victoria and her ladies were marvelling over a plate showing a pair of young ladies with sleeves so voluminous that they resembled nothing so much as butterflies with their small round heads nestling between their gaudy wings.

'The French always go too far,' said Harriet. 'How could anyone have a conversation wearing sleeves like that?'

'I think these styles are for women who only want to be admired from afar,' said Emma. 'I saw Mrs Norton wearing something similar at the opera last week. But as no one wants to be seen speaking to her, I suppose the sleeves are no impediment.'

Victoria looked up. She wanted, very much, to know more about Mrs Norton. 'Why does nobody want to be seen speaking to Mrs Norton?'

Harriet and Emma looked at each other. Harriet shook her head, but Emma, who had deduced the reason for the Queen's curiosity, leant forward.

'You must know, Ma'am, that Mrs Norton's husband brought a case against her last year for criminal conversation.'

Victoria remembered Lehzen's embarrassed explanation of the term.

'Mr Norton, an odious man, alleged that his wife had been having relations with Lord Melbourne. And went so far as to prosecute.'

Victoria blushed and looked down at her hands.

'William was called as a witness and made to answer all kinds of impertinent questions in court, but fortunately the jury would have none of it and the case was dismissed.'

'So Lord Melbourne was innocent?'

Emma looked at the Queen's shining young face, and chose her words with care. 'Of course, William was friendly with Mrs Norton. I believe he sympathised with her plight in being married to a most uncongenial man. He is, as you know, a man who is always easy in the company of women.'

'How monstrous that he should be put to the misery of a trial.'

'I feel sure that the Tories were behind it, Ma'am. I believe they persuaded Norton to bring his case. They would like nothing better than to bring Melbourne down.'

Victoria stood up, and so Harriet and Emma did likewise. 'I wonder that Lord Melbourne does not marry again?'

'I think, Ma'am, that his experience of marriage was not a happy one, and perhaps he has been reluctant to repeat it.'

Emma had been in political life long enough to know that the Queen had many questions she wished to ask about Lord Melbourne's marriage if only she knew how. And because she was very much enjoying her place at court and her new status as the Queen's confidante, she decided to speak.

'Caroline, his wife, Ma'am, was charming but, I regret to say, unstable. They were very happy at first, I believe, but then Caro made the acquaintance of Lord Byron. He was an awful man, of course, quite depraved yet devilishly handsome. Caro was completely enamoured of him, and behaved in a way that was most unbecoming in a married woman. Poor William was made a laughing stock. I believe his mother wanted him to divorce her, but he refused. When Byron threw Caro over, she was quite distraught; there was talk of committing her to an asylum. But William would not abandon her. He is a man of great feeling.'

Victoria's mouth fell open. 'How could any wife do such a thing?'

'Caro was not an ordinary woman, Ma'am. She was a Bessborough, and I am afraid her upbringing left much to be desired.'

'And yet Lord Melbourne stuck by her?'

'Yes, Ma'am. He cared for her until her death a few years ago. And then he went back to politics. He could not, of course, have become Prime Minister with Caro at his side.'

'What a sad story, and yet Lord Melbourne always seems so cheerful.'

Once again Harriet and Emma exchanged glances. Emma Portman continued, 'I think, Ma'am, that if you had known him last year you would not say that, but his mood, of late, is much improved.'

'My husband thought he was ready to give up politics after the Mrs Norton affair,' said Harriet, 'but now he seems quite happy to be Prime Minister.'

'I am very glad that he did not give up,' said Victoria. 'I do not think that I could have managed half so well with someone else.'

Harriet and Emma smiled, and so did Victoria, but for different reasons.

Since moving to Buckingham Palace, Victoria had done everything she could to separate herself physically from her mother. She had been quite successful, but there were some occasions where protocol left the Queen no choice but to be at her mother's side.

One of these instances was the weekly service in the Chapel

Royal. Victoria would drive over the short distance from Buckingham Palace, but it had become her custom to walk back across The Mall. This habit had become known to the public, and crowds would gather on a Sunday morning waiting for a glimpse of their Queen.

The sermon that morning had been on the fourth Commandment, *Honour thy father and mother*. Victoria had been conscious of her mother's eyes upon her as the priest talked about the respect due to a parent being the model for belief in God. She shifted in her pew and wished that Lord M was with her. She had asked him to come with her on previous occasions, but he had told her that he was not a church-going man.

As the organ played, Victoria got up to leave the chapel, and as precedence demanded, her mother followed immediately behind.

When they reached the steps of the chapel, there were a few cheers from the people waiting outside. Victoria felt her mother's hand on her shoulder, and had no choice but to walk out arm in arm with her.

'Such a beautiful sermon, do you not think, Drina?'

'Fisher was certainly eloquent, Mama. But I don't think I have ever found a sermon too short.'

A little girl ran out from the crowd and held out a small bunch of flowers to Victoria. She bent down and took them, and a murmur of appreciation went up from the crowd.

'Oh, how charming.'

The Duchess said nothing, but then another slightly bigger girl came from the other side with a posy for her, and she too bent down and went so far as to plant a kiss on the little girl's cheek.

'You see, the people do not forget the mother of their Queen.'

'No, Mama. You have always been popular with the people.'

Victoria tried to move on, but the Duchess once again put her arm through hers, a gesture that made the crowd sigh with pleasure. How lovely to see their young Queen walking with her mother.

Victoria realised that there was no escape.

'So, Drina, are you happy with the Duchess of Sutherland as Mistress of the Robes?'

'Very happy. She is so charming and elegant.'

'And what about Lady Portman?'

'I like her very much. She told me that she once danced a polka with Papa.'

'It is possible. She is certainly old enough.'

'I find her most amusing.'

'But both these ladies are married to friends of Lord Melbourne, Drina. I think it is not wise.'

'They are not my only ladies, Mama, and it is quite normal for the ladies of the household to be connected to the party of government.'

The Duchess shrugged. 'Quite usual, perhaps, I am not knowing. But what I think is not so usual is for you to be surrounded only by Melbourne's friends. There is no one there to tell you what he is really like.'

'I think I know what he is really like, Mama. I believe Lord Melbourne to be the most capable of men. He has been invaluable to me since I came to the throne.'

'Of course, he has. But I warn you, Drina, as your mother, I wish you to be on your guard with him.'

'On my guard? What on earth can you mean, Mama?'

Victoria's voice rose on this last remark and she saw a woman in the crowd give her a curious glance.

'He is not, I am thinking, quite reliable. You must know that last year he was accused of a criminal conversation with a married woman.'

'Of course! And I also know that he was acquitted.'

The Duchess rolled her eyes. 'Even an English jury will not find their Prime Minister guilty, Drina.'

'Is it impossible for you to imagine that he might have been acquitted because he was innocent, Mama?'

The Duchess laughed. 'Oh, Drina, your Lord Melbourne may be many things, but he is not innocent.'

Mother and daughter made the rest of the journey back to the Palace in silence, and Victoria thought she might manage to escape without another lecture from her mother. But as they walked through the Marble Arch and into the courtyard of the Palace, her mother turned to her again. This time the Duchess leant towards her and her face was soft. Victoria caught a whiff of lavender and felt for a moment such regret that things between them could not be more easy.

'Dearest Drina, I think perhaps that I have failed you as a mother. I have been leaving you together too much with Baroness Lehzen, who is not really understanding the ways of the world.'

The Duchess put her hand to Victoria's cheek and stroked it tenderly. 'I want to tell you something, *Liebes*. Something I think that only a mother can be saying.' She opened her eyes wide.

'You must be careful with Lord Melbourne. You are a young girl, and he, well he is *ein Herzensbrecher*. A stealer of hearts. You should take care, Drina, that he does not steal yours.'

'Really, Mama, there is no danger of that. You forget I am the Queen and he is my Prime Minister.'

'I am sure that is what you are believing, Drina, and maybe it is true. But I am seeing the way your cheeks are making a rose every time you see him.'

Chapter Twelve

*D*INNER WAS NOT A CONVIVIAL MEAL THAT EVENING, as the Queen appeared to have lost her appetite. Since she was only picking at her food, it meant the other diners were not really able to enjoy their fricassée of oysters, or veal ravigote engelée, as the moment Victoria put down her fork all the plates were whisked away by the footmen standing behind every chair. No one, of course, could continue eating when the Queen had finished. This had a dampening effect on the conversation, as every diner was anxious to partake of as much food as possible before the Sovereign stopped eating.

Although she would not admit it, even to herself, Victoria's loss of appetite had everything to do with her mother's warning. Was Lord M really a *Herzensbrecher*? She had felt that he alone, of all the men who surrounded her at court, liked her for herself, not just for her position. But perhaps, as her mother said, he liked all women. She looked down the table to where he was laughing with Emma Portman and felt a pang of something she did not quite recognise. Did he laugh so merrily when he was with her, she wondered. She put down her spoon and got to her feet. The rest of the table did likewise, the ladies following Victoria as she led the way to the drawing room, the gentlemen escorting them as far as the dining-room door.

The gentlemen did not linger after the Queen and her ladies had gone to the drawing room. Although Melbourne was partial to the Palace port, he had no desire to drink it in the company of Conroy. As he got up from the table, he found to his displeasure Conroy accompanying him to the door.

'The Duchess was wondering, Melbourne, about the seating arrangements for the Coronation.'

Melbourne was irked by the way that Conroy had addressed him as an equal. But as ever, his politeness in replying was in inverse proportion to his annoyance. 'Indeed, Sir John. Is there something in particular that the Duchess wishes to know?'

'Her Royal Highness wants to know if her brother King Leopold will be attending, and her nephews, Albert and Ernst? She is concerned that the Queen might have forgotten the Coburg side of the family.'

Melbourne gave Conroy his most engaging smile. 'Oh, I think that would be most unlikely. The Queen, as you know, has the most astonishing grasp of detail. But sadly protocol forbids the presence of another monarch at the Coronation, which would preclude the attendance of King Leopold. I think that their Serene Highnesses Prince Albert and Prince Ernst would hardly like to attend without him.'

Conroy bowed his head. 'You have the advantage of me, Melbourne, when it comes to protocol. I shall explain that to the Duchess. But I think, or rather the Duchess thinks, it would be wise if the Queen were to invite her cousins to visit in the near future.'

'Indeed? Then I suggest that you or rather the Duchess should make that suggestion to the Queen herself. She alone issues invitations to the Palace, a freedom that she rather enjoys as I believe it is the first time she has been at liberty to choose her companions.'

Melbourne walked out of the dining room without looking back.

In the drawing room, Victoria looked up at once as he walked in. 'Ah, Lord M, we were just about to play Piquet. Would you care to join us?'

Melbourne felt Emma looking at him from one corner of the room, and Conroy from the other. He knew that every exchange of his with the Queen, however innocent, was being scrutinised.

'Will you forgive me, Ma'am, if I decline? There are some government matters I must attend to.'

Victoria frowned. 'I think I can excuse you, but I shall expect you in the Park tomorrow for our ride. I don't enjoy it without you.'

Melbourne smiled; his efforts at discretion were no match for the Queen's guilelessness. 'In that case, Ma'am, I shall be there.'

Chapter Thirteen

'I THINK I WILL WEAR THE RED HABIT TODAY, JENKINS.'
Victoria put up her arms, and Mrs Jenkins pulled the riding costume over her head. It was made of scarlet gabardine with gold lace on the facings and braid on the skirts, secured by a row of gold buttons that Mrs Jenkins was fastening with a buttonhook.

She looked at herself in the mirror and smiled. The door opened, and Lehzen came in behind her, and curtseyed to her reflection.

'Don't you think my new habit is perfectly splendid?' Victoria said. 'I wish I could wear it all the time. I feel so happy without my stays.'

Lehzen looked mildly scandalised, and Jenkins repressed a smile.

Victoria noticed. 'Oh, Lehzen, surely I can say that I don't like wearing a corset. It's so nice to be able to bend over and move my arms around. It's boring to be trussed up in a corset all the time, like a chicken.'

'It is part of being a woman, Majesty.'

'Not just women, Lehzen. Lord M told me that my Uncle

George was so fat that he used to wear stays in order to keep his waistcoat buttoned.'

'Lord Melbourne is so well informed.'

Victoria put on the high-crowned riding hat and turned around in front of the looking glass to admire herself. 'If only I could wear this to the Coronation Ball, then I could dance all night in perfect comfort.'

'You are the Queen, Majesty. There is no one to stop you.'

'True. I shall ask Lord M. But I am afraid he will think I have lost my wits.'

'I doubt that, Majesty.'

Hyde Park was still shrouded in mist when Victoria rode into Rotten Row accompanied by her groom and Lord Alfred Paget, her equerry. Melbourne was waiting for her, as always, by the gates to Apsley House.

When he saw her, he smiled. 'How charming you look today, Ma'am. I believe that is a new riding habit.'

They cantered along at quite a pace, dust flying before them, until they reached the northern limit of the Park. Victoria reined in her horse, and they turned down along the Serpentine.

'I think our rides in the morning are quite my favourite part of the day, Lord M. If I didn't have the Park to look forward to, I don't think I would ever get out of bed.'

As they crossed the bridge spanning the Serpentine, Victoria turned to him, and said in a rush of words, 'We talk about everything on our rides, but you never talk about your past, Lord M.'

'My past, Ma'am? I am afraid that is neither edifying nor entertaining.'

Victoria looked out across the water. 'I wonder that you have never married again.'

Melbourne paused, and then, 'Caro was not a model wife by any means. But she suited me well enough, and I have never found anyone to replace her.'

'But didn't you mind when she ran away with Lord Byron?'

'Mind?' Melbourne gripped the reins of his horse. 'Yes, I minded.'

'And yet you took her back afterwards. I don't think I could do such a thing.'

'Perhaps, Ma'am, you are too young to understand.'

Victoria kicked her heels into her horse's side and rode off. Melbourne hesitated briefly and then followed her. When he was alongside she turned and said, 'I am old enough to be Queen, Lord Melbourne.'

'I meant no disrespect, Ma'am. But in my experience the young cannot always understand the compromises of age.'

Victoria bit her lower lip. 'I think she, your wife, I mean, behaved very badly.'

'I agree, Ma'am, that is how it must look, but Caro was not like other women. I found it easier to forgive her than to turn her away.'

'I could not do it.'

'I very much hope you will never have to, Ma'am.'

Victoria felt her cheeks burning. She did not understand why he was being so short with her. She had meant no offence by asking about his wife. As they reached Apsley House she turned her horse's head in the direction of the Palace.

'I shall go in now. I think I will look over the army lists before the next Privy Council.'

'I think that would be wise, Ma'am.'

'Yes,' said Victoria. 'I think perhaps I have been neglecting my duties of late. I don't think I will ride out tomorrow, but go through my boxes instead. I have had so many charitable requests, I really must attend to them. The Baroness will help me, I am sure.'

'The country is fortunate to have such a diligent Queen, Ma'am,' said Melbourne as he turned his horse towards Park Lane. And they went their separate ways, both riders thinking of the words they wished they had said.

Chapter Fourteen

 T HE SMELL WAS SO STRONG THAT VICTORIA HAD TO
    put her handkerchief in front of her face.

'Is it always like this in the city, Lehzen?'

'That is Billingsgate on your left, Majesty. The fish market.'

Victoria looked out of the window and saw a small boy pushing a trolley loaded with fish heads and bones along the side of the road.

'Look at that. What do you think he could want with all those fish heads?'

'Probably he is collecting them to sell for soup, Ma'am.'

'Oh.'

Victoria was relieved when they left the fish market behind. Through the window she could see the white towers that were her destination.

The carriage clattered across the cobbles and came to the drawbridge, which was guarded by two Beefeaters who saluted as they approached.

Victoria looked up at the ancient stone arch and saw that the underside was covered in dark green moss. She shivered.

'I keep thinking of Anne Boleyn.'

'She was a foolish woman, I believe,' said Lehzen.

'But to have her head cut off! I think it was somewhere here. Oh, I wish Lord M were here. He would be able to tell us everything and make a story out it.'

Lehzen drew her lips together in a thin line.

The carriage circled the White Tower and drew up outside a building on the left of the outer wall. The footman pulled out the carriage steps and Victoria walked into the Jewel House.

'If you will allow me to lead the way, Your Majesty.' The Keeper of the Queen's Jewels was sweating, even though the air inside the thick stone walls was dank.

He produced a large key and made a great show of unlocking the vault. The doors opened reluctantly.

The interior of the vault was dark and musty. Victoria coughed. The Keeper looked around in dismay.

'I apologise, Ma'am, for not having aired the chamber. I should have made preparation, but we have never had a woman, I mean a Queen, visit here before.'

Victoria inclined her head. 'I wanted to see the crown before the Coronation.'

'If you would like to sit down here, Ma'am, I shall bring over the casket.' The Keeper put a studded leather case on the table and opened it with a click. Victoria gasped as a ray of light hit one of the stones in the crown, throwing up a skein of dancing pinpoints that skittered around the gloom of the vault.

She stood up to take the crown out of its case. It was heavy; she guessed it weighed as much as Dash, perhaps even more. Lehzen stepped forward to help her, but Victoria shook her head. 'I think I must do this myself.'

Reaching up, she placed the crown on her head. It was, as she had suspected, far too big. When she let it go, it settled right down over her forehead, listing over her right eye.

'I have a looking glass here, Ma'am, if you would like to see the effect.'

He brought out a silver hand mirror with a monogram on the back. When Victoria looked at it curiously, the Keeper muttered apologetically, 'It belongs to my wife, Ma'am. She thought you might need it.'

'Your wife is very thoughtful. I am indebted to her.'

Victoria picked up the mirror. She thought that the tinsel crown she had made for doll No. 123 was a much better fit. She tried tilting the crown so that it perched on the back of her head, but it looked even more precarious. If she put it on straight, the head band rested half way down her nose, and all she could see was a diamond filtered blur. She put it down on the table with a thud.

'This will not do.'

'No, Ma'am.' The Keeper's voice throbbed with apology. 'Perhaps you would like to try this.'

He produced a coronet from another case. This was an airy knot of diamonds with clusters of sapphires round the head band.

It was a perfect fit. Victoria turned her head from side to side and admired the way in which it caught the light in her eyes.

'This is much better.'

'Yes, Ma'am, it is the Queen Consort's crown.'

Victoria took off the diadem. 'Unfortunately, I am not a Queen Consort, but a Queen Regnant. The State crown must be altered to fit my head. I cannot walk down the aisle in Westminster Abbey with a crown that is too big for me.'

'But the Coronation is on Thursday, Ma'am!'

'Then it is a good thing that I had the foresight to try it on.'

'But I worry, Ma'am, that it will always be too heavy for you. There are so many stones.'

'I am not concerned about the weight, merely the circumference.' She turned to Lehzen.

'Do you have a ribbon or some such so that I can leave the keeper with an accurate measurement?'

Lehzen pulled a lace from her pocket and wrapped it round the Queen's head, tying a knot where the ends met over her forehead. She handed it to the Keeper. 'Now there can be no excuse for it not fitting.'

Victoria heard the Keeper give a deep sigh as she left the room.

Back in the safety of the carriage, Victoria allowed herself to laugh. 'The Keeper's expression when I tried on the crown. I was trying so hard not to laugh. But really he should have checked it before.'

Lehzen gave her a sidelong glance. 'I am surprised that Lord Melbourne did not attend to it, Majesty. He is always so anxious to be of service.'

Victoria's smile faded. She sat up a little straighter in her seat. 'Lord Melbourne is the Prime Minister. He cannot attend to every single detail. The size of my crown is hardly an affair of state, Lehzen.'

'No? But what could be more important, Majesty?'

Victoria turned to look out of the window. She had asked Melbourne if he would come with her to the Tower, but he claimed that he was very busy at the moment preparing for the Coronation. As Lehzen pointed out, however, what could be more important really than a crown that fitted? Victoria congratulated herself on insisting that she try it on. Everything, all the trappings of state, had been designed for men, large, portly ones. She could barely lift the gold forks or the chased crystal goblets that her uncles had used. Even the knives and forks in the state cutlery service were enormous.

She had resolved not to show any discomfort after her mother had once said to her, at a state banquet at Windsor while the King had been alive, 'What tiny hands you have, Drina. Perhaps we should get a special place setting made, more suitable for someone of your size.'

Conroy had been smiling by her side. 'Do you think that's wise, Duchess? Your daughter has a little tendency to plumpness. We do not want to encourage her to overeat.' It was an exchange she had never forgotten. But now she decided that even if her mother had not meant it kindly, she was quite right. Her hands were small, and there was no reason at all why the Queen of the greatest country in the world should not have cutlery that was the right size – or indeed, a crown that fitted.

It was a thought that normally she would have shared with Lord Melbourne. He was always such an attentive listener. She never felt with him that he was simply waiting for her to finish so that he could make his own, superior, point. She could tell Lehzen, of course, but the Baroness was not the same as Lord M.

Chapter Fifteen

THE ORCHESTRA HAD ALREADY STARTED PLAYING, AND the music was drifting up from the ballroom to the Queen's bedroom. Victoria could not help tapping her foot as they started to play one of her favourite polkas. There was a muttered exclamation from Monsieur Philippe, the hairdresser who was brought in on special occasions. He was doing something very complicated with curling tongs, and Victoria's sudden movement had made him burn his fingers.

'I am sorry, Monsieur Philippe, but it's hard not to move when you hear music. Are you nearly finished?'

'*Oui, Votre Majesté.*'

Monsieur Philippe spoke French with an accent that Victoria was not familiar with, but as his speech was largely confined to *oui*, *non*, and *eh voilà*, she had no problem following him. Tonight she had asked him to do her hair in a style called *à l'impériale*. The hair was drawn back in a chignon, with two waterfalls of ringlets hanging down over each ear. Harriet Sutherland had started wearing her hair like this, and Victoria had heard Lord Melbourne compliment the Duchess on how elegant she looked.

'*Et voilà, votre Majesté.*'

Victoria turned to face the mirror, Monsieur Philippe standing proudly behind her. But her reflection made her stiffen in horror. Where the tall Duchess could carry off the elaborate hairstyle, on Victoria it looked absurd, more like a lap dog than a great lady.

'Oh. But I look ridiculous.' She felt unwelcome tears pricking in her eyes.

'I so wanted to look elegant,' Victoria almost wailed, 'but these ringlets make me look like Dash!'

Lehzen moved out of the shadows. 'I think you look very fine, Majesty.'

'No, I don't! I look silly and everyone will laugh at me.'

'No one laughs at the Queen, Majesty.' Victoria covered her face with her hands, biting her lip with the effort of not crying.

There was a rustle and a murmur behind her. Finally a soft voice said, 'Would you like me to do your hair in a pendant braid, Ma'am? I think it's a style that would suit a face like yours.' Victoria turned round and saw a girl of about her own age, who wore her hair in two coiled plaits that looped around her ears. 'I'm Skerrett, Ma'am, Mrs Jenkins's assistant.'

Mrs Jenkins stepped forward in high Welsh dudgeon. 'You must forgive Skerrett, Ma'am, for speaking out of turn. She is new to the Palace and doesn't know our ways.'

Victoria looked and saw the mortification on Monsieur Philippe's face, the indignation on Jenkins's, but her eye was drawn to the remarkably neat way in which Skerrett had arranged her own hair.

'I think, Monsieur Philippe, that you have executed the style admirably, but it does not suit me. You may leave us.'

Monsieur Philippe walked out of the room backwards, every sinew of his body expressing outraged pride.

Victoria looked at the new dresser. 'I think I should like to try the style you suggest. Can you do it quickly? I don't want to be late for my own ball.'

'Oh yes, Ma'am. I do my own hair in five minutes.' Skerrett clapped her hand over her mouth, realising she had been over-familiar.

Jenkins frowned. 'Are you sure this is wise, Ma'am? Skerrett has never done your hair before and you don't want any more delays.'

Victoria put up her chin; the tears had subsided now and she felt more in control. 'If Skerrett does my hair half as well as she does her own, I will be quite satisfied.'

Just as Skerrett had finished fastening the second pendant braid in position around Victoria's left ear, the door opened and Emma Portman came in.

'I came to tell you how splendid everything looks in the ballroom, Ma'am. I haven't seen anything so magnificent since your Uncle George's day. I can't wait to see the Grand Duke. I hear he is most handsome.'

'Oh yes, I meant to ask Lord M how I should address him. Is he a Royal Highness or an Imperial Highness, I wonder. And does he speak English? I certainly don't speak any Russian. Where is Lord M? He would have the answer; he always does.'

A flicker passed across Emma Portman's face. 'I am sure he will be here soon, Ma'am.'

'But he should be here now. He must know that I can't walk in without him.'

Emma looked at the floor. 'Perhaps, Ma'am, it would be better if you did not wait for him. If he has been delayed, you do not want to keep your guests waiting.'

Skerrett put the last pin into the Queen's hair. 'I hope that's to your liking, Ma'am.'

Victoria looked at herself in the glass. 'Yes. That is much

better. Thank you.' She turned to Emma. 'But you think Lord M will be here soon?'

'Yes, Ma'am, as I said. But I think it would be a mistake to wait for him. The dancing can't start until you open the ball.'

Victoria watched as Skerrett settled her tiara into position. 'You are right, I suppose. Lord M always says that punctuality is the politeness of princes. Please will you tell the Lord Chamberlain that I will be there shortly.'

Emma left the room with alacrity.

Victoria took another glance at herself in the looking glass, and smoothed down the brocade of her skirts. This dress, with full sleeves dropped on the shoulder and the train sweeping out behind shimmering with gold thread, felt like the most grown-up thing she had ever worn.

'You look like something out of a fairy tale, Ma'am,' Skerrett said softly.

'The Queen doesn't need to hear what you think, Skerrett,' said Jenkins crossly.

Victoria smiled. 'I just hope there won't be a bad fairy to cast a spell over me.'

Skerrett smiled back.

The door opened again, and Victoria turned, expecting to see Emma, but instead her mother was standing in the doorway with Conroy and Flora a little behind her. 'Oh, Drina, I have come to escort you into the ball.'

She walked into the room and took a proper look at Victoria. 'But how charming you look.' The Duchess went over to her daughter and adjusted the diamond necklace round her throat so that the pendant lay exactly between her clavicles.

'My little girl, all grown up. I am so proud.'

Conroy said to Victoria, 'It is time to make your entrance,

Your Majesty. Of course, this is the first time that many of the guests will have seen you, so I am sure I do not need to remind you to behave with decorum. I would not advise drinking champagne, for example.'

'Remember that you must not dance more than twice with the same man,' said the Duchess. 'People notice these things.'

'And you will, of course, open the ball with the Grand Duke, Ma'am, as he will be the highest ranking guest,' added Lady Flora, anxious as always to display her knowledge of protocol.

Victoria said nothing. They walked down the corridor to the Grand Staircase, and Victoria gasped as she saw how the crystal chandeliers sparkled in the candlelight.

The hum and chatter of the ballroom went silent as people turned to see the Queen. Victoria started down the staircase, her head held high, but she missed her footing, and for a second she thought she would fall down the staircase. But Lehzen was right behind her and gripped her by the elbow. 'I have got you, Majesty.'

'You understand now, I think, Ma'am, why we did not think it was safe for you to walk down the stairs alone, with your uncertain balance,' Conroy said. 'What a mercy you did not fall down the stairs in front of all these people.'

Victoria took her arm out of Lehzen's grasp, and without looking back, she walked down the staircase, her eyes scanning the crowd for the only person she wanted to see.

The messenger from the Palace walked up the stairs of Dover House. The door was opened by the butler.

'I have a message for Lord Melbourne from Lady Portman.'

'His Lordship is not at home to anyone.'

'Lady Portman told me to say that she knows what day it is, but the Queen is asking for him.'

The butler nodded. 'Wait here.'

His master, the butler knew, was sitting in the library, looking at the box that he kept in the third drawer of his bureau. The decanter of sherry he had placed there this morning would be almost empty by now. As much as he did not want to disturb his lordship on this day, the butler realised that the message should not be ignored.

He opened the door to the library and saw Melbourne exactly where he had left him early that morning. He cleared his throat, and Melbourne looked round, irritated. 'I told you I was not to be disturbed.'

'I know, my lord, but it is a message from the Palace. From Lady Portman. She says that the Queen is asking for you.'

'Emma should know better.'

'Lady Portman says that she knows what day it is, my lord, but the message could not wait.' Melbourne sighed. 'I have laid out your dress clothes, my lord.'

Melbourne waved him away and the butler retreated. The messenger was waiting in the hall. He looked up. 'Well?'

The butler nodded. 'You may tell Lady Portman that his lordship will be there soon.'

Victoria settled herself on the throne. At least now her feet could touch the ground. She signalled to a footman to bring her a glass of champagne. Drinking it quickly, she looked over at Emma Portman, who was standing to her right. 'Have you heard from Lord M?'

Emma's smile was strained. 'William is on his way, I am quite sure.'

Just then the Majordomo announced, 'His Imperial Highness, the Grand Duke Alexander of Russia.'

The guests melted before the Grand Duke, who walked up the red carpet toward Victoria. He was tall, with a magnificent blond moustache that tickled her hand as he brushed it with his lips.

'*Bienvenue en Angleterre, votre grande Altesse Impériale.*' Lehzen had insisted that the Russian royal family spoke French at court.

'I am delighted to be here, Your Majesty.' The Grand Duke smiled wolfishly.

Victoria smiled back. 'You speak English.'

'I had an English nanny. My father is a great admirer of your country.'

'I must say I am relieved. I have no Russian, you see.'

'Perhaps one day, when you visit my country, I will be permitted to teach you a few words.'

'I shall look forward to that.'

The Grand Duke put out his hand, 'And now, Your Majesty, will you do me the honour?'

Victoria stood up and took the Russian's hand. He looked very splendid in his uniform, his shako draped over one shoulder, and a stripe of gold braid down the leg of his trousers. She could see that all the women in the room were looking at him with admiration. But handsome as he was, there was something slightly alarming about the red lips under the moustache.

At a signal from the Lord Chamberlain, the orchestra started to play a gavotte and the Grand Duke led Victoria to the top of the set. For a few minutes the sheer pleasure of dancing drove all other thoughts from her mind. This was the first ball where she had not been under the irksome control of her mother and Conroy. As the champagne began to flow through her system, she found herself smiling with pleasure.

The Grand Duke looked down at her as they crossed each other in the dance. 'I did not know that a Queen could dance so well.'

'Have you danced with so many, then?'

The Grand Duke laughed and took her hand to lead her down the set.

The gavotte was followed by a polka, and the Grand Duke picked her up in the turn as if she were a feather. Victoria felt flushed and exhilarated; the Grand Duke was very different to the Lords Alfred and George who were her usual partners. Perhaps it was because he was also royal, but he had no qualms about taking her firmly by the waist or hand, liberties that would never be attempted by one of her subjects. And then she wondered what it would be like to dance with Lord M.

When the dance finished Victoria took another glass of champagne and was gratified to see Conroy watching her. She drained her glass. The Grand Duke did likewise.

'You drink champagne like a Russian, Your Majesty.'

'I think you may call me Victoria.'

'And you must call me Alexander.'

'Very well, Alexander.' She looked up at him and smiled. She saw a glimpse of pink tongue as he smiled back. She felt herself sway slightly, but then the music started again and Alexander was leading her into another dance. As he whirled her round the floor, she thought she saw a familiar back, but then the man turned and she saw that she had been mistaken.

'What a face, Victoria. Did I step on your foot?'

'Oh no. I just thought I saw someone, that's all.'

'Someone you want to see?' Victoria nodded. 'Then I envy this man.'

Victoria felt the unwelcome colour coming to her cheeks. 'Oh, you misunderstand me.'

'Then you must be blushing on my account.'

Victoria was relieved when the dance came to an end. She curtseyed to the Grand Duke and turned to see the Baroness standing behind her.

'I think I need to go to the retiring room, Lehzen.'

'Come with me, Majesty.'

The retiring room was in an anteroom that opened out of the Picture Gallery. Mrs Jenkins and Skerrett were there, armed with sewing kits to repair the damage that enthusiastic but unskilled dancing was doing to the gowns of the guests. In the back of the room was a screen behind which were the chamber pots.

As Victoria and Lehzen came in, Lady Flora emerged from behind the screen. For a moment she stood in profile with one hand resting at her waist, and Lehzen gasped.

'What is it, Lehzen?' Victoria asked. 'Have you seen a ghost?'

'Not a ghost, Ma'am.' Lehzen leant in close and whispered to Victoria, 'If you look at Lady Flora in profile, Majesty,' Victoria turned her head, 'you will see. I believe she is with child.'

Victoria gasped. 'But she is not married!'

'No, indeed.' Lehzen's eyes narrowed with excitement. 'But when she came back from Scotland six months ago, I believe that she shared a carriage with Sir John Conroy.' She paused and raised her eyebrows. 'Quite alone.'

Victoria put her hand over her mouth. 'It seems incredible. She is so pious.'

'Nevertheless. The signs are unmistakable.'

Victoria turned to Lehzen, her face flushed from the champagne and the excitement. 'Do you think Mama knows?'

'I hardly think so.'

Victoria's eyes glittered.

At the back of the anteroom was a gallery that led to the private apartments. Victoria stepped inside to clear her head. But as she leant against the wall facing the portrait of her grandfather George III as a young man, she heard a step behind her. Conroy was walking down the gallery. He must have been in the Duchess's apartments.

He saw Victoria and made a stiff little neck bow. 'Ma'am.'

For a second Victoria thought she might let him pass by, but the champagne brought the outrage she felt to a head.

'Why aren't you dancing, Sir John? With Lady Flora? I believe she is your preferred partner.'

Conroy looked down at her, and his lips twitched. 'I am about to dance with your mother.'

Victoria put her head back. 'If my mother knew what you were really like, she would never dance with you again!'

Conroy shook his head indulgently. 'You never *could* take champagne,' he paused, 'Ma'am.'

He turned away from her and walked down the corridor.

Melbourne slowly made his way down the Grand Staircase. Penge, the steward, looked up and opened his mouth to announce him, but Melbourne shook his head. He did not want to draw attention to his late arrival.

From years of experience he could see that the ball had reached its zenith: enough champagne had been drunk to heighten all emotions, to add colour and sparkle to the most leaden courtier. In a few minutes the mood would begin to turn, and like roses just past their prime, the flowers of the dance floor would begin to fade and droop.

He looked around the ballroom. Cumberland was dancing with surprising grace with that awful German wife of his. The Duchess of Kent was in the arms of Conroy; Melbourne had always assumed that she was in love with him but the look on her face confirmed it. It was a pity, of course; Conroy was a charlatan, but as the Duchess was hardly in a position to remarry, he could hardly blame her for seeking consolation.

His eyes found the Queen. She was waltzing with the Russian Grand Duke. As she swept past him, he caught her eye and smiled. Victoria smiled in return, but there was something about the way her eyes widened that made Melbourne wonder how much she had had to drink. As she and the Russian circled round the room, Melbourne noticed that her steps, though graceful, were not always steady; there was also something about the way in which the Grand Duke's hand was holding her waist that he did not like.

'You have been missed.' Emma Portman was looking at him, one eyebrow raised in reproach.

'The Queen seems quite happy,' Melbourne said as the royal couple waltzed by.

'Do you think the Grand Duke is a possibility?'

'For the Queen's hand? Out of the question. He is the heir to the throne. He could not live here, and the Queen could hardly move to St Petersburg.'

'Pity. I never knew Russians to be so handsome.'

Melbourne said nothing. He noted the deepening flush on Victoria's cheeks. When the Grand Duke whispered something in her ear, she turned her head away from Melbourne.

'Are you going to watch her all night, William?' Emma said acerbically.

Melbourne shook his head. 'She is so young and artless. Never has a thought but expresses it directly. I tremble sometimes at her guilessness. And yet . . .'

He broke off. Emma looked at him and finished the sentence. 'And yet you cannot keep your eyes off her.'

Melbourne shrugged, but then leant forward, noticing a movement on the dance floor. 'Do you see where the Grand Duke has his hand?'

Emma narrowed her eyes. 'I think he could be sent to the Tower for less.'

Melbourne looked around him and caught the eye of Lord Alfred Paget, one of the Queen's equerries. He beckoned him over. 'I think, Lord Alfred, that it might be time for the Grand Duke to find a different partner. Perhaps you might distract him, tactfully, of course, but make sure you get him away from the Queen. He has, I think, been taking liberties.'

Alfred Paget looked indignant. 'Outrageous. I will attend to it at once.'

He walked over and tapped the Grand Duke on the shoulder. Alexander ignored him at first, but Alfred, the youngest of six brothers, was used to demanding attention.

'Your Imperial Highness, there is a messenger from Petersburg.'

'Tell him to wait. I am dancing with the Queen.'

'I believe it is urgent, Sir.'

Alfred, whose lissome figure disguised surprising strength, put his arm on the Grand Duke's shoulder and firmly steered him away from Victoria and out of the room. Melbourne stepped forward.

'You seem to be without a partner, Ma'am. Would you do me the honour?'

Victoria turned round at the sound of Melbourne's voice. Her face lifted into a smile.

'I would be delighted.'

The band was now playing a waltz, and as Melbourne put his hand on her waist, Victoria felt safe for the first time that evening.

'I was worried that you weren't coming.'

'I had some matters to attend to.'

'I thought perhaps you might be cross with me.'

'With you, Ma'am? Never.' Melbourne looked down at her tenderly.

'You dance very well, Lord M.'

'I am glad to hear it, Ma'am, but I think you are being kind. I am afraid my dancing days are almost over.'

'That's not true. You are my favourite partner tonight.'

Melbourne gave a theatrical sigh. 'Nevertheless, I am too old to dance as I used to.'

'You are not old, Lord M!'

Melbourne looked over Victoria's shoulder and saw the trio of Conroy, the Duchess, and Lady Flora staring at them.

'At the risk of being thrown into the Tower, I must contradict you there, Ma'am. I cannot deny my advancing years, even to please you.'

Victoria laughed. 'Well, I never think there is any difference between us, Lord M.'

The music came to an end, and Melbourne let go of Victoria's hand and bowed. 'Ah, here is Lord Alfred for the next dance.'

Victoria looked reluctant. 'But I want to dance with you. I have so much to tell you.'

'He will be very disappointed if you refuse him, Ma'am. And besides, he dances the best polka in the country.'

Melbourne slipped away as Lord Alfred came forward to claim the Queen.

One polka succeeded another, and by the end Victoria was

breathless and thirsty. Lord Alfred brought her a glass of champagne; she drank it greedily and asked for another.

She was about to drink that when she heard an unwelcome voice. 'Excuse me, Ma'am,' Victoria spun round to see the sallow, disapproving face of Lady Flora Hastings, 'but the Duchess thinks that perhaps you have had enough champagne.'

Swaying slightly, Victoria locked eyes with Lady Flora and said, a little too loudly, 'Mama sent *you*, to tell me what to do!'

The band had stopped playing, and so her words rang out across the ballroom. There was a frozen moment as Lady Flora looked at her in incomprehension, then her face crumpled at this public humiliation. She turned and stumbled out of the ballroom. As a deep sigh ran round the guests, Victoria stood transfixed, angry, and afraid. She felt for the first time a wave of something like disapproval. There was a voice in her ear.

'It is very hot in here,' said Melbourne. 'Perhaps you would care to step out onto the balcony, Ma'am, and get some air.'

She felt his hand under her elbow and was grateful for the support. She was a little unsteady on her feet. When they stepped out onto the balcony, she felt the cool night air on her face like a blessing.

Melbourne turned towards her. 'You look a trifle fatigued, Ma'am, if I may say so. Perhaps it time that you retired.'

'But I don't want to retire. I want to go on dancing, with you!'

Victoria leant in towards him. Melbourne put out his hands as if afraid she would fall, and for an instant they stood in a half embrace. And then he leant back and said softly, 'Not tonight, Ma'am.'

Chapter Sixteen

*D*ASH PICKED UP THE BALL AND BROUGHT IT BACK TO Victoria. When she threw it again, the ball landed at the feet of the Duchess, who had just entered the gallery. The Duchess kicked it out of her way.

Victoria paused. She had summoned her mother to challenge her about Lady Flora and Conroy, but now that the Duchess was in front of her, she did not quite know how to approach the subject.

'Did you sleep well, Drina, after the ball?' The Duchess looked at her daughter with meaning.

Victoria was about to reply when Dash brought the ball back, barking. She stooped and picked it up. She decided that she must plunge straight in. 'Mama, you must send Flora Hastings and Sir John Conroy away immediately. I have reason to believe that they have been involved in a . . .' she took a deep breath, 'a criminal conversation.'

The Duchess, who had been walking down the gallery towards her, stopped in amazement. 'Are you losing your mind, Drina? What is this nonsense you are saying?' The Duchess opened her large blue eyes and shook her head like a baffled china doll.

'Surely you have noticed that Lady Flora is with child?' said Victoria.

'With child?' The Duchess's voice was incredulous.

'Yes, Mama. And I believe Sir John to be responsible.'

The Duchess shook herself, and to Victoria's surprise and annoyance, she smiled. 'What are you saying? Who told you this ridiculous thing?'

Victoria said angrily, 'Baroness Lehzen told me that they shared a carriage from Scotland together six months ago.'

The Duchess laughed in her daughter's face. 'The Baroness told you? She knows so much about what goes on between a man and a woman, of course.'

Victoria squeezed the ball in her hand. She wanted very much to throw it at her mother. 'I cannot allow this . . . this corruption to invade my court.'

The Duchess tossed her blonde ringlets. 'Really, Drina, I would advise you not to listen to gossip. It is not becoming in a Queen.' Turning her back on Victoria, she walked away down the long corridor.

Without thinking, Victoria threw the ball at her mother's departing back, but her aim was off and she hit a Meissen vase given to her by the Elector of Saxony. It shattered with a resounding crash. Thrilled by all the excitement, Dash started to bark.

Victoria found herself shaking with fury. She had thought her mother might be upset, might indeed be angry, but this contemptuous dismissal was worse than anything she had imagined. She would not be brushed off. If her mother would not accept the truth, then she would have no choice but to prove it.

She confided her plan to Melbourne on their ride that day.

'Sir John and Lady Flora? You cannot be in earnest, Ma'am.'

'Indeed I am, Lord M. The Baroness says that they shared a carriage from Scotland together, quite alone. Tomorrow I am to take the Coronation Oath. How can I swear to serve my people faithfully when my own household is tainted by corruption? They must both leave court at once.'

Melbourne sighed. 'You don't know that it is true, Ma'am, and I would beware of making accusations, as Lady Flora has powerful friends. Her brother, Lord Hastings, is the leader of the Tories in the Lords, and he will not take kindly to having a scandal attached to his sister.'

'How can I look Sir John in the face, knowing he has behaved so shamefully?'

'I know you do not care for him, Ma'am, but I think there are easier ways of dismissing him than accusing him of getting a child on Lady Flora.'

'Even if it happens to be true?'

'Think of the scandal, Ma'am.'

'Is that all you care about? Avoiding a scandal?'

A spasm of pain passed over his face. 'I do know, Ma'am, how difficult and painful a scandal can be.'

Victoria paused and then she said slowly, 'So you think I should just do nothing.'

'Much the best thing, Ma'am. If your suspicions are correct, in a few months there will be no denying the evidence. Wait and see, Ma'am, wait and see.'

'But I must have the truth.'

'The truth, in my opinion, is vastly overrated.'

'You are, I believe, what is called a cynic, Lord Melbourne. But I am not.'

Without waiting to hear Melbourne's answer, she dug her heels into her horse's side, urging it into a gallop, and did not look round until she reached the Marble Arch. Behind her was her groom and Lord Alfred, but there was no sign of Melbourne.

Lord Alfred approached her. 'Lord Melbourne has gone back to Dover House, Ma'am. He sends his apologies and asked me to tell you that he feels he is too old to keep up.'

Victoria frowned. 'I see. He has never had this problem before.'

Lord Alfred smiled. 'You were going very fast, Ma'am.'

When she had changed out of her riding habit, Victoria asked Lehzen to fetch Sir James Clark, the court physician.

'Are you ill, Majesty? Perhaps you are nervous on account of the Coronation.'

'I am perfectly well, thank you, Lehzen. No, I want Sir James to enquire as to Lady Flora's state of health. Mama refuses to believe me, so the only answer is to have a medical examination.'

Lehzen nodded. 'Indeed, Majesty.'

'You agree with me, then? That we must get to the bottom of this . . . this affair?'

'If the Duchess will not believe you, then you must make certain, Majesty.'

Victoria sighed. 'Lord M thinks that I should do nothing.'

Lehzen leant towards her. 'Of course, Lord Melbourne has been leading a most irregular life in the past. Perhaps he does not care to condemn this behaviour.'

Victoria heard the note of spite in Lehzen's voice. 'I think he does not care for scandal, but in this case Lord Melbourne is wrong.' She spoke more loudly than normal, as if trying to convince herself.

Lehzen returned half an hour later with Sir James, who was

as emollient as he was eminent. He had risen to the heights of his profession by his meticulous attentions to the late George IV – humouring every vagary of the King's fancies about his health while refraining from pointing out the inconvenient truth that the Sovereign's habit of eating three grouse washed down with port for breakfast was perhaps the cause of his maladies. Sir John, whose bulbous and be-veined nose suggested that he too did not refrain from the finer things of life, had long ago discovered that the most fashionable kind of doctor was one who listened with great attention to every symptom and gave them all due significance before dispensing a medicine that was as expensive as it was harmless.

The doctor made Victoria a very low bow, which turned his already florid face even redder. 'Your Majesty. How may I be of service? Do you require something to steady your nerves before the Coronation? My patients of the fairer sex seem to find a tincture of laudanum most efficacious at such times.'

Victoria raised her blue eyes to his bloodshot ones. 'Do you have many patients, Sir James, who are about to be crowned in Westminster Abbey?'

The doctor made a noise that could have been a laugh or a groan of apology. 'You have the better of me, Ma'am.'

'But in answer to your question, I do not require your services myself. There is another . . . matter that I would like you to attend to.'

Sir James raised a tufted eyebrow.

Victoria began to walk up and down. It had all seemed so simple in her head, but now she found that she did not quite know to broach the subject. 'It has come to my attention, Sir James, that a certain lady may be in a . . . condition that is not compatible with her . . .' Victoria looked at Lehzen for assistance.

'With her status, Majesty.'

'Her status?' The doctor looked puzzled. 'Ah, I see. You believe the lady to be in an interesting condition, without the benefit of marriage.'

"Yes. I think she has been involved in a criminal conversation with a certain gentleman.'

'A shrewd assumption, Ma'am.'

Victoria stopped pacing. 'But I must have proof, Sir James.'

The doctor swallowed. 'Proof, Ma'am?'

'Yes. I want you to examine the lady.'

Sir James pulled at his side whiskers with a meaty hand. 'May I enquire as to the lady's identity?'

It was Victoria's turn to swallow. 'Lady Flora Hastings.'

There was a pause as Sir James considered this. The doctor was tugging at his whiskers so hard now he seemed likely to pull them out. 'If I might venture to ask, does the Duchess know of your suspicions, Ma'am?'

'I have discussed the matter with my mother, but she is not disposed to believe me.'

Sir James sighed. 'I see. I must warn you, Ma'am, that I anticipate some difficulty in effecting this examination. If Lady Flora is not willing, I can hardly force the issue.'

'I imagine that a doctor of your experience would be able to ascertain the facts just by looking at her.'

'You flatter me, Ma'am. I find that in cases of this kind, it is very difficult to rely on the eye alone. So many other factors come into play – dress, digestion, even a particular way of standing. A sway-backed posture can be most deceptive.'

Victoria tapped her foot impatiently. 'I can assure you that this is not a question of posture, Sir James.'

'No, Ma'am.'

'I must know the truth, and I am asking you to find it out, Sir James.'

'Yes, Ma'am.'

The doctor looked as if he was about to say something else, but Victoria turned her back on him. When she had heard his footsteps retreating into the corridor, she turned to Lehzen. 'You must tell the Lord Chamberlain that Sir John and Lady Flora are not to have cards for the Coronation. I cannot have them there in the circumstances.'

Lehzen frowned. 'I think, Majesty, that if you do this, then everyone will understand that you believe the scandal.'

Victoria lifted her chin. 'Precisely.'

Chapter Seventeen

THE DUCHESS FROWNED WHEN SIR JAMES WAS announced. 'I did not send for you, Sir James.'

Sir James looked down at the floor and then at the ceiling, anywhere but at the Duchess and her companion. He cleared his throat noisily. 'I have come, Ma'am, at the request of the Queen.'

The Duchess looked at Lady Flora, who was sitting beside her. The other woman closed her eyes and swayed slightly. 'But no one is being ill here, Sir James, so I have no need of you.'

Sir James shifted from foot to foot. 'The Queen was most insistent, Ma'am.' His eyes flicked over to Lady Flora.

The Duchess bridled and, standing up, glared at the doctor. 'There is nothing for you to do here. You may leave us.'

Sir James twisted himself into a corkscrew of apology. 'With respect, Ma'am, I am afraid that I cannot do that. The Queen would like some information regarding Lady Flora.'

The Duchess tried to laugh. 'Does my daughter persist in this ridiculous fantasy? You may tell her that there is no more truth in it now than there was this morning.'

Sir James said nothing, but did not move.

Lady Flora lifted her head. 'I will answer your questions, Sir James. I have nothing to hide.'

But this answer did not relax the spiral into which the doctor had contorted himself. 'I am afraid, Lady Flora, that the Queen is requesting an . . . examination. For the avoidance of doubt.'

There was a gasp from the Duchess. 'It is impossible! I will not permit such a thing. Drina has lost her mind.'

But Lady Flora stepped in front of her mistress and addressed the doctor directly. 'There are two things in life that I hold dear, Sir James. One is the Crown and the other is my faith. If the Queen thinks that I would do anything to bring either into disrepute, then I am willing to prove her wrong.'

She paused for a second, wiping a bead of sweat from her forehead in an impatient gesture. Then she steadied herself and looked Sir James in the eye. 'But I insist on my own physician being present, Sir James,' the corners of her mouth flickered into the imitation of a smile, 'for the avoidance of doubt.'

The doctor was so eager to leave the room that he fell through the doors as they were opened by the footmen. It was a comical sight, but neither of the women in the room laughed.

Chapter Eighteen

IT WAS THE SOUND THAT WOKE HER. A SOFT SUSURRATION, as if a giant flock of wood pigeons had landed outside the Palace. As she listened, the noise began to break up, become more distinct. Individual voices seemed to break through, but the words floated away on the breeze before Victoria could catch them. At last one voice more piercing than the rest penetrated her sleep-befuddled brain. 'God Save the Queen,' it went, followed by others in a descant of celebration.

Victoria jumped out of bed and went to the window. Beyond the Marble Arch she could see a heaving carpet of colour: flags, bonnets, upturned faces. There must be thousands of people out there. Her people, she thought, as she felt the breath coming out in a long, shuddering sigh. She had been Queen for a few months now, but today the responsibility pressed down upon her shoulders like a physical weight. Today she would swear the Coronation Oath, which had been sworn by the countless Kings and the four Queens who had preceded her.

She thought of all those eyes in the Abbey that would be looking at her. How many of them would be waiting for her to make a slip, to prove their suspicion that she was unworthy of the great office bestowed upon her? Victoria bit her lip, but then she put her shoulders back and lifted her chin. She would not make a mistake. She had been chosen for this role by a divine providence that had left her, the daughter of George III's sixth child, heir to the throne. If her uncles had been less profligate, there would have been a dozen legitimate children between her and the throne, but they had been so distracted by the pleasures of the flesh that the crown had come to her. Victoria knew that there had been a reason for this, a divine purpose, and she was determined to prove worthy of it.

Picking up a cushion for an orb and a parasol for a sceptre, she rehearsed the words of the Oath. 'By the grace of Almighty God, I, Victoria, do solemnly swear to serve my country.'

Her voice sounded thin in the high-ceilinged room. She hoped that they would be able to hear her in the Abbey. She thought of her uncles; with their loud booming voices, it was easy for them to be heard. But as Lord M said, there is nothing wrong in talking quietly; it only makes people listen harder. Victoria smiled when she thought of her Prime Minister. He would be there today, of course, and she had made sure that he would be standing in her eye line. It was a pity that there had been that stupid disagreement in the Park yesterday. But that would soon be resolved when Sir James had performed his examination.

The interconnecting door opened, and Lehzen came in, her wide face shining with affection. 'You should be in bed, Majesty. It is still so early.'

'Oh, I can't sleep any more, Lehzen.' She gestured for the Baroness to join her on the window seat. 'Look out there, Lehzen. So many people.'

'Waiting for their Queen.'

'I trust I shall be worthy of them.' She squeezed her governess's hand. 'I mean to be a great Queen, Lehzen.'

'I have no doubt of that, Majesty.'

Victoria saw tears in her governess's eyes. 'Thank you, Lehzen.' She leant forward and kissed the Baroness's cheek. 'For everything.' Feeling a rough tongue lick her bare foot, Victoria leant down and picked up Dash. 'Oh Dash, are you jealous? I am grateful to you too, of course.'

And she laughed. But Lehzen did not smile. 'It has been the greatest honour of my life to serve you, Majesty.'

The State coach was waiting for her at the foot of the steps, the gilded mouldings winking in the sunlight. As Victoria walked carefully down the steps, anxious not to trip on her heavy crimson mantle, she could not help thinking of Cinderella's pumpkin. But this was no enchantment, this was the coach that her forebears had taken to the Abbey. She had wanted Melbourne to come with her, but he had said it would be against precedent: the only companions that Sovereigns might have in the coach were their consorts. So she would have to travel alone.

As the carriage pulled out into the Mall, she could feel the wave of cheering rocking her. The seat of the coach was a little low, so that she had to half stand to wave at the crowds. As she lifted her hand, there was another roar, and she was almost blown backwards. But the sound ignited a glow of happiness within her. She remembered the day when she had followed the horizontal and then the vertical lines of the family tree to their inevitable conclusion. Of course, Lehzen had told her, she was only the Heir Presumptive; it was still possible that Queen Adelaide might have a living child. But Victoria had known then that it was her destiny to be Queen, her fate to be sitting where she was now in a golden coach bathed in the adoration of her subjects.

The great nave of the Abbey lay before her, the seats on either side gaudily crimson with the peers in their State robes. She stood in the doorway and felt the eight train bearers lift the heavy mantle in readiness for the procession. She heard the organ play the first bars of Handel's *Zadok the Priest*, which was her cue to start walking. But her feet would not move. She was conscious that every eye was upon her, waiting for her to step forward. This was a disaster. She willed herself to do it, but it was as if her legs belonged to someone else.

And then she saw him. Lord M. Smiling at her, his hand a little outstretched as if to say, *Come on, you have nothing to fear*. She smiled back and took her first step.

In a bedroom in the north wing of the Palace, a room that was never warmed by the sun, Lady Flora waited for the doctors.

Victoria shivered as she stood in the shift that all monarchs wore before they were invested with the robes of State. She felt her heart beating so loudly she wondered if the Archbishop could see it through the muslin. How vulnerable she felt, standing there in front of all the nobility in their crimson velvet, wearing only a muslin tunic. The Archbishop was intoning the words of the ceremony. Even as she listened to the great sonorous sweep of the words – Almighty God, kingdom, honour, and glory – she was looking for Lord M. He gave her a little nod of approval. She turned her eyes back to the Archbishop, and when he asked, *'Will you to your power cause Law and Justice, in Mercy, to be executed in all your judgements?'* she replied in her clear high treble, *'I will.'*

The purple robe of State trimmed with ermine was placed on her shoulders. She sat down on the throne, which had been prepared with a specially high cushion so that she would not disappear into its gothic depths. The Archbishop picked up the Ring of State, and to Victoria's dismay he started to push it on to her middle, not her ring, finger. He pushed hard against the unexpected obstacle, and Victoria tried not to cry out in pain as he forced it over her knuckle. She winced as he placed the orb in her right hand and the sceptre in the other. She hoped that the pain would not show.

But then the Archbishop was holding the crown over her head, intoning the words that had been used since the time of Edward the Confessor. Finally he put it down. It perched there for a moment, teetering on her head, and then it settled, and a feeling of serenity washed over her. She was the Queen of this great nation, anointed by God.

The trumpets sounded and the boys of Westminster School sang out, 'Vivat, vivat, Regina.'

With a great rustle, all the peers and peeresses picked up their coronets and placed them on their heads. Out of the corner of her eye, Victoria saw Harriet raising her long white arms like a swan and her mother with tears running down her face.

Lady Flora lay down on the bed and closed her eyes. The doctors talked in low voices at the other end of the room. She felt for the words of her favourite psalm: I lift up mine eyes to the hills, from whence cometh my strength. My help cometh from the Lord, who made heaven and earth. *She ran through the psalm as if strolling down the garden path to her childhood home, finding comfort in the familiar tread of the rhythm. When she got to the end of the psalm, she started again at the beginning.*

The organ swelled, and the choir began to sing the *Hallelujah Chorus*. Victoria sat very still as the peers of the realm approached one by one to pay homage. If she moved her head by so much as a fraction, the crown tilted down over one eye. As the Keeper had warned her, the weight of the jewels was too great. She managed to keep her posture through the Dukes and Marquesses, but when halfway through the Earls, an elderly peer called Lord Rolle missed his footing on the steps to the dais and was about to tumble at her feet, Victoria put out a hand to save him from falling over and felt the crown slip down over one eye.

Luckily Lord Rolle righted himself before it could slip down over the other eye, and she was able surreptitiously to wedge it back in place. But the episode had jolted her out of her trance. As she saw Lord Rolle tottering back to his place, his robes laden with dust and his coronet askew, she felt the laughter rising inside her. Her corset dug into her as her lungs filled with air.

A Queen could not laugh at her Coronation – she knew this – but somehow the idea of a laughing Queen made her want to laugh even more. In the aisle, she could see the scowling face of her Uncle Cumberland and his boot-faced Duchess, but even their obvious hatred was not enough to quell the revolution inside her. Just as the volcano of mirth inside her was about to erupt, she saw Melbourne coming up the steps, as a mere viscount one of the last to pay homage. He raised his eyes to hers and almost imperceptibly shook his head. That moment of recognition was enough to stop the hysteria from catching hold, and she felt herself subside..

The doctors pulled down their sleeves and fastened their cuffs. The maid helped them into their jackets and they left the room. Flora did not move.

At last it was over. The peers had all sworn their fealty and returned to their seats in coroneted ranks. The Archbishop and the other clergymen took their places at the head of the procession, and Victoria knew this was her cue to stand up. She did so with enormous care so as not to dislodge the crown. As she walked down the steps, her eight train bearers stumbled over themselves to pick up the robes of State. She stepped forward and felt the robe go taut. For a moment she thought she would be pulled backwards, but then there was a whispered command from Harriet Sutherland, *Altogether now, go*, and Victoria dared to step forward. To her relief her train came with her.

The procession made its way down the aisle, Victoria listening to Harriet's murmur of *one, two, one, two*, as she tried to set the pace for the maids-of-honour. As they moved down past the choir stalls into the nave, the soldiers began to open the great west door of the Abbey, and for the first time Victoria heard the roar of the crowd over the swell of the organ. It burgeoned as she grew closer and closer to the entrance.

Now the doors were fully open and the sun flooded into the gloom of the Abbey, refracting from the diamonds in Victoria's crown into a thousand points of light. There were so many people. A bigger crowd than she had ever seen. Everywhere there were flags, banners, and even balloons. On another day she might have been overwhelmed by the numbers, but today Victoria could feel her people's love in every fibre of her body. Her mouth was stretched into its broadest smile, and her subjects smiled back. She loved her people then; they were at one.

A mile away, Flora Hastings felt her stomach contract, and she turned her face to the wall.

Chapter Nineteen

ASH WHINED IN PROTEST AS VICTORIA POURED THE warm water over his back. 'Come on, Dashy, keep still. You know you need a bath.'

Dash looked at her reproachfully as if to say that today of all days, he might be spared the indignity of being washed.

'I want to finish this, before I have to get changed for the fireworks.'

For the first time since she had woken up that day, Victoria was alone. As soon as Jenkins and Skerrett had taken away her Coronation robes, she had decided that the only thing she wanted to do now was to give Dash a bath.

The colour of the water turned a satisfying grey as the grime from Dash's squirrel hunts was washed away. When he was finally clean and Victoria let go of her grip on the dog's collar, he ran away from her, shaking himself frantically to get rid of the excess water.

Just then Penge announced that Lord Melbourne was waiting for her in the drawing room. The steward could not help but grimace as water landed on his silk stockings.

Victoria tried not to laugh, and failed. 'Dash, come here, you wicked boy. Penge, tell Lord Melbourne I will be there presently.'

In front of the looking glass, Victoria pulled at the braids on either side of her face so that they hung at a more becoming angle.

Melbourne was standing at the window as she walked in, and Victoria saw something melancholy in the set of his shoulders. But as he turned round he gave her such a warm smile that she knew that she had been imagining things.

'Oh Lord M, I am so glad to see you. What a day it has been. I thought I would never keep myself from laughing when Lord Rolle rolled over.'

Melbourne looked down at her, a tender light in his sea-green eyes. 'But fortunately, Ma'am, your natural dignity prevailed.' He paused and then said in a deeper voice, 'I came to tell you how splendid you were today, Ma'am. No one could have done it with more dignity.'

Victoria looked up at him. 'I knew you were there all along, Lord M, and that made it easy. I find that everything is more . . . tolerable if you are present.'

Melbourne made her a little bow. 'You are too kind, Ma'am.' When he spoke it was in his best drawing-room tone. 'Yours is the third Coronation I have attended and undoubtedly the best. Your Uncle George's, although magnificent, was rather spoiled by the presence of his errant Queen banging on the door of the Abbey to be admitted. And your Uncle William's show was a very drab affair. A Coronation is not the time for economy; the people like a spectacle. Today they got one.'

'Did you hear how they cheered me when I came out of the Abbey? I thought I would be blown over.'

'You are the symbol of a new era, Ma'am, and your people are thankful. They were tired of old men, and they know how fortunate they are to be ruled by a young and beautiful Queen.'

Victoria felt herself blushing. 'I hope I am worthy of their love.'

Melbourne did not reply, but he held her gaze. This time it was Victoria who looked away first. 'I am so looking forward to the fireworks tonight. I hope it won't rain.'

'I have already made arrangements with the Almighty, Ma'am.'

Victoria pointed at him. 'How can you expect me to believe that, Lord M, when I know you never go to church?'

They were laughing together when Lehzen came in. Her face was set. 'Excuse me, Majesty, but Sir James Clark is here. He would like to speak with you.'

Victoria watched the smile fade from Melbourne's face. For a moment she wished with great intensity that she had taken his advice and done nothing about Lady Flora. But remembering her mother's laugh when she had broached the subject of Flora and Conroy, she nodded to Lehzen. 'You may show him in.'

As Sir James came in, he bowed to Victoria but avoided looking at her directly. 'Forgive me, Ma'am, for venturing to disturb you on such a day, but I thought you would want to know the results of the . . . visit to Lady Flora.'

'Yes indeed, Sir James.'

The doctor looked at the parquet floor as if he thought the marquetry might yield him the secret of eternal life. 'I must tell you, Ma'am, that upon examination, I found Lady Flora to be,' he swallowed, '*virgo intacta.*'

Victoria did not recognise the phrase. 'But is she with child, Sir James?'

The doctor went an even deeper shade of crimson and shook his head. Melbourne stepped forward. 'The one generally precludes the other, Ma'am.'

Glancing at the regret etched onto his face, Victoria realised her blunder. 'I see. Thank you, Sir James. That will be all.'

The doctor contorted his face into a grimace of apology. 'Before I go, I should explain, Ma'am, that I believe that the um, swelling, which could indeed be mistaken for a pregnancy, is the result of a tumour. I believe Lady Flora to be gravely ill.'

Victoria said nothing. The doctor backed out of the room, followed by Lehzen. When they had gone, Victoria turned to Melbourne, and said with passionate regret, 'I should have listened to you, Lord M.'

Melbourne shook his head. 'It is always easier to give advice, Ma'am, than to take it.'

Later that evening, when walking out on the balcony to see the fireworks, Victoria felt a ripple of something among the assembled courtiers that she did not immediately recognise. It was dark so she could see the faces only when they were lit by the gaudy colours of the illuminations.

Her mother was standing at the other end of the balustrade with Conroy at her side, and when the pyrotechnic device that spelt VR began to explode in the sky, Victoria saw the resentful bruise of her mother's face change from red, to blue, to gold. Conroy's face remained in shadow. Victoria knew she should say something to her mother, address the rift that was opening between them. Just then another shower of gold came down from the sky, and she saw her mother lean on Conroy's arm, and the small hard knot of rage that had been there since Ramsgate burnt in her chest. She had been wrong about Flora and Conroy, but that did not mean that she had been wrong about everything. Her mouth filled with bile as she saw her mother look up at Conroy and smile.

There was a sigh behind her, and she sensed Melbourne's presence. 'The illuminations are magnificent, Ma'am. A fitting end to this great day.'

Victoria felt the anger subside a little.

There was a gasp from the courtiers on the balcony and cheers from the crowds in The Mall below as the centerpiece of the display, a life-size profile of Victoria, was set alight. Victoria turned to Melbourne. 'How funny, I am standing here watching myself go up in smoke.'

'That is one way of describing the spectacle, but I see you as a beacon of light inspiring the nation.'

'You always put things so happily, Lord M.'

'In this case, Ma'am, I am merely being accurate.'

The burning profile was beginning to disintegrate. The coronet collapsed in the middle, and the nose and chin caved into each other. Victoria sighed. 'This is the best day of my life and also the worst. Can you believe that?'

Melbourne's face glowed green from a final rocket. 'I can, but only because I remember what it was like to be young. When you are my age, you find that the world is not so extreme. The mountains and valleys have worn down to a comfortable plateau.'

'Is that all I have to look forward to? Comfort? I think I should prefer to be happy.'

'As you grow older, there is a lot to be said for being comfortable, Ma'am. But I don't expect you to believe me. When I was your age I too wanted to be happy.'

Victoria felt a quick tug at her heart. 'And were you? Happy, I mean?'

'Yes, I believe I was.'

'With your wife? What was she like?'

'Caro? When I first met her she was captivating. I had never met anyone so vivid or so unexpected. I could never predict what she would say or how she would take things.'

Victoria said, 'I think I should find that rather tiring.'

Melbourne looked out over The Mall. 'And you would be right, Ma'am, I daresay.'

Victoria's effigy collapsed on itself at last. The unilluminated sky seemed diminished. A chilly breeze sprang up from nowhere, and the crowds below in The Mall began to move: a murmuring stream of people beginning to flow towards home, their head full of the glory of the day and the radiance of their Queen.

Chapter Twenty

*I*T RAINED EVERY DAY FOR TWO WEEKS AFTER THE Coronation. The weather was so bad that Victoria was forced to give up her daily rides with Lord M and amuse herself with indoor pursuits. She practised the piano; she attempted a portrait of Dash; she even looked at Blackstone's *Commentaries*, but nothing, whether frivolous or serious, dispelled the cloud that hung over her, as oppressive as the grey skies outside.

The ripple she had noticed among the courtiers on the balcony the evening of the Coronation, she now knew was disapproval. No one said anything, but Victoria felt the stiffness of the curtseys, the awkwardness of the bows, the failure to look her in the eyes. More than once she had come into a room and heard the conversation stop as surely as if a candle had been blown out.

One morning she had gone so far as to ask Harriet and Emma if something was troubling them. Harriet had looked at the floor, and Emma had said that the weather was putting them all in low spirits. It was not much of an answer, but Victoria was grateful for the effort. That evening she had asked Lehzen what people were saying about her, and Lehzen had said she did not know.

But Victoria knew that Lehzen was lying. The truth was that since the Coronation Lady Flora had gone into a decline. She had taken to her bed in the Duchess's apartments and had not been seen in public for a fortnight.

Victoria had sent Sir James to enquire after Lady Flora's health, but he returned saying that his services were not required. The Duchess and Conroy remained in the north wing and were only seen at church. Although in other circumstances Victoria would have welcomed this, now their absence felt ominous, as fraught as the thunderous skies outside.

Normally she would have found some respite in doing her boxes with Lord M.

Since the Coronation, however, that pleasure had been dimmed by the shadow cast by the invalid in the north wing. She had not mentioned Lady Flora to Melbourne since they had heard the results of Sir James's examination, and he had not brought up the subject, but she knew it was as present in his mind as it was in hers.

She heard the doors opening at the end of the corridor and Melbourne's quick step echoing on the parquet. 'Good morning, Ma'am.'

'I am so glad to see you. I can't tell you how much I miss our rides.'

'Indeed, Ma'am. But this is not the weather for riding.'

There was a silence. Melbourne glanced about him as if he had lost something, finally looking Victoria in the eye. 'I am afraid, Ma'am, that I hear reports Lady Flora is likely to die.'

Victoria put her hand to her mouth. 'Surely not. Why, she looked quite healthy only a month ago. I know Mama is nursing her, but she always likes to exaggerate these things.'

'In this case, though, I am afraid that the Duchess does not exaggerate.'

Victoria looked annoyed. 'I can't believe it. How can this happen?'

Melbourne said as gently as he could, 'I believe, Ma'am, that Lady Flora has been ill for some time; that is generally the way of these things. She has had a sickly cast to her countenance for a while. And, of course, the recent events have most likely precipitated her decline.'

Victoria turned away from him. 'I have sent Sir James with offers of help, but she refused to see him.'

'I can imagine, Ma'am, that in the circumstances Lady Flora would not want to see Sir James.'

Victoria looked at him sideways, her shoulders drooping. 'You think I should have sent someone else?'

'Indeed, Ma'am, I think the only visitor that Lady Flora would welcome at this juncture would be yourself.'

Victoria turned round to face Melbourne, her face mutinous. 'You want me to go?'

'It is not a question of what I want, Ma'am.'

There was a long silence. Victoria looked at the floor. Finally, she lifted her chin, and an expression of defiance fired up in her face. 'Well, I think this is all . . . a . . . storm in a teacup. I see no reason to gratify my mother by taking this seriously. I suggest, Lord Melbourne,' Victoria only ever called her Prime Minister by his full name when she was angry with him, 'that we stop gossiping and start on my boxes.'

Melbourne bowed his head. 'As you wish, Ma'am.'

Victoria sat down and opened the red box. It took her a full ten minutes to invite Melbourne to take a seat beside her. They worked on through the boxes methodically, without the usual chat and badinage, and as a result accomplished a great deal but were left feeling unsatisfied. Victoria did not, as she usually did, offer Melbourne a glass of madeira, and he left for the House rather earlier than usual.

After he had gone, Victoria decided that she could not bear to stay cooped up in the Palace, and ran out into the garden with Dash at her heels. For a moment she stood with her face turned up to the rain, feeling the drops fall into her mouth and run down the back of her neck. She stared at the grey sky and said quite loudly, 'It's not my fault!' and then shook her head at her own folly.

Hearing a noise behind her, she turned round and saw Lehzen. 'Majesty, why are you standing here in the rain?'

'Melbourne says that Lady Flora is dying!'

Lehzen's face made it clear to Victoria that she had heard the same thing. But she made an effort to conceal her knowledge, and put on her bright governess smile.

'We know that she is ill, Majesty, but I have known cases like hers to recover. If she is dying, it is because she has lost the will to live.' Realising that she had said precisely the wrong thing, Lehzen hurried on. 'You know how religious Lady Flora is. I think she is wanting to be in heaven.'

Victoria was silent, and Lehzen, knowing she had blundered again, said with desperation, 'If you stay out here in the rain, Majesty, you will catch a chill, and then we will have two invalids in the Palace.' She touched Victoria's arm, trying to guide her back inside, but the Queen shook her off.

'Leave me alone.'

'But Majesty, you are wet through. At least let me fetch you an umbrella.'

'I don't want anything from you, Lehzen.' Victoria marched

away down the shrubbery, leaving Lehzen staring after her, shaking her head.

The rain continued to fall. The newspapers started to talk of the Book of Job. The farmers stared at their ruined crops. In the clubs, and in the corridors of the House, there was no fresh air to blow away the vapours of rumour that swirled around the recumbent form of Lady Flora.

The conversations grew more heated as the weather remained damp. There was outrage in White's, the club favoured by the Tories.

'Hastings had it all in a letter from his sister. The Queen asked Sir James Clark to perform an examination.'

'On Lady Flora? But the woman was born with a crucifix in her hand!'

'Nevertheless, the Queen believed her to be with child.'

'Must have been an Immaculate Conception, as the Papists say. There is no more determined spinster in the country than Flora Hastings.'

'Sir John Conroy was meant to be the guilty party.'

'Conroy! But his interests lie elsewhere, surely?'

The Duke of Cumberland, who did not normally care for White's, where he felt the members did not accord him the respect that was due to a Prince of the Blood, found the card room of the club much more congenial than usual. He made sure to drop in every day to relish the latest morsel from the feast of the Hastings affair. He was too wary, of course, to comment, but the angle of his eyebrow and the sigh that he gave whenever his niece's name was mentioned were enough to let his listeners know what he thought of the business.

Even in Brooks's where the Whigs predominated, there was no avoiding the ripples of scandal. When Melbourne walked through the great drawing room, conversations stopped, and members, even fellow ministers, looked down at their cards, instead of stopping him with a smile.

If Melbourne knew why the conversations stopped when he passed by, he gave no sign of it, his air of weary languor undisturbed. Only his butler knew that he sat up late all night in the library at Dover House, the decanter at his side.

The only amusement that the rain could not affect was the theatre. Victoria was looking forward to seeing *La Sonnambula* by Bellini. She loved opera very much, and Bellini in particular. Sitting in the dark of the Royal Box listening to opera was the only time she permitted herself to cry in public.

Sometimes she would imagine herself standing on the stage, commanding the audience with the purity of her voice. How she envied La Persiani, her favourite singer. Not just for her voice, but for the ability to express her emotions perfectly.

Victoria had learnt from an early age to keep her feelings in check in public, to make her face as smooth and as imperturbable as that of one of her dolls. But it could be hard work. Sometimes when she went to bed she felt the muscles of her cheeks ache from the effort of keeping the slate blank.

But here she could relax and let the music do its work. She could feel the hairs on her arms stand up as the diva on stage began to sing the famous sleepwalking aria. It was a moment of pure enjoyment, the first she had had since the Coronation. Her eyelids fluttered as she let herself sigh with pleasure.

Then something changed. The music continued, but her dreamy reverie was broken. He was here; she knew it even before she turned around to see Melbourne standing there, his face set. He leant down and whispered in her ear. 'I am sorry to disturb you, Ma'am, but I am afraid this cannot wait.'

His face was very close to hers. Victoria could smell water of limes and tobacco.

'Lady Flora?'

'Yes, Ma'am. I am afraid the end is near.'

'I see.'

Victoria got up and, with a regretful backwards glance at the stage, walked towards the door of the box. In the red and gilt corridor, she said, 'You think I should go to her?'

Melbourne nodded. 'I think you will regret it if you don't.'

Victoria put a hand against the red velvet wall. 'I am afraid, Lord M.'

Victoria felt Melbourne touch her hand with his own. The brush of his skin jolted her with a current of warmth. She turned her head to look at him.

'I know, Ma'am. But I also know what courage you have.' Melbourne's voice was reassuring.

'Very well. Must I go tonight?'

'I believe tomorrow could be too late, Ma'am.'

Victoria could hear the tenor launching into the love duet as she followed Melbourne down the corridor, to the foyer where her carriage was waiting.

Penge led the way to the room in the north wing where Lady Flora lay dying. Victoria had wanted to change out of her opera dress, but in response to a look from Melbourne, she had decided to go up as she was. As they walked down the corridor, Victoria noticed that the red carpet underfoot had given way to a thin drugget. There were no pictures on the wall. The candles in the sconces hissed and guttered; they were tallow, not the beeswax always used in the royal apartments.

At the door of the bedroom, Victoria hesitated. She turned to Melbourne. 'You will come with me?'

Melbourne shook his head. 'There are some things, Ma'am, you must do alone.'

Victoria hesitated. Then she put her hand on the door and pushed it open.

The smell hit her first. Sweat, fever, and something that could only be decay. She wanted to put her hand over her face, but forced herself to keep her arms down by her sides. It took a moment to see Lady Flora in the room, which was lit only by one candle.

The dying woman was huddled in a pile of bedclothes in the middle of the bed, her shrunken form dwarfed by the coroneted half tester hanging above her. Her face was yellow against the white sheets, and her lips had begun to pull back over her teeth as if the skull was already showing beneath the skin. Her breath was heavy and effortful. Victoria could hear the rasp of the exhalation from her side of the room. Digging her nails into her palms, Victoria advanced slowly to Flora's bedside. Flora's head was turned towards the wall. She clasped a Bible to her thin chest.

The nurse who had been sitting there got up in a flurry of confusion and curtsied clumsily. Victoria gestured for her to go, and then, painting on her brightest smile, advanced to where Flora could see her.

'Good evening, Lady Flora. I am sorry to find you in ill health.'

Lady Flora turned her head, and her eyes gleamed at the sight of Victoria, but she said nothing, only the laboring, agonizing breath.

Unnerved, Victoria found herself talking loudly. 'Is there anything we can do for you? Some beef tea? Peaches perhaps? The ones they grow in the hothouses at Windsor are a real delicacy. I believe that they could tempt you back to health.'

Flora put up a feeble hand as if to say _enough_, and, with great difficulty, spoke with something approaching scorn. 'I am beyond peaches.'

Victoria shook her head. 'Don't say that, Lady Flora! I am sure that with rest and care you will soon be on your feet again.'

Flora gasped, 'I am going to a better place,' and she clutched her Bible.

There was a silence broken only by Flora's awful breathing. At last Victoria could bear it no longer. 'I have wronged you, Lady Flora. I have come to ask your forgiveness.'

Flora tapped her Bible and said, 'Only God can forgive you.'

Victoria rocked back a little on her heels. 'Well, I intend to ask for His forgiveness too.' She swallowed. 'I believed something that was not true because I wanted to believe it, and I did you a great injustice.'

Flora closed her eyes. For a long, awful minute, Victoria imagined that she would not open them again, but then the red-rimmed lids parted. 'Your subjects,' Flora gasped, 'are not dolls to be played with.' She stared at Victoria with great intensity. Lifting her head with an agonising effort, she said, 'To be a Queen, you have to be more than a little girl with a crown.'

And then Flora subsided back on to the pillows, spent, a dribble of saliva leaking from the corner of her mouth.

Victoria felt Flora's words burning across her forehead. Impulsively she reached down and picked up the invalid's hand and pressed it to her lips. The flesh felt cold and waxy, as if already belonging to a corpse. Flora did not stir, the only sign that she was still alive the terrible rhythm of the jagged breaths.

Victoria put down the cold hand and backed away towards the door.

Melbourne was waiting for her outside. 'You weren't in there very long, Ma'am.'

'It was long enough,' and Victoria hurried past him down the corridor, not wanting him to see the tears that were threatening to demolish her composure.

She felt his steps coming after her, and heard him say, 'I imagine it was most upsetting, Ma'am, but I think you must know that you have done the right thing.'

'That can hardly make up for the wrong I have done her,' said Victoria through her tears.

'You made a mistake, and you have apologised.'

'I have been so foolish,' she sobbed.

'Perhaps, but everyone is capable of folly, even a Queen.'

'I wish I could believe you, Lord M.'

'You must believe, Ma'am. After all, I am older and wiser than you.'

He touched her elbow and walked with her back to her apartments, where Lehzen was waiting for her. 'Good night, Ma'am.'

'I won't be able to sleep a wink,' Victoria answered, but felt a great weariness steal over her.

Lehzen took her by the arm. 'Don't worry, Majesty. I will make you some negus and then you will be sleeping like a baby.'

Victoria leant on her for a moment and closed her eyes. When she opened them again, Melbourne had gone.

Chapter Twenty-One

VICTORIA WOKE UP THE NEXT MORNING TO SEE THE sun shining through the windows. She jumped out of bed, Dash at her heels, and looked out over the Park. She would go riding today. Then she remembered the events of last night, and her sudden elation at the sunshine evaporated.

She wondered how long it would be now. Even as she reproached herself for such an uncharitable thought, she could not put aside the hope that Flora's death would come sooner rather than later. The waiting was the worst part.

She did not have to wait long. Victoria was in the morning room playing a duet with Harriet Sutherland when the doors opened and the Duchess flew in, her face stiff with grief. 'My poor Flora is dead!'

Victoria's fingers froze on the keys. She heard Harriet's mumble that she hoped that Ma'am would excuse her, and the rustle of her skirts as she hurried from the room. Victoria stood up. She shut the piano lid as carefully as she could. 'Oh, Mama, that is terrible.'

The Duchess narrowed her eyes. 'You drove her to her death, Drina.'

'But I went to see her last night. To apologise for my . . . mistake.'

'Mistake! You send doctors to humiliate a dying woman!'

'And I said I was sorry.' Victoria tried to keep the note of panic out of her voice.

'Do you think that is enough, Drina? To say you are sorry, like a little girl who is breaking a glass? Anyway, it is not me you should apologise to, but Sir John. You accused him, and he too is innocent.'

At the mention of Sir John's name, Victoria felt the rage beginning to build behind her eyes. All her mother could think of was her precious Conroy.

'Of that particular crime, perhaps. But he is guilty of far worse, Mama!'

The Duchess's head snapped back as if she had been hit. 'What are you saying? Sir John has always been like a father to you. And you have repaid his kindness with this . . . this slander.'

Victoria took a step forward, possessed by the desire to take her mother by the shoulders and shake her. 'Kindness? Is that what you call it? Locking me up at Kensington like a prisoner, laughing at me about my height, my voice, my ignorance. And you laughed with him, Mama!'

The Duchess put up her hands as if to ward off a blow. 'Drina, please.'

But Victoria would not, could not stop. 'Ever since I can remember, Mama, you have looked at him first, then me!' Her voice was threatening to break, but Victoria kept the tears at bay by the fierceness of her anger.

The Duchess looked at her, bewildered. '*Wovon redest du?* What are you talking about? I think you are not yourself, Drina.'

Victoria knew that she could not hold in her emotions much longer. She pulled back her shoulders and lifted her chin, and said slowly and clearly, with every shred of dignity she possessed, 'This audience is over, Mama. You have my permission to withdraw.'

The words hung in the air between them. Thinking that her mother might break through them and touch her, Victoria found herself longing to feel her mother's arms around her. The Duchess quivered, as if resonating to an invisible chord that held them together. But then she dropped her gaze and slowly, as if sleepwalking, left the room.

Victoria wept.

Chapter Twenty-Two

THERE WERE CROWDS LINING THE ROUTE FOR LADY Flora's cortège: the sort of crowds that usually marked the passing of a statesman or a minor member of the royal family, not the funeral of the spinster daughter of a Tory peer. The men removed their hats and the women bowed their heads as the hearse went by, pulled by six black horses whose plumes fluttered in the breeze.

Behind the hearse came the line of carriages sent by mourners. There were ragged cheers as the crowd recognised the crest of the Duke of Wellington, and a more muted acknowledgement of the arms of the Duke of Cumberland. This was a solemn crowd, here to pay their respects to a woman they had barely heard of a week before, but whose passing they now felt most deeply.

As the long line of carriages sent by Tory grandees clattered past, there was a murmur of expectation. This crowd was waiting, and as the last carriage came into view, they got what they wanted. A low boo began swelling in volume as it passed from one end of the crowd to the other. There were no jeers, no shouts – after all, this was a crowd in mourning – but as the carriage sent by the Queen rolled past, the royal arms clearly visible on the door, there was no doubt as to how the crowd viewed this belated gesture of contrition.

Victoria had stayed in the Palace on the day of the funeral. She had tried to visit the Duchess in her apartments, but the Duchess had sent word that she was indisposed.

The following day Victoria had gone riding in the Park with Melbourne, and had noticed that the bystanders did not wave and smile as they usually did. When she remarked on this, Melbourne shook his head. 'Oh, there is no accounting for people in the Park, Ma'am. Shall we have one last gallop?' But as she thundered past a knot of men, she heard one of them shout something that sounded like 'fame'. This puzzled her all the way back to the Palace.

She had hoped that Melbourne would stay to dine, but he said that he had business to attend to at the House.

That night as Victoria lay in bed, she heard the wind rattling the windows and thought of the shout she had heard that morning in the Park. *Fame, lame, game,* and then the blood flooded to her face as she realised that the word the men had dared to shout had been 'shame'. She lay in the dark with her eyes open. Perhaps she had been mistaken; perhaps the men had been arguing with each other. But in her heart she knew that they were shouting at her, despising her for what she had done.

The next day Victoria noticed that there were no newspapers in her sitting room. When she asked Penge where they were, he said in a stilted way that he believed that they had not yet been delivered. Victoria frowned and decided to find Lehzen, who would know what was going on.

As she walked down the Picture Gallery to Lehzen's closet, a door opened beside the portrait of George III. To her dismay

Sir John Conroy walked out in front of her. She stopped dead, wondering whether to turn on her heel and walk away. She had not seen Conroy, except at a distance, since the night of the Coronation Ball. His long white face was lit up by a smile that added to Victoria's sense of unease. He was carrying a paper in his left hand. From where Victoria was standing it looked like some kind of cartoon.

She acknowledged his presence with the curtest of nods, and made to walk straight past him. But Conroy, whose smile did not falter, took a step in front of her. 'Good day . . .' He paused just long enough for it to be insolent, 'Ma'am.'

Victoria said nothing. She knew from long experience that he had something to say, and unless she actually pushed past him there was no way to avoid it. If only Lord M had come early. Conroy would not dare attempt anything in his presence.

Still with that odious smile pasted across his features, Conroy held out the paper in his hand, using his other hand to hold it taut so that she could see exactly what was on it. She looked at it silently. It was a vulgar cartoon of a woman naked from the waist down lying on the bed with her legs in the air. Peering between them were three figures, two men and a woman. From the set of his sideburns she was pretty sure one of the men was Lord Melbourne; from the profile she guessed the other was Conroy. Behind them, the figure of a small, plump girl with a rapacious grin stood on her tiptoes trying to see what was going on. From the tiny coronet perched on her head, she realised the girl was meant to represent Victoria herself. The caption read, *Lady Flora's Distress*.

Victoria looked away quickly and tried to keep her face as still as possible.

'The Press can be so cruel, Ma'am.' Conroy's smile got even

wider. 'Shall I leave this with you? So that you can peruse it at your leisure?'

Summoning up every vestige of self-control she possessed, Victoria kept her face completely still as she swept past Conroy. She would not give him the satisfaction of seeing her flinch.

When the messenger came, Melbourne was in the library at Dover House reading one of St John Chrysostom's homilies. Ever since he had first come across the Cappadocian saint during the nadir of his marriage to Caro, he had found a perverse consolation in the certainties of a man who had never had an unfaithful wife or an unruly party to govern. The fourth-century saint preached against extravagance of any kind, urging his followers to heed Christ's example by spreading their bounty among the poor. There was a phrase that always made him smile: 'How can you bear to relieve yourself in a silver chamber pot, when the poor go hungry?'

Melbourne looked at the magnificent walnut panelling of his library, the tapestry of Solomon meeting the Queen of Sheba hanging on the opposite wall, and the Lawrence portrait of Caro hanging above the mantelpiece. He sighed at his own hypocrisy. He had done very little for anyone. He had failed to protect the Queen from the consequences of her own folly over Flora Hastings. The gossips had it that he was too indulgent with his monarch, and in this case he knew that they were right. He should have insisted that Flora Hastings, that crucifix-wielding virgin, was the last person in the world to have an illicit liaison, and that the blackguard Conroy was far too calculating and self-serving to risk a scandal by seducing his mistress's lady-in-waiting. But Melbourne had been, as ever, too squeamish. Just as he had averted his eyes when Caro had thrown herself at Byron in public, he had drawn back from risking his friendship with Victoria by telling her that she was wrong.

Caro and Victoria were alike in that impulsive need to assert themselves without thinking of the consequences, and he could not resist either of them. Melbourne smiled wryly as he recalled how he had tried to comfort Victoria by telling her that everyone was capable of making a mistake, but he was the fool who had made the same mistake twice. The Queen was now the eye of a storm of scandal and conjecture, just as Caroline had been. And he had failed to prevent it both times.

Melbourne took another long draught from the schooner of brandy beside him. He tried to concentrate on the convictions of his stern mentor, but for once he found no comfort in applying his mind to one so different from his own.

The butler brought in the letter on a silver salver. 'From the Palace, my Lord.'

To his surprise the note was not from the Queen but from Emma Portman.

William,
  The Queen has locked herself in her bedroom and refuses to speak to anyone. But she will, I suspect, talk to you. There is the Inspection of the Troops this afternoon and I am concerned she will not appear. Please come.
  Your friend, Emma

Melbourne finished the brandy in his glass and stood up, feeling the ache in his bones. As he walked towards the door, he caught sight of himself in the looking glass. The face that looked back at him, unshaven and crumpled, looked like that of an old man. Melbourne straightened his shoulders and pulled his stomach in.

'Tell Bugler to fetch the shaving water. I must get ready to go to the Palace.'

The butler was too well trained to smile, but there was a slight twitch to his lips and he nodded. 'Certainly, My Lord.'

The clocks were striking eleven as Melbourne's carriage turned into The Mall. The trees along the route were hung with flags, and stands had gone up for spectators in Horse Guards Parade. He could see knots of people lining the route that the Queen would take that afternoon to inspect the troops but, Melbourne noted with unease, there were not many bonnets among them. Bonnets were the difference between loyal subjects turning out to cheer their Queen and a querulous mob that could be rented by anyone with deep enough pockets.

Melbourne wondered if any of the Tories would really stoop so low, and then he thought sadly that perhaps they didn't have to. After the funeral Lord Hastings had published in *The Times* the letter from his sister that outlined her treatment at the hands of the Queen. Lady Flora had asked that the Queen be treated with the spirit of Christian forgiveness as she was too young to be wholly responsible for her youthful folly, but Melbourne doubted whether there would be much sympathy for Victoria. Flora Hastings, dour and sanctimonious in life, in death had become a martyr sacrificed on the whim of a spiteful young Queen. To send doctors to ascertain whether Flora was a virgin was bad enough, but to humiliate a dying woman was, to the public mind, unforgivable.

Of course, it would pass, Melbourne thought – in the end

every scandal lost its piquancy – but for now the people were feasting on the carrion of the young Queen's reputation. There was much talk of her youth and inexperience. He had been told that Hastings had described her as a spiteful chit; there had even been hints in the Tory press that the Queen was not of sound mind and a Regent should be appointed.

Melbourne hoped that people would see the hand of the Duke of Cumberland behind this; nothing would suit the Duke better than to be appointed Regent while his niece was declared mad. But people still remembered what had happened to the Queen's grandfather, George III, and there was the general belief that young unmarried women were susceptible to hysteria, which could only be cured by marriage and motherhood.

Although Melbourne reflected that no one who had ever met Victoria could be in any doubt as to her sanity, there was no easy way to make that clear to her subjects. All too many of them would be willing to believe that the Queen was mad. The important thing now was not to stoke the fire. The Queen must carry on as normal.

Emma Portman was waiting for him at the entrance to the Palace. 'Oh, William, thank goodness you're here! We have all tried to speak to her, but she has locked the door and won't come out. The only sound from her bedroom is Dash barking.' She stopped and put her hand on Melbourne's arm, her usual expression of worldly detachment transfigured with alarm. 'You don't think, do you, that she could have done something . . . foolish?' She lowered her voice. 'I keep thinking of Caro.'

Melbourne frowned. The Long Gallery through which they were walking had footmen posted at both ends, and while they looked impassive, he had no doubt they were listening to every word. He did not want servants' gossip to fuel the rumours of the Queen's instability. Caro, of course, had tried to kill herself several times, but in this respect he knew that his Sovereign and his late wife had nothing in common.

'I am sure the Queen is simply fatigued after the strain of the last few weeks.'

'I hope you are right, William.'

'Of course I am right,' said Melbourne with a touch of impatience.

As they climbed the staircase to the Queen's Apartments, the Duchess appeared on the landing, accompanied by Conroy. They were both wearing full mourning. Melbourne bowed to the Duchess and gave Conroy the barest possible nod.

'I suppose you are on your way to see the Queen, Lord Melbourne. Well, I wish you luck.' Conroy showed his teeth in his most awful smile.

The Duchess's ringlets fluttered beside him. 'She would not see me this morning, her own mother. She left me standing at the door like a creditor.'

Conroy continued, 'I hope her . . . indisposition does not last. It would be such a pity if she were to miss the inspection. People might think there was something . . . wrong.'

The Duchess broke in. 'This is not what I am bringing her up for all those years. To hide in her bedroom. Refusing even her mother.' Melbourne found himself surprised to hear a note of real distress in the Duchess's voice.

Emma said soothingly, 'The Queen has refused everyone, Ma'am. Harriet and myself, Baroness Lehzen – no one has been admitted.'

The Duchess flinched. 'Why would she want to see any of you if she would not be seeing her own mother?' Then she looked at Melbourne, and a look of distaste crossed her face. 'But I suppose she will be seeing you, her precious Lord M.'

Melbourne gave her a smile almost as wide as Conroy's. 'I sincerely hope so, Ma'am. But I suspect that it will be hunger rather than my presence that will open her door. It is getting on for noon, and I have never known the Queen to miss a meal.'

The Duchess looked at him blankly and walked on, Conroy at her elbow.

'That was nicely done, William,' Emma said approvingly. 'I could have bitten my tongue out for mentioning Lehzen. They hate each other, of course.'

'I think the Duchess is genuinely worried about her daughter. Conroy, of course, is another matter.'

'I think we both know what he wants,' said Emma, 'an incapacitated Queen with the Duchess as Regent.'

Melbourne shuddered. 'What a thought! Lead on, Lady Portman. It is time that the Queen showed herself to her people.'

In the anteroom outside Victoria's bedroom, the ladies-in-waiting were huddled in an anxious group. They looked up in relief on seeing Melbourne. Only Lehzen looked less than pleased. She shook her head at him, 'It is all a great fuss for nothing. Just some nerves.'

Melbourne gave her a special bow. 'I am sure you are right, Baroness. You know the Queen better than any of us, but I should like to try my luck if you are in agreement.'

Looking a little mollified, Lehzen gestured for him to go ahead.

Melbourne knocked firmly on the double doors. 'Your Majesty, may I have a word?' There was a long moment, and then the door opened. Lehzen sniffed loudly as Melbourne walked through the door and closed it behind him.

Victoria had pulled a Paisley shawl over the lacy froth of her nightdress. Her hair was down, streaming over her shoulders. She looked pale, and her eyes had dark shadows beneath them. She also looked very young, but there was a dullness in her eyes he had not seen before. She went to sit on the window seat with Dash by her side.

'I am sorry you are indisposed, Ma'am. But I think you will be revived by your regiments. The Household Cavalry in full fig is a sight for sore eyes.' Victoria said nothing. Her hand was convulsively smoothing Dash's long silky ear. Melbourne took a step forward. 'Come now, Ma'am. You don't want to keep your troops waiting.'

Victoria looked up at him, her voice low and expressionless. 'I can't go anywhere. Have you seen that?' She pointed at the cartoon of *Lady Flora's Distress* that was lying on her dressing table. 'How can I go out?'

Melbourne glanced at it. 'I hadn't seen it, but it makes no difference.'

Victoria let go of Dash's ear, and the spaniel jumped gratefully to the floor. This time when the Queen spoke, her voice had a bit more spirit. 'How can you say that? I am the object of public ridicule.'

Melbourne laughed. 'If I had stayed in my room every time I was mocked in the press, I would not have seen daylight for the last thirty years.' He moved another step closer to her. 'When I took Caro back, somebody – Gillray, I think – drew her as a shepherdess leading me as a lamb on a ribbon. My surname was Lamb then, and I suppose it was irresistible. It caused me pain at the time, but I have survived it, as you see.'

He smiled at her, willing her to smile back, but Victoria looked at the floor. Then she whispered so low that he could hardly hear it, 'It's all my fault. Everything is ruined.'

Melbourne saw that attempts to laugh Victoria out of her depression would be in vain. Victoria's distress was more than injured pride. She was afflicted with remorse. He gestured to the space on the window seat beside her. 'May I, Ma'am?'

At her nod, he sat down next to her. He wanted very much to put his arm around her shoulders, to comfort her, but knew that was the line he could not cross. It was already against all the rules of protocol that he was alone with her in her bedroom. To touch her was tantamount to treason, and, of course, there were all the other reasons why he should not touch her as he would another woman.

'I can't go on, Lord M, not any more.' The words were a young girl's, but there was a desperation behind them that was adult.

Melbourne took a deep breath. A lock of Victoria's hair was brushing his hand; he longed to wind it round his finger as once he had with . . .

'I don't think I ever told you why I was late for the Coronation Ball.' Victoria turned her head to look at him, surprised. Melbourne continued, 'Did you know that I had a son, Ma'am? His name was Augustus, and that day was his birthday. I suppose he was what the world calls feeble-minded, but I found him sensible enough.'

Victoria turned her whole body to face him now. Melbourne felt her gaze as directly as a candle flame. 'After Caro died he became very afraid of the dark, and he could not go to bed unless I was there holding his hand.' He paused, and Victoria leant forward as if afraid of losing a single word. 'You know, I think I was never happier than in those moments, watching my poor son drift off into sleep.'

Melbourne made himself continue. 'When he died three years ago, I thought that there was no longer any point to my existence.'

Victoria's lips trembled. 'Oh, Lord M, how can you say that?'

Melbourne smiled. 'But I no longer feel that way, Ma'am. Since I became your Prime Minister and, I hope, your friend, I have found a reason to continue.'

The blue eyes opposite his were glistening. He felt the pressure of her small hand on his, and the touch spurred him on. 'Now you must do the same, Ma'am. You must go out there today and smile and wave, and never ever let them see how hard it is to bear.' With a great effort Melbourne stood up, relinquishing her hand.

Victoria got to her feet, but her face was still a foot below his. In a low voice, almost a whisper, she said, 'Thank you, Lord M. I will do my best.'

Melbourne gave her what he hoped was a fatherly nod. 'Now I think I should send your ladies in, Ma'am. You will want to look your best on the Parade Ground. And if I might say so, the dress uniform is most becoming.'

For the first time that day, Victoria smiled.

That was the smile that she kept on her face as she rode out on Monarch, her favourite white mare, through the Marble Arch to the Parade Ground. She was wearing her riding habit, cut in the style of the Windsor uniform, that Melbourne had mentioned. Like the men's uniform it was a royal blue with red facings and gold buttons down the front, and there was a matching cap with a peaked brim. She knew that she looked her best.

As she steered Monarch through the arch, Victoria waited for the cheer from the crowd that always heralded her appearance. But it was not forthcoming. Fortunately, this absence of enthusiasm was disguised by the band that preceded her down the Mall. The music was loud, even if not always in time or in tune. Victoria kept her gaze fixed on the plumes fluttering from the guardsman's helmet directly in front of her. Despite the music and the clatter of the horses' hooves, she could feel the silence of the crowds. She knew without looking around that there were no flags waving for her, no children being held up by their parents to catch a glimpse of their Queen.

Although the distance from The Mall to the Parade Ground was less than half a mile, Victoria was conscious of every inch. Her cheeks were aching from the effort of keeping her face composed as she rode past the people who had once made her feel so loved.

The Parade Ground was lined with boxes for the spectators. To the left were the wives and daughters of the military, to the right were the politicians, and in the middle was the Royal Box. The Duchess of Kent was sitting in the front row with Conroy to her left and, to Victoria's great surprise, the Duke of Cumberland on her right.

A voice called out, 'Long live the Duchess of Kent' and the Duchess, despite her deep mourning, allowed herself a beaming smile. Conroy gave a small nod, as if he too was being acknowledged by the crowd. Cumberland glared straight ahead. No London crowd, even one that was being supported by prominent Tories, was so venal that it would cheer for Cumberland.

Victoria was to enter the Parade Ground through a ceremonial arch. Behind it was a small awning where she pulled up Monarch to compose herself for the ordeal ahead. The inspection of the regiments would take at least an hour as the troops filed past her. Normally she looked forward to seeing all her soldiers tricked out in their finery, but today she knew every eye would be watching and waiting for her to falter. She also knew that Melbourne was right, that she would have to find the courage to continue just as he had.

A Queen could not hide from her subjects. And yet today would be the greatest test. The crowds had come not to celebrate their Queen but to condemn her, and what made this so much harder to bear was that she knew she deserved it. For a moment she hesitated – perhaps she could say that she was feeling faint and go back to the Palace – but then she heard another cheer for the Duchess of Kent. The thought of the look of triumph on Conroy's face stiffened her resolve.

Victoria took a deep breath and dug her heels into Monarch's flanks. As she came through the arch, a shaft of sunlight broke through the crowds and refracted off the metal breastplates of the Guardsmen so that she was dazzled. But in that moment of temporary blindness she heard the low hiss of the crowd, which swelled as she rode out in front of the cavalry.

Keeping her face as immobile as possible, Victoria guided Monarch to the spot where she would acknowledge the salutes of the troops. She longed to look up at Melbourne in the stand behind her, but she knew that she could not avail herself of that comfort. The hissing of the crowd was now amplified into actual boos, and she heard one voice from the back of the crowd cry out, 'What about Flora Hastings?' Another voice took up the name and then another until Victoria thought her head would explode. But she would not give them the satisfaction of showing what she felt. Biting the insides of her cheeks so that she would not cry, she kept her face in an impermeable smile. Only when she heard a woman shout 'Mrs Melbourne' did her lip quiver.

But just when Victoria thought she could bear it no longer, there was a drum roll and the cavalry band started playing the national anthem. The familiar chords drowned out the noise of the crowd, and Victoria raised her hand to salute her troops. As the columns of soldiers began to weave through each other like red and black ants, Victoria heard the words floating across the Parade Ground,

> God save our gracious Queen!
> Long live our noble Queen!
> God save the Queen!
> Send her victorious,
> Happy and glorious,
> Long to reign over us,
> God save the Queen.

The deep voices of the Household Cavalry resonated around the square. Victoria thought of all the monarchs who had come before her. Somehow they had managed to endure; she must, she would do the same. When the crowd began on the second verse, Victoria listened to the words as if she had never heard them before.

> Thy choicest gifts in store
> On her be pleased to pour,
> Long may she reign.
> May she defend our laws,

> And ever give us cause,
> To sing with heart and voice,
> God save the Queen.

Her arm was stiff from holding it in the salute, but she would not falter now. As the anthem came to an end, she resolved that she would do everything in her power to give her people cause to sing with Heart and Voice in the future. Lady Flora's whispered admonition came back to her, 'To be a great Queen, you must be more than a little girl with a crown.'

There was a silence after the singing. Generally there were cheers and applause when the anthem came to an end, but today there was only the rhythmic one–two of the soldiers marching to fill the gap. Victoria stared straight ahead, her hand still at her temple.

Then from the back of the crowd came a shout. It was a child's voice, thin and clear: 'God Save Queen Victoria!'

Book Two

Chapter One

THE LINE OF DIGNITARIES WAITING TO BE PRESENTED stretched all the way along the antechamber of the Guild Hall. There must be at least sixty men there, thought Victoria, as she tried to keep her smile in place. She wished that the tiara she was wearing were not quite so heavy. She had selected it to impress the burghers who would be present at the Lord Mayor's Banquet, but now regretted her choice. She could feel the headache beginning to press down behind her eyes.

The Lord Mayor's breath tickled in her ear. 'I believe you know Sir Moses Montefiore, Ma'am.'

Victoria smiled at the portly man bent over her hand. 'Indeed I do. I am glad to see you again, Sir Moses.'

She was pleased to see someone she recognised. Sir Moses had been knighted at her first investiture. He was the first Jew to have been honoured in this fashion, and Victoria felt proud of having set that precedent.

'And how is Lady Montefiore?' Victoria remembered the joy on the wife's face at the investiture ceremony. Of all her duties, conferring titles was one of her greatest pleasures. It was a role that only she could perform, and there could be no doubt as to its popularity.

Sir Moses beamed with pleasure. 'Very well, Ma'am, but she will be even better when I tell her that you have enquired after her.'

'I shall send her a card for my next Drawing Room.'

Sir Moses's smile grew even wider. 'Her cup will run over, Ma'am. You are most gracious.'

Victoria nodded. Before moving on to the next man, she glanced at Melbourne, standing on her other side, to see if he had noticed the interaction. Melbourne was always encouraging her to make small talk on occasions like these, and she wanted him to see she was making progress. To her surprise she saw that he was looking not at her, but consulting his pocket watch. Although his inattention made her want to frown with vexation, the Lord Mayor was murmuring another introduction, so she had no choice but to smile at the man who was now standing expectantly in front of her, waiting to make the bow he had been practising all morning.

It wasn't until the Queen had been shown into the small antechamber where she was to wait while all the guests were seated at the Banquet so that she could make her grand entrance, that she was able to talk to Melbourne.

'Do you have a more pressing engagement, Lord Melbourne?' As she very rarely called him anything other than Lord M, her irritation was clear. But Melbourne did not look nearly as remorseful as Victoria expected. He frowned as he put his pocket watch away.

'I confess, Ma'am, that I am distracted. There is an Anti-Slavery Bill going through the House of Commons at the moment, and I am concerned that it will go against my government.'

Victoria was confused. 'But I thought that slavery was abolished years ago. I remember as a child I had a cup which had a poor slave in chains on one side and him freed on the other.'

Melbourne looked grave. 'The slave trade has been outlawed, Ma'am, for many years. But slavery itself continues in some of our territories, the Caribbean islands in particular. The Jamaica planters say that they cannot harvest their crops without slaves to cut the sugar cane for them. And the Tories have decided to support their cause in the hope of getting rid of my government.'

Victoria began to pace up and down the room, her footsteps echoing indignantly. 'But how can the Tories be so wicked? Surely they must know that your cause is the righteous one? I can't believe that Wellington, the man who fought for liberty at Waterloo, would stoop so low.'

Melbourne's lips twitched. 'Wellington is a politician now and a Tory, and he looks for advantage where he can. The Tories think they can muster a majority against my government on this issue – there are many members with interests in sugar, and so Wellington and his friends will use it to bring me down.'

Victoria stopped pacing. 'Isn't there something I can do? If I support your cause in public, surely no one will dare to disagree.'

Melbourne looked rueful. 'I am afraid that I have not taught you as well as I should have, Ma'am. You have no power to intervene in the business of government. You can advise, encourage certainly, and even warn, but you can never insist.'

Victoria looked at Melbourne. 'I see. But then what is to happen?'

Before he could answer her, the door opened to admit her mother and Conroy. Victoria had not wanted her mother to attend the banquet at all, but Melbourne had told her that it was vital, after the Flora Hastings affair, that she appear to be on good terms with the Duchess, in public at least. Victoria had reluctantly agreed to invite her mother, but had refused to share a carriage with her. Conroy's presence was the Duchess's retaliation; if she could not ride with her daughter, she would not ride alone.

The Duchess had spots of colour on each cheek. Appearing in public always excited her. 'Such cheering from the crowds as my carriage went by, Drina! It was most gratifying.'

Conroy bowed to Victoria. 'I think it is time, Ma'am, that your mother had a title that reflected her popularity with the people. Queen Mother seems fitting.' He gave her a smile which made it quite clear he knew the crowds had not cheered Victoria's carriage with the same enthusiasm.

Victoria bridled. She looked at Melbourne, but he was looking at the floor. 'I see no reason to change your title, Mama. After all, the name you bear belonged to poor dear Papa.'

She had the satisfaction of seeing Conroy's smile fade, but before she could say any more, the Lord Mayor came to usher her in to the Banqueting Hall.

As she took her place at the dais, she looked instinctively for Melbourne, but he was nowhere to be seen. Conroy noticed the look, and as he passed behind her to take his seat he said, 'If you are looking for Lord Melbourne, I am afraid you will be disappointed. A messenger arrived from the House, and he has been obliged to return there. I understand that his government is likely to fall. These are uncertain times, Ma'am, uncertain times,' and once again he smiled, with undisguised pleasure at the thought of Melbourne's downfall.

Without betraying by a muscle that she had heard his remark, Victoria sat through the interminable speeches that followed the banquet, wondering if Conroy could possibly be right, and if so, what would happen then.

Looking out at the glittering array in front of her, the successful men in their court dress complacent in their prosperity, satisfied to be eating in the presence of the Queen, she imagined doing all this without Melbourne at her side, to give her a reassuring glance or a raised eyebrow when a speech became particularly florid. She decided that Conroy was trying to frighten her. The Whigs were still popular in the country, and surely the government would not fall because it supported the abolition of slavery, which must after all be the attitude of all right-minded people. Still, she felt a tug of fear at the thought of Melbourne's distracted face as he checked his pocket watch. Then the Lord Mayor turned to propose the Loyal Toast, and she was forced to put aside her preoccupations and smile on the assembled company as their most gracious Sovereign.

The next day Melbourne sent word that he would not be able to ride out, so Victoria went round the Park with her groom and her equerry. Lord Alfred was easy company; his family, who had been courtiers for generations, had learnt from the cradle the art of talking pleasantly to monarchs about nothing. As he chattered on about Lady Lansdowne's new barouche and the rivalry between Lady Vesey's twin daughters for the love of the younger Fitzgerald son, Victoria allowed herself to be swept along quite happily into a world where new liveries and matrimonial prospects were the only things that mattered.

In the afternoon she sat for her portrait, wearing her Coronation robes. Hayden the artist had put her in a pose where she was standing and looking back over her shoulder. It was a difficult stance to maintain, particularly as the crown, even the paste replica that she was wearing, was so heavy. Moving her head a little, she heard Hayden cough in disapproval. She tried to straighten up and said to her ladies, who were sitting in a semicircle in front of her, 'It was just like this at the Coronation. I was worried the whole time that the crown would slip down over my nose. The affair was so nerve wracking, I felt as if my heart was beating fast enough for the Archbishop to see it through my shift.'

There was another cough of irritation from Hayden.

Harriet Sutherland looked at the artist enquiringly. 'I suppose I may talk?' Hayden nodded, and the Duchess continued, 'No one would ever have known, Ma'am. From where I stood you looked quite at ease. Melbourne said that he had never seen a monarch look so serene at their Coronation.'

'Did he really?' said Victoria, forgetting that she was meant to be silent, and earning another cough from Hayden.

Emma Portman jumped in to rescue her. 'Oh yes, Ma'am, William said the same thing to me. And I have to say I agree. Yours is the third Coronation I have attended and by far the most satisfactory. Your Uncle George had a most magnificent ceremony, but he was so fat that he could hardly squeeze himself onto his throne, and of course there was all that unfortunate business with his wife Queen Caroline trying to gain admittance. Then your Uncle William's Coronation was a very threadbare affair – no music to speak of, and no balls or parties after, so disappointing. No, as William said, you have restored the splendour of the monarchy, Ma'am.'

Victoria smiled. Apart from talking to Melbourne himself, she liked nothing better than to talk about him. Judging from the frequency with which Harriet and Emma mentioned Melbourne's name, they enjoyed talking about him too.

'But I am worried about Lord M. He seems so distracted at present.'

This time Hayden did not even attempt to mask his irritation with a cough. 'Please, Ma'am.'

Victoria reverted to her Queenly pose, but Harriet picked up the thread. 'I think he is worried about the anti-slavery vote, Ma'am.'

Emma put her head on one side and said, 'It's curious; a year ago, William would have been delighted to relinquish the reins of office. He was always complaining how tedious the business of government was and how much he would prefer to be in the library of his house in the country, Brocket Hall. But now he is quite different. Don't you think, Harriet?'

Harriet said eagerly, 'Oh yes, my husband says that he has never seen Melbourne so engaged. He seems to have had a new lease of life.'

Emma nodded. 'I don't think I have seen him so happy for a long time. Not since,' she paused, uncertain of what she was going to say next, 'well, not since he was a much younger man.'

Victoria listened in happy silence.

A mile away in the House of Lords, Melbourne was attempting to make himself heard over the clamour from the Opposition benches. 'And I say to the Noble Lord, slavery in all its forms is an affront against civilised society. I must repeat to the House that a point of principle cannot be set aside simply because it is inconvenient.'

There were roars from his supporters, but they were lost in the jeers and catcalls from the Tories. Melbourne could see the Duke of Cumberland on the other side of the House, nodding vigorously, the scar on his cheek more livid than ever. The Duke had no holdings in Jamaica, but was supporting the sugar lobby because as an Ultra Tory he longed to see the end of the Whigs, whom he blamed for every evil from the Reform Act to the failure of the harvests.

'Lord Hastings.' The Lord Chancellor gave the nod to the speaker on the other side of the House.

Hastings got to his feet and began to bemoan the unjust treatment of the sugar planters and the effects that the ruin of their business would have on the domestic economy. Hastings had no interests in the Caribbean either, but he too was using the issue against Melbourne, whom he held to be complicit in the scandal surrounding his sister Flora.

Melbourne turned to Sutherland, who shook his head. 'There will be a vote tonight, and I think it's going to be damn close.'

Sutherland sighed. 'Too many people have money in the sugar plantations. They don't hold with slavery at home, but so long as it suits their pocketbooks . . .'

'The world has always run on self-interest, Sutherland. You have been in politics long enough to know that.'

'But still. Even Wellington is supporting the motion. I thought he was a man of principle.'

'The Duke is a politician.'

'Must the one exclude the other?'

'In my experience, Sutherland, there is no principle strong enough to withstand a man's desire to become Prime Minister.'

'You won't back down on this bill to save your ministry? I believe the Queen will take it hard.'

Melbourne looked down at his boots. 'Yes, I think she will. But even if I concede this, there will be something else. The Tories want power and will find a way to bring me down.'

Sutherland smiled. 'And you would rather be defeated on a

bill that you believe in? You have principles, Melbourne, even if you do your best to appear a cynic.'

'Every government must fall eventually.'

As he walked out of the chamber, Melbourne thought of the Queen, and felt his face slip. She would, as Sutherland said, take it hard, but then, he thought, so would he. He did not care so much about losing his position; he had been in office for seven or so years now and had had his fill of power. He would not miss the endless stroking and cajoling that was necessary to keep his motley coalition of aristocratic Whigs and fiery radicals together. He was tired of trying to explain to angry men that power must be exercised with discretion.

He had enjoyed it once, of course, the feeling that the whole world looked to him, but after Augustus's death, he had found it harder and harder to relish the game ahead. Since Victoria had come to the throne, however, he had found a new purpose. His role was to educate the girl into a credible Queen: she had all the right instincts, or most of them anyway, but had not been taught the ways of government. She did not realise how delicate the relationship was between monarch and Parliament, that her power was a façade that could not be leant upon. He wondered if he had taught her to understand that a change of Prime Minister was an inevitable part of political life. If the vote went against him, he would find out.

In Buckingham Palace, Victoria and her ladies were playing cards in the Blue Drawing Room. But when the Queen missed two bids in a row, Harriet suggested that perhaps they should play the piano instead.

Victoria stood up, and her ladies followed. She began to move around the room restlessly. 'I wonder what has happened to Lord M. He usually looks in after dinner. Do you think, perhaps, that he has had an accident? I believe he has a new horse, and it is rather frisky.'

Emma and Harriet looked at each other, and Emma said, 'I think it is more likely that he will have been detained at the House by the Anti-Slavery Bill. I suspect, Ma'am, that if the debate is prolonged we may not see him at all tonight.'

Victoria went over to the window that looked out over the Mall. Nothing that Harriet or Emma could say or do would distract her from looking out into the darkness waiting for a glimpse of Melbourne's carriage.

After what seemed to Victoria's ladies like an age, they heard the sound of horses coming through the Marble Arch. 'That's his carriage now,' said Victoria. 'See? I told you he would come.'

As Melbourne drove through the Arch, he saw the small neat head silhouetted in the window of the Queen's private sitting room. He felt the ache of what he was about to do constrict in his chest. Getting out of the carriage, he heard his knees crack in protest, every part of his body resisting what must come next. Walking through the Picture Gallery on his way to the Queen's private apartments, he caught a glimpse of himself in the mirror and he noticed that his hair had much more grey in it than the last time he had looked.

Victoria was waiting for him at the door of the sitting room. Behind her stood Harriet and Emma, who gave him an enquiring glance. He shook his head imperceptibly. But Victoria was too excited to notice.

'Oh, Lord M, the others had quite given you up, but I knew you would come. I have been longing to talk to you all day. So many things have happened. I have had a letter from Uncle Leopold saying that he is coming to visit, and a request from Mama about raising her allowance, and I managed to get Dash to sit still long enough to finish my picture of him.'

Melbourne looked at the eager face, the shining blue eyes, and he forced himself to smile. 'That is a feat in itself, Ma'am. If you can persuade Dash to sit still, then I am sure that no feat of diplomacy involving the crowned heads of Europe will be beyond you.'

Victoria laughed, but it was not her normal unselfconscious peal; there was a staginess about it that suggested to Melbourne that she too was playing a part.

'I wonder if the crowned heads will be quite so amenable to sweetmeats as dear little Dashy?'

'Everyone is susceptible to something, in my experience, Ma'am. But I suspect it may be easier to find Dash's heart's desire than it is to discover King Leopold's.'

Victoria laughed again. 'Actually I know exactly what Uncle Leopold wants – to marry me to my cousin Albert as soon as possible. He thinks I need a husband to steady my giddy ways.'

Melbourne saw Emma Portman looking at him over Victoria's shoulder. He knew they were waiting for him to deliver the news. But the Queen carried on talking, almost as if she did not want to give him the chance to speak.

'I told him that I had no intention of marrying at present, indeed probably not for three or four years. And when I do, it certainly won't be to a boy like Albert. When he came to visit three years ago, he had no conversation and started yawning at half past nine.' She looked up at Melbourne. 'So you see, Lord M, I am not always so diplomatic.'

Melbourne waited to see if she intended to say more. Finally he said in a low voice, 'I have something to tell you, Ma'am. As you know, I have come from the House. I am afraid to say that the Jamaica bill, outlawing slavery in that island, passed with only five votes. As a result,' he hesitated, finding this even harder than he had anticipated, 'I have decided to resign my ministry.' His voice sank almost to a whisper.

Victoria's voice, by contrast, was bell-like in its clarity. 'Resign? But why on earth would you do that, if the bill has passed?'

Melbourne sighed. 'The Tories, Ma'am, are like hyenas. Once they sense a weakness they will worry my government until they destroy it completely. I would rather go now, on my own terms.'

Victoria looked at him blankly. 'But who will be Prime Minister?'

Melbourne said quickly, 'That depends on you, Ma'am. As the Sovereign it is your job to appoint a new Prime Minister. I should send for the Duke of Wellington. He is the senior Tory.'

'Wellington? But he is so brusque, always talking to me as if I were one of his junior officers.'

Melbourne smiled. 'I doubt that he will want to be Prime Minister again, Ma'am. I imagine that he will recommend that you summon Sir Robert Peel; he leads the Tories in the Commons and is very much the coming man.'

Victoria started walking around the room distractedly. Harriet, Emma and Melbourne followed her with their eyes. 'But I don't know Sir Robert Peel! How can I be comfortable with someone I don't know?' She stopped walking and turned to him. 'I have decided not to accept your resignation, Lord M.' She put her head on one side and smiled as bewitchingly as she knew how.

Although Melbourne understood the intention behind the smile and was touched by it, he persevered. 'I am afraid, Ma'am, that you cannot refuse me in this.'

Victoria's smile became steely. 'Really? I thought the Prime Minister served at the pleasure of the Crown.'

"Indeed, Ma'am, but I must remind you that I still have the right to resign.'

Victoria met his eyes, then said, with a note in her voice that made Melbourne tremble, 'Do you really mean to forsake me?'

Melbourne looked away, unable to bear the directness of the appeal in her face. When he spoke, he found himself talking to her hands, which were clasped tightly together. 'I am afraid I have no choice, Ma'am.'

Victoria unclasped her hands and smoothed the folds of her dress. 'I see. Then I think I must retire. Good night, Lord Melbourne,' and without turning to look at him she swept out of the room, Harriet and Emma following in her wake. Emma gave him a sympathetic glance, as if she knew how much this exchange had cost him. But, he thought, no one could really know the damage that had been done.

Chapter Two

THE RAIN HAD BROUGHT DOWN ALL THE BLOSSOMS from the cherry trees in the Palace gardens, and they littered the paths like confetti. But Victoria did not notice the blossoms or the puddles beneath her feet. She did not care that it was raining steadily, that her new pink-sprigged muslin was sodden, or that the braids on either side of her ears were clinging to her face, or indeed that her ladies-in-waiting were huddling under an umbrella.

Victoria was using her umbrella not to shield herself from the rain but to cut a swath through the plants in the shrubbery. There was something satisfying about seeing the proud heads of the tulips fall under her onslaught. Slash, slash, slash. Having reduced the border to a scene of devastation, Victoria looked about her for something else to destroy.

Harriet Sutherland approached and said gently, 'Don't you think we should go back inside, Ma'am? It is very wet, and I should hate you to catch a chill.'

'You go inside if you want to. I am as happy to be here as anywhere.'

Harriet retreated to her umbrella. Victoria continued to storm along the shrubbery, remembering a bed of peonies by

the fountains that she would take particular pleasure in deci-
mating. Lord Melbourne had once told her that peonies were
his favourite flower.

But as she turned, she heard another voice behind her. 'Drina!'

Victoria stopped. To her surprise she saw the Duchess of
Kent walking towards her, carrying an umbrella.

When she reached Victoria, she stopped and put her free
arm around her daughter. Victoria bristled; she had hardly
spoken to her mother, let alone embraced her, since the death
of Lady Flora, but then she smelt the lavender water the
Duchess always wore. For once Victoria allowed herself to relax
and rest her head on her mother's shoulder.

'My poor Drina. I came as soon as I heard about Lord
Melbourne.'

'Oh, Mama! What am I going to do? He is the only one
who understands me.'

Victoria felt her mother's heart beating under her cheek.
'Not the only one, Drina.'

Victoria said nothing, allowing herself for once to feel the
comfort of her mother's presence. She looked up at her mother
and saw the tenderness in her face. 'But it is so hard.'

'I know, Drina. But I will help you, and perhaps it will be
better to have someone in your family at your side.'

Victoria felt the tears coming to her eyes.

'People are always saying that you are too close to Lord
Melbourne. Now they will see that you are your own woman.'

The tears were rolling down Victoria's cheeks now. The
Duchess set down her umbrella and put her arms around her
daughter.

'Never mind, *Liebchen*. You must not worry so. I will take
care of you, you know this.'

Just for a moment, for the first time in years, Victoria allowed herself to dissolve into her mother's embrace. She felt safe in the circle of those lavender scented arms, to be her mother's little *Maiblume* again.

That evening Melbourne attended a reception at Holland House, but did not stay long. On the way back from Kensington, Melbourne told his coachman to take a detour through Piccadilly, rather than passing Buckingham Palace. As the carriage turned into Trafalgar Square, past the half-built column to the Admiral Lord Nelson, Melbourne thought of Victoria's face the night before when she had asked him if he really intended to forsake her. Suddenly the library at Dover House lost its appeal, and he found himself directing the coachman down a certain side street in Mayfair.

Melbourne had not been to Ma Fletcher's nunnery for at least a year, so his presence caused a flurry of excitement. Ma Fletcher herself was all graciousness and tact, and when she clapped her hands, half a dozen girls presented themselves in the drawing room in various states of undress. Melbourne looked over at them and tried not to yawn. He could not quite summon the enthusiasm that was required. But then he noticed that one of the girls, a little blonde girl of no more than twenty, had an eager expression on her face that he found intriguing. He pointed to her and was rewarded by a beaming smile of triumph.

Ma Fletcher gestured to the girl. 'This is Lydia, my lord. A very popular choice.'

Melbourne followed Lydia up the staircase to a large bedroom on the first floor. It smelt of beeswax and cologne, but underneath there was something darker – a mixture of sweat and desire. Melbourne took off his coat, sat down in the armchair near the fire and loosened his neckcloth. Lydia came towards him and let the robe she wore fall down over her bare shoulders. She came and sat down on his lap, and as Melbourne put his hand on her thigh, he allowed himself to imagine how it would feel to have another young woman in his arms. Lydia laughed and began to undo the buttons on his breeches. Melbourne looked at the bare nape of her neck and asked, 'How old are you, Lydia?'

Lydia looked up. 'Nineteen next month, sir.'

'How young you are.' He sighed. 'I suppose I must seem very old to you.'

Lydia shook her head vigorously. 'Oh no, my lord. There are plenty that come in who are much older than you. And you have all your own hair, which is more than I can say for most of my gentlemen.' She ran her fingers through Melbourne's grey-blond locks, and smiled encouragingly.

There was something in the tilt of her head that made him lean forward and ask, 'Tell me, Lydia, how old do you think I am?'

The way her eyes clouded over in panic before she regained her professional smile was enough to make him realise it had been a mistake to ask.

'Oh, my lord, you are surely not a day over forty?'

Gently Melbourne disengaged Lydia's hand from his fly. He stood up and reached for his coat. The girl made a little wail of disappointment.

'Did I say something wrong, my lord? I'm not good with ages, I know, but you don't look old, not at all. Won't you come and lie down with me? I promise you won't regret it.'

Melbourne said gently, 'I find that my inclination has changed. But don't worry, I will tell Mrs Fletcher that it was not your fault.' He felt in his waistcoat pocket and found a gold sovereign.

'Here,' he pressed the coin into her hand. Lydia's expression of delight told him that he had managed to assuage the slight to her professional pride.

In the carriage going home, Melbourne smiled at his own folly. When he got to Dover House, he called for brandy. The butler returned with the decanter, and as Melbourne took a long draught, he noticed that his fly buttons were still undone.

Chapter Three

THE PALACE CLOCK STRUCK ELEVEN AS VICTORIA MARCHED up and down the inlaid parquet of the Throne Room. The last chime had barely faded when the Duke of Wellington was announced. Victoria turned and held out her hand, smiling as best she could at the great general. She had known him since she was a child, but always found his ramrod stature and brusque manners alarming.

'Thank you for coming, Duke. I am sure you know why I have asked you here today. I would like you to form an administration.'

Wellington spoke carefully. 'I am honoured, Ma'am. But I am afraid I must decline. I am too old to serve as Prime Minister again. You must send for Sir Robert Peel, who is the only man who can command the House at the moment.'

Victoria tapped her foot. 'But I don't know Sir Robert Peel, and I have known you all my life, Duke!'

Wellington moved his great leonine head from side to side. 'Nevertheless, Ma'am, I must still decline.'

Victoria tried another tack, and said with as much force as she could muster, 'Will you really refuse your Sovereign,' she paused, 'and commanding officer?'

Wellington smiled. 'A good soldier knows when to retreat, Ma'am, and I am afraid that this is a battle you cannot win.'

Victoria sighed. 'You are most disobliging.'

'If I might say so, Ma'am, I think you will find Sir Robert to be a most able fellow. I realise that you have been used to dealing with Melbourne. While Peel does not have the Viscount's ease of manner, he is the only man who can command enough support on both sides to form a government that has any chance of succeeding. You may not want him, but the country needs Peel.'

Victoria said nothing.

'Then I bid you good day, Ma'am.'

Wellington walked backwards for two stiff steps, and then turned and left the room. Victoria resumed her pacing. Everything she had heard about Sir Robert Peel suggested that he would not be at all congenial. Emma Portman had told her that he had no greater vice than Calculus and disapproved of waltzing. How was she expected to be comfortable with a man who took no pleasure in life? There must something she could do.

She summoned the footman and asked him to bring her writing desk directly. Dashing off a note to Melbourne asking him to visit her at his early convenience, she told the footman to send it by messenger to Dover House. Surely Melbourne would relent when he knew that she had tried with Wellington and failed. He would not be so cruel and uncaring as to leave her in the hands of Sir Robert Peel.

But as the day went on there was no sign of Melbourne. Victoria attempted one of the new Schubert duets with Harriet Sutherland, but try as she might she could not find the tempo. At last she gave up and started to pace up and down the music room. Her ladies stood in a semi-circle waiting for her to stop.

'I don't understand what can have happened to Lord Melbourne. I sent a letter this morning. He usually comes straight away.'

Victoria saw Harriet and Emma look at each other. Before she could ask them what that look meant, the Duchess of Kent came into the room unannounced. She was clearly in a state of excitement.

'Drina, I am just hearing about what happened with Wellington. What a pity. But you must not worry, I have a plan.'

Victoria smiled. 'A plan, Mama?'

The Duchess walked over and took Victoria's hands in hers. 'Yes, *Liebes*, I have talked to Sir John and we think that the best thing to do is to summon Robert Peel.'

Victoria broke away from her mother at the mention of Conroy. 'I see. Well, I thank you for your concern, but as it happens I have a plan of my own.' She turned to Emma Portman. 'Your carriage is unmarked, isn't it, Emma?'

Emma nodded, puzzled. 'Be so good as to have it brought round. Lehzen, I shall need you to come with me.'

Lehzen turned to the Queen. 'Where are we going, Majesty?'

'Dover House.'

The Duchess drew in her breath sharply. 'But Drina, Lord Melbourne has resigned. A Queen cannot go chasing after her Prime Minister. Do you really want another scandal?'

Victoria ignored her and walked out of the room, followed by Lehzen. 'What will people think?' wailed the Duchess. But there was no reply.

Melbourne sat in his favourite armchair in the library. It was by no means the smartest chair in his possession; the green leather was worn and cracked in places, but it had belonged to his father and no other chair was as comfortable. He had picked up a volume of Gibbon, hoping to distract himself by reading about the excesses of Ancient Rome. But the words refused to make themselves intelligible. He kept thinking of the note from the Palace. *Please come,* she had written, *at your earliest convenience.*

He knew that he should reply, explain to her that things were different now that he was no longer her Prime Minister. He could not just go to the Palace; people would assume that she had summoned him to form a government. It would be wrong for him to go until she had appointed a new Prime Minister. But as he thought of the letter he should write, he also thought of Victoria's small face and shining blue eyes, and could not summon the resolve he needed.

A sound disturbed his reverie. The door opened behind him, and without looking round he barked, 'I thought I said I wasn't to be disturbed.'

There was a cough, and then a small, high, utterly familiar voice said, 'I hope you will forgive me, Lord M.'

The Queen was here in his library. Melbourne leapt to his feet, frantically tugging down his waistcoat and pulling his neckcloth into position.

'Your Majesty. Forgive me, I was not expecting visitors.'

Victoria smiled. She rather enjoyed seeing Melbourne caught off his guard. 'Evidently.'

She looked around the room. Every surface was covered in piles of books and drifts of paper. There was a dish with a half-eaten pie on the desk and an empty decanter. It was not a room fit for a Queen. Melbourne thanked God he had kept his boots on.

'You always talk about your library, so I am glad to see it at last.'

'If I had known you were coming, Ma'am . . .' He gave her a little bow.

'As you did not reply to my letter, I thought I should come to you.'

'Alone, Ma'am?'

'No, Lehzen is outside.'

'I see. But what am I thinking? Please come and sit down.'

He led her over to the chair he had been sitting in, but she shook her head and took the one opposite. 'I won't deprive you of your favourite chair, Lord M,' she said, smiling.

Melbourne looked at her and, at her nod, took his seat. It felt very odd to see the Queen sitting opposite him when five minutes ago he had been imagining her presence.

'What can I do for you, Ma'am?'

'I saw the Duke of Wellington this morning. He says that he is too old to be Prime Minister and that I should send for Robert Peel.' She put her head on one side and looked at him appealingly.

'I thought that might happen. But there is no cause for alarm. Sir Robert Peel is not such a bad fellow. A little serious perhaps, but honest and straightforward. You should have no trouble with him.' He forced himself to give her a reassuring smile. 'Do you remember the day of your accession, Ma'am? You were playing with your dolls, and I wondered if such a young girl could really be Queen?'

Victoria lifted her chin. 'I wasn't playing with the dolls. You asked me about them.'

Melbourne wanted to laugh at her vehemence. 'The point is that as soon as I heard you speak I knew that you were a Queen in every sense, Ma'am. It has been the greatest privilege of my life to serve you, but you will manage very well without me.'

'But I don't want to!'

Melbourne leant towards her. 'Even Queens have to do things they don't like.'

Victoria began to pout. 'It seems to me that I am never to do anything I *do* like. Why can't you just come back? You haven't lost a vote yet. I am sure you could manage.'

Melbourne hesitated, and then, in a voice quite different to his usual amused tone, he said, 'You know, Ma'am, that I don't believe in much. But there is one thing that I do believe in, and that is the British constitution in all its tattered glory. For me to return without the support of the House would be unconstitutional, and nothing,' he paused, and his voice grew lower, 'not even my devotion to you, will stop me from doing my duty.'

Victoria stared back at him blankly. 'I see.'

'As I said, Peel is not a bad fellow. Just remember that if he suggests anything you don't agree with, tell him that you need time to consider. If in doubt, always delay.'

She hesitated, and then said in her usual tone, 'And will you come to dinner tonight, Lord M? So I can tell you all about it?'

Melbourne blinked. This was much harder even than he had imagined. 'Not tonight, Ma'am. Not until this matter is settled, and even then I cannot be with you as constantly as I have been.'

Victoria stood up, and when he too had got to his feet, she said, 'But why not? You may not be my Prime Minister, but you are still, I think, my friend.'

She looked up at him as she said this, and Melbourne felt the force of her clear blue gaze. He lowered his eyes and said as gently as he could, 'I think you must understand why.'

He paused and then added a little more strongly, 'A monarch cannot be seen to favour one party only. You must dine with Robert Peel.'

Victoria turned her head away from him. He saw, with a pang, the delicate ear surrounded by the thick braid. But he must continue. 'He will probably ask you to make some changes to your household. Harriet Sutherland and Emma Portman are married to Whig ministers. Sir Robert will want you to have some Tory ladies about you.'

Victoria looked back at him, and he could see that there were red spots on her cheeks.

'Tory ladies? No, thank you!'

This time Melbourne averted his gaze. 'Remember, Ma'am, that I would ask the same thing in his position. A Prime Minister cannot function if he feels that he does not have the confidence of his monarch.'

To his surprise, Victoria did not protest at this, and a flicker of something he did not recognise passed over her face. She smoothed down her skirts with that quick deft gesture that she had, and said crisply, 'I shall disturb you no longer, Lord Melbourne. Thank you for your advice.'

At the door he saw Lehzen, who was waiting in the hall, frown as they came out. Partly for her benefit, Melbourne said, 'You will send for Peel?'

'Don't worry, Lord Melbourne. You may not be my Prime Minister, but I still listen to you. I will talk to Peel directly.'

'A wise decision, Ma'am.'

Victoria did not reply. She pulled her veil down over her

face, so that she would not be seen by any passersby, and got into the carriage, Lehzen bustling in her wake. She did not look back.

Victoria had put some thought into the location of her first meeting with Sir Robert Peel. She always received Melbourne in her private sitting room, but that was too intimate for the Tory leader. The Throne Room would be more imposing, and while she saw Melbourne alone, she decided that she would have her ladies with her. She had not met Peel before, and it was important that she had all the support at her disposal.

At three o'clock, the time Peel was expected, she was looking at the designs for the coinage with her ladies. The drawings were laid out on a table in front of her, together with a proto-type of the new crown piece.

Victoria sighed with exasperation when she examined them. 'I have no chin in this one, and two chins in the next one. How can they say it is an accurate likeness when none of these images looks the same?' She tapped her foot in temper.

Harriet picked up the coin and held it out to her, with her most emollient smile. 'But look at the coin itself, Ma'am. It is more convincing in relief, I think.'

Victoria's foot tap turned into a stamp. 'But I look like a goose wearing a crown!'

Before Harriet and Emma could protest, the door opened and Penge announced Sir Robert Peel.

Victoria held out her hand for Peel to kiss. As he was uncommonly tall, he had to bend right over and she saw a patch of pink at the top of his head where his hair was thinning. This gave her confidence.

'Good afternoon, Sir Robert. I was just inspecting the designs for the new coins. I am not sure that I am satisfied with them. Tell me, what do you think of this?'

She pointed to the coin on the table. Peel picked it up and examined it carefully, taking out his eyeglass so that he could peruse every detail. Finally, and with great deliberation, he said, 'I see nothing wrong with it, Ma'am. Indeed, I would say it is an excellent likeness.'

Victoria had not expected to like Sir Robert Peel, and now she knew that she had been correct.

'An excellent likeness. Really?'

Her voice was so icy that Harriet and Emma looked at each other in alarm, but Peel did not seem to feel the *froideur* and carried on in just the same tone. 'Yes, Ma'am. Most coins are quite crude in their detail, but this one is remarkably accurate.'

Victoria stared at him with distaste. The profile on the coin was quite hideous; it was out of the question that her likeness should be immortalized in this way. Melbourne, of course, would have seen that at once. She shook her head. 'Nevertheless, it will not do.'

Peel was about to say something more, but Emma Portman gave him a warning glance and he stayed silent.

Victoria continued, 'But you are here on business, Sir Robert.'

Relieved to be on safer ground, Peel nodded, and then glanced at the ladies-in-waiting who stood behind the Queen like a praetorian guard in petticoats. He swallowed and said, 'Perhaps if I might have a private audience, Ma'am.'

Victoria raised her chin, considering her next move. She

decided that it would be better to conduct this part of the audience alone, so she nodded her head in regretful dismissal and in a rustle of silk umbrage they left the room.

Picking up Dash, who was growling at Peel's feet, Victoria settled herself on a sofa. She did not invite Peel to sit, which left him hovering in front of her like a reluctant heron. After waiting a moment, Victoria raised an eyebrow and said, 'Well, Sir Robert?'

Peel put his thumb in his waistcoat pocket, a gesture he often adopted when addressing the House of Commons. 'I am here to assure you, Ma'am, that I have enough support in the House to form a government.'

Victoria inclined her head with the smallest possible movement, making it quite clear to Peel that he might have the support of the House, but here in the Palace things were different. Peel, however, had faced down more alarming audiences than a teenage girl, even if she was the Sovereign. He put the other thumb in his waistcoat and faced the Queen as if she were the leader of the Opposition.

'As you know, Ma'am, any government serves at the pleasure of the Crown.'

Victoria played with Dash's ear. 'I do know how the constitution works, Sir Robert.'

Peel tried to ignore the frostiness in her tone. 'And of course, Ma'am, you know that it is essential that the Crown,' he hesitated, remembering that he was not, after all, in the chamber, and continued in a less rhetorical tone, 'that is, yourself – must appear to be above party politics and favour neither side over the other.'

Victoria raised her head to look at him, and it was all he could do not to take a step back. 'Have you come to give me a lesson in government, Sir Robert?'

Peel took a deep breath, and said boldly, 'There is the question of your household, Ma'am.'

'My household?' repeated Victoria slowly.

Peel decided to plunge in, and in what he imagined to be his most reasonable voice, said, 'Two of your ladies, Ma'am, are married to Melbourne's ministers, and your maids of honour are all the daughters of Whig peers. If you were to replace one or two of them with ladies who are connected to my side of the House, then there would be no danger of you appearing to favour one side over the other.'

The Queen sat up very straight, and Peel noticed Dash tense too, as if ready to pounce on an unsuspecting mouse.

'You want me to give up my ladies, my closest and dearest friends. Whatever next, Sir Robert? My dressers? The housemaids? Do you want to surround me with spies?!'

The anger in Victoria's voice surprised Peel, who explained, 'It is not my intention to deprive you of your friends, Ma'am, merely to ask you to be friendly to all.'

Victoria flicked an imaginary speck of dust from her skirts. 'I absolutely will not give up my ladies, Sir Robert!'

Peel spoke without thinking. 'What, not even one?'

Victoria looked at him for a second, and then, 'I think I have made myself clear. Good afternoon, Sir Robert.'

Peel hesitated, wondering if he should say anything more, but he caught a flash of blue and realised that there was no point. He started to turn before remembering that he was meant to back out of the room. He took a few awkward steps and then, as the Queen seemed to be preoccupied with her dog, he turned and walked away as fast as he could.

Victoria waited until Sir Robert was out of sight, if not out of earshot, and taking Dash's muzzle she said playfully, 'Your mama isn't going to be told what to do by Sir Robert Peel, or by anyone else.'

And Dash, hearing the note of adventure in his mistress's voice, wagged his tail as hard as he could.

Sir Robert did not go home directly. Instead he told the coachman to call at Apsley House, or as the Duke of Wellington liked to call it, Number One London. He found Wellington in his library. From the other man's high colour and slightly crotchety manner, Peel suspected that he had woken him from an afternoon nap. This made him regret his impulse to visit, but he felt that he must tell someone about his audience with the Queen.

Wellington turned to him, his pale blue eyes assessing. 'Have you come straight from the Palace? Would you like some tea? No, by the looks of you, you want something stronger.' He gestured to the butler. 'Brandy and soda.'

Then to Peel, 'I take it that your audience was not successful?'

Peel took a gulp from the schooner of brandy that was put before him. 'She dismissed me like a footman caught stealing the silver.'

Wellington raised an eyebrow. 'It appears the Queen has her grandfather's temper. But she cannot refuse you.'

Peel sat down heavily in one of the buttoned leather chairs. 'I am afraid she has. She won't change a single lady.'

Wellington made a sound halfway between a bark and a snort. 'Nonsense, man, go back and offer her someone charming like Emily Anglesey. I am sure Her little Majesty would swap her for a busybody like Emma Portman.'

Peel drained his glass and said with feeling, 'I am sorry,

Duke, but I cannot form a ministry on the basis of Lady Anglesey's charms.'

Wellington tapped him on the shoulder, and as Peel looked up he felt how powerful the Duke's presence on the battlefield must have been.

'Can't or won't? No stomach for the fight, eh? You need to win her over like Melbourne does.'

Peel got to his feet; clearly this visit had been a mistake. He said stiffly, 'I am afraid I do not have Lord Melbourne's ease of manner.'

Wellington laughed at his offended face. 'Or his way with women, Peel. She would be yours if you would just flirt with her a little.'

Peel longed for his own drawing room and the sympathy of his wife. His job was to form a government, not to pander to the fancies of eighteen-year-old girls. 'I had not realised that flirting was a prerequisite for being Prime Minister, Duke. And now, if you will excuse me, I will detain you no longer.'

For the second time that day Sir Robert Peel left a room feeling that he had been wronged.

Chapter Four

I T WAS AN UNHAPPY DINNER AT THE PALACE THAT night. Victoria sat one end of the table and the Duchess of Kent at the other, and as they would not speak to each other, it fell to the household to keep some semblance of conviviality. Lord Alfred Paget told a long and involved story about his attempts to teach his dog Mrs Bumps to play chess. Harriet and Emma tried to embellish the anecdote until it became almost a conversation. Emma volunteered that her aunt had a cat who played piquet, and Harriet confided that there was a parrot at Ragsby who kept score in the billiard room. Normally this was the sort of absurd banter that Victoria delighted in, and the courtiers looked at her to see if she would raise a smile.

But the Queen did not appear to be diverted, dissecting her food with her knife and fork as if it were a laboratory specimen. The Duchess, meanwhile, made no attempt at all to follow the conversation, and ate as much as she could in total silence.

Victoria looked at her mother scraping up the last morsel of *quenelles de brochet* from her plate, and sighed. If only Lord M were here, he would find a way of making everything easy. That was not a skill that Robert Peel possessed, judging by his performance that afternoon. She had not been expecting to be charmed, but he had not even been civil. Striding in and proposing to take away all her friends; it was as if he had forgotten who he was talking to. How could Melbourne have left her to deal with such an uncouth man? She put down her knife and fork with a clatter, and the footmen swooped in and cleared the plates, despite the Duchess protesting that she hadn't finished.

After dinner, Victoria sat looking at a volume of *La Mode Illustrée*. She liked the new neckline that skimmed the collarbone and neck. Lord M had once told her that she had fine shoulders. Inviting Harriet and Emma to sit down next to her, she showed them one of the dresses she particularly admired. Harriet, who was generally considered to be one of the best dressed women in London, pointed to a style that she thought would look especially becoming on Victoria, and they spent a happy half an hour turning the pages, discussing passementerie and the ideal depth of a lace flounce.

When they got to the last page, Emma looked at Victoria. 'I know, Ma'am, that you will have to make some changes to your household now that there is to be a new administration, and I think that I should be the one to go. Harriet is so much more accomplished than I am, and I think her taste will be invaluable to you, whereas I can hardly play the piano and am scarcely a leader of fashion.'

Harriet shook her head. 'No, Emma, you have wisdom and experience. Sutherland always says that you are the best man in the Cabinet. Without Lord Melbourne, I think the Queen will need your counsel more than ever!'

'You are too kind, Harriet, but I think that the Queen needs a younger companion. I am old enough to be her mother.'

Both women looked over at the Duchess of Kent, who was on a sofa near the fire, her eyelids drooping.

Victoria, who had been listening to this exchange in silence, looked up. 'The point is that I find you both invaluable. You are not just my ladies, you are also my friends, and I have no intention of losing either of you.'

Harriet and Emma looked at each other. Emma spoke first. 'But Ma'am, it is customary for the ladies of the household to change when the ministry does.'

'But that's ridiculous. What right does Robert Peel have to tell me who I should be friends with?'

Harriet said gently, 'I think, Ma'am, that he would find it difficult to form a government if he is not seen to have your support.'

Victoria gave them both a knowing smile. 'Precisely.'

Emma and Harriet looked at each other again, surprised by Victoria's reaction.

Victoria got to her feet and when the whole room was standing, she addressed them both. 'So you see, ladies, there is no question of either of you resigning.'

Harriet made a deep curtsey, and Emma followed suit.

The Duchess woke up from her reverie and said plaintively, 'But where are you going, Drina? I want to talk to you. You should not always be acting alone. It is dangerous.'

Victoria turned to her, her eyes glittering. 'But I am not acting alone, Mama. I have my ladies.'

The Duchess snorted. 'You forget, Drina, that blood is thicker than water.'

Victoria stopped. 'Do you really believe that, Mama? Perhaps you should tell Sir John Conroy!'

The Duchess threw up her hands in despair. 'You are so childish, Drina. Sir John and I only want to serve your interests. That is all I have ever wanted.' The Duchess reached for her handkerchief and started to dab at her eyes.

Victoria hesitated; her mother never cried in public. She turned back and sat down next to her. 'I know, Mama, that you are worried, but there is no need. I have learnt how to handle myself.'

'I think, Drina, that is a matter of opinion. You visited Dover House alone against my advice, and now I believe that you have told Sir Robert that you refuse to give up your ladies.' The Duchess glared at Harriet and Emma, who were huddled together on the other side of the room.

'Yes, Mama, I did. But I did not do so on a whim. I know what I am doing.'

'You think you do, but Sir John says that you are playing with fire. This country needs a Prime Minister, and if it seems that you are preventing the country from being governed, then the country will blame you.'

Victoria stood up. 'As you say, Mama, blood is thicker than water. Perhaps you should trust my judgement rather than Sir John Conroy's.' Turning her back on her mother, she walked quickly out of the room, Emma and Harriet following in her wake.

The next morning, Emma Portman went to Dover House at an hour that she would generally consider too early to be civilised, but rules had to be relaxed at times like this. Melbourne's butler told her that His Lordship was still in bed, but Emma took no notice and proceeded directly up the stairs to the bedroom. The butler attempted to protest, but the gleam in Lady Portman's eyes told him that resistance was useless.

Melbourne was lying in bed reading *The Times* when Emma burst in. He saw the butler's apologetic face and nodded that it was all right. Emma sat down at the end of the huge four-poster.

'Really, Emma, you might have given me some warning. I am hardly presentable.'

'My business couldn't wait, and I am too old to be shocked by your whiskery chin or the egg on your dressing gown.'

Melbourne looked down and saw that there was indeed a patch of congealed yolk on the lapel of his Paisley robe. 'Well, then, you must take me as I am, Emma. But what is this business that couldn't wait for me to receive you in the library like a respectable married lady?'

'The Queen saw Peel yesterday.'

'I know. I told her it was the only sensible course.'

Emma looked at him searchingly. 'But did you know that she told him that she would not give up any of her ladies?'

Melbourne sighed. 'No. In fact, I told her that she would have to make changes to her household, or Peel would not feel he had her confidence.'

'I saw Peel as he was leaving. His ears were bright red as if she had boxed them!'

Melbourne sighed again. 'But how can Peel not have persuaded her that it was in her interests to make changes? It would not be right for her to be seen as the Queen of only one party.'

Emma Portman laughed. 'You know perfectly well why he couldn't persuade her. She won't change her ladies because she means to have you back, William.'

Melbourne got out of bed and rang the bell for his valet. 'That is not her decision to make,' he snapped.

'Nevertheless, that is her intention.' Emma arched an eyebrow. 'You can't blame her really. Why put up with a clod like Peel if she can have her charming Lord M?'

The door opened, and the butler came in, followed by one of the royal messengers who held out a letter to Melbourne. 'From the Queen, my lord.'

Melbourne tore it open and frowned.

'You see,' said Emma smiling, 'there is your summons.'

Melbourne made a sound that from a less urbane man would have been considered a snort. 'I hope that in the last year I have taught the Queen the difference between inclination and duty.'

Emma walked over and gave him a kiss on the cheek. 'I am sure that was your intention, William. But you forget the Queen is also a young girl who likes to get what she wants.'

Half a mile away on St James in White's club, the stronghold of the Tory party, the Duke of Cumberland was making his way through the library. If he saw that some members turned their back on him, he gave no indication of noticing; he was too intent in reaching Wellington, who was holding court with a cabal of Tory party grandees, including Robert Peel, at the end of the room.

The Duke strode into the middle of the group, his scar livid against his cheek, and without greeting anyone, he attacked. 'Can it really be true that the Tory party, the party of Burke and Pitt, has been defeated by the caprice of an eighteen-year-old girl?' He turned his bloodshot blue eyes on Peel, who took a step back.

'I cannot form a government, sir,' the flat northern vowels were evident in his voice, 'without the support of the Sovereign.' He returned Cumberland's stare without flinching.

Cumberland put his finger to his temple, and turned to Wellington. 'Do you think, Wellington, that her behaviour is altogether rational? To make such a to-do over her ladies. It reminds me of my father. He was not altogether rational at the beginning of his . . . sad affliction.'

Peel raised an eyebrow. 'Are you saying that the Queen is not of sound mind, sir?'

'I am saying that she is not strong enough for the business of government. What she needs is guidance. When my father was ill, there was a Regent appointed. Why should we not do the same?'

Wellington leant back against the mantelpiece and surveyed Cumberland with a cool stare. 'I am sure that the Duchess of Kent would be ready to step in and, of course, *she* is very popular with the people.' Wellington's emphasis was clear; the Duchess had the kind of public support that Cumberland lacked.

Cumberland stared back at him with dislike. 'I think the Duchess is hardly capable of being Regent unaided.'

Wellington smiled. 'Oh, I am sure Sir John Conroy would be more than happy to advise her. I believe he is very ambitious.'

The colour in Cumberland's face went darker. 'A German ninny and an Irish mountebank – I hardly think that will do.'

Peel spoke from his corner. 'So who did you have in mind, sir?'

Wellington took a step towards Cumberland. 'Oh, I believe the Duke thinks that a Regent should come from the British royal family, am I right?'

Cumberland drew his lips back into something approaching a smile. 'Quite right, Wellington. The Duchess has a claim as the Queen's mother, but she would need a co-Regent of royal blood.'

Wellington nodded. 'Well, let us hope that it won't come to that. Another Regency would not be a good thing for the country.'

Cumberland tried not to show his annoyance. 'Better a Regency than a hysterical girl on the throne.'

Peel cleared his throat. 'I wouldn't say the Queen was hysterical, sir. In fact, she seemed to me to be quite calm.'

Cumberland turned his head sharply. 'But she has behaved completely unreasonably, has she not?'

Wellington smiled. 'I daresay that in the Queen's mind, her behaviour is quite rational. I imagine that she thinks by refusing to give up her ladies, she will get Melbourne back.'

'But that is unconstitutional,' spluttered Cumberland.

'So is replacing a sane monarch with a Regency, Your Royal Highness,' said Wellington with exaggerated courtesy. Peel's lips twitched.

'Something must be done,' grumbled Cumberland, ignoring the implied insult.

Wellington nodded. 'Yes, we need a Prime Minister. She will send for Melbourne now, but I wonder what he will do?'

'Whatever she wants, of course; the man is besotted with her,' said Cumberland.

'Perhaps, but even Melbourne might baulk at becoming the Queen's second lapdog,' said Wellington, 'and whatever you think of his politics, the man knows his duty.'

Peel looked at Wellington and then at Cumberland. 'His

notions of political economy are sadly deficient, but he is a man of honour.'

Cumberland looked at them both incredulously. 'Honour and duty indeed! This is not a novel by Sir Walter Scott. Melbourne's a man and a politician; he will do whatever suits his own interest.'

Wellington's smile did not waver. 'Well, that remains to be seen, but for now we are in his hands.'

Cumberland seemed about to berate them further, but evidently thought better of it. Giving them both a curt neck bow, he turned on his heel and left them, the club members darting away from him like frightened sheep.

Peel turned to Wellington. 'I suppose if the Queen won't see reason . . . then at some point we might have to consider the idea of a Regency.'

Wellington narrowed his eyes. 'It's possible, of course, but of one thing I am certain – the people would rather have Tom Thumb on the throne than be ruled by the Duke of Cumberland. Half the country thinks he murdered his valet and the other half believes he fathered a child on his sister. Little Vicky may be young and foolish, but she isn't a monster. Or at least not yet.'

Chapter Five

VICTORIA WAITED FOR MELBOURNE IN HER PRIVATE sitting room. She opened one of her boxes and tried to concentrate on a paper about the appointment of the Dean of Lincoln Cathedral, but could not focus her attention. She closed the lid of the red dispatch box and examined her reflection in the looking glass on the chimney piece. She was wearing the pink dress that Melbourne had once called becoming, but in the mirror she thought it made her face look sallow. Was there time to change?

She looked at the Boulle clock on the malachite console; it was nearly eleven o'clock. If she changed her dress now, then Melbourne might arrive, and she did not want to keep him waiting. She pinched her cheeks hard and bit her lips, trying to bring a little colour into her face, but she still looked pale. It had been so difficult to sleep last night. She wondered if Lord M would notice; he was so observant usually.

Before the clock had finished chiming eleven, the footman opened the door to admit Melbourne.

Victoria saw at once that his smile was not as warm as she had hoped, but she did not let her own smile waver as she held out her hand to him. 'Dear Lord M, I can't tell you how glad I am to see you.' She smiled conspiratorially. 'Don't you think I have arranged things marvellously?'

Melbourne said without expression, 'You have been most resourceful, Ma'am.'

'Sir Robert wanted to take all my ladies away and replace them with Tory spies.'

To her great relief, she saw Melbourne's lips twitch as he replied, 'Peel is a fine politician and a man of principle, but I fear he has never understood the fairer sex.'

He looked at Victoria then and she held his gaze. Then in a lower voice, she said, 'I have missed you, Lord M.'

Melbourne raised an eyebrow. 'It has been all of a day and a half.' He took a step towards her and she looked up at him eagerly, but he spoke with great seriousness.

'I have come here to tell you, Ma'am, that it would not be in your interests for me to return as Prime Minister.'

Victoria had to repeat the words in her head before she could understand their meaning, and then she said in astonishment, 'Not in my interests? But it is all that I desire in the world.'

Melbourne bowed his head and continued in that same grave voice, 'You flatter me, Ma'am. But I cannot allow you to jeopardise the position of the Crown on my account.'

Victoria felt as though her head would burst. It had never occurred to her that Melbourne might not come back once she had dealt with Peel. And now he was talking to her as if she were a recalcitrant child instead of his Sovereign.

She lifted her chin. '*Allow me*, Lord Melbourne?'

Melbourne continued, 'Peel was quite within his rights to ask you for changes in your household. After all, your ladies are ones that I put forward.'

Victoria felt her stomach lurch, and her breath started to come in short fast bursts. 'But my ladies are my friends. If I lose them as well as you, then I have no one. It will be like Kensington with Mama and Sir John all over again. I don't think I could stand it.' She felt tears coming to her eyes, and bit her lip. 'Sir Robert Peel does not understand this, but I think that you must, Lord M.'

Melbourne sighed, his handsome face struggling to keep his composure. Victoria thought that he must yield, but when he spoke it was again in that hateful voice. 'I'm sorry, but if I agree to form a government now, you will be the loser, Ma'am. Critics, and I have many, will say that I have manipulated you, a young and impressionable woman, for my own political advantage.'

Victoria said fervently, 'But that isn't true. I am not a piece of clay to be moulded by any hand.'

He looked at her then and said slowly and carefully, 'No, you are not a child any more, and that is why you must try to understand that it doesn't matter who you like or don't like.'

Victoria bridled; how could he not understand that she needed his support, not a lecture on the duties of being a Sovereign? 'Of course it matters! I am the Queen,' and as she spoke she saw him shake his head.

'Vic–,' then he caught himself, 'Your Majesty, surely you understand what's at stake here?'

Victoria pulled her shoulders back, and with as much force as she could muster she said, 'Lord Melbourne! You forget yourself!'

But Melbourne's face did not change. Usually so mobile, it seemed to be made of granite. His gentle expressive eyes were hard, and his perpetually smiling mouth was set into a grim line. Victoria felt as if her heart would break; she had trusted him completely and now he was telling her that he would not do the only thing in the world that she wanted.

At last she said in a small voice, 'Don't you want to be my Prime Minister?'

When he spoke it was as if the words were being squeezed out of him. 'Not in these circumstances, Ma'am. The relationship between the Crown and Parliament is a sacred one, and I will not allow you to put it in danger.'

And before she could reply, Melbourne said in a thick voice, 'You must excuse me, Ma'am,' and without waiting for her permission, he turned his back on her and walked quickly out of the room.

Conroy was on his way to the Palace from his lodgings in Bruton Street, when a messenger presented him with a letter asking him to call at Cumberland House. Conroy's supple mind began to calibrate the points at which the Duchess's interests and Cumberland's might coincide, and he made his way to St James's Palace, where the Duke had apartments, with a sense of anticipation. With Melbourne out of the way and Cumberland as any ally, there could be any number of possibilities for advancement.

Cumberland received him in the armoury, a room where every inch of wall was covered in weapons. A shaft of light fell on a row of mounted sabres and bounced around the room, temporarily dazzling Conroy.

Cumberland stood under a chased silver axe, looking like a man who would not flinch at an execution. As Conroy was announced, the Duke was taking a large pinch of snuff, and proceeded to sneeze violently. When the explosions had finished, he narrowed his eyes at his visitor.

'There you are, Conroy,' he said.

Conroy heard the impatience in the other man's voice and said smoothly, 'I came as soon as I got your message, sir. Although I must confess that I was a little surprised to receive it. I am, as you know, very close to the Duchess of Kent, with whom you have not always been on friendly terms.'

Cumberland sneezed again. 'Things have changed, Conroy.' The Duke took a couple of steps towards his visitor and said in a stage whisper, 'I am worried about my niece. It seems to me that she has taken leave of her wits,' he paused and then with a pious roll of his eyes, 'like my poor father.'

Conroy lowered his eyes, while he tried to fathom the Duke's intention. The Queen was of a nervous disposition, prone to hysteria like all young women, but to question her sanity, likening her to the mad King George III, was premature. But as this was clearly a prelude to something more, he nodded gravely. 'I believe you are right, sir. She has been of a nervous disposition ever since she was a child. It is possible that the strain of her position has disordered her senses.'

'Exactly!' One side of Cumberland's mouth rose in agreement. 'I thought you might agree with me. Papa used to talk to himself and scream at nothing in particular. Does my niece do anything like that?'

Conroy returned the Duke's smile. 'The Queen's behaviour has certainly been . . . erratic. There was the Hastings affair and now this business of her ladies. Do you know that she actually went to Dover House for a *tête-à-tête* with Melbourne?'

'Such behaviour is not becoming in a monarch,' said the Duke, shaking his head. 'Of course, no one wants to believe that the head that wears the crown is less than sane, but if that is the case then we must not shirk our duty.'

Conroy bowed in agreement. 'No, indeed, sir.' He waited for the Duke to continue, wondering what cards he intended to play.

The Duke waved a hand. 'I am sure the Duchess must be very concerned about her daughter's welfare. I worry, of course, about the country. It may be that between us we can come to some arrangement.'

Conroy looked up. 'Regarding a Regency, sir?'

Cumberland nodded. 'Of course, as her mother, the Duchess is the obvious choice. But I don't think Parliament will want another woman in charge, especially as she is a foreigner. If the Duchess had a co-Regent, from the British royal family,' he gave another of his lopsided smiles, 'I think there could be no possible objection.'

Conroy smiled back. 'I feel confident that the Duchess would agree, sir.'

'We will need evidence, though. You would think her recent behaviour would be enough, but Wellington and Peel are damnably cautious.'

'Evidence?'

'Some indication that the Queen's state of mind is disordered.'

'I understand, sir.'

'Good.' The Duke took out his snuff box again and tapped a pinch onto his hand and then put it to his nose. Three sneezes later, he looked at Conroy as if surprised to find that he was still there. 'Well, I think that is everything I wished to say. You may leave us.'

Conroy walked silently from the room. The Duke's arrogance was insufferable. If Conroy had doubted the rumours that

Cumberland had murdered his valet, he now thought them entirely credible. Dismissing him as if he were a servant, rather than an invaluable ally. If only he were in a position to act alone, but Conroy knew if the Duchess was to have any hope of obtaining the power and influence that were rightfully hers (and his, naturally), they needed Cumberland's help.

Of course, when it came to it, Conroy had no intention of supporting a co-Regency. The Duchess already had an advisor, but the Duke was the only person at present who could bring the matter of the Regency to a head. This exercise in logic made Conroy feel calmer, and by the time he had walked across The Mall to Buckingham Palace and the Duchess's apartments his serenity was restored.

He found the Duchess going through her accounts with her dresser Frau Drexler. When he came in she was sighing. 'Oh, Sir John, do you know that Madame Rachel my dressmaker will give me no more credit? Soon I will be forced to dress in rags. It is not right that the mother of the Queen should be humiliated in this way.'

Conroy smiled. 'Oh, I don't think you will have to worry about your bills in the future, Duchess. I have some news that I think will interest you very much.'

He looked at Drexler, and the Duchess waved her out of the room.

Conroy sat down on the sofa next to the Duchess. He sat a little closer perhaps than was entirely proper, but he knew the Duchess was a woman who responded to physical proximity. The closer he got to her, the more power he had.

'I have just come from seeing the Duke of Cumberland.'

The Duchess turned to him in amazement. 'Cumberland! But why? He is my enemy.'

Conroy put one strong hand on the Duchess's lace-mittened one. 'That may have been true in the past, but now I believe that you have more in common than you realise.'

The Duchess raised her liquid blue eyes to his. 'But what can I have in common with that dreadful man?'

'The Duke is worried, as we are, about the Queen. He believes that the strain of her position is becoming too much for her wits.'

The Duchess shook her head. 'No, no, Drina may be head-strong and wilful, but she is not mad.'

Conroy took the hand beneath his own and squeezed it. 'Not mad exactly, but . . .' he paused, looking for the right word, 'overtaxed. The Duke feels, and I agree with him, that what she needs is a period of quiet and seclusion where she can regain her strength.'

The Duchess's hand trembled in his. 'Quiet and seclusion?'

'Yes. Of course for that to happen a Regent would have to be appointed to take care of the business of government.'

The Duchess looked down at the hand that clasped her own. 'A Regency. It is what I always hoped for, to be able to guide my daughter instead of being always shut out. But I don't understand why this . . . Cumberland would want this.'

'He imagines that you would need a co-Regent.'

The blonde ringlets shook. 'No, Sir John, this cannot be. I cannot betray my daughter to help that man.'

Conroy berated himself for having gone too fast. 'I think that the only person you would be helping, Ma'am, would be your daughter. I think she is in danger at the present of losing all credibility with the public. A period of reflection away from the pernicious influence of Lord Melbourne could only be beneficial. And of course, if you are Regent when she is fully recovered you will be able to hand back the throne. If it were left to the Duke,' he paused and looked into the Duchess's eyes meaningfully, 'well, let us say that the Duke desires the throne very much and I doubt he would give it up once he had got it.'

He held the hand tightly now and interlaced his fingers through hers. Sensing that she needed more reassurance, he continued, 'A short spell as Regent would be enough to show your daughter and indeed the country what is due to you as the Queen Mother. You would get the respect that you deserve, and of course all the dresses that you need.'

The Duchess took her hand away. 'You think I would do this for some dresses?'

Conroy put on a face of deep contrition, and extended his hand in supplication. After a long moment the Duchess gave him hers again.

'I think that you would only act in your daughter's best interests, Duchess. But it would give me great pleasure to see you dressed as befits your station. A woman like you should be resplendent.' As he said this, he raised the lace-mittened hand to his lips and kissed it.

The Duchess gave a deep sigh. 'I must talk to Drina. She should understand what will happen if she is not sensible.'

Conroy's voice was low and urgent. 'With respect, Ma'am, you must not mention our plan to your daughter. I think she would not understand that our motives are entirely disinterested, and I believe she might use it against you. Much better to say nothing and be prepared to act, if there should be some further sign of mental instability.'

The Duchess stood up, and Conroy followed suit. 'I do not trust Cumberland, Sir John.'

Conroy stood in front of her and clasped her elbows with his hands. 'No, Ma'am, neither do I. But it is better, I think, to act with him, than to let him act alone. That is the only way that we can protect the interests of the Queen.'

The Duchess looked at him, her face clouded with indecision. Conroy pressed on.

'Tell me, Duchess, that you know I am right.'

He tightened his grasp on her elbows until she nodded and then said in a tremulous voice, 'We will protect her together.'

Judging that he had now made his point, Conroy relinquished his grip on the Duchess and made her a deep bow before taking his leave. Once he was outside the Apartments he stood leaning his forehead against a marble pillar, the stone cool to his heated flesh.

Chapter Six

A WEEK HAD PASSED SINCE MELBOURNE HAD RESIGNED as Prime Minister, and the country was still without a government. Word had got out that the Queen refused to give up her ladies for Sir Robert Peel, and talk of what was known as the Bedchamber Crisis filled the clubs and corridors. Peel had written to Victoria the day after their interview to tell her that without her cooperation in the matter of her household he would be unable to form an administration. She had replied that she would not give up her friends. Victoria had enjoyed writing that letter, but there had been no word from Melbourne since their last disastrous meeting. She had been so sure that Melbourne would applaud her stratagem, but instead they had quarrelled and now she was alone.

That afternoon she took Emma Portman aside and asked her if she knew why Melbourne did not come to the Palace.

Emma looked embarrassed. 'I imagine, Ma'am, that he is waiting for you to decide on your Prime Minister. He does not want to be seen to interfere.'

Victoria shook her head in disbelief. 'But what am I to do? Peel won't form a government unless I accede to his outrageous demands, and Lord M, who must know how much I depend on you and Harriet and all my ladies for support, says that I must do as Peel wishes. He was quite sharp with me the last time we met, and I have not heard from him since. Tomorrow is my birthday.' Victoria's face crumpled. 'Do you think he will come to my celebration? I do not think I will enjoy it otherwise.'

'I cannot say, Ma'am. But I suspect he will not come to the Palace until a Prime Minister has been appointed.'

That night, Victoria lay in bed listening to the chimes of the clock in her room as they signalled every passing quarter of an hour. Usually she fell asleep as soon as she laid her head on the pillow, but tonight she could not get her mind to settle. She could not believe that Melbourne could be so hard-hearted. She felt angry and bereft at the same time. Without him at her side, all the little pleasures of being Queen were denied to her. She had looked forward to doing her boxes in the morning with him at her side, but without him there to explain and enlighten, the names were just names and the papers merely chores.

Imagining what it would be like to go through the appointments with Sir Robert Peel made her shudder. Peel, she sensed, was a man who did not connect amusement or pleasure with the performance of a public duty. From their brief meeting, she knew that he would lecture her instead of trying to educate her without making her feel stupid, as Melbourne did. Peel would not, she thought, care for her feelings. And besides, he was a great awkward lump of a man. He was not a man she would ever care to dance with.

The chimes rang out again: ten, eleven, twelve. Midnight. It was now officially her birthday. Nineteen years old. Victoria decided that she could lie in bed no longer. She got out of bed, pulled on her wrapper, and put on her slippers. She thought about waking Lehzen, who slept in the room behind the interconnecting door, but she knew the Baroness would fuss over her and scold her for wandering about in her nightdress. And besides, she could not talk to Lehzen about Lord Melbourne.

She lit the candle by her bed, and wandered out into the long corridor, Dash pattering along at her side. It was a full moon, and as she entered the Picture Gallery the faces of her regal ancestors gleamed in the silvery light. She looked at the portrait of Elizabeth Tudor, whose mouth was set into a hard line. In the past she had wondered why Elizabeth had chosen to be painted looking so disagreeable, but tonight she thought she understood. Elizabeth, a woman on her own without a husband, didn't care for being liked; she wanted to be respected, or even feared.

To the right of Elizabeth was Charles I with his family. Lord Melbourne was very fond of that picture; he said that the painter had done a splendid job of showing how a man could be magnificent and foolish at the same time. 'Look at the stubborn set of his mouth,' he would say; 'that is the one quality that is unforgivable in a King. Monarchy is fundamentally absurd and it is a foolish Sovereign who forgets that.' Victoria had looked askance at that remark, and Melbourne had laughed at her. 'Do you think I am being disrespectful, Ma'am? Perhaps I am. There is no greater supporter of a constitutional monarchy than myself, but the structure can only hold if neither side leans on it too heavily.' Victoria looked at the sulky droop of Charles's lips. She hoped that her portrait, the one in her Coronation robes, would not reveal a quality that did not do her credit.

There was a bark from Dash, and the spaniel chased along

the corridor after some unseen prey. Victoria hoped that it wasn't a mouse; she had had a horror of mice since one had scampered over her face one night when she was sleeping in Kensington Palace. She had woken up screaming with horror. Mama had refused to believe that such a thing could have happened, but Victoria could still feel the tiny claws scrabbling across her chest and the awful soft slide of the tail. Since then she had insisted that Dash sleep on a cushion at the end of her bed. She would rather be disturbed by his snuffling and snoring than that terrible rapid scurry.

Dash was scratching at the wainscoting underneath the full-length portrait of her grandfather George III. Victoria had a particular dislike for this picture since Conroy had told her she had a look of her grandfather. As the King in this picture had bulbous blue eyes and an expression of bewildered confusion, she had not taken this remark as a compliment. She suddenly felt tired and, deciding that she might at last fall asleep, she bent down to pick up Dash, who she knew would not leave unless forcibly removed.

Dash was not going to leave his prey without a struggle. Trying to pull him away from the skirting board, Victoria started as a voice behind her said, 'But Drina, what are you doing here? All alone in the middle of the night?'

She looked round and saw her mother, whose hair was tied up in curl papers so that she looked like a porcupine. Her face, lit up by the candle she was carrying, was full of shadows.

'I couldn't sleep, Mama.'

'But you should not be walking around in the middle of the night in your nightgown. You will catch cold, and if the servants should see you there might be some gossiping. I think maybe you are missing having me in your room. You always used to sleep so well when you were in the bed next to mine.' She put her arm round Victoria and squeezed her shoulder.

'I cannot expect to sleep so well now that I am Queen, Mama. I have so many responsibilities.'

The Duchess held the candle up to Victoria's face as if searching for something in it. 'I hope they are not too much for you, *Liebchen*. I think it is hard to be so young and to have so many cares.'

'Not so young, Mama. It is past midnight, so I am nineteen now.'

The Duchess smiled and kissed her daughter on the cheek. 'But you must not catch cold on your birthday. Let me take you back to your room, and I will stay with you until you fall asleep. I don't think you will worry if your mother is there.'

Victoria turned to follow the Duchess when out of the corner of her eye she saw a rapid movement and the flash of something pink, and she gave a little scream of terror. 'Did you see that, Mama? I think it was a mouse or even a rat.'

As if to confirm her words Dash started to whine and bark, his muzzle pressed up against the skirting board.

The Duchess said, 'You are trembling, Drina. Surely you cannot be so frightened of a little mouse.'

'But you know how much I hate them, Mama. Since that mouse crept over my face.'

'That was never happening, Drina. It was just your imagination.'

The Duchess moved her hand to her daughter's cheek. 'You must not start at shadows, Drina. Or people will whisper about you.' She looked up at the white face of George III gleaming above them in the moonlight. 'They remember your grandfather.'

Victoria looked at her in confusion. 'My grandfather? What are you saying, Mama?'

The Duchess shook her head. 'It is not what *I* am saying, Drina. But maybe you are needing some rest and quiet.'

Victoria looked up again at the bovine face of her grandfather, and her mother's meaning began to dawn on her.

The Duchess continued with passionate fervour: 'But you mustn't worry. I will protect you, Drina, I will not let them take it away from you.'

Victoria shivered, but this time it was with anger, not fear. When she spoke, all trace of her earlier tremors had gone. 'There was a time, Mama, when I needed your protection, but instead you allowed Sir John to make you his creature.'

The candle in the Duchess's hand shook, casting discordant shadows around the room. When she spoke, the fury in her tone matched her daughter's. 'Sir John at least cares for my existence. You have banished me from your affections.'

Victoria retort was immediate. 'Whose fault is that, Mama?'

The Duchess stared at her before she walked quickly away, her curl papers fluttering.

Victoria watched her go and, turning her back on her ancestors, started to walk back to her bedroom. Her cheek still felt warm from where her mother had touched it.

The next morning was bright and fair. In the kitchens of the Palace, Mr Francatelli, the Queen's pastry chef, was putting the finishing touches to her birthday cake. He had been working on it for weeks, baking the fruitcake layers a month ago and steeping them in brandy so that they went the colour of mahogany wood. Then he had iced each layer and had made the columns that supported one tier on top of the other. Now he was working on the *pièce de résistance*, a model of the Queen with her lapdog Dash executed in sugar.

In the Throne Room the wife of the vicar of St Margaret's Westminster was trying to keep her young charges in order as they waited to sing the national anthem. Her husband had been delighted to volunteer her Sunday School class to sing on the Queen's birthday, but, she thought ruefully, he had never had to keep eight seven year olds quiet in a palace. The children squealed with delight as Francatelli wheeled in a trolley bearing the birthday cake.

'That's the biggest cake in the world, I think.'

'I bet it's bigger than the Queen herself.'

'Look up there, you can see the Queen. playing with her little dog!'

The vicar's wife moved with a swiftness born of long experience to intercept a small and rather grimy hand from patting the head of the sugar spaniel.

'You come away from there, Daniel.'

The footmen started to open the double doors, and the vicar's wife motioned for her young charges to get in line under a banner on which was painted *Happy Birthday, Your Majesty*.

'Do we sing now, Mrs Wilkins?'

'No, that's the Queen's mother, the Duchess of Kent.'

'Who's that man with her? Is that her husband?'

'No, child, her husband is dead. That, I believe, is Sir John Conroy.'

'He looks like her husband.'

'You are an impertinent boy, Daniel Taylor. Please keep your opinions to yourself.'

A hush fell in the room as the footmen at the door signalled that the Queen's party was coming down the Picture Gallery. Mrs Wilkins looked at her charges, and as Victoria walked into the room, smaller than the vicar's wife had believed possible, she nodded to them to start singing.

> *God Save our gracious Queen!*
> *Long live our noble Queen!*
> *God save the Queen!*
> *Sent her victorious, happy and glorious.*
> *Long to reign over us,*
> *God save the Queen.*

The children were, as ever, off-key, but the Queen smiled and clapped at the end of the verse. Mrs Wilkins gestured to Eliza, the smallest member of the choir, to present the bunch of violets. The Queen buried her face in the flowers and said, 'They smell wonderful. What a delightful birthday greeting.'

The children, even Daniel, beamed with pride. Then, at a signal from Baroness Lehzen, Mrs Wilkins gestured to the children to make their curtseys and bows and to follow her.

When they were safely ensconced in the Palace kitchens eating the ices that had been provided for them by the Baroness, Daniel asked, 'Does the Queen have a husband, Mrs Wilkins?'

'No, not yet.'

'Is that why she's so sad?' said Eliza.

'The Queen ain't sad,' scoffed Daniel.

'She is too. I saw tears in her eyes when I gave the flowers. Real tears.'

'Probably crying because she had to look at your ugly mug.'

As Mrs Wilkins stepped in to separate the two children, and to comfort Eliza, who was indeed a plain child, she thought of the Queen's small and stricken face, and wished that she too could be comforted so easily.

In the gilt-embellished vastness of the Throne Room, Victoria tried to admire her magnificent birthday cake. She could not help but exclaim with delight when a stool was brought so that she could appreciate the sugar figurine of herself and Dash sitting on the top tier of the cake. The representation was so accurate that she could make out the pendant braids around her ears and the tiny crown on Dash's collar.

It was truly ingenious and touching. Instinctively, Victoria turned round to point out the sugary Order of the Garter to Lord M, who would surely enjoy such a thing, only to remember with a lurch in her stomach that he was not there. She had waited by her window for an hour this morning, hoping for a glimpse of his carriage, but there was no sign of him.

'May I offer you my congratulations on your birthday, Ma'am?' Conroy was bowing to her. 'The first of many as Queen, I trust.' As he said this, he gave a waxy smile, and Victoria heard the threat that lay beneath the words. She wondered why he was here; Mama must know that she would not appreciate his presence. She looked over at her mother to show her displeasure, but the Duchess was looking out of the window.

Victoria turned away from him without replying, and Harriet rushed forward to fill the awkward silence. 'I have arranged all your presents on this table, Ma'am. There is a jewelled dagger here from the Shah of Persia, and the most ingenious silver musical box from the Corporation of Birmingham that shows you sitting on your throne and waving as it plays *Rule Britannia.* Let me set it in motion for you.'

Victoria stared listlessly as her small clockwork Doppelganger jerked her tiny hand up and down.

'Very ingenious.' She turned to Lehzen. 'Please make sure that you thank them from me.'

She picked up the jewelled dagger, which had a ruby the size of Dash's eye on the handle, and thought that she had a Palace full of weapons that she was not allowed to use.

Emma Portman came bustling in, carrying a parcel wrapped up in brown paper and string that she placed in Victoria's hands.

'From Lord Melbourne, Ma'am.'

Victoria sat down to open the parcel. He had not forgotten her birthday after all. Under the layer of wrappings was a wooden box with a brass plate on the top that said, *Presented to Her Majesty Queen Victoria on the occasion of her nineteenth birthday from her devoted servant Lord Melbourne.*

Quickly she opened the box. Inside, nestling in a bed of blue velvet, was a brass tube. She picked it up and saw that it had an eyepiece at one end.

'Oh, Ma'am,' said Emma, 'I believe it is a telescope. How typical of William to choose such an unusual present.' Her voice was encouraging, as if she knew that Victoria needed to be convinced.

Victoria picked up the telescope and put it to her eye. She could see nothing, but then Emma reached down and showed her how to extend the instrument. 'You have to pull it out like this, Ma'am, in order to see anything. Try now.'

Victoria put her eye to the glass again and trained it on the ceiling. She made out the dimpled hand of a cherub holding a lyre; she could even see the dust that lay in drifts on the cornice. As she lowered the instrument, she saw a mouth set in a line of fury. Putting the telescope down, she found that the mouth belonged to her mother.

'Oh, Ma'am, look, there is a card here from Lord Melbourne.' Harriet pressed the letter into her hand.

Victoria's heart began to hammer in her chest when she saw the familiar handwriting. She broke the seal and saw with a lurch of disappointment that the letter was only two lines long.

> *To help you see things differently, Ma'am.*
> *I am as ever, your loyal and obedient servant,*
> *Melbourne.*

Victoria let the letter slip to the floor, where Dash picked it up like a trophy and ran with it round the room, yelping with delight.

'And here is my present, Drina.' Victoria looked up to see her mother holding out a parcel. She was not smiling.

'Thank you. Mama.'

'It is not much, I know, but then I do not have unlimited funds at my disposal.'

Hearing the bitterness in her mother's voice, Victoria said as lightly as she could, 'I do not need expensive gifts, Mama. It is the thought that counts.'

She tore open the paper to reveal a book. It was an edition of *King Lear* bound in red Morocco leather.

'Shakespeare, Mama?'

'Why don't you open it? I have marked a passage that I think you should be reading.'

Victoria looked at the book in her hands. She felt the force of her mother's gaze and the presence of Conroy standing behind her. She forced herself to open the book slowly, trying to keep her hands from trembling.

The book fell open easily, and she saw that two lines had been underscored in red ink. *How sharper than a serpent's tooth it is, to have a thankless child.*

'Why don't you read them, Drina?' said her mother, her voice full of meaning.

Victoria shut the book with a snap. She stood up and was about to walk out when she saw a sudden movement at her feet. At first she thought it was Dash, but then there was a flash of pink, and a large brown rat ran over her foot.

Her screams were so loud that afterwards the servants claimed that the brilliants on the chandelier rattled. She tried to stop, but kept feeling that sudden movement across her instep. Nowhere was safe.

Lehzen was behind her now. 'Do not worry, Majesty, Dash has caught it now. Look, he has it in his mouth.'

But Victoria screamed even louder. Then she took her arm back as far as her corset would allow, and hurled the volume of *King Lear* at the window overlooking the balcony with all her strength. The glass broke with a satisfying crash. Victoria stopped screaming and began to laugh, rocking back and forth on her heels, the noise getting even louder as she saw Dash trotting around the room holding the rat between his teeth.

A pair of strong hands gripped her shoulders and held her

still. She looked up and saw Conroy looking at her and smiling. That smile felt like a band around her heart.

'You are not yourself, Ma'am. It seems that the excitement of the day has been too much for you. Baroness, I think you should take the Queen to lie down. I will send for Sir James.'

Victoria tried to speak, but the words would not come. Her voice was hoarse from all the screaming, so she shook her head as hard as she could.

'Really, Ma'am, I must insist. You are under strain; the cares of office are clearly too much for you. A period of rest and seclusion is what you need. It is fortunate that you are among friends here, but think of the reputation of the monarchy if anyone else were to witness one of these episodes.' Conroy spoke firmly and calmly, as if he were restoring order after a period of anarchy.

'Don't you agree, Duchess, that your daughter needs a spell of quiet retirement?' Conroy turned towards Victoria's mother.

'My daughter needs to be taken care of, I think.'

Victoria wanted to protest, but instead she found that she was weeping. Lehzen gripped her elbow. 'Come with me, Majesty, it is better so.'

Victoria heard the loyalty in Lehzen's voice. Knowing that the Baroness at least would never betray her, she allowed her former governess to lead her from the room.

Lehzen helped her out of her corset, and Victoria lay down on her bed and immediately fell asleep. When she woke up, she saw Lehzen leaning over her and beside her Sir James Clark, who was licking his lips nervously.

'I believe you are overtired, Ma'am.' He picked up her wrist and grimaced as he listened to the pulse.

Victoria turned her head away from him and saw her mother

standing on the other side of the bed with Conroy next to her, his face a mask of sympathetic concern. A great feeling of weariness came over her. How easy it would be to close her eyes and wait for them to go away. But when she saw that Conroy had his hand on her mother's elbow as if she were a marionette, a wave of anger made her sit up.

'Really, Ma'am, your pulse is most irregular. I think a period of complete rest is essential.'

Victoria took a deep breath and snatched her hand out of the doctor's grasp. Looking at Conroy, she said as loudly as she could, 'That is out of the question, Sir James. There is absolutely nothing wrong with me.'

'But, Ma'am, these episodes of hysterical behaviour often recur. The Baroness tells me that you have an engagement at the Palace of Westminster this afternoon. Surely it would be wiser to cancel?'

'It would be so unfortunate,' said Conroy, 'if you were to find yourself . . . indisposed in such company. I believe that there is to be a very large gathering of peers and Members of Parliament to see your portrait unveiled.'

Victoria clasped the sheet with her hand, and sat up as straight as she could. 'I believe I have made myself clear. I saw a rat, that is all. You all have my permission to leave. Except for you, Lehzen. I wish to talk to you about the arrangements for the unveiling.'

Sir James Clark was about to protest, but Conroy put his hand on his arm. 'We must do as the Queen says, Sir James. It is evident that she believes that she is quite well.' He ushered the doctor and the Duchess out of the room.

When they had gone, Lehzen was about to speak, but Victoria put up her hand to stop her. 'No, Lehzen, I am not staying in bed. I merely had a shock. Mama's . . . present, and then the rat – it was unsettling, no more.'

'But, Majesty, you look tired. I think it would be good for you to rest.'

Victoria looked up at her governess's worried face. 'I will rest now, Lehzen, but I must go to the ceremony this afternoon. Otherwise there will be gossip about me, and there has been too much of that already. You know what Lord M says: a monarch must be seen to be believed.'

Lehzen flinched at the mention of Melbourne, but she nodded. 'I understand, Majesty.'

'Besides, who wants to spend their birthday in bed?'

Lehzen put her hand to her mouth. 'Oh Majesty, I am nearly forgetting. I have something for you.' Fumbling in her skirts, she pulled out a small parcel and placed it in Victoria's hand.

Inside was an enamelled miniature of a young girl with long red hair. Victoria looked at it and recognised the girl as Elizabeth Tudor. Clearly painted earlier than the portrait in the gallery, this was a picture of a girl who had not yet hardened into monarchy. The face was wary, but the eyes were soft. She was looking out of the picture as if searching for someone to trust, but the set of her mouth, the jut of her chin suggested that she knew what it was to be disappointed.

Victoria smiled. 'Elizabeth Tudor. Thank you, Lehzen. I like it very much.'

'She was a great Queen, Majesty. Nobody thought that she was capable of ruling alone, but she brought peace and prosperity to the country.'

Victoria looked at Lehzen. 'The Virgin Queen. Do you think, Lehzen, that I should follow her example?'

The governess looked confused, but then she lifted her eyes

to the Queen. 'I think, Majesty, that there are some women who are always needing a man, but I think that it is not necessary for a Queen.'

'I don't think Conroy would agree with you!'

Lehzen smiled. 'No, Majesty.'

Victoria leant over and took her hand. 'But even a Queen needs friends, Lehzen.'

Conroy lost no time in sending a note across to St James's Palace and received a message asking him to wait on the Duke of Cumberland at his earliest convenience. He left at once, before the Duchess of Kent could ask him where he was going.

This time the Duke did not have his snuff box, and stood up as Conroy was announced. 'I was perturbed by your note, Conroy. Hysterics, you say, over a rat?'

Conroy nodded. 'I am afraid you could hear her all over the Palace. I sent for Sir James Clark at once, naturally.'

Cumberland traced the scar on his cheek with his finger. '*Was* there a rat, or could it have been an hallucination? My father, you know, used to see a red dog.' He looked at Conroy hopefully.

Conroy shook his head. 'I believe there was a rat, sir, but the Queen's reaction was extreme. Sir James believes she is suffering from hysteria.'

Cumberland pursed his lips. 'Then it is our sad duty to raise the question as to the state of her wits. I think that Wellington and Peel will have to come round to my point of view when they hear of this episode. The country is still without a ministry, and my niece is unhinged by a rodent.'

He said the last words with relish. Conroy could see the Duke was already assuming power, and added swiftly, 'The Duchess wants no harm to come to her daughter.'

Cumberland gave him a quick glance, annoyed by this reminder of their alliance. He waved his hand with a gesture of royal hauteur. 'Indeed. The Duchess and I will care for her together.'

Conroy bowed. 'The Duchess will be reassured to hear that, sir.'

Cumberland considered him. 'There is not a moment to lose.' He pulled out his pocket watch. 'I must go to White's; I daresay that Wellington will be there at this hour.' Cumberland picked up his hat from the table and started for the door.

Conroy realised he was being dismissed. 'The Duchess will need to be informed of all . . . developments, sir.'

Cumberland looked round, surprised to find Conroy still there. 'Indeed.'

There was a pile of dresses on a chaise in Victoria's dressing room. She had intended to wear the pink figured silk, but when she put it on she found it would not do. Although Lehzen had protested that it was most becoming, Victoria had declared that it was a hateful colour and she looked like a stick of rhubarb. Then she sent for Harriet Sutherland, who suggested the cream brocade, but Victoria decided that made her look like a dumpling. Now wearing a blue silk, she was looking at herself in the mirror, with Harriet, Emma and Lehzen waiting for her to speak. Victoria could tell from the expression on their faces that she was being unreasonable, but none of them knew what it was like to walk out into a room full of strangers when every single one of them was looking at you.

'This dress makes me look like a . . . a delphinium!'

'A glorious flower, I always think, Ma'am,' said Harriet with a little curtsey.

'But I want to look like a Queen!'

'You *are* the Queen, Ma'am,' said Emma. 'How could you look like anything else?'

Victoria was about to answer when one of the pages came in, looking breathless. 'Excuse me, Ma'am, but the Duke of Wellington is here. He is requesting an audience.'

Victoria noted the look of surprise on the faces of her ladies. 'I see. Tell him I will be with him presently.'

The page left, and Victoria turned to Emma. 'Do you think he has changed his mind about forming a ministry, Emma?'

Emma considered this. 'I would be surprised, Ma'am. The Duke is not a man who changes his mind.'

'Well, I hope he is not here to persuade me to give in to that horrid Peel and surround myself with Tory harpies.'

Emma smiled. 'The Duke is brave, but he is not foolhardy, Ma'am.'

Mrs Jenkins came into the room holding the blue sash of the Order of the Garter. She was about to put it down when Victoria said, 'Thank you, Jenkins, I shall wear it now.'

Jenkins adjusted the Order on Victoria's arm so that it was secure. Victoria took a deep breath.

'I feel as if I am going into battle.'

Lehzen picked up the miniature of Elizabeth and handed it to her. 'Perhaps you should have this, Majesty, to remind you of what is possible.'

Victoria nodded and put it in her pocket.

Wellington was waiting for her in the Throne Room. As he bent over her hand, she could see that he was examining her face with care, as if looking for something.

Conscious that the Duke was at least a foot taller than her, Victoria sat down and invited him to do likewise. There was a momentary pause, and then Wellington spoke. 'I have come to enquire after your health, Ma'am.'

Victoria looked at him in surprise. 'I am quite well, thank you.'

The Duke nodded and smiled. 'I am most glad to hear it, Ma'am. I heard reports at the Club of an . . . incident at your birthday celebration, and I was concerned.'

Victoria narrowed her eyes. 'But I am in perfect health, Duke, as you see.'

Wellington put his hands on his knees in a gesture that announced that he was about to do business. 'Then you must be aware that it is time that you called someone to form a government, Ma'am. I know Peel is not a charmer like Melbourne, but he's sound enough.'

Victoria lifted her chin. 'If you say that Sir Robert is sound, then I must believe you. But I will not give up my ladies. They are not just my friends; they are my allies.' She paused and looked directly at him. 'You were a soldier, Duke. Would you want to go into battle alone?'

Wellington shifted in his seat. 'I was not aware you were fighting a war, Ma'am.'

Victoria did not smile back. Sitting up a little straighter, she felt the shape of the miniature in her pocket. 'That is because you are not a young woman, Duke, and no one, I suspect, tells you what to do. But I have to prove my worth every single day, and I cannot do it alone.'

The Duke considered this, and the craggy plane of his face erupted into a broad smile that made his whole face blaze. If Victoria had been a soldier, she would have willingly followed him into battle. 'Then, Ma'am, I do not blame you for sticking to your guns.'

Victoria felt herself subside in relief, but the Duke continued, 'And yet your greatest ally, Viscount Melbourne, is not at your side?'

Victoria looked at the floor and shook her head. 'He and I are not . . . in agreement.'

'That is unfortunate. It seems, Ma'am, that you need a new plan of attack.'

Victoria waited for him to continue, but he picked up his cane and looked at her for permission to leave.

She stood up and he followed suit. Bending down, he said, 'As you know, I knew your father, Ma'am. But I must tell you that I believe that I would rather have you at my side on the battlefield.'

He gave her a crisp neck bow and left.

Victoria put her hand to her cheek. It was burning hot.

The carriages were lined up all the way along Whitehall. Melbourne put his head out of the window and, seeing that there was no movement, decided that he would get out and walk. He had not intended to go to the portrait unveiling, but he had received a message from Wellington asking him to meet him there, and knew it would be churlish to refuse. Wellington no doubt would want him to use his influence with the Queen to persuade her to make some changes to her ladies. He would have to explain that his influence with the Queen did not extend that far.

It was important that Wellington should understand that the Queen's stubbornness was not of his making, but something quite her own. The irony was that everyone thought that he had encouraged her to resist Peel. Sutherland, Portman, Lord John Russell had all called on him, asking when he was going to form a new administration, and when he had told them that he had no plans to return as Prime Minister, they had looked baffled.

As he walked along Whitehall, he saw that the reason for the delay was a flock of sheep that was being driven down the middle of the road by a shepherd wearing a smock. The shepherd looked quite unconcerned about the chaos he had created. Melbourne looked at the shepherd's ruddy face and unhurried manner and envied him his independence.

Melbourne had thought that he would feel equally sanguine about his decision, that there would be sustenance in doing the right thing, but in truth even St Chrysostom had not assuaged his sense of loss. The day before had been the first since the Queen had come to the throne when they had not met or communicated by letter. He knew there would be a lessening, he was not Prime Minister after all, but he had not anticipated how much he minded the silence of his study, the relentless ticking of the clock marking out the hours that were no longer punctuated by red boxes or rides in Rotten Row or by a small clear voice calling for Lord M.

Melbourne heard the conversations around him turn to whispers as he walked up the steps to Westminster Hall. One voice was saying, 'Screaming like a banshee, apparently. Had to be held down by six footmen,' but it stopped when Melbourne came into view.

Inside he saw that the Hall was packed with peers and Members of Parliament who had come to see the unveiling of the Queen's portrait, but also to assess which way the political wind would blow. He saw the Duke of Sutherland standing with Lord John Russell and Lord Durham, and could tell from their furtive expressions that they had been talking about him. To distract himself he looked up at the great wooden hammerbeams of the roof. They had been there since the time of the Plantagenets and had survived the great fire of 1834 that had burnt down the rest of the Parliament building. There had been some people that night who would have been quite happy to see the whole building destroyed, but Melbourne had ordered that the Hall should be saved. His concern and a lucky shift in the direction of the wind had meant that apart from a few scorch marks, the ceiling at which Charles I had looked when he was being tried for his life had been preserved. At the end of the Hall, on a wooden dais with the easel covered by a red velvet cloth, was Hayden's portrait of the Queen in her Coronation robes. The picture, commissioned by Parliament, would hang in the new buildings whenever they were finally built.

Melbourne wondered if the Queen knew the history of the Hall. Perhaps it would make her think more seriously about the consequences of her behaviour. The country could not function without a government. It could, on the other hand, as the ten years of the Interregnum had shown, survive without a monarch.

He felt a hand on his shoulder and turned round to see the hawk-like visage of the Duke of Wellington. 'Found you at last, Melbourne,' said the Duke.

'Perhaps we should go somewhere more private?' Melbourne gestured to an area behind the portrait where they would not be in the public gaze.

As they walked over, Wellington said briskly, 'You have played this very smartly, Melbourne. Our little Queen is such a Whig supporter that she won't surrender a single bonnet to my party. I wonder how she comes to be so stubborn?'

Melbourne waited until they were safely behind the dais before replying. 'I advised the Queen that she should make some adjustments among her ladies, Duke.'

Rather to his surprise, the other man gave a short bark of a laugh. 'And she don't listen to you, either? Women.'

Then Wellington drew a little nearer and in a lower voice, said, 'Well, if she ain't listening to you, who is telling her what to do? Cumberland thinks she is listening to voices in her head, like her grandfather.'

'The old King? But he was mad,' said Melbourne, astonished.

Wellington tapped his nose with his finger. 'Precisely.' Then, in an even lower voice, 'And what's more, Cumberland is agitatin' for a Regency bill.'

Melbourne's heart lurched, but he kept his gaze steady. 'I assure you, Duke, that the Queen is as sane as anyone in this room. The only voice she is listening to is her own.'

To his great relief, the other man gave a sharp nod of agreement. 'I'll take your word for it, Melbourne. But the longer this business of her ladies goes on, well, it don't look good. If the Queen ain't right in the head, then something must be done.'

'What do you mean?' said Melbourne, in a louder voice than he had intended.

Several bystanders looked round.

Wellington put his finger to his lips, and looked at Melbourne steadily. 'If the Queen won't appoint a Prime Minister, then Parliament will have to appoint a Regent. Must have someone sensible at the heart of things.'

Melbourne could hardly believe that Wellington, of all people, would give credence to such an absurd suggestion. 'You cannot mean that, Duke,'

Wellington shook his head and cast a shrewd glance at Melbourne. 'Perhaps not.'

And then, leaning in and pointing a finger at Melbourne's chest, 'But *I* am not the man to put those rumours to rest, Melbourne.'

Melbourne looked into the old soldier's flinty blue eyes and realised that he was being given an order.

There was a change in the sounds around them, and heads started to turn towards the doors of the Hall. The royal party was arriving. Wellington gave Melbourne a nod and made his way over to where the senior Tories were standing. As the group shifted to accommodate him, Melbourne saw that Cumberland was talking urgently to Sir Robert Peel.

The great door opened, and Melbourne saw Victoria silhouetted against the afternoon sun. He was struck by how small she was, and yet there was something essentially regal about the resolute tilt of her head and the steady pace at which she walked through the chamber, flanked, and that was the only word for it, by her ladies.

The Queen stopped at the foot of the dais where she was greeted by James Abercrombie, the Speaker of the House of Commons. He was the kind of Scotsman who never used two words when he could use twenty. Clearing his throat with elaborate care, he began his speech. 'I would like to extend the welcome of this the mother of Parliaments to Your Majesty on the occasion of the presentation of this portrait of Your Majesty to the nation, by Charles Hayden, Fellow of the Royal Academy. May I request that you do us the honour of unveiling this pictorial tribute in front of this audience of your most loyal and devoted subjects?'

As he uttered the last line, several heads swivelled to look at Cumberland, who looked neither loyal or devoted. There was a hush as the Queen climbed the steps to the dais. She stood beside the covered easel, surveying the crowd as if she were looking for someone. Then she put her hand on the golden rope that was to pull the velvet cloth down from the front of the picture. Someone had misjudged the relative heights of the easel and the monarch, so the Queen had to stand on her toes and stretch out her arms to reach the rope. She looked precarious and a little absurd. Melbourne saw Cumberland raising an eyebrow and looking round at his neighbours as the Queen tried and failed to tug the rope so that it released the cloth.

Her face was going pink with the exertion, and she frowned with frustration. She gave a little jump, as if hoping that by pulling on the rope with all her weight it might eventually give way. Melbourne heard a snigger behind him, and when he looked, he saw that faces all around him were struggling to contain their mirth. He saw Victoria squaring her small shoulders to make another attempt, and before he had time to think about what he was doing he was standing beside her and saying, 'May I be of assistance, Ma'am?'

Victoria turned her head, and her face blossomed into a smile that Melbourne thought that he would remember for the rest of his life.

'I should be most grateful. It seems I can't manage unaided.'

Melbourne reached up and took the rope out of her hands. 'Then it will be my pleasure to serve you, Ma'am.'

Their hands touched, and Victoria looked at him enquiringly. 'Do you mean that . . .' she trailed off, hope shining in her eyes.

'I mean, that if Your Majesty should do me the honour of asking me to form a government, I would consider it my privilege to accept.'

He could see that Victoria was not really attending to his words but scanning his face for his meaning. He smiled at her and at that moment pulled down the cloth covering the portrait.

There was a gasp from the audience, but whether it was from the splendour of the portrait or the spectacle of the Queen standing by the side of her former Prime Minister, was impossible to tell.

In the painting Victoria looked out over her shoulder at the world. Hayden had resized the Crown, so that instead of perching precariously, it fitted Victoria's head as if it had been made for her. Her hair was in plaits around her ears, and the bright colours of the State robes and the royal standard behind her throne gave the painting a mythic air, as if she were not just the Queen but the symbol of Sovereignty itself.

Victoria looked up at Melbourne. 'Do you like it, Lord M?'

It had been less than a week since she had last called him by that name, but Melbourne felt a foolish lift in his heart.

'No painting can truly do you justice, Ma'am.'

She smiled back at him. 'It is better than those horrid cartoons where they draw me as a dumpling.'

'I trust that no one will draw you as a dumpling again, Ma'am. At least not while I am Prime Minister.'

Victoria laughed. 'Then I hope you will remain in office as long as I am Queen.'

Abercrombie appeared at the Queen's elbow. 'If you would be so gracious as to permit me to present to you some of the members who have subscribed to the portrait.'

Victoria glanced at Melbourne. 'Yes indeed. I believe that I have finished talking to the –' and she paused and smiled – 'Prime Minister.'

'I believe so, Ma'am.'

Abercrombie's eyes widened as he led the Queen over to the line of MPs waiting to be presented. Melbourne followed a couple of paces behind, knowing that this would be the fastest way to signal to his peers that he had decided to return to government. As the Queen made her way down the line of men, acknowledging their greetings with her small quick smile, she would from time to time look back over her shoulder at Melbourne as if to reassure herself that he was still there.

On the other side of the room Cumberland, who was standing next to the Duke of Wellington, was convulsively tracing the scar on his cheek with his finger as he watched his niece proceed along the receiving line, her slight figure dwarfed by the forest of men around her.

'And that is the Lord's Anointed. The French knew what they were doing when they adopted Salic Law.'

Wellington permitted himself a smile. 'Women can be an infernal nuisance, but the public like having a young Queen. Makes the country feel youthful, don't you know?'

'No one wants a Queen who has lost her reason.'

'Oh, I think the Queen looks sane enough. Look how she has got Melbourne back. I think there is no doubt that she will keep her wits about her.'

Cumberland heard something in the Duke's tone that made him turn round. 'I wonder if Robert Peel agrees with you,

Duke. Denied his chance of being Prime Minister because the Queen wouldn't give up a single petticoat.'

'Sir Robert knows that we will be in office soon enough,' Wellington raised an eyebrow at Cumberland, 'but only in the right circumstances.'

Victoria was almost level with them both on the other side of the room. When she saw Wellington, she glanced at Melbourne and then back at the Duke and smiled. A smile that was returned.

Cumberland, who saw this exchange, decided that there was no point in remaining. He stalked out of the Hall without saying goodbye, his finger still tracing the scar's signature on his cheek.

Melbourne dined at the Palace that night, and the household were able to finish their food without interruption as the Queen listened with delight to his stories of the court in George III's day. After dinner the Queen played a duet with Harriet Sutherland.

Melbourne was only half attending to the music; he was looking at the Queen's small head and observing the way that she sucked in her cheeks as she encountered a difficult passage.

'The Queen looks very happy tonight,' said Emma Portman. He hadn't noticed her behind him. Melbourne answered without taking his eyes from Victoria.

'So young but with such responsibilities. She should not have to bear them alone.'

At that moment Victoria glanced up from the keyboard, and seeing Melbourne looking at her, she smiled at him, showing her small white teeth. Emma watched the exchange, then said slowly, 'You know your days are numbered, don't you, William?'

Melbourne was still gazing at the Queen as he replied, 'Of course. Every Prime Minister knows that.'

'No, I don't mean that. She is very young, as you say, but one day soon she will marry, and then . . .'

'And then she will look to her husband, not to me,' Melbourne said. 'Yes, Emma, I know.'

Emma knew better than to say more.

The playing stopped, and Victoria got up and walked over to where they stood. 'Do you care to play cards, Lord M? I have missed our games of Piquet.'

Melbourne looked down at her and smiled. 'So have I, Ma'am. So have I.'

Book Three

Chapter One

'THERE IS A LETTER FOR YOU, MAJESTY, FROM Brussels.' Lehzen produced the letter from a pocket in her skirts.

Victoria sighed. 'I don't want to read it now, Lehzen. Not today.'

Lehzen put the letter on the dressing table and retreated. Skerrett was unpinning Victoria's hair from the elaborate style she had worn for the State Opening of Parliament. Victoria looked at the letter balefully. Today had been exhausting; she had been on view from morning till now. Riding to Parliament in the glass coach, waving and smiling to the crowds all the while, whether they waved back or not, and then in Parliament itself she had been under the scrutiny of all those grey men, as she mentally called the members of the House of Lords and the Commons. The worst thing was having to read the speech that outlined the government's plans for the next Parliamentary session. It was always so long and with such cumbersome phrases.

She had complained to Lord M that it was like reading the sort of sermon that put her to sleep when she went to church, but Melbourne had laughed and said that no one could fall asleep when she was talking or they would be arrested for treason. But even Lord M could not understand the effort of keeping her voice steady as she read the speech in front of that audience. Every time she looked up from the page, as Lord M had encouraged her to do, she would see some red-faced peer cupping his hand to his ear in a pantomime of deafness, or some cadaverous MP smirking because he considered her pronunciation peculiar. She never looked up to the right, where she knew that the Duke of Cumberland was sitting, waiting and hoping for her to make a mistake. There were very few instances in which she would have preferred to have been born a man, but today's ordeal made her wish for a baritone voice that never struggled to be heard.

There had been one moment when she had felt quite hoarse and had wished for a sip of water. Knowing, however, that everyone was watching for such a sign of weakness, she had swallowed and continued, allowing herself at the end of the sentence to look up and catch Melbourne's encouraging smile.

All she wanted to do now was to fall into bed, close her eyes and fall asleep, but the letter was still lying on the dressing table. It was from her Uncle Leopold, her mother's brother, who five years ago had been asked by the new country of Belgium to be its King. Before Victoria was born, he had been married to Princess Charlotte, the heir to the English throne, until she had died in childbirth together with their child. To be King of Belgium was some consolation for not being the husband of the Queen of England, but not quite enough, so Uncle Leopold had decided that to be uncle of the Queen of England was a grave responsibility he must fulfil whether his niece liked it or not. He wrote to her at least once a week with advice on how she should conduct herself as Queen. If she did not reply immediately he wrote again reproachfully, reminding her that he was the only person who would offer her disinterested advice, because '*My dear niece, I write to you not only as uncle to niece but as one Sovereign to another. So you would do well to listen to what I say and remember that your welfare is my only concern.*'

Although Victoria longed to write back that the welfare of his subjects should be his only concern, she was not quite brave enough. She wondered what would be in this letter; the last one had been a lecture on her folly over refusing to give up her ladies to Sir Robert Peel. '*The duty of a constitutional monarch is to put public duty before the exercise of personal inclination. I know that you are attached to your ladies and of course to the estimable Lord Melbourne, but you must realise that by such a blatant display of personal attachment you lay yourself open to charges of partiality and bias. The Queen of England must be seen to be above the machinations of party, and to preside not to interfere. If you do not realise the folly of your behaviour, then your people may cease to revere you as their monarch, and begin to wonder why they are being reigned over by a thoughtless young girl.*'

She had torn that letter up and sat down to write to her uncle that she never wished to hear from him again. But even as her quill scratched furiously across the paper, she knew this was a letter she would never send.

The next day she decided that the best revenge was to write with such blandness that Leopold would be forced to wonder if she had read his insults. So she had written a long and rambling letter asking about her Coburg cousins and telling him in excruciating detail about all her recent ecclesiastical appointments. As King of the Belgians, Leopold had become a Catholic, and Victoria felt no little satisfaction in reminding him of her position as Head of the Church of England.

'Will that be all, Ma'am?' Skerrett hovered behind her. 'Would you like me to put your curl papers in?'

'No, you may go,' and the young dresser curtseyed and left the room.

Picking up the letter, Victoria lay down on the bed. When her moment of repose was interrupted by Dash, she pulled the dog up and ran her fingers through his soft curly coat. 'What do you think Uncle Leopold is going to lecture me about now, Dash? He wouldn't like it if I wrote to him and told him how to run his foreign policy. I am just as royal as he is, in fact much more so, as my country has existed for a thousand years and his for just five.'

Dash looked up at her in adoration, his long tail wagging. Victoria kissed him on the nose. 'If only everyone could be like you, Dash, how easy my life would be.'

Dash licked her hand in agreement. At last Victoria picked up the letter and broke open the seal. To her surprise it was not the usual long missive but a brief note that informed her that he would be visiting the following week, because he wished to talk to her about her cousin Albert. Victoria threw the letter across the room, which made Dash bark in alarm.

The interconnecting door opened, and Lehzen appeared in her wrapper, her hair in papers, her broad face worried. 'Is something wrong, Majesty? Are you unwell?'

'Yes! Something is very wrong! My Uncle Leopold has announced that he is coming to stay so he can talk to me about Albert. How dare he! I have no intention of getting married for years, and when I do it won't be to a milksop like Albert.'

Lehzen nodded. 'I think your Cousin Albert is not really a match for you.'

'Do you remember when he came with Ernst a few years ago? When there was dancing, he started to yawn and say that he was too tired to take part. Imagine anyone being too tired to dance!

And he was so dull, always asking me how many acres there are in Windsor Great Park and whether I had ever visited the Royal Mint. Ernst is not so bad; at least he smiles occasionally and likes dancing, but Albert is such a baby. I mean he is only three months younger than I am, but it might as well be three years.'

'When is King Leopold arriving?' Lehzen asked.

'Next week. I don't understand how he can just assume that I will be happy to receive him. I suppose he has already written to Mama, and she has told him he will be welcome. I expect the pair of them have been hatching this visit together. But I won't have it. Nobody is going to choose my husband for me.'

'No, Majesty. It must be your choice.'

'Uncle Leopold doesn't care whether Albert and I are suited; he just wants to make sure that the Coburgs are on the throne of every country in Europe. It makes him feel like an Emperor instead of the King of a country that didn't even exist five years ago. Who are the Coburgs, anyway? Just a minor princely family that have married well.'

Lehzen coughed. 'Your mother is a Coburg, Majesty.'

'Yes, but my father was from a royal line that stretches back to William the Conqueror.'

'I am sure the King will understand when you tell him that you have no plans to marry at present.'

Victoria laughed. 'He will put his head on one side and say,' she adopted a heavy German accent, '"Ah my little *Maiblume*, that is because you are a young girl who does not understand the way that the world is working. That is why you must listen to your elders."'

She sighed. 'Uncle Leopold, Mama, they still think they can control me but I won't be told what to do, by them or by anyone else.'

She sounded so fierce as she said this that Dash growled in sympathy, which made both women laugh. Lehzen put her hand on Victoria's, a gesture which she only allowed herself when they were together in private.

'Please don't worry, Majesty. No one can make you do anything that you do not agree with. Not any more.'

'No,' agreed Victoria. 'Not any more.'

The next morning, when Melbourne came to go through her boxes, Victoria had the miniature of Elizabeth Tudor that Lehzen had given her by her inkwell.

Melbourne noticed it at once, and glancing at Victoria for permission, he picked it up to examine it. 'This is a lovely thing. What an arresting woman your predecessor was.'

'I wonder what her voice was like. I find it so hard to make mine loud enough to be heard.'

Melbourne looked at her. 'I am sure that people listened to her because she was the Queen, just as they listen to you.'

'You don't think my voice is too slight for a Queen? I thought people looked very disgruntled yesterday, Uncle Cumberland especially.'

'Your Uncle Cumberland has looked disgruntled ever since I have known him. If others looked displeased, it is because they do not like my policies, not the way in which they are delivered. In my opinion, Ma'am, you have a very beautiful speaking voice, and there could be nothing more dignified than the way in which you conducted yourself yesterday. Indeed, if I might say so, you were a great deal more regal than your late uncle, who could only get through the speech by consuming great quantities of snuff. I believe that the finer points of our policies were lost in the resulting explosions.'

Victoria laughed. 'You always say the right thing, Lord M.'

'I assure you, Ma'am, that the Tories do not agree with you. But you look listless this morning. Is something the matter?'

'I am plagued by uncles. First I have Uncle Cumberland staring at me like a gargoyle, and now my Uncle Leopold has written that he is coming to stay.'

Melbourne smiled. 'How delighted you look at the prospect, Ma'am.'

'He wants me to marry my Cousin Albert.'

Melbourne looked at the miniature in his hand. 'I believe you did not take to your cousin the last time you met him.'

'Indeed I did not.'

'Not all Queens marry, Ma'am.' Melbourne put the miniature of the Virgin Queen back on the desk.

Victoria looked at it and then at Melbourne. 'Do you think she was lonely?'

Melbourne paused, and then replied, 'I believe she found . . . companions.'

Victoria glanced at him. 'Well, I have no intention of marrying at present.' She went on, 'I have not seen so many happy marriages.'

Melbourne sighed. 'Neither have I, Ma'am, neither have I.'

Seeing the pain in his face, Victoria realised that while she had spoken lightly, he had spoken from the heart. Before she could say anything more, Lehzen appeared in the doorway, looking apologetic but determined.

'Forgive me, Majesty, for interrupting, but there is a messenger from the House who says he must speak with Lord Melbourne urgently.'

Victoria saw an expression of alarm flicker across Melbourne's face, which was quickly replaced by his usual half smile. He made her a regretful bow. 'Forgive me, Ma'am, but I believe I must attend to this.' He began to back away from her.

'Of course.' Victoria nodded but then, before she could stop herself, she added, 'Lord M, you will return?'

Melbourne turned and looked back at her. 'Yes, Ma'am.'

Victoria nodded and watched him go.

She was reminded that Lehzen was still in the room as the Baroness made a noise somewhere between a sigh and a click of disapproval.

Victoria addressed her directly. 'Is there something wrong, Lehzen?'

Lehzen hesitated, and then blurted out, 'He will not be your Prime Minister for ever, Majesty.'

'Do you imagine that I am unaware of that, Baroness?'

Lehzen put a hand to the wall for support. 'No, Majesty, but sometimes I worry that you are unprepared. You rely on him so much and he cannot always be there.'

'Indeed.' Victoria's tone was icy.

The older woman bowed her head. Then said in a low voice, 'I have cared for you, Majesty, since you were a little girl. It has been my vocation. So you must forgive me if sometimes I am caring for you beyond my position. Where you are concerned I am forgetting everything except your happiness.' At the end of this speech her voice was so quiet that Victoria strained to make out the words. When she had finished, Lehzen began to back out of the room.

'Wait!'

Lehzen stopped, and Victoria went over to her and took her hand. 'I know how much you care for me, Lehzen, and I am grateful, but I have to make my own way.'

Chapter Two

LEOPOLD I, KING OF THE BELGIANS, WAS A MAN OF HIGH colour and an even higher opinion of his own talents. As a young man he had been extremely good looking and had turned the head of the greatest match in Europe, Charlotte the Princess of Wales, only child of George IV and heir to the English throne. Her father had looked for a more illustrious bridegroom than a penniless younger son from an obscure German duchy, but even he could not deny that Leopold cut a dashing figure in his Hussar's uniform.

In the end, Charlotte's infatuation and Leopold's glamour had won the day, and George had consented to the marriage. His daughter had inherited much of her mother's wilfulness, and the sooner she had a husband to keep her in check, the better. Leopold and Charlotte, who had been genuinely in love, were delighted when Charlotte had discovered that she was expecting a child soon after their wedding.

Leopold had thought so much of that child and how it would seal the place of the Coburgs at the heart of European power for ever. But as the pregnancy progressed and Charlotte grew fatter and more breathless, the doctors had begun to look grave and to produce their instruments of torture: the leeches, the cupping bells. Leopold begged his wife to send them away, but she felt that she must listen to them because she was carrying the heir to the English throne. When the doctors told her that she was getting too fat, she had even stopped eating the *marrons glacés* that she loved beyond anything. But, as Leopold had known all along, all the doctors and their rigmaroles could not save his son, who was born large, handsome, but quite dead, or his wife, who had been consumed by a fever that killed her the next day.

Leopold had mourned his wife most sincerely, but he had also mourned the loss of the dreams that had come with his marriage. In the year that followed, as the unmarried brothers of George IV scrambled to find themselves wives in order to secure the succession, he saw that there might still be an opportunity, albeit a slim one, for the Coburgs to find a way to the British throne. He had suggested to his brother-in-law, Edward the Duke of Kent, who like his other brothers was scouring Europe for a suitable Protestant princess, that he might care to pay his addresses to Leopold's widowed sister Victoire. She was pretty, fertile – she had borne her first husband two children – and unlike some of the horse-faced young women on offer from Brunswick or Mecklenburg Strelitz, had some experience of how to please a husband. Leaping at the suggestion, Edward had abandoned Madame St Laurent, his mistress of the past twenty-five years, in Nova Scotia, to sail to Germany, where he wooed and won Victoire in less than a week.

Of course the alliance was far from ideal. Edward's older brother William, the Duke of Clarence, had also got married, and his children would take precedence in the line of succession. But as Leopold wrote to his sister, '*This Princess Adelaide does not have your experience with men, my dear sister, or your evident skill in this area.*' Victoire had repaid his faith in her by falling pregnant a few months after the marriage.

They were living in Victoire's home in Amorbach, as the Duke's debts meant that he could not afford to support a wife in London, but Leopold had urged his sister to return to England for the birth. '*Otherwise they will not view the child as English. But make sure you take a midwife with you. The English doctors are nothing more than butchers.*' Following her brother's advice, Victoire had embarked on the difficult journey across Europe when she was seven months pregnant, with her husband, her silver, a parrot, and Frau Siebold the midwife. There were times when it looked as though the future heir to the throne of England might be born in a hired post-chaise somewhere in rural Normandy, but the Duchess had held on until the royal party arrived in England, where she gave birth to a small but healthy little girl.

Leopold had, of course, been present for the christening in St James's Chapel, where there had been an unseemly dispute about what the infant should be called. Her father had wanted to call her a royal name like Elizabeth or Mary, with Charlotte as a second name, but the King, who resented the idea that his despised younger brother's child might one day become Queen, had vetoed this idea. So there had been much rumination around the font, with names being suggested by the parents and rejected by the petulant monarch. At last agreement was reached on calling the baby Alexandrina, after her godfather, Alexander, the Emperor of Russia. Then there was a question of a second name. The King's watery and malevolent blue eyes fixed on his sister-in-law, and he said with disdain, 'Use one of the mother's names.' More confusion ensued as the Duchess's first name, Marie-Louise, sounded too Catholic, so in the end they settled on Victoire, which was anglicised as Victoria. It was a funny-sounding name, one that the Archbishop who was conducting the ceremony stumbled over. Afterwards, though, the Duke of Kent walked up and down the chapel holding the baby in his arms, chanting, 'Alexandrina Victoria, Alexandrina Victoria,' and saying to anyone who would listen, 'Do you know, I think it has a most triumphant sound. Victoria is quite a fitting name for a soldier's daughter, don't you think?'

Leopold had agreed, of course, although he could not help reflecting that he had fought at Waterloo, while the Duke of Kent had spent the last twenty years commanding a garrison in Nova Scotia under threat of nothing more serious than intemperate winters. Still, Leopold had been pleased that a name from his side of the family had been included.

It had been a surprise when his niece had decided to style herself as Victoria on her accession. He had reproached her for not consulting him: *'Do you think that to choose a name that is so unfamiliar to your subjects is entirely wise, my dear niece?'* But now he thought that perhaps she had been right. There was some sense in choosing name that distanced her from her Hanoverian predecessors. For all its strangeness, the name Victoria sounded like the beginning of a triumphant new era.

Nevertheless, thought Leopold, as his carriage started its progress up The Mall, the young Queen had not yet covered herself in glory. The Flora Hastings affair had shown a shocking failure of sense and propriety, followed by the unfortunate business with Peel over the composition of the Queen's household, and above all her unreasonable attachment to Lord Melbourne. Leopold had no grudge against Melbourne personally, but his influence over Victoria was not healthy. His niece, of course, would never accept that she had anything in common with her mother, but it must be said that they were both in the thrall of powerful men.

What Drina – Leopold mentally corrected himself, what *Victoria* – needed was a husband to control her youthful impulsiveness. Ever since his poor sister-in-law, Louise, the wife of his brother Duke Ernst, had given birth to a son three months after the birth of Victoria, Leopold had thought that there could be no better pairing than that of his niece and nephew, the infant Albert. As Albert had grown up, proving himself to be a true Coburg with his seriousness, his industry, and his ambition, Leopold had become more and more convinced of the felicity of his plan.

When he had brought his nephews over three years ago, it was unfortunate that Victoria had not taken to Albert, who had been overcome with shyness. But young men and young women grew up so quickly. Albert had left behind his adolescent awkwardness, and while he was not an accomplished flirt like his older brother, he was certainly handsome.

On meeting Albert, many people had remarked to Leopold on the likeness between the nephew and his uncle, which Leopold always acknowledged with a smile. There was nothing to suggest that Albert and he were anything more than nephew and uncle. And indeed it was quite possible that their relationship was no closer than that.

Poor Louise, his sister-in-law, so unhappy with his brother Ernst, the Duke of Coburg, had been very kind to him during his first awful grief. They had comforted each other as best they could, and when Albert was born nine months later, Leopold taken a keen interest in his future. When Louise, finally unable to bear Ernst's dissolution, had eloped with her equerry, Leopold had not found it in his heart to blame her. Publicly, of course, he had deplored her behaviour, but he had also written *sub rosa* to promise that he would keep an eye on the two sons she must know she would never see again. She had not answered his letter. But Leopold had kept his word, making sure that Albert's education was worthy of a future occupant of the British throne.

Six years ago, when it had become clear after Queen Adelaide's final miscarriage that there was nothing to stop Victoria becoming the next Queen of England, Leopold had encouraged a correspondence between the young cousins (making sure he received copies of the correspondence). This epistolary relationship had been fitful, but as Leopold lost no opportunity to remind both parties, it was the beginning of a great alliance. The distressing fact that Victoria's correspondence had become even more lackadaisical since she had ascended the throne, he attributed to the distraction offered by Lord Melbourne. It was time for the two cousins to meet again. He had no doubt that once he had had a chance to talk to Victoria in person, she would see that his suggestion was the only sensible course.

With their marriage, the triumph of the Coburgs would be complete. He was now King of Belgium; there was another nephew married to the Queen of Portugal; and he had no doubt that his family would soon be preeminent in the courts of Europe, thanks to their personal charms, proven fertility, and unalloyed ambition.

Leopold allowed himself a little smile as he drove through the Marble Arch. Before he alighted from the carriage, he took out a little mirror that he always kept in his waistcoat pocket, and examined the angle of his toupee. Only when the King of the Belgians was satisfied that his wig was securely and becomingly in place, did he step down from the carriage to greet his niece.

But Victoria, he was displeased to see, was not waiting for him on the steps. Instead he was greeted by Baroness Lehzen, who made up for her mistress's shortcomings with a gratifyingly deep curtsey.

'Welcome to Buckingham Palace, Your Majesty.'

'I am delighted to see you here, Baroness, but I confess I expected my niece.'

Lehzen lowered her gaze. 'The Queen has had much official business to deal with this morning, but she hopes that you will wait upon her this afternoon.'

'What business could there be that is more important than greeting her uncle, who has travelled across Europe at considerable inconvenience to see her?'

'I am sure, sir, that if the Queen had had more notice of your intentions, she would have arranged things accordingly.'

Leopold looked at her and smiled. 'You are a model of loyalty, Baroness. It does you credit that you will not acknowledge my niece's thoughtlessness.'

The Baroness shook her head. 'Her Majesty lets nothing stand in the way of her duties.'

'Not even Lord Melbourne?'

Lehzen pursed her lips. 'If you will follow me, sir, I will show you to your apartments.'

At three o'clock Leopold walked down the red-carpeted staircase on his way to the Throne Room, where he was told that Victoria would receive him. He noted with approval that the place was in a good state of repair; the cornices had been freshly gilded and the chandeliers were free of wax. He had taken a proprietary interest in the Palace ever since he had walked its corridors imagining it as his home one day.

As he was announced by the steward, Leopold glanced around. The small figure of Victoria was evident in the middle of the room, flanked by her ladies. Standing a little way off to the right he saw his sister and the tall figure of Conroy.

He advanced towards his niece and with a beaming smile kissed her upon both cheeks, the greeting of one monarch to another. Then he stood back and allowed himself to look her up and down. 'How fortunate, Victoria, that you have inherited your excellent posture from the Coburg side of the family. Your lack of inches cannot be helped, but a small Queen with a slouch would be a national tragedy.'

Victoria gave a tight smile. 'Welcome to Buckingham Palace, Uncle Leopold.'

Leopold gave an extravagant sigh, and brushed away a tear or rather the intention of a tear. 'Forgive me. Being here is making me think of my poor dead Charlotte. If she had lived, this would have been my home.'

Victoria made a small, impatient movement. 'Of course I remember, Uncle Leopold. After all, how could I forget?'

She looked at Leopold steadily, until her mother broke the impasse by rushing forward to embrace her brother. 'Dear Leopold, I am so happy to see you.' Putting her head to his ear she whispered in German, 'Are you going to talk to her about Albert?'

Victoria tapped her foot and said in English, 'Why should Uncle Leopold need to talk to me about Albert, Mama? Has he had an accident?'

Leopold disengaged himself from his sister's embrace. He

knew that if his plan was to have any chance of success it was essential that it should not involve Victoria's mother.

'On the contrary, Albert has finished his studies and is a most admirable young man. You could not hope for a better husband.' He smiled winningly at his niece, who did not smile back.

'Then he must have changed since the last time I saw him. He didn't smile, he didn't dance and he fell asleep at half past nine.'

'When you last met, three years ago, I believe you were still playing with dolls. It is possible for people to change, Victoria. I know at your age that seems impossible, but that is why you need wiser heads around you.'

Victoria began to move towards the door, her ladies forming a silken phalanx behind her. She said over her shoulder, 'I think I manage quite well.'

Leopold's smile did not falter. 'Of course you have the excellent and devoted Lord Melbourne. But he will not be at your side for ever, my dear niece.'

The Duchess nodded, the blonde ringlets trembling. 'Every woman needs a husband, Drina. Even a Queen.'

Leopold followed Victoria as she walked towards the door, forcing her to slow down. 'And if, heaven forbid, you were to be gathered to the Almighty God tomorrow, then your most wicked Uncle Cumberland would be King.'

Victoria lifted her chin in defiance. 'I believe that in my predecessor Elizabeth's time – a Queen who never married, by the way – just to mention the death of a monarch was an act of treason.'

Leopold smiled. Seeing from the spots of colour on her cheeks that he had repaid her earlier rudeness in not greeting him when he arrived, he gave her a little bow. 'I merely point out the facts.'

Victoria swept out, saying, 'You must excuse me. I have government business to attend to. But I am sure you and Mama will have a great deal to say to each other.'

Leopold could not help but admire the perfect carriage of his niece's small neat head as she walked away from him. She had, he realised with surprise, a dignity that transformed the impetuous, unformed girl into a credible Queen. She would have to be managed, of course, but Leopold, who had made the study of royalty his life's work, was impressed.

The moment was broken by his sister, who was overjoyed to have a new sympathetic audience for her grievances against her daughter. She said in a torrent of German and English, 'You see how impossible she is? She listens to no one except her precious Lord M. She ignores me completely. After all I have done for her. You know, Leopold, sometimes I think I should like to move back to Amorbach and live in peace and seclusion, instead of spending all my time worrying about a girl who has no respect for her family.'

Leopold saw Conroy, who was standing by the window, flinch as the Duchess mentioned Amorbach. He was certain that his sister's comptroller had no intention of spending the rest of his career in a German backwater.

'My dear sister, you should not alarm yourself. Now that I am here, I am sure that Victoria will come to understand where her duties lie.'

'Not when she is always with Lord Melbourne,' said his sister, shaking her head. 'You know that she refuses to let me style myself as the Queen Mother or to give me enough money so that I can dress like the mother of a Queen? It is all that wicked Melbourne's doing. Before he came between us, we were always so close. Before he came she listened to me . . . and to Sir John.'

Conroy nodded at the Duchess's words. 'The Queen needs a husband to guide her, sir. The Duchess and I have done everything in our power to direct her, but she will not be governed. Marriage is the only way that she will be curbed.'

'And Albert is such a good boy. He will make sure that Victoria understands what is due to her mother.'

There were times, thought Leopold, when allies were more dangerous than enemies. It struck him that perhaps the only way to ensure that Victoria would marry Albert would be if the Duchess and Conroy were to vehemently oppose him. He could see that Conroy, who had been frustrated in his hopes of exercising power through Victoria, still entertained the prospect of doing so through her husband. Those hopes, of course, were misplaced, as the only person who would be influencing Albert, when he came to marry Victoria, would be Leopold himself.

He kept these thoughts to himself, but nodded and said, 'I am here, of course, to promote the match, but it seems to me that we must proceed with caution. If, as you say, Sir John, Victoria will not be governed, then it is better to suggest and to entice than to command. That, I suspect, is how her Lord Melbourne is able to control her. I think it would be sensible for us to do the same.'

The Duchess put her hand on his arm. 'Oh, I am glad you are here, Leopold. You are so wise always.'

Leopold noticed Conroy's frown at the Duchess's words. 'If you will excuse me, Ma'am, sir.' Conroy gave an abrupt bow and left the room.

When he had gone, Leopold considered his sister. Although he knew she was managed by Conroy, he wondered if she might come to see the advantages of breaking with him, if it meant Victoria marrying Albert. But women, even Coburg women, could not always be relied upon to act in their own self-interest.

'I wonder, my dear sister, if perhaps you should consider parting with Sir John. I am afraid that Victoria will never give you the respect you are due, while he remains at your side.'

'What can you mean, Leopold?' The Duchess's rather full lower lip began to tremble.

'I think that at some point you will have to choose between your . . . companion and your daughter. You cannot have both.'

Tears sprang into the Duchess's eyes. 'But Leopold, he is everything to me. I cannot live without him.'

Leopold sighed. 'Then, my dear, perhaps you should think of returning to Coburg.'

The Duchess covered her face with her hands, and her shoulders began to heave. 'She is so ungrateful. I am so lonely, a poor widow twice over. Sir John is my only comfort; without him I will have nothing. He is the only person who notices me.'

Leopold put an arm around her. 'I understand how hard it is to be alone, *Liebes*, and I can see that Sir John is most attentive. You might have some happiness in Coburg with him at your side. If you wish to go, then I will do everything in my power to help you.'

The Duchess looked up at him, bewildered. 'You think I should go back to Coburg, with Sir John?'

'It might be better than to remain here to be slighted by Victoria. You will suggest this plan to Conroy?'

From the look on her face, Leopold knew that he had planted the first seed of doubt in his sister's mind.

'I don't know that Sir John would care to leave England. He has so many interests here.'

'But surely no interest could compete with ensuring your happiness, my dear sister. Not if he is as devoted to you as you say.'

The Duchess shook her head. 'It is not something we have ever talked of. But why should I go into exile, after all? I have earned my place here in England as the Queen Mother.'

'Of course you have, my dear. But if Victoria continues to be obdurate, it is worth considering. Perhaps you should discuss it with Sir John.'

Leopold saw his sister bite her lip. 'Perhaps,' she said, but she did not meet her brother's eyes.

'My dear sister, we must talk of pleasanter things. I believe we are to go to the opera tomorrow, and I understand that there is to be a costume ball at Syon House.'

The Duchess was distracted, as he knew she would be, by this talk of parties.

'Indeed. The Duchess of Richmond's costume balls are famous. I am to be Columbine and Sir John is to be Harlequin. What about you, Leopold?'

'I have decided to appear as the Emperor Augustus. I find a laurel wreath most becoming.'

Victoria was not the only person who was not overjoyed by the visit of the King of the Belgians. When Ernest, Duke of Cumberland, saw the notice of King Leopold's visit in the

Court Circular, he made a noise which made his wife look up in alarm, fearing some kind of apoplexy. The Duchess was a German princess a few years younger than her husband, who nevertheless had been widowed twice. There was talk that the speedy death of the first two husbands had not been unconnected to their choice of wife, but the rumours had not deterred the Duke from marrying her twenty years ago. They had one son, who to their mutual sorrow had begun to lose his sight at the age of ten, and was now completely blind.

The Duchess could not help feeling that her son, even with his limitations, would make a far more suitable monarch than the present Queen. She had, of course, been her husband's confidante in all his attempts to become Regent, and had railed with him daily against the injustice of a system where a foolish girl could take the throne ahead of a man of experience. But as she kept reminding him, the Duke was still the Heir Presumptive to the throne. If anything should happen to Victoria – and young girls, even irritatingly robust ones like the Queen, could be unexpectedly vulnerable – Ernest would be King not just of Hanover but of Great Britain as well.

'But what is the matter, my dear?'

'That mountebank Leopold is staying at the Palace. King of the Belgians, indeed. What's Belgium, I should like to know . . . a made-up country that didn't exist five minutes ago. I remember when he was a cavalry officer without a penny to his name, making eyes at Charlotte Wales.'

'He has done well for himself, then.'

The Duke snorted. 'He married well, like all those Coburgs. Of course that's why he's here.'

Frederica looked puzzled.

'Leopold has come here to fix a match between Victoria

and one of the Coburg boys. He's determined to keep the English throne in the family.'

The Duchess looked at her husband, who was pacing up and down the drawing room, his scar pale against his florid cheeks. She sympathised with his frustration, although there were moments when she thought that she would be quite happy to go to Hanover and live out their days peacefully as King and Queen. Having spent the early part of her life trying to change her circumstances, she now saw the virtues of being satisfied with what was possible. It was true that Hanover could not compare to Britain in size or wealth, but in her heart Frederica felt that it was better to be King of somewhere than to be always living in expectation. She would never say this to her husband, though. She cast around for some other way to channel his anger.

'Well, if Leopold is proposing a match, perhaps you too should find Victoria a husband.'

The Duke turned to look at his wife, then jerked his head in the direction of the music room, where their son was playing the piano. He played very well by ear, and if you listened to him you would never know he was blind. 'You don't mean?' he said, raising an eyebrow.

'No, I think our poor boy will be quite happy to succeed you as King of Hanover. I was thinking of your nephew.'

'George Cambridge?' To her relief Frederica saw that her husband had stopped pacing and was standing in the middle of the room with his hand tracking the scar on his cheek with his finger, a sign that he was concentrating.

'Yes. He is a personable young man but not clever. I am sure you could . . . direct him.'

Cumberland stopped and smiled at his wife. 'How lucky I

am to have married you, my dear. You are always so resourceful. My brother owes me a fortune, but if his son marries the Queen I might get my money back with interest. And it would be a fine thing to keep the throne in the British royal family.'

'Indeed. You should call on George and make him aware of the opportunity that presents itself.'

'I am surprised he hasn't thought of it already. But then I suppose he takes after my brother Adolphus, who has never been very bright.'

'You have been blessed with the brains in your family, my love.'

Cumberland took his wife's hand. 'And in you, I have found my equal.'

Chapter Three

'WHY THE LONG FACE, LORD M?' VICTORIA LEANT across the desk in her private sitting room, where she and Melbourne were engaged in going through the red boxes. When Melbourne did not immediately reply, she went on, 'I am so happy to see you. You can't imagine how tiresome my Uncle Leopold is being.'

Melbourne looked up from the paper he was reading. 'At the risk of being impertinent about one of your family, I must say I remember him as being vain and self-seeking.'

Victoria laughed. 'Nothing has changed. He wears a wig now, and he plans to marry me off to my Cousin Albert.'

'I do not think that marriage between first cousins is wise, Ma'am.'

Victoria gave him a keen look. 'If that is what you are worried about, Lord M, then you have no reason to be alarmed. I told him it would never do!'

Melbourne paused and then stood up, saying, 'If I look concerned, Ma'am, it is not on account of your Uncle Leopold. I fear that there has been an uprising in Wales by a group, a mob really, who call themselves Chartists.'

Victoria came to stand beside him. 'What a curious name.'

Melbourne sighed. 'So called because they have written a charter demanding universal suffrage, annual elections, a secret ballot, and even payment for MPs. Their ideas are impossible, of course, but they have much support among a certain class.'

Victoria looked puzzled. 'But their ideas are so extreme. You have always told me the British are not a revolutionary people.'

Melbourne shook his head. 'As you know, Ma'am, there was a poor harvest this year and last. When people are hungry, they can fancy themselves radicals.'

Victoria nodded her head. 'I see. But is there danger from these – these Chartists?'

Melbourne looked out of the window. He could see the Marble Arch and beyond that the flag-lined expanse of The Mall. To the left lay the magnolia stucco squares and terraces of Thomas Cubitt's Belgravia, which was rapidly challenging Mayfair as the most fashionable address in London. But if he turned his head to the right and looked over the railings that surrounded the Palace, he could see the crooked roofs of the Pimlico rookeries. If he opened the window, he fancied the smell of poverty would reach even here into the Palace itself. Of course the Queen was quite safe here, surrounded as she was at all times by the Household Cavalry, but it was salutary nonetheless to remember how close they were, even here, to the forces of unrest.

When he turned to Victoria, he made sure that the expression on his face was that of reassurance. 'Oh, no, Ma'am, the rioters in Newport were armed only with pitchforks and scythes. The garrison there dispatched them with no difficulty. The ringleaders have been brought here to be tried for treason. If we make an example of them now, it will deter others in the future.'

He caught Victoria's gaze. 'There is no cause for you to

worry. That is my job. Your safety is the only thing that disturbs my peace of mind.'

He must have stared at her a little too intently, because Victoria flushed and said brightly, 'Will you come to the opera tonight? La Persiani is singing *Lucia di Lammermoor*. I know you prefer Mozart, but I don't think I can bear an evening with Uncle Leopold alone.' She smiled.

Melbourne declined. 'I don't think that my presence is necessary. You forget that the Grand Duke will also be there. I seem to remember that you rather enjoyed his company at the Coronation Ball.'

Victoria looked at her hands. 'The Grand Duke is an excellent dancer and he can be agreeable company, but,' she raised her pale blue eyes to his, 'he is no substitute for you, Lord M.'

Melbourne saw the appeal in her eyes and wondered if she understood how flirtatious she was being. She was so young and so innocent compared to the women he had always surrounded himself with, but there was a directness in her gaze that was unsettling. He had to remind himself that she had no idea what she was doing.

He bowed and gave her his most urbane smile. 'You flatter me, Ma'am, and like all men I am susceptible to flattery.'

'Perhaps I should try that with Uncle Leopold!'

'I should have said, all men apart from your Uncle Leopold.'

The sound of Victoria's silvery, delighted laugh stayed with Melbourne for the rest of the day.

Victoria took special care over her toilette for the opera. After extensive conferring with Skerrett, they decided to do her hair in a coronet of plaits high on her head, a style which made her neck look longer as it rose out of the low neckline of her dress.

'I think that tonight I shall wear Queen Charlotte's diamond necklace.'

'Yes, Ma'am, I shall fetch it presently.' Jenkins went off, rattling the bunch of keys round her waist, and came back with the faded green leather box, which she put in front of Victoria. When she opened it, both women gasped as the diamonds sparkled in the candlelight.

'Yes, I shall definitely wear this,' said Victoria and she handed the necklace to Jenkins to fasten round her neck.

Skerrett, who came back into the room carrying the flowers for Victoria's hair, squeaked with astonishment when she saw the necklace. 'It looks like your neck is on fire, Ma'am.'

Victoria looked at herself in the mirror with satisfaction. The necklace did indeed look as though it had its own inner furnace. As Skerrett fixed the matching tiara onto the crown of her head, Victoria was satisfied with her appearance.

She had been pleased when Melbourne had told her that the Grand Duke Alexander, having made his Grand Tour of Europe, had decided to come back to England before going back to St Petersburg. He was an excellent dancer and his conversation was charming. But his reappearance now was fortuitous; he would be a useful shield against Uncle Leopold. Tonight, for example, she had invited the Grand Duke to join her in the Royal Box, knowing that because Belgium had no formal alliance with Russia it would be impossible for Uncle Leopold to join them.

Uncle Leopold had not been happy when she had told him that for diplomatic reasons she would have to share the Royal Box with the Grand Duke.

'But you can sit with Mama, Uncle Leopold. I know you have so much to discuss.'

He had protested that to show such favour to the Grand Duke might be misinterpreted, but Victoria forestalled him. 'Oh, don't worry about that. Lord M will be there too. He will make quite sure there isn't a diplomatic incident.'

Leopold had pursed his lips, but said nothing more.

The orchestra of Her Majesty's Theatre played *God Save the Queen* and then the Russian national anthem when Victoria entered the Royal Box with the Grand Duke. When the Russian anthem came to an end, the Queen and the Grand Duke sat down. They did not, it was noted, glance over their shoulders to see if the chairs were in the right position. Royal since birth, they just assumed they would be there.

Her Majesty's Theatre, which had been His Majesty's Theatre until Victoria came to the throne, was full. Donizetti's version of Sir Water's Scott's *The Bride of Lammermoor* was already a success, but tonight the audience was interested in the spectacle off as well as on the stage.

There was the Royal Box, where the Queen sat next to the Grand Duke of Russia, whose diamond-encrusted orders sparkled as brilliantly as Victoria's necklace. Behind the two royal personages were the Prime Minister and Lady Portman, condemned by protocol to stand throughout.

On the other side of the royal circle was the box containing the King of the Belgians and his sister the Duchess of Kent. There had been a cheer when they had taken their places, a cheer that was claimed as their rightful tribute by both brother and sister. But Sir John Conroy who stood, as always, directly behind the Duchess, had no doubt as to whom the cheer belonged.

There were no cheers for the Duke of Cumberland as he entered his box accompanied by his wife and his nephew Prince George of Cambridge. The Prince had the bulging blue eyes and uncertain chin of the Hanoverians. He was wearing his uniform and looked as if he would rather be in his regiment's mess than at the opera.

When the overture came to an end, and La Persiani came on to the stage to sing her first aria, there were quite as many opera glasses trained on the Royal Box as there were on the diva.

The Duke of Cumberland had been delighted to see that Leopold was not in the Royal Box, but he had been less pleased that the Grand Duke was sitting next to his niece. He would be Tsar of all the Russias one day, so he was not a serious contender for Victoria's hand, but he was exotic in a way that Cumberland feared that his nephew George was not.

'The Queen is getting awfully cosy with the Russian, George. I think you should go over there and pay your respects, before she sits on his lap.'

George gave a magnificent sigh. 'As long as I don't have to stay for the second Act. I have heard better singing in the mess.'

Perhaps the only person watching the stage with the attention that La Persiani's performance deserved was the Queen herself. As Lucia sang of her undying love for Edgardo, tears came to Victoria's eyes and one trickled down her small white cheek.

The Grand Duke, who had been watching Victoria's profile

with attention, pulled out a handkerchief of imperial propor-
tions and offered it to her. She took it with a smile.

'Thank you. I feel quite overcome.'

The Grand Duke leant over to her and said in a low voice,
'We do not have so many opportunities to cry, you and I.'

Victoria nodded. 'You are right, of course. I suppose that is
why I love opera so much.'

'You have a Russian soul.'

'Or an English one.'

At that moment the music swelled as Lucia reached the end
of the aria and collapsed on the stage in a swoon. Her performance was lost on the audience, who were watching the heir
to the Russian throne smile at their Queen.

In the interval Prince George presented himself at the Royal
Box. Victoria looked at him in surprise. 'I did not know you
cared for opera, George.'

George's milky face blushed as he struggled to reply. Finally
he said, 'I suppose it is a new interest, Cousin Victoria.'

She smiled. 'Then I shall insist on you being my companion
next time I come.'

Victoria turned to the Grand Duke. 'May I present my
cousin Prince George of Cambridge?'

George gave the Russian an adequate but not fulsome bow.
The Grand Duke nodded and said, 'I had the honour of
inspecting the Prince's regiment. Such magnificent uniforms.'

His tone implied that the uniforms were the only things
that had been magnificent. As the implied insult worked its
way through to George, his colour rose even further. He wanted
to say that at least his men were a disciplined fighting force,
not a bunch of drunken Cossacks, but he had to resort to
glaring at the impertinent Russian instead.

'Isn't Lucia wonderful?' Victoria asked her cousin. 'Did the mad scene make you want to cry?'

George was relieved to be asked a question that he could answer truthfully. 'It certainly did.'

He stood there for a few minutes longer, feeling all the while the eyes of Cumberland upon him, but then the music began again and he made his excuses and left.

Leopold had watched the entire exchange through his opera glasses. He had understood immediately what Cumberland intended by bringing Prince George. Even though he knew that George was decidedly inferior to Albert in looks and intellect, he was nonetheless relieved to see that Victoria did not betray any kind of excitement at his appearance. She seemed rather to prefer the company of the Grand Duke, but Leopold was happy to dismiss his presence as a harmless flirtation. The marriage of two Sovereigns was a practical and diplomatic impossibility. The last time it had been attempted, between Mary Tudor and Philip II of Spain, it had not been successful for either party.

After George left, Leopold's attention was diverted to the stage where a very pleasing ballet was taking place. But Leopold's appreciation of the shapely calves of the dancers was interrupted by the Duchess, who was looking at her daughter through her own opera glasses.

'Look at Drina. I believe she is flirting with the Grand Duke. It is most unsuitable.'

'My dear Marie-Louise, do not alarm yourself. The Grand Duke can only be a harmless diversion. Even Victoria is not so foolish as to imagine that there could ever be more than a flirtation between them.'

The Duchess sighed. 'I hope you are right, brother. But she is capable of every kind of foolishness.' Conroy made a noise of assent.

Leopold turned his gaze from the stage to the Royal Box. Victoria's face swam into vision, much magnified, and he saw to his surprise and alarm that there was an expression on her face that looked very much like the softening one would expect of a woman in love. But who was she looking at? When Leopold tilted his glasses to follow her gaze, the handsome face of Lord Melbourne swam into view. Melbourne was, Leopold noted, returning Victoria's look with equal affection.

Leopold put the opera glasses down. His sister was right; Victoria clearly was capable of every kind of foolishness. Could she seriously imagine that Melbourne could be more to her than a Prime Minister? No, it was impossible – even Victoria could not be so deluded. But he knew what he had seen and it troubled him deeply. He decided against mentioning it to his sister. The one thing calculated to provoke Victoria into doing something irrevocably foolish would be an intervention by her mother. No, he must be the one to talk to Victoria. And having decided on his course of action, Leopold turned his attention back to the stage, where to his disappointment the dancers had been replaced by a chorus of sturdy Scottish Highlanders singing in Italian.

The Queen's party, of course, was the first to leave the theatre. The Grand Duke escorted Victoria down the staircase to the entrance on the Haymarket, where her carriage was waiting. As she came out she was gratified to hear a few cheers from the crowd that had assembled outside.

The Grand Duke turned to her and smiled. 'Your people love you, Victoria.'

'I think they like to see their Queen. I am sure that you are greeted with the same enthusiasm in Russia.'

'Perhaps. But your people are free to cheer as they like, while mine are not. The cheers of serfs are not the same as those of citizens.'

Victoria saw that the Grand Duke's eyes were clouded as he bent over her hand to kiss it.

'Good night, Alexander,' she felt self-conscious using his name, but he had called her Victoria.

The Grand Duke clicked his heels in farewell.

As she climbed into the carriage, she heard a noise and felt Dash jumping up to kiss her hands. 'Oh, my dear little Dashy, what a lovely surprise!'

She picked up her dog and hugged him to her. The handsome blond head of Lord Alfred Paget, her equerry, appeared at the carriage window. 'I hope you are not offended, Ma'am. But he was pining for you at the Palace, so I took the liberty of bringing him with me to meet you.'

'How very thoughtful of you, Lord Alfred. I cannot imagine a more delightful companion for the ride back. Dash loves to hear about the opera, don't you, Dashy?' And the little dog wriggled in delight as she scratched his tummy.

'I hope you will not object to a human passenger, Victoria.' She looked up and to her annoyance saw her Uncle Leopold. Without waiting for her reply, the King of the Belgians pushed past Lord Alfred and seated himself opposite her.

Victoria shrank back to her side of the carriage, clutching Dash in her arms. She was tired, and the last thing she wanted was an enforced tête-à-tête with her uncle. But there was nothing she could do, unless she asked the soldiers to remove him, which would cause a diplomatic incident. This thought made her smile and she pulled Dash's ear and whispered in his ear, 'You don't know how pleased your Mama is to see you, Dashy.'

Leopold took a match from his pocket and lit the candle next to his seat. It illuminated his face from below, making him look almost demonic. 'My dear niece. You know I have always tried to be a father to you.'

Victoria fiddled with her dog's ears. 'You have certainly written to me often enough. Hasn't he, Dash?'

Leopold sighed. 'Please talk to me and not to your lapdog. I have something important to say to you.'

Victoria held her dog's face up next to her own. 'And we are listening.'

Leopold ignored the pertness. 'You say you do not want to marry Albert, but I would ask you if you intend to marry someone else?'

Victoria looked at him, and said coldly, 'I have no plans to marry anyone at present.'

Leopold put his hand to his head to check the position of his hairpiece. 'You do not, I hope, imagine that your Lord M could ever be more than your Prime Minister?'

Dash yelped as Victoria tugged his ear in fury. 'I will not dignify that suggestion with an answer.'

'Then, as one Sovereign to another, I would advise you to be careful,' Leopold said.

Victoria retorted, her voice taut with irritation, 'And as one Sovereign to another, I must advise you not to interfere.'

'Perhaps you are too young to understand how dangerous your situation is. The country is in a volatile state. I am most

concerned about the disturbances in Wales. All revolutionary
movements start like this, with popular discontent.'

'Lord Melbourne says I have nothing to fear from the
Chartists. He says that there has been a bad harvest, and when
people are hungry they fancy themselves radicals.'

'Your Lord Melbourne is not infallible, Victoria. I am afraid
that even the British Crown is vulnerable.'

Victoria made a noise somewhere between a snort and a
laugh. But Leopold continued unperturbed, taking some
matches from his pocket and striking one of them in front of
her, revealing her sulky face.

'You think that your monarchy burns brightly, Victoria, but
all it takes is a little draught from the wrong direction. Marry
Albert and start a family that your subjects can be proud of.
Otherwise . . .' Leopold blew out the match.

Victoria clutched Dash even more tightly and said nothing
for the remainder of the mercifully short journey.

Chapter Four

$\mathcal{V}$ICTORIA'S UNCLES WERE NOT ALONE IN TAKING A KEEN interest in her matrimonial status. In drawing rooms up and down the country, there was a feeling that a young personable Queen of marriageable age must be in want of a husband. In Brooks's club, the bastion of Whig values, there was much talk of the Queen's duty to provide an heir to the throne more in tune with the times than the Duke of Cumberland. Across the street in White's, the Tory stronghold, there was an equally strong feeling that the Queen should marry because it was the only way to curb the pernicious influence of Lord Melbourne.

But while it was generally agreed that the Queen must marry, there was no agreement as to who the ideal husband might be. In the servants' hall at Buckingham Palace, there was much speculation on the subject. Indeed, Penge, the Queen's steward, had gone so far as to establish a running wager on the likely runners and riders. He had put his sixpence on Prince George. Having served briefly in the household of Princess Charlotte when she had been married to the then Prince Leopold, he had no desire to work for another Coburg prince. The Coburgs were, in his trenchantly held opinion, 'the worst kind of foreigners'.

When he had been pressed by Mrs Jenkins as to the nature of his objections, he had mentioned that the King of the Belgians had not only complained about the dampness of the sheets on his bed but also failed to grasp the level of emoluments due to the Palace's personnel. 'The Coburgs are money-grabbing, sausage-eating mountebanks who have no place on the British throne. What we need is a British bridegroom.'

Mrs Jenkins, who had seen the care with which the Queen had dressed for her night at the opera, was inclined to support the candidacy of the Grand Duke. 'Such a handsome young man, what a lovely couple they would make.' Penge had said that a union between the Queen and the heir to the Russian throne was a diplomatic impossibility, but he was prepared to take her money if she was foolish enough to wager it. Mrs Jenkins, who liked to believe that love conquered all, persisted in supporting her candidate.

The chef, Mr Francatelli, who had no love for Mr Penge, decided to back Prince Albert of Saxe-Coburg-Gotha; and Brodie, the hall boy, declared that if he had a sixpence he would put it on Lord Alfred Paget, as he was always laughing with the Queen. Penge and Mrs Jenkins raised their eyebrows at Brodie's choice, but neither felt obliged to point out that Lord Alfred was not the marrying kind. Miss Skerrett, the junior dresser, said that she did not have a sixpence to wager on the Queen's matrimonial prospect, but that it seemed to her that the only man she really cared for was Lord Melbourne. And in this, the junior dresser was perfectly in accord with Leopold, King of the Belgians.

The morning after her encounter with Leopold, Victoria herself knew only that she was enormously relieved to be in the Park riding as usual with Melbourne at her side. Although she loved the opera and found the Grand Duke an agreeable companion, she felt altogether more at ease riding through Rotten Row with her Prime Minister. She had gone to meet him just as usual just behind Apsley House, the Duke of Wellington's house, on the corner of the Park. But Melbourne, most unusually, was not there and had kept her waiting for a full five minutes.

When he did arrive, he was dusty and apologetic. 'Forgive me, Ma'am. I received a message just as I was setting out, and had to act immediately.'

Victoria smiled at him. 'It must have been important. I don't think I have ever seen you so out of countenance before.'

Melbourne looked ruefully at his dusty clothes. 'I did not want to keep you waiting.'

He looked at her with concern. 'I wonder if it is wise for you to open the almshouses tomorrow, Ma'am. It is an open space and I believe there will be a crowd. I think it may not be altogether safe.'

Victoria turned to him in surprise. 'But I must go. These almshouses are dedicated to my father's memory. It would be disrespectful not to attend. And as to being safe, well, you always tell me that a Queen must be seen to be believed.'

Melbourne shook his head. 'In general I believe that to be true, but I have just heard that the Newport rioters have been sentenced to death, and I fear there may be repercussions.'

Victoria looked at her Prime Minister. 'That seems a very harsh punishment. Is it necessary to execute them? I believe they did not hurt anyone. Indeed, I believe the only dead were among the Chartists themselves.'

'Better that a few should die now, Ma'am, than an armed insurrection later.'

'You feel it might come to that?' Victoria asked.

'Yes, Ma'am. I do.'

'I see. Nevertheless, I shall still attend the ceremony.'

'Very well, Ma'am.'

They rode along in silence for some minutes. At last Victoria could bear it no longer. 'What did you think of *Lucia*? I never spoke to you about it.'

Melbourne shrugged. 'It was not Mozart, Ma'am.' Then, turning his head towards her, he asked, 'And you? How did you enjoy the evening? You seemed to be well attended.'

Victoria smiled, pleased that they had moved on from the Newport Chartists. 'The Grand Duke is amusing, I daresay. It is refreshing to talk to someone who understands the cares of my position. But he is too foreign to be entirely comfortable, I think.'

'And what about Prince George of Cambridge? He was being most attentive, I thought.'

Victoria made a grimace. 'We never liked each other as children. He always used to say that girls had no business being Queens.'

'And what did you say?' asked Melbourne.

'I said that when I was Queen I would send him to the Tower like all traitors!'

Melbourne laughed. 'Quite right! And what do you think of him now he is grown up?'

'Well, he is not so short or so fat as he once was, but I don't think his opinions about the fitness of women for the throne have changed much.'

'Oh?' Melbourne drew up his reins and his horse's head to face Victoria. 'That is unfortunate, as I think he would like to be a candidate for your hand.'

'George thinks he would like to be my husband?' Victoria looked at him in amazement.

Melbourne nodded. 'I believe so, Ma'am. And, of course, an English marriage would be very popular in the country.'

Victoria raised her blue eyes and looked straight at him. 'An English marriage?'

'Would go down very well, Ma'am.'

Victoria beamed at him. 'Then I shall bear that in mind, Lord M.'

Victoria's father, the late Duke of Kent, had been distinguished, even among George III's famously profligate sons, for his extravagance. He had spent most of his adult life abroad, in Canada, partly because of his military career but more particularly because he wanted to escape his many creditors.

On her accession to the throne, Victoria had been surprised to find that so many of her father's debts remained unpaid. As there had been a grant made by Parliament to the Duchess for that express purpose after the Duke's death, Victoria was doubly mortified. She had declared that she would pay off her father's outstanding debts at once, even if it meant that she and her mother would have to forgo new bonnets. Melbourne had laughed and said that he did not think that such a hardship would be necessary, and he observed that she was very frugal in comparison with her predecessors on the throne.

After clearing the debts, Victoria thought that it was time to do something more positive to honour her father's memory. Her father, she believed without much evidence, had been charitable in his impulses, and she wanted to do something that would make his generosity concrete. Her mother had been unhelpful, suggesting the thing that would have pleased her father most was to see his widow properly established. 'He always liked me to look elegant, Victoria. He was always buying me nice clothes.' Victoria had replied that she thought there might be a more permanent tribute to her father's generosity than a new parasol.

She had, of course, consulted Lord M, who had advised her to do something philanthropic. 'There are statues of your uncles all over London, and while they decorate the skyline, they are of little practical use.' Victoria had listened, as she did to everything Lord Melbourne said, with attention, and started to look about for a suitable undertaking.

Harriet Sutherland, whose family took philanthropy very seriously, had directed her towards a project for building alms-houses for the relief of the poor in the parish of Camberwell. 'There are old people there, Ma'am, living in conditions of great poverty, having worked diligently all their lives. To think that they can live so wretchedly only a mile from the Palace.' Visiting the parish with the Duchess incognito, Victoria had been appalled by the conditions she found there. Although she did not dare get out of the carriage for fear of being recognised, she saw children in rags begging on the streets and an old woman in a dusty black dress that had once been of good quality sitting on the pavement with a small bundle by her side and a parrot in a cage.

She had asked the footman to enquire as to the woman's circumstances and had discovered that she had been a lady's maid who had lost her place on account of her age. Without children or a pension, the woman had no way of supporting herself or her parrot. Victoria had been moved by the parrot, its plumage dusty but its yellow eye bright. She had felt quite indignant with the old lady's former employers. How could they have cast her out on the streets like that? Harriet had told her that it was quite common. 'Not everyone with servants, Ma'am, has been brought up to understand that there is an obligation on both sides.'

Victoria had wanted to relieve the woman's situation at once, and as she never carried money had been forced to ask Harriet to lend her some. Harriet suggested that it might be better to have her conveyed to the Palace where she could be given a meal and some direction as to the future.

The plight of Mrs Hadlow, the lady's maid (the Mrs was an honorific), had convinced Victoria to build almshouses where the respectable poor could see out their days in peace. She had contributed a major part of the funds for the project on the understanding that they would be called the Duke of Kent's Almshouses. Mrs Hadlow and her parrot were to be among the first tenants.

The buildings had been built most handsomely, thought Victoria, as her carriage drew up outside the little square. The low two-storey buildings with their red front doors and their neat front gardens looked like the epitome of genteel comfort, a splendid contrast to the squalor she had witnessed there before. The roofs and railings were hung with flags and bunting, and a brass band started to play the national anthem as Victoria's footman pulled down the carriage steps.

In the middle of the square was a plinth with a dedication to her father's memory covered in a velvet cloth. Victoria was to make a short speech before dedicating the plinth and declaring the almshouses open. She had not wanted the ceremony to be an elaborate affair, but the visit of her uncle had meant that she had been forced to invite him, and Melbourne had suggested that to make the ceremony more amusing she should also invite the Grand Duke. She had thought this was an excellent suggestion but had been less pleased when she heard that the Duke of Cumberland was mortally offended not to have been asked. She had no intention of including him, but Melbourne had said that to exclude him would cause an unnecessary scandal and he was sure that she did not want to do anything that would detract from honouring her father's memory. So Victoria, mindful of what had happened the last time she had ignored her Prime Minister's advice, had relented and asked the Cumberlands and the rest of her father's family.

It was with some trepidation that she stepped out of the carriage. Sitting in the stands around the plinth were all the people who caused her distress: her mother, Conroy, the Cumberlands, who had brought Prince George, and Sir Robert Peel. In a way she had not anticipated, what had begun as a tribute to her father had somehow become a test of her authority. This feeling of alarm was exacerbated by the presence of a line of soldiers from the household regiment separating the royal party from the crowd gathered in the street. Victoria felt as if she was being scrutinised from every angle. She looked about her. There was only one face, she realised, that she wanted to see, but there was no sign of him. She forced herself to smile at the warden of the almshouses, who was being presented to her by Harriet Sutherland.

Then she sensed him standing just behind her, and felt a warm tide of relief run through her body.

'Forgive me, Ma'am, for not being here when you arrived, but the crowds are so thick that my carriage could hardly make its way through them.'

Victoria turned and smiled. 'I forgive you, Lord M. But can you tell me why there are so many soldiers? I know my father was a military man, but I feel it destroys the peaceful character of the event.'

Melbourne looked at her. 'As I mentioned before, I fear there may be some disturbance from the Chartists, Ma'am.'

Victoria looked out over the crowd and shook her head. 'But do Chartists wear bonnets, Lord M? Because there are a great many of them out there today.'

Now it was Melbourne's turn to smile. 'Actually, Ma'am, some Chartists do believe that women should have the vote.'

Victoria laughed. 'Now you are teasing me.'

'No, Ma'am, I assure you I am quite in earnest.'

Victoria gestured to a group of children waving flags. 'And will they give the franchise to infants as well?'

'No, Ma'am, I don't think even the Chartists would go that far.'

The Queen followed Melbourne up onto the dais alongside the plinth. There was a small scuffle as the Grand Duke and Prince George vied for the position closest to her. George, who had taken a dislike to the Russian prince not only because he perceived him as a possible rival for Victoria's affections, but also because the Grand Duke's uniform was so much more magnificent than his own, said with what he imagined was icy hauteur, 'We are fortunate, sir, that your father the Emperor can spare you to attend the opening of an almshouse.'

The Grand Duke, who did not perceive George to be a rival in any way, said, 'My father and I are great admirers of British institutions, your Queen in particular.'

George moved to stand in front of him, but found that the Russian blocked his path. They stood there uncomfortably close, neither of them ready to give way.

Observing this little contretemps, Melbourne permitted

himself a small smile, then glanced to see if Victoria had noticed the rivalry between her two admirers. But she was looking at the plinth and biting her lip, a sign, he knew, that she was nervous. She said in a small voice, 'Should I start, Lord M?'

'If you feel ready, Ma'am.'

She stepped a little closer to the dais, and he saw that the hand carrying the piece of paper on which she had written her speech was trembling. In a high and slightly quavering voice she began, 'I never knew my father, but I know that he believed in Christian charity above all things.'

Melbourne heard the Duke of Cumberland mutter to his wife, 'The only charity my late brother indulged in was supporting the mistress he discarded when he married. And even that didn't last long.'

Melbourne turned to see if the Duchess of Kent had over-heard this remark, but fortunately she was flanked by her brother and Sir John Conroy and too taken up by their company to pay attention to her brother-in-law. The Queen was too far away to hear anything her uncle was saying.

'So it gives me great pleasure to dedicate these almshouses to his memory.'

To the sound of applause from the dais and from the crowd, the small figure of the Queen walked over to the plinth to unveil the plaque in her father's memory. The Grand Duke and Prince George moved at the same time, both it seemed with the idea of helping the Queen. They stood there, on either side of the plinth, George glaring at the Grand Duke, the Russian pretending that the English prince did not exist.

When Victoria saw the situation, it was all she could do not to smile. 'Thank you so much, but I believe I can manage unaided.'

She stared at them long enough for both men to retreat a little, then stepped forward and pulled the string which removed the velvet cloth. To her relief it came off without a hitch, revealing a plaque with the unmistakable Hanoverian profile of the Duke of Kent.

She turned and looked out over the crowd. 'And now it is my great pleasure to declare these almshouses, for the relief of the poor and elderly of this parish, open.'

There was another round of applause from the crowd and a few cheers of God Save the Queen, but there was also a harsher, more strident, noise. The Queen heard it and was turning to Melbourne when a rock landed with a great crash on the plinth, narrowly missing Victoria herself. Then the noise from the crowd solidified into a chant of 'Justice for the Newport Chartists! Justice for the Newport Chartists!'

Victoria felt Melbourne's hand on her arm, pushing her behind him, and for a moment in the crush she rested her cheek against the wiry broadcloth of his coat and laid her arms around his waist. Despite the noise and confusion, the acrid breath of panic all around her, despite the scratchy wool against her skin, Victoria felt as if she had been wrapped in the finest cashmere, cocooned completely from the chaos around her. This, she thought, was what safety felt like.

Then a shot rang out over the crowd and Victoria was startled from her reverie. She said urgently, 'Lord M, don't let them shoot. Remember the bonnets.'

Melbourne turned to her, his green eyes bright and hard, but seeing her face he softened. 'Don't worry, Ma'am, I won't let anyone be harmed. But you must go back to the Palace at once.'

'I don't want to leave you. You are the only person that . . .'

Her words were lost in another volley of gunfire. Melbourne looked over the Queen's head and saw Prince George on the left with his hand on his sword making his way towards the crowd like a knight errant and the Grand Duke looking equally martial on the right. Neither of them was suitable for what he had in mind, so it was with a sigh of relief that he spotted the fair, imperturbable face of Alfred Paget. He called him over urgently. 'Lord Alfred, I believe the Queen is leaving. Can you escort her and the Duchess back to the Palace?'

Lord Alfred, with a skill forged by his experience on the field of diplomatic levees rather than in the smoke of battle, managed to shepherd the reluctant Victoria through sheer force of suggestion towards the carriage, while simultaneously collecting the Duchess, conveying to her with a mere frisson of the eyebrow that in such a moment of upheaval her place was by her daughter's side.

Victoria allowed herself to be placed in the carriage without protest, but as she leant against the glass and saw Melbourne talking to the officer in charge of the troops, his face alive with concern, she felt the pain of leaving him so acutely that it brought tears to her eyes.

Seeing this, her mother put her hand on her daughter's cheek. 'Don't be scared, *Liebes*. No harm will come to you. I promise.'

But Victoria turned her face away, looking back out of the window for one last glimpse of him. He was standing in the middle of the crowd with the commanding officer. She willed him to look round, and when he lifted his head, it seemed as if he must look right at her. But then the carriage lurched forward through the crowd, and he disappeared from her view. Victoria leant back against the buttoned leather seat and closed her eyes.

Melbourne saw the carriage drive away and thought he glimpsed the small white face of the Queen at the window. Feeling a great sweep of relief that she was leaving, he turned back to the Captain and said with more conviction than before, 'You must disperse the crowd peacefully. Make sure that your men only fire in the air. I do not want anyone to be harmed. Do you understand me, Captain?'

The Captain nodded reluctantly. He thought that Lord Melbourne was not a solider; if he had been, he would know that the more people that were harmed now, the less likely it would be that such things would happen again.

Melbourne was looking for Emma Portman, wanting to make sure that she would be with the Queen for the rest of the day, when he heard a voice just behind him. 'Lord Melbourne, may I have a word?' Melbourne recognised the clipped English of the King of the Belgians. He tried to control his irritation.

'Can it wait, sir? I am somewhat preoccupied at the moment.' He gestured at the mêlée in front of them. Prince George and the Grand Duke were standing with their swords drawn, and it was unclear whether they were ready to fight the crowd or each other.

Leopold shook his head. 'I think not.'

Melbourne sighed and regarded Leopold with weary resignation. 'I see. Then, sir, I am at your service.'

Leopold gestured for Melbourne to follow him to a spot behind the plinth where they could not be overheard, as unlikely as that seemed in the general hubbub. But the King, thought Melbourne, would lose no opportunity to set himself apart.

The King leant forward so that his mouth was very close to Melbourne's ear. 'I wish to talk to you about my niece.'

Melbourne took a step back, squaring himself off against the other man. 'Indeed?'

Leopold gave him a smile that suggested that they were both men of the world. 'You must agree, I think, that the sooner she is married the better. Her reign so far has been troubled. A husband, children would steady her giddiness.'

Melbourne paused, and then, 'I do not see any urgency for the Queen to marry. What is most important, I think, is that she chooses wisely.'

He looked over at the two princes. Leopold followed his gaze.

'I could not agree more. And there could be no better choice than her Cousin Albert. He is a serious young man, and I have taken a great interest in his education.' He turned his head to face Melbourne. 'And of course he is of a suitable age.'

Melbourne's face did not move. 'I believe the Queen did not take to him the last time they met.'

Leopold smiled at his niece's foolishness. 'She was too young to have an opinion. Victoria will change her mind, but only, I think, if she understands that such a marriage is in her best interest.' In a lower voice, 'I believe, my lord, that you could persuade her of that.'

The other man gave a mirthless smile. 'I am not a magician, sir. The Queen tends to hear only what she already thinks.'

Leopold put his head on one side, and said slyly, 'Come, Lord Melbourne, you are too modest. I have seen the way my niece looks at you.' He blinked slowly as if to suggest the flirtatious guiles of the coquettish Queen.

Melbourne said as evenly as he could, 'I think, sir, that you exaggerate my influence.'

'If you say so, Lord Melbourne. But I am sure that on

reflection a man of your,' he paused, 'experience, will understand what needs to be done.'

Another volley of shots spared Melbourne from having to reply. He gave the King the briefest of nods. 'You must excuse me, sir,' and he set off towards the surging crowd.

Leopold watched him go. He had achieved his aim. Melbourne knew now that his relationship with Victoria was under scrutiny.

Chapter Five

 HE NEXT MORNING, VICTORIA WAITED AS USUAL FOR
Melbourne in her sitting room, the pile of red boxes
in front of her. She had dressed for the interview with care,
wearing her new sprigged muslin and with her hair in the
plaits around the ear that Lord M had once told her he thought
charming. The events of the day before had been confusing,
so puzzling in fact that she had gone to bed without any supper.
But then in the middle of the night she had woken up, and
feeling restless had got out of bed.

There was a full moon, and the gardens of the Palace were
bathed in silvery light. She saw an animal, perhaps a rabbit,
run across the lawn down to the lake. Here in the Palace, it
was hard sometimes to remember that she was right in the
middle of London. And yet the almshouses were less than two
miles from where she was now. It had been a relief to hear
that no one had been harmed that afternoon; she was glad that
Melbourne had listened to her.

She had expected to hear from him that evening, but to her
surprise he had not called in after dinner or even sent a note.
In a way she had been relieved because she needed time to
examine her feelings; she could still feel the rough scratch of

the wool of his coat against her cheek. That contact, rushed and accidental though it had been, had moved her in a way she could not explain. It was as if she had found something that she did not know she had been looking for.

As she made her way round her bedroom, the moon was so bright she did not need a candle. She saw the box containing the telescope that Melbourne had given her for her birthday. She opened the box and pulled out the instrument, extending it to its full length. Kneeling down on the window seat, she put it to her eye and tried to find the moon. At last the lens revealed the lunar landscape, and she gazed with awe at the shadows it revealed.

It had not been at all the present she had been expecting from Lord M on her birthday, but now she thought she understood its significance. He had been suggesting to her that she should try and look at things differently, to view her life and affairs from a different perspective. Of course, at the time he had wanted her to accept that he could no longer be her Prime Minister, but he had come to understand that his place was at her side. Now, as she looked through the magnifying glass of the telescope, she thought that perhaps it was time that she looked at Melbourne from a different angle.

He was her friend, her advisor and her confidant, but, she wondered, could he perhaps be something more. Her body had known it at once – that sudden contact had been electrifying – but her mind had to acknowledge this new perspective. If she really was going to marry, could there be a more suitable or more desirable husband than the man who already filled her thoughts? It would be an unorthodox choice, she knew, that would provoke some protest. Uncle Leopold would not approve, but surely it must be better for her to marry a man she loved than to enter into a calculated marriage of convenience.

There was the Royal Marriage Act, which made it impossible for a member of the royal family to marry without the Sovereign's consent, but she was the Sovereign. She knew, of course, that there would be objections from her uncles, and perhaps from those beastly Tories, but in the end, who could stop her?

It would be difficult, she thought, turning the brass eyepiece of the telescope around in her hand, to tell him her decision. She wondered if he might perhaps guess, since he was always so perceptive, but even if he did, any – and here she gripped the telescope very tightly – any proposal would have to come from her. A Sovereign always had to be the one to propose.

She sighed and tried to imagine how she would say it. The only way would be to stand very close to him so that she could feel his warmth but would not have to meet his eyes. She did not think that she would be able to say what she must under the scrutiny of that green gaze. But she must do it, and without delay. She remembered the quotation that Lord M always used when he wanted to do something, 'There is a tide in the affairs of men, which, taken at the flood . . .'

She would take it at the flood.

When the door to her sitting room opened just after the clock struck nine, she looked up with a smile, but instead of her Prime Minister she saw Emma Portman, who uncharacteristically looked uneasy.

'Emma? I was expecting Lord M.'

'I know, Ma'am, which is why I came to tell you that he has gone to Brocket Hall.'

'Brocket Hall? Why would he go there now?'

Emma Portman lowered her eyes. 'I am not sure, Ma'am. Perhaps he felt the need for some country air.'

'But he always tells me he thinks there is nothing more bracing than a walk down St James's.'

Emma gave a smile that did not reach her eyes. 'I am afraid that even Lord Melbourne can be inconsistent, Ma'am.'

Victoria stood up suddenly, knocking the pile of boxes to the floor. Emma began to stoop to pick them up, but Victoria put a hand out to stop her.

'Never mind those. Is your carriage here, Emma?'

Emma nodded slowly, her face apprehensive.

'I should like to borrow it, if I may. Or rather I should like us to make an excursion together.'

Emma looked at the Queen, and asked a question to which she already knew the answer. 'Where will we be going, Ma'am?'

'To Brocket Hall. I have something of great importance to say to Lord M.'

Emma Portman took a deep breath. 'It is a considerable journey, Ma'am. Perhaps it might be better to send a messenger. I am sure that William would come back to town directly.'

But Victoria, who was pacing up and down, said, 'No, it cannot wait. There is a tide, Emma, in the affairs of men, which taken at the flood leads on to fortune.'

'I cannot argue with Shakespeare, Ma'am.'

'Good. But we must go at once. And we must go incognito, of course.'

'Of course,' said Emma Portman, her voice echoing her mistress's with a dying fall. If Victoria noticed her lack of enthusiasm, she gave no sign of it, and was already setting off down the corridor with her quick light tread.

The journey to Brocket Hall, which lay in the county of Hertfordshire, took just under two hours. Victoria insisted on driving straight there, without stopping. She sat on the edge of her carriage seat, playing with her veil and trying out in her head the speech she would make to Lord Melbourne. Every so often she would look across at Emma and remark on the weather or the scenery, but it was clear that her head was too full of her thoughts to permit ordinary conversation.

At last, to Emma's great relief, the carriage turned into the elm-lined drive that led to Brocket Hall, a Palladian mansion faced with Portland stone.

'There, Ma'am, if you look out onto my side of the carriage you will have your first glimpse of the house. I believe it was built during the reign of your great-great grandfather George II, and is considered one of the finest examples of the period.'

Victoria glanced out of the window, but the house was not what she had come to see. 'Did you ever meet Lord M's wife, Emma?'

'Caro? Yes, of course. She is, was, a cousin of sorts.'

'What was she like? Was she very beautiful?'

'Beautiful? No, I wouldn't say that. But she was uncommonly lively. If she was in a room it was impossible to look at anyone else.'

'I see. But she was an immoral person, was she not?'

Emma smiled. 'Because of her imbroglio with Byron? I wouldn't call her immoral. I think she was reckless, but I believe he dazzled her, and she did not have the strength to resist him.'

'You sound as if you think she was not to blame!'

'I felt sorry for her, Ma'am. If you had seen her after the *mésalliance* ended, you would understand. It was as if all the spark in her had been extinguished. He was a terrible man, so attractive but completely without heart. He brushed poor Caro aside as if she were thistledown.'

'But she broke her marriage vows, Emma. How can you feel sorry for a woman who does that?'

Emma glanced at Victoria's small face and saw the spots of colour in her cheeks, the shining blue eyes, the eager mouth. 'She will not be the first married woman to do so, Ma'am, or the last.'

'Well, I think her behaviour was shocking. I have never understood why Lord Melbourne took her back after she had treated him so shamefully.'

'I never admired him more, Ma'am. His mother, his friends, the party all tried to convince him to divorce her, but he would have none of it. He said that he would not desert her in her hour of need. And he looked after her for the rest of her life, even though, I am afraid, she was most of the time half out of her wits.'

Victoria shook her head. 'She didn't deserve him.'

Emma, in turn, shook her head. 'At the beginning she was very lovable, and then . . . well, I think William held himself responsible.'

The carriage began to slow down as it reached the house.

Emma looked at the Queen. 'If you will permit me, I will go first, Ma'am. I know the butler here, and can warn him to be discreet.'

Victoria lowered the thick black veil down over her face. 'You think that anyone will recognise me wearing this?'

Emma tried not to smile.

Hedges the butler was coming down the steps as the coachman opened the door, his face creased with worry. When he saw Emma, he made a deep bow. 'I am so sorry, my lady, my master did not tell me that you were coming.'

'That's all right, Hedges. He didn't know.'

Hedges's face was now crumpled with concern. 'I hesitate to say this, Ma'am, but as you are such an old and trusted friend of the family, I must tell you I am afraid you will not find his lordship in the best of humours. He arrived last night with no warning and was most unlike himself.'

'Thank you, Hedges, I shall prepare myself for the worst.' She lowered her voice.

'I have brought with me a visitor, a most *distinguished* visitor, to see Lord Melbourne.' The butler looked puzzled, but when he glanced at the small veiled figure in the carriage, a glimmer of understanding began to pass over his wrinkled features. 'I see, your ladyship.'

'She is here incognito, is that understood?'

Hedges nodded. 'Perfectly, my lady.'

'Good. Now you had better tell your master he has visitors.'

'He is in the Park, your ladyship. I believe he has gone down to the copse by the lake, the place he calls the rookery.' He accompanied this with a lift of his eyebrows, as if he was not answerable for the location.

Emma nodded. 'Thank you, Hedges. I think we will walk down to meet him.'

Unable to wait any longer, Victoria climbed down from the carriage. 'Is everything all right? He is here, isn't he?'

Emma took her by the arm and walked a little way down the path with her, so that they were out of earshot.

'Yes, Ma'am, William is here. The butler says that he is over there.' She pointed to the copse on the other side of the lake, which was bisected by a grey stone bridge.

Victoria followed her gaze. 'Then I shall go and find him.'

'Would you like me to go first and tell him you are here? He might not be ready for you.'

Victoria laughed. 'Oh, Emma, Lord M and I don't stand on ceremony with each other. Why, he often comes to the Palace unannounced. Why should this be any different?'

'Very well, Ma'am.'

Victoria started to walk down the gravel path that led to the bridge, but when Emma made to follow, she turned back and said, 'I think, Emma, that you might prefer to sit down in the house.' When it looked as though the older woman might protest, Victoria said with some firmness, 'I believe I can manage alone.'

'If you are sure, Ma'am.'

'Quite sure.'

Emma watched the small figure in the voluminous dark veil walk briskly down the hill and across the bridge to the other side. When she turned, Hedges was standing beside her. They looked at each other, acknowledging the scene before them, and then Lady Portman reasserted herself. 'I find I am thirsty after my journey. Would you order me some tea?'

'Certainly, my lady.'

Victoria saw him first, the dark green of his coat against the grey stone of the seat. He had his face turned away from her, looking at a clump of oak trees whose green-fringed branches were speckled with the black forms of the rooks. He sat perfectly still, his head resting against the stone, until the rooks, sensing the approach of the Queen, began to wheel and circle in alarm, their cries echoing across the water of the lake. Melbourne stood up slowly, his shoulders expressing his reluctance at being disturbed. But as he made out the unmistakable figure walking towards him, his posture changed into something alert and wary.

He waited until she was a little closer before acknowledging her with a wave of his hand. He did not speak until Victoria stood before him and lifted her veil, whereupon he said, 'It is you then, Ma'am. I couldn't be sure.'

Victoria looked up at him. 'The butler said this was a favourite spot of yours.'

Melbourne turned and gestured to the trees behind him, where the birds were screaming in protest at the intruder. 'I come for the rooks, Ma'am. They are sociable animals. A gathering like this is called a Parliament. But they are altogether more civilised than their human equivalent.'

They stood listening to the eldritch shrieks of the birds. Victoria bit her lip and then said, 'I am sorry to disturb you, Lord M, but I had to talk to you.'

Melbourne made her a little bow. 'Brocket Hall is honoured by your presence, Ma'am.'

'I came here with Emma Portman. Incognito, of course.'

Melbourne's lips twitched. 'Of course, Ma'am. But your presence cannot be entirely disguised.'

Victoria put her hand up to fasten her veil, which was billowing behind her in the wind. The rooks answered her gesture with an eddy of cawing.

'You see, Lord M. Yesterday . . . yesterday I realised something.'

Melbourne's gaze did not leave her face. He waited for her to go on, and when she hesitated he said quietly, 'Yes, Ma'am?'

Victoria spoke quickly, as if she must get rid of the words before they burnt a hole in her mouth. 'I think perhaps that I am speaking now as a woman and not as a Queen.'

She hesitated again, but Melbourne continued to look at her until she was ready to go on. 'At the beginning I thought that you were the father that I never had, but now I feel,' she looked up, 'I *know*, that you are the only companion I could ever desire.'

As she said this, a shaft of light broke through the clouds above them and shone directly onto Melbourne's face, so that he briefly turned his face away. And then, as the sun went back behind the clouds, he faced Victoria and took one of her hands in his. Even through her white kid glove she felt the touch of his hand as if it were a red-hot coal burning into her palm.

With his other hand, but never taking his eyes off Victoria, he gestured to the birds behind him.

'Did you know, Ma'am, that rooks mate for life? Every year they court each other as they build their nest, renewing those little civilities that make a marriage sparkle. We could learn so much from them.'

Victoria heard his words, but all she could feel was the hand that was holding hers tightly. Melbourne hesitated as he looked at the upturned face but then he continued, 'If I had watched the rooks more closely, then perhaps my wife would have felt more attended to.'

Victoria said with indignation, 'She should never have left you! *I* would never do such a thing.'

Melbourne swallowed and then he said with great seriousness, 'No. I believe that when you give your heart it will be without hesitation.'

And then in a lower voice, 'But you cannot give it to me.'

Victoria almost laughed. Did he not understand what she had come here to tell him?

'I think, Lord M, that you have it already.' She lifted her face as close to his as the difference in their heights permitted. Although she knew he would not want to take advantage of a Queen, surely if she were to make it clear that she would not mind at all if he were to kiss her, then he might overcome his scruples. She closed her eyes, waiting. But instead of leaning forward, she felt his hand let go of hers.

When she opened her eyes she saw lines between his nose and his mouth that she had never noticed before. He spoke with determination. 'No, my dear, you must keep it intact for someone else.'

He looked back at the rooks as if they might have some message for him, then, turning back, said with awful clarity, 'I have no use for it, you see.' He tried to smile. 'Like a rook I mate for life.'

It took a moment for Victoria to understand what he had said, a moment to comprehend that everything that she had thought, had hoped for, was not to be. She had been mistaken; he cared not for her, but the memory of the wife who had betrayed him.

She knew she must leave before the tears came. With a voice that was as dignified as she could make it, she said, 'I see. Then I am sorry to have disturbed you, Lord Melbourne.' She pulled the veil down over her face and walked and then ran away from him as fast as she could, the cries of the rooks covering the sound of her tears.

From the drawing room of Brocket Hall, Emma Portman watched the small figure of the Queen crossing back over the bridge. From the way she was tacking diagonally across the path as if she could not see the way ahead, it was clear to Emma that the Queen was crying.

She rang the bell and asked Hedges to have the carriage brought round, as they would be leaving immediately. Hedges nodded, but before he disappeared he said with a sadness that spoke of great affection, 'My master has not had the happiness he deserves, my lady.'

'No. But he has served his country well, I think.'

The butler bowed his grey head and went to call the carriage. Emma Portman waited for her Queen.

Victoria walked up the hill and got into the carriage She did not raise her veil. She saw Emma get into the carriage beside her, but could not find the words to speak. What could she say? That the only man she had ever loved, ever would love, had rejected her because he preferred the memory of his dead wife – a woman who had treated him shamefully.

Victoria felt bereft of that moment of clarity she had felt when she had leant against Melbourne at the almshouses. She had not been safe after all; he did not care for her at all, only for the wicked, adulterous Caroline – who had humiliated him, while she, Victoria had done nothing but show him love and affection. Thinking of how much she hated Caroline and what a monster she must have been made her feel a little better. It was easier to blame the dead wife than the husband who stayed faithful to her memory. How quickly everything had gone from hope to despair. She thought of how he had smiled at her when she had lifted her veil and then the thrill of pure happiness she had felt when he had taken her hand, not as her Prime

Minister, but as a lover. She thought her face would break apart from smiling so hard, but then he had started talking about rooks, and though he still held her hand like a lover, his words had pushed her away. Her only chance of happiness gone for ever. She did not know how she could bear it. The sole consolation was that no one apart from the two of them would ever know what had passed between them.

In a minute, when she had regained her composure, she would say something to Emma that would make it clear she had come here to consult Melbourne on a matter of state. But that made her think of the red boxes and the happy hours they had spent every morning going through her papers, the jokes they had made about rural deans, the day she had received a zebra from the Emir of Muscat. They had been such happy days, but now they were gone. She wondered if she would ever be able to face Melbourne again. How could she speak to him now as she used to? Everything was ruined. The tears began to roll down her cheeks, and she felt Emma throw her a swift glance. Victoria turned her head away. She did not want Emma to see her crying. She closed her eyes, trying to pretend that none of this was happening, and that she was still the girl she had been on the journey to Brocket Hall.

A smooth metal object was placed in her hand. 'Might I suggest a sip of brandy, Ma'am? I find it is very efficacious when suffering from . . . travel sickness.'

Victoria raised the flask to her lips and felt the fiery liquid scald her throat. She coughed at the shock of it, but as the initial burn began to mellow into a more general warmth, she raised it to her mouth again.

After her third tot, she found she could say, 'Thank you, Emma, the brandy is most helpful.'

'I always keep some with me when I am travelling, just in case,' Emma lied. Hedges had pressed the flask into her hand as they were leaving.

As Victoria felt the warm tide course through her body, the initial misery began to recede, to be replaced by an over-whelming surge of fatigue. Within a minute she was asleep, her head falling onto Emma's shoulder.

To Emma's relief, Victoria slept all the way back to the Palace. When the carriage pulled in through the Marble Arch, Emma saw Lehzen standing by the door, her face taut with worry. As the carriage stopped, Victoria woke up with a start. With a pang, Emma saw the young Queen's face crumple as she remembered what had happened to her. She signalled to Lehzen to come and help. Before Victoria had the chance to speak, Emma said, 'The Queen is most fatigued from her journey. She needs to go straight to bed. With some negus perhaps.'

As Victoria climbed down from the carriage, she almost threw herself into Lehzen's arms. Emma saw the governess's face, the sympathy but also the tiny gleam of triumph.

Chapter Six

$\mathscr{L}$ EOPOLD MADE IT HIS BUSINESS TO BE INFORMED OF everything that went on in the Palace, so news of Victoria's excursion to Brocket Hall reached him before dinner from his valet, who had conjured it from Brodie the hall boy. Leopold, therefore, was not surprised and indeed rather relieved when his niece did not appear that evening. It was pleasant to have a meal where he could finish every course in peace, and he felt that Victoria's decision to stay in her room suggested that her mission, whatever it was, had not been successful.

The next morning, he found his sister walking in the gardens. She looked worried. 'Do you know where Victoria went yesterday? No one will tell me, and now she is in her room refusing to see anybody.'

Leopold looked at his sister. He decided not to tell her about Brocket Hall. If the visit had not been a successful one for Victoria, then the Duchess would no doubt say something tactless, and Leopold did not want the rift between mother and daughter to widen any further.

'Why don't we go and see her together? I hardly think she will refuse to see both of us. It is important, I feel, that we should talk to her about Albert. It is time that he came to England, I think.'

'Dear Albert, such a good boy. He reminds me so much of you at that age.'

Leopold smiled. 'Yes, I believe that Albert has turned out very well. He is a true Coburg.'

They found Victoria lying down on a chaise longue in her sitting room, clutching Dash like a hot water bottle. Lehzen tried to stop them coming in, but the Duchess just pushed past her, with Leopold in her wake. 'Where did you go yesterday, Drina? No one could tell me where you were. I was so worried, I thought something had happened to you.'

Victoria did not look up at them. When she spoke her voice was flat and expressionless. 'It doesn't matter, Mama.'

Leopold walked around the chaise longue to face her. He looked at her swollen eyes and said gently, 'Wherever you went, it seems it did not make you happy.'

Victoria turned her face away. Leopold continued smoothly, 'I wonder if this is a good time to talk about the visit of your Coburg cousins.'

Victoria said nothing, but Dash gave a yelp, as if he were being squeezed too tightly

'No? In that case, I think I shall attend to my preparations for the Duchess of Richmond's ball. I am rather pleased by my costume. Please don't ask me what I am wearing; I want it to be a delicious surprise.'

Dash, who by now had come to associate Leopold with cruel and unusual treatment at the hands of his mistress, began to bark at the King of the Belgians, and Leopold decided to make his escape. He had a letter to write that must be sent at once.

The Duchess came round to kneel in front of Victoria and

put her hand to the tearstained cheek. 'Dearest Drina, why are you so melancholy? I think it is because you are alone. Please invite dear Albert to visit; he would be such a good companion for you.'

Victoria's lower lip began to tremble, but biting it hard, she picked up a pillow and threw it across the room, where it knocked over a small harp in the corner of the room, causing it to fall to the ground with a boom of tingling strings.

Victoria looked savagely at her mother. 'I don't want a stupid boy like Albert, Mama! Or anyone else.' She got up and went into her bedroom, slamming the door behind her.

Her mother hovered, wondering if she should knock on the door and ask to come in, but then she saw Lehzen watching her and decided that she did not want to humiliate herself in front of the governess.

'Drina is not herself today, Baroness. She would be so much happier if she had a husband, I think, and children to love.'

Lehzen said, 'I am sure you are right, Ma'am, but of course you remember that I am not an expert in these matters.'

When the Duchess had left, Lehzen tapped gently on the bedroom door. 'You can come out now, Majesty; they have all gone.'

There was no answer from behind the door. Only when Dash came back from chasing Leopold and started to whine and scratch to be let in was the door opened, but only the dog was admitted.

Nevertheless, Lehzen continued to stand by the door. It felt like the only action she could take that would protect her mistress. That feeling was confirmed when a few minutes later she saw Conroy walking down the corridor towards her.

When he saw her he gave her his most opaque smile. 'Ah

Baroness, are you standing guard? In case your charge disappears again? I hear she went to Brocket Hall without an escort, but of course you knew that.'

Lehzen was not quick enough to disguise her surprise that Conroy should be so well informed. Victoria had not told her that she had been to Brocket Hall, but she had had her suspicions. She was surprised, though, that Conroy knew. She could only assume he had paid one of the servants.

'I am no longer the Queen's governess, Sir John.'

Conroy nodded. 'Or her confidante, it seems. We are but the playthings of princes, Baroness – to be discarded at their pleasure.'

There was a note of something approaching melancholy in his voice that made Lehzen turn and look at him. 'You shouldn't worry, Sir John. I do not think the Duchess will be discarding you.'

Sir John shook his head. 'I had such hopes of bringing some rigour to the monarchy. But instead "Queen Victoria"' – his voice dripped with disdain – 'has been allowed to squander the goodwill of the country in a series of squalid episodes. And chasing after Melbourne all the way to Brocket Hall is yet another embarrassing blunder. '

The Baroness turned on Conroy. 'You have no right to speak about the Queen in such a way!'

'But why not? Like you I have been watching over her since she was a little girl. I want her to be a great Queen, not an embarrassment to her country.' He looked at the door and sighed.

'The only hope now is that she marries a man who can control her.' And with that Conroy walked off, without waiting for Lehzen's reply.

Conroy had been seriously perturbed by the news that the Queen had visited Brocket Hall. He could only guess as to why she would abandon protocol and decorum to visit her Prime Minister incognito at his country house. Although he had observed her growing infatuation with Melbourne with dismay, it had never occurred to him that she might consider him as a potential husband. Surely even a nineteen-year-old Queen could not be so foolish as to imagine that she could marry a man in his fifties, who was a confirmed *roué* to boot? Not to mention that he was her Prime Minister and her subject.

There could be no more unsuitable husband in Europe, a fact that was obvious to everybody, except perhaps to the Queen herself. What Victoria needed was to marry a prince like Albert of Saxe-Coburg-Gotha. The prince was a serious young man who would listen to advice from his aunt, the Duchess, and, he thought, from his aunt's advisor. Thanks to Melbourne, it was too late to influence Victoria directly, but Conroy saw a glimmer of hope in the compliant form of Prince Albert.

First, however, she must be persuaded to marry him. That was Leopold's object in coming here, of course, but so far all he seemed to have achieved was to drive Victoria into the arms of Lord Melbourne.

Conroy wondered how the Prime Minister had responded to the visit from the Queen. There were some men who would not have hesitated to take advantage of the situation, but much as he disliked Melbourne, Conroy did not believe him to be one of them. Conroy would have liked nothing better than to be able to look down on Melbourne, but his behaviour over the Bedchamber Crisis had shown that in extremis, he would always put his country before his personal inclination.

Still, if Victoria had proposed and he had refused, his position now would be most awkward. Indeed, the only thing to relieve the embarrassment would be for the Whig government to fall or, more likely, the Queen to marry. Conroy smiled to himself. If Melbourne were to decide that it was in the Queen's best interests to marry, then a wedding seemed quite likely.

The question was which of the various candidates for the Queen's hand would Melbourne favour? He would not support the Russian Grand Duke, as the prospect of a marriage between two Sovereigns would not appeal to his political sensibilities. It would not always suit Russia and Great Britain to be allies, and they could hardly be anything else if their monarchs were husband and wife. It was likely that Melbourne would favour an English match, but the opportunities were limited to her first cousins: Cumberland's blind son and Prince George of Cambridge. The blindness meant that Cumberland's son was not suitable, an opinion clearly shared by his own father, whose patronage of Prince George had not gone unnoticed by Conroy. But George was such a dull boy, and moreover had been heard in the clubs moaning about how he didn't want to marry the royal dwarf. Conroy wondered if Melbourne had heard those rumours, and whether it might be wise to alert him to George's unsuitability as a bridegroom.

Given the less than cordial relations between himself and Melbourne, Conroy decided to see what happened at the ball that evening. George would be there and if there was any sign of Victoria favouring him, then Conroy would intervene. But he doubted it would be necessary. Victoria was a foolish girl, but not so foolish she could not see that Prince George was a first-class booby.

For the first time since Melbourne had come back as Prime Minister, Conroy began to feel hopeful again. Melbourne would come to see the advantages of the Queen marrying Albert, and once the wedding had taken place, then he, Conroy, would be uniquely placed to guide the bridegroom through the difficulties of his position. Of course Leopold had great sway over Prince Albert, but he would have to return to Belgium eventually. There was so much to do, and there might yet be a way in which to do it.

He found the Duchess in her apartments trying on her costume for the ball. She was dressed as a character from the *Commedia dell'arte*, with a black domino, a tricorne hat, and a gold mask that covered most of her face. When she saw him she lowered the mask and smiled with delight. 'What do you think of my costume?'

'I think it is splendid apart from the mask. It is a shame to cover a face as charming as yours.'

The Duchess giggled happily. 'You are being foolish, Sir John. No one wants to look at me.'

'Forgive me, but you are mistaken about that. I, for one, want to look at you, very much.'

The Duchess stretched her neck with pleasure at the compliment, like a cat. 'You are being absurd, Sir John, but I can't say that it isn't nice to be noticed.'

'How could anyone possibly do otherwise?'

The Duchess tossed her head. 'My daughter hardly knows I exist.'

Conroy took her hand and looked into her eyes. 'That will change when Victoria marries Albert. He will make her understand how fortunate she is to have such a mother.'

'But she says she will never marry Albert, or anyone else.'

'Young girls often say things they do not mean.'

'Perhaps. But she has such a *tendresse* for her Lord Melbourne,

I think it will be hard for her to feel affection for someone else.'

'Young girls have been known to change their minds, Ma'am.'

'I hope so.'

'So do I. My greatest desire is for you to take your rightful place as the Queen Mother.'

The Duchess sighed. 'Oh, Sir John, what would I do without you?'

Skerrett picked up the long red wig and settled it on Victoria's head.

'What do you think, Ma'am?'

Victoria looked up and regarded herself in the mirror. The red hair did not altogether suit her, but what did that matter now? She had decided some time ago to go to the Duchess of Richmond's ball as Queen Elizabeth, but now, she thought, there was a melancholy prescience in her choice. It looked as though she too would be a virgin queen, unable to find a man she cared about enough to marry, who also returned her affections.

'I think it looks very suitable.'

She did not want to go to the ball at all. She had been writing a note to the Duchess to say that she was unwell, when Lehzen had told her that the Grand Duke was going, which made her think that to cry off might cause a diplomatic incident. Besides, the Grand Duke was a very good dancer. Not as good as Melbourne, of course, but she would never dance with him again.

Skerrett pinned the wig into place, then held out the dress

with the heavy farthingale that was so stiff it could stand up
on its own. Victoria climbed into it, and the dresser began to
fasten the hooks at the back. When it was done, Victoria was
surprised by the weight of her costume. She realised that there
was something rather military about the stiff, jewel-encrusted
bodice and the heft of the skirt. It was more like a suit of
armour than a ball dress, and the thought gave her comfort.

Skerrett handed her a long pearl necklace with a ruby
pendant, which clanked against the jewelled bodice like a sabre.
For a brief moment Victoria thought how splendid it would
be to carry a weapon: to know that one could settle things not
with words but with deeds. She remembered Elizabeth's speech
at Tilbury, the one where she talked about having the body of
a feeble woman but the heart and mind of a king. She imagined
herself saying those words sitting on a white palfrey in front
of her troops.

The door opened, and a footman came in, carrying a corsage
of orchids on a silver tray. 'With Lord Melbourne's compliments, Your Majesty.'

Victoria looked at the waxy white flowers in disbelief. Lord
M was sending her flowers after what had passed between
them?

'Would you like me to pin them on for you, Ma'am?'

Victoria shook her head. 'No. I don't think I shall wear
flowers tonight. They do not suit my costume.'

'In that case, Ma'am, I shall run along and fetch the crown.'

Victoria stood alone looking at herself in the mirror. She
now had to entertain the possibility that Melbourne would be
there tonight. She had assumed that he would keep away, but
the flowers suggested otherwise. How could she face him? But
perhaps it would be better to see him in a crowd of people,

where they would not have to talk to each other, than to face him for the first time alone over the red boxes.

On her dressing table was the miniature of Elizabeth that Lehzen had given her. Victoria picked it up and compressed her mouth into the same hard line as the woman in the portrait. She was so immersed in her impersonation that she did not notice Emma Portman walk in behind her.

'How splendid you look, Ma'am.'

Victoria turned around. Emma, dressed as Diana, Goddess of the Hunt, was carrying a bow and a quiver of gold-tipped arrows.

'Do you really think so?'

'Yes, Ma'am. Although perhaps a little stern.'

Victoria relaxed her face. 'I was trying to look like this portrait. She doesn't look very happy.'

'I think the painter did not catch her true expression. By all accounts she was a great wit.'

Emma saw the flowers lying on the table. 'What beautiful flowers. Oh, there is an orchid. Where did they come from?'

Victoria did not look at her as she replied, 'Brocket Hall.'

Emma gasped. 'But I thought William had closed the green houses after Caro . . . He must have opened them again for you.'

Victoria turned to look at Emma and said slowly, 'I do not think he would do anything for me.'

Emma shook her head. 'Do you know how hard it is to grow an orchid? You misjudge him, Ma'am.'

'Lord Melbourne cares only for the memory of his wife.'

There was a pause and then Emma said gently, 'Is that what he told you, Ma'am?'

Victoria nodded. She did not trust herself to speak.

Emma hesitated; she knew it might be more politic to let the Queen believe Melbourne's fiction, but when she saw the misery in the other woman's face she could not help herself. 'Then that is what he wants you to believe. But these flowers, Ma'am, well . . . I think they are not a sign of indifference.' She sighed.

Victoria turned away, and Emma slipped out of the room.

The orchids glistened in the candlelight. Victoria picked up the corsage and looked at the strange exotic blooms. Emma said that he had grown them specially for her. She found the pin underneath the spray and attached the corsage to her bodice.

Skerrett came in with the replica of Elizabeth's coronet. 'Are you ready, Ma'am? The carriage is waiting.'

Victoria took the coronet and placed it on top of her wig. 'Queen Elizabeth is ready.'

The ball at Syon House was to be the most magnificent of the season. The honey-coloured stone of the house was lit up by strings of Chinese lanterns that also punctuated the gardens leading down to the Thames. Strolling in the gardens were Roman centurions with classical goddesses, Madame de Pompadour with Louis XV, court jesters with Circassian slave girls, medieval knights with Titania, Queen of the Fairies. All kinds of monarchy – French, Roman, Egyptian – were represented, except of course English; as the Queen was expected, it would be *lèse-majesté* to come as one of her forebears.

Dressed as Circe, the sorceress who had beguiled Odysseus, the Duchess of Richmond stood at the top of the grand staircase that led into the ballroom to greet the guests. Her husband the Duke was dressed as a Beefeater; he had not wanted to wear fancy dress at all, but his wife had insisted, and this costume was English, at least.

Leopold had come as the Emperor Augustus, a costume which he felt reflected his status nicely. He only wished that a laurel wreath was still part of modern dress, as it set off his profile so well. His pleasure was only momentarily marred when he saw that the Duke of Cumberland had also come as the first Roman Emperor; but his frisson of displeasure soon turned to satisfaction when he saw how much better his legs looked in a toga. Cumberland's were scrawny affairs, and if a man was to show his legs at their age it was essential to sport a shapely calf. In Cumberland's wake came his wife, who was dressed as Lady Macbeth complete with dagger, and Prince George, who had come as a Knight of the Round Table.

Looking around for his sister, Leopold saw her on the other side of the room with Conroy. They had both come as characters from the Venetian *Commedia dell'arte*, and carried masks, hers gold, his black. Leopold sighed. It was unwise of his sister to declare her allegiance to Conroy quite so publicly, but both mother and daughter were regrettably prone, as the English put it, to wear their hearts on their sleeves.

The guests milled about in the ballroom, spilling out through the French doors to the gardens below. The orchestra played in the background, but the dancing could not start until the Queen arrived to open the ball. A large number of nymphs and goatherds hoped fervently that she would not be late.

There was a ripple of excitement at the Grand Duke's arrival. He and his attendants were dressed as Cossacks, in white shirts open at the neck, and voluminous trousers tucked into high red boots. Round their waists they wore heavily embroidered sashes, out of which the chased silver handles of their daggers poked. On their heads they wore Shapkas, or Astrakhan caps. As the band of Cossacks swaggered through the room, there was excitement among the nymphs and some feeling of unfair play among the jesters and harlequins. Fancy dress was acceptable on the premise that everyone looked faintly ridiculous, whereas the Russian costumes only enhanced their native glamour. Prince George of Cambridge, who as Sir Lancelot felt he had chosen a costume that was just about acceptable for a Guards officer, now regretted his knitted chain mail and uncomfortable breast plate, and cast covetous glances at the red boots of the Cossacks. As the Grand Duke and his entourage swept past, he made a barely adequate bow, but found that the chain mail caught in his neck hair, and he spent an uncomfortable moment trying to lift his head. Cumberland, who was standing behind him, gave him a poke between the shoulder blades that was extremely painful, and snarled in his ear, 'This is a great opportunity to charm your cousin. In my younger days I always found that young ladies were always at their most receptive when dancing. Carpe diem, George. Carpe diem. You must be as attentive as possible.'

George tried to put the thought of the young Cumberland being attentive to the ladies out of his mind, and muttered, 'I will stick to her like a bloody limpet, Uncle, but it's all up to her. What can I do, she's the Queen and has to make all the running. I can't make up to her as I would to a normal woman.' As he said this, his eyes strayed to a nubile-looking nymph who he thought was smiling at him across the dance floor.

Cumberland said sharply, 'Nonsense! Faint heart never won fair lady, boy. She is a nineteen-year-old girl, and you are Sir Galahad.'

George looked at his uncle, who irritatingly had the advantage of height over him, and said, 'Sir Lancelot, actually.'

Cumberland shrugged. 'I don't care who you are as long as you make eyes at her and not at that blasted nymph!'

The champagne and claret cup were flowing freely, which only exacerbated the feeling of restless anticipation: where was the Queen? A rumour went around that she was indisposed; someone's lady's maid had heard it from Lady Portman's coachman, and the tension in the air, especially among the nymphs, was palpable.

But then the room went silent and the stable clock could be heard chiming eleven. Victoria dressed as Gloriana appeared in the doorway with Emma Portman and Lehzen who had come as a Rhine maiden, behind her. The Duchess greeted her with a low curtsey, her diaphanous Circe costume revealing a scandalous amount of thigh. The Duke almost dropped his staff in surprise; he had not seen so much of his wife's leg in years.

'Welcome to Syon House, Your Majesty,' said the Duchess, who was too overwhelmed by the presence of royalty at her ball to realise that her legs were being revealed to her guests. Victoria, who had noticed, took pity on her.

'I am very glad to be here. And Duchess, what a charming costume. May I feel the material – is it silk?' Leaning across to stroke the pleated silk she deftly arranged the folds of the skirt so that the Duchess's legs were covered.

'I had it woven in Venice, Ma'am.'

'It drapes so beautifully.'

The Duchess smiled with pleasure and hoped that her arch-rival Lady Tavistock had seen the exchange; she was looking forward to recounting the conversation later. Emma Portman smiled at Lehzen. It was reassuring to see that their charge was capable of behaving with such tact, a quality that in Emma's opinion could not be overrated.

Before Victoria could take a step on the staircase that led down to the ballroom, Leopold was at her side. As he was in his opinion the only other reigning monarch present, the Grand Duke being merely the heir to the throne, he wanted to assert his right to lead her into the ball before Cumberland, who as King of Hanover might think that he was entitled to the same privilege. He got there just in time, and gave the Queen's paternal uncle a little glance of triumph as he took Victoria's hand to lead her into the dance.

'You look very splendid, Victoria. I believe you are dressed as one of your regal predecessors.'

'Elizabeth Tudor, the Virgin Queen.'

Leopold winced slightly at Victoria's emphasis, but she continued looking up at him with chilly blue eyes.

'I think I have a lot to learn from Elizabeth. She did not allow herself to be controlled by anyone.'

'Indeed. But I think I prefer you as Queen Victoria, my dear niece.'

They continued to dance in silence, and then Leopold noticed the flowers pinned to Victoria's bodice.

'Such exotic blooms. I have not seen such a flower before.'

'They are called orchids, Uncle. They come from the East, and are extremely difficult to grow.'

Leopold looked at the flowers and then at his niece's face, hearing something in her tone that troubled him. 'But where did your orchids come from, Victoria? I do not think they came from the Orient.'

'No, these orchids were grown in the glasshouses at Brocket

Hall.' Victoria looked around her uncle's shoulder as if she was searching for someone.

Leopold said nothing; he knew who his niece was looking for, but reassured himself that the letter he had sent that morning to Coburg would soon address that situation.

As the music came to a close, Leopold escorted Victoria off the dance floor, where she was immediately approached by the Grand Duke on the left and Prince George on the right. George, who felt that Lancelot would have enjoyed drinking champagne, was a little unsteady on his feet, but nonetheless managed to get to the Queen's side first. 'Cousin Victoria, or should I say Cousin Elizabeth! May I claim this dance?' He attempted a low and what he hoped was a chivalric bow.

Before Victoria could answer, the Grand Duke was beside him kissing Victoria's outstretched hand. 'May a Cossack dance with the Queen?'

Victoria looked at her two suitors. She had no desire to dance with either of them, but the Grand Duke was definitely the lesser of two evils. George was clumsy at the best of times, and she thought that her feet would not survive the suit of armour.

She pretended to consult her dance card and then she smiled at the two men. 'I understand that Cossacks can be dangerous if thwarted, so I will dance with you first and then with you, Sir Galahad.'

George looked sulky. 'Actually I am Sir Lancelot.'

Victoria did not hear him as she was swept onto the floor by the Grand Duke, who was even better at dancing than she remembered. He was just sending her into a complicated spin when out of the corner of her eye she saw the figure whose arrival she had been waiting for with a mixture of excitement and dread. Melbourne had come as an Elizabethan courtier, the Earl of Leicester, dressed in a doublet and hose. He knew that she was going to the ball dressed as Gloriana, so his choice of costume made her heart tighten. She stumbled a little, and the Grand Duke put out his hand to steady her.

'Perhaps my Cossack ways are too rough for you.'

'Not at all. It was my fault; I was distracted.'

The Grand Duke smiled, showing his white teeth. 'Distracted? When you are dancing with a Cossack? I hope it was by your Sir Galahad; it would give me great pleasure to use my friend here to avenge my honour.' He patted the dagger at his belt.

Victoria laughed with exaggerated delight, knowing that Melbourne would be watching. 'Although it would give me great pleasure to see you challenge my Cousin George, I must remind you that in this country duelling is illegal.'

'That is too bad. I think your cousin would benefit from an encounter with a Cossack.'

'I am sure he would.'

Then the Grand Duke leant down and said in a gentler voice, 'If it is not your cousin who distracts you from me, then it must be someone else. I do not see anyone else here who is a suitable candidate for your hand.' Seeing the look on Victoria's face, he added, 'But perhaps he is an unsuitable candidate.'

Victoria blushed in confusion.

'I am sorry to embarrass you. But we cannot love where we please, you and I. Or at least we can love but we cannot marry.'

'I don't think I shall ever marry.'

'No? Perhaps you are right. Better to reign alone than to marry without love.' The Grand Duke looked down at her and sighed. 'But you, I think, have a choice whereas I do not.'

Victoria saw the shadow pass across his face.

'No one can force you to anything, surely?'

'You don't know my father, your esteemed godfather. He has very definite ideas about my marriage. My wishes are of no interest to him.' He gave Victoria a look intended to convey the possibility that she might have been one of his wishes.

Victoria smiled and was about to say something when the music stopped. Private conversation became impossible as Prince George, goaded into action by his uncle, came forward to claim his prize. 'I believe that this is my dance.'

Victoria glanced towards where Melbourne was talking to Emma Portman. Satisfied that he was looking at her, she took George's outstretched hand with a brilliant smile.

Emma saw the Queen's manoeuvre and said to Melbourne, 'I hope that Queen Elizabeth has saved a dance for the Earl of Leicester. They were devoted to each other, I believe.'

Melbourne looked at her sideways. 'You are very well informed, Emma, as always. But I do not think that the Queen has time to dance with an old man.'

'Oh, I think she might spare a dance for you, for the Earl of Leicester's sake.'

'I wonder.' Melbourne looked over to where Victoria was dancing with George, a bright fixed smile on her face.

'What beautiful flowers she is wearing, William. They must be from an admirer.'

'Yes Emma, I suppose they must.'

Victoria's feet were bruised by the end of her dance with George. He had stepped on them on every turn, and because his feet were encased in armour he seemed unaware of the fact. Their conversation was similarly clumsy.

'The ball is very splendid, is it not?' Victoria asked, thinking she must say something.

George frowned, and stepped on her foot again. 'Yes. Tolerably good show, I suppose, but if you really want to see something splendid, you should come to one of our regimental balls. They are quite something.'

'Really?'

'Yes. In fact it would be an uncommonly good show if you were to come to the next one. My regiment would be tickled pink to dance with the Queen.'

'I am not sure I can promise to dance with all of them,' said Victoria, wincing as he stepped on her foot again.

'Oh, you won't have to dance with the junior officers. They wouldn't expect it.'

Victoria raised an eyebrow. 'Really?' she said again.

George did not hear the warning note in her voice and carried on cheerfully about the splendours of his regiment, and how she would be a great asset to his standing among his fellow officers.

When the music stopped, Victoria saw to her horror that George was about to lead her into the next dance. 'You must excuse me, George. I think I shall sit this one out.'

'Then allow me to accompany you.'

'No indeed. Not when there are so many nymphs who are hoping to dance with Sir Galahad.'

'Actually, Victoria, I am Sir Lancelot.'

Victoria smiled and made her way towards the retiring room. Lehzen was at her side immediately.

'Are you quite well, Majesty?'

'Apart from my feet, which may never recover from my dance with Prince George.'

In the retiring room she looked at herself in the mirror and adjusted her wig. There was colour in her face after the dancing. She looked at the spray of flowers on her breast; the petals of the orchids looked cool and untouched. She wondered if she would speak to Melbourne tonight. She decided that if he approached her, she would not ignore him, but she would do nothing herself. She would not look at him, let alone smile. Things could not be as they had been.

As she came out of the retiring room, with Lehzen walking behind her, she saw Cumberland and George standing with their backs to her.

'Why aren't you with her, George? Every moment is precious. Don't you want to be the most powerful man in the country?' Cumberland was pointing his finger at George, but George, who had obviously spent the interval since their last dance refreshing himself with claret cup, swayed slightly and said, 'It's no use, Uncle. Even if I were Victoria's husband, I would never be the master in the house. I don't want to spend the rest of my life dancing attendance on a midget.'

Lehzen, who was also listening to this exchange, made an exclamation of disgust, which caused the two men to turn around. Victoria had the satisfaction of seeing their faces freeze as they registered her presence. She walked past without looking at them, and as she left them behind she heard Cumberland say in fury, 'Sir Lancelot indeed!'

Victoria saw Lord Alfred Paget on the other side of the ballroom making his way towards her, but before he reached her, she heard the voice she had been waiting for.

'Would you do me the honour, Ma'am?'

'I am afraid I have promised this dance to Lord Alfred.'

'I hope there is somewhere on your card for me.'

Victoria pretended to consult her card. Alfred immediately saw that he was *de trop* and made a little bow to Victoria. 'If you would excuse me, Ma'am, for this dance. I believe our hostess needs my assistance. I hope that Lord Melbourne will take my place.'

Melbourne looked at Victoria and she, not trusting herself to speak, simply nodded.

They danced in silence for a minute or two. Melbourne could feel Victoria trembling through the heavy carapace of her dress. Finally he spoke. 'I see that you have not been short of partners, Ma'am. I saw you dancing with Prince George. I hope he was suitably attentive.'

'I think he wants to dance with the Queen, but not necessarily with me,' said Victoria. 'I overheard him telling Uncle Cumberland that he didn't want to spend the rest of his life dancing attendance on a midget.'

'Then he is even more of a fool than I took him for,' said Melbourne angrily. He looked at Victoria more closely. 'You cannot be insulted by a man of such limited intelligence.'

'Perhaps he was just telling the truth as he saw it.'

Melbourne shook his head. 'He is an idiot, and you are to pay him no mind, Ma'am.'

'You think he is an idiot because he does not choose to be my husband?' Victoria said, looking up at Melbourne with challenge in her eyes.

Melbourne did not reply, but then as the dance caused them to move apart, he saw the flowers pinned to her dress. Victoria blushed at his glance.

'They are very beautiful. The flowers.'

Melbourne put his hand a little further round her waist. 'Then they are worthy of you.'

Victoria heard something in his voice which made her turn away in confusion. 'I didn't know if I would dance with you tonight.'

Melbourne looked at her intently. 'I hope that Queen Elizabeth would not desert her Leicester.'

Victoria raised an eyebrow. 'Leicester was her companion?'

Melbourne locked eyes with her. 'He was. He had a wife at first, but then she died.'

Victoria did not look away, although she found the conversation almost unbearable. What did he mean?

'But even though he was free, they never married?' she asked.

Melbourne paused as they turned the corner of the dance floor, and then in a lower voice he said, 'I think he and the Queen both knew that they were not in a position to marry. However strong their inclination.'

Victoria looked up at his melancholy green eyes. 'Was their inclination very strong?' she said softly.

Melbourne replied almost in a whisper, 'Yes. I believe it was.'

Victoria felt her heart flood with relief. He was telling her that he did care for her after all, but then she sighed because he was also telling her they could never marry. She would not let her guard down again. She lifted her chin. 'Elizabeth was a great queen. I mean to learn from her example.'

Melbourne nodded, satisfied that she understood. 'She had a long and glorious reign, Ma'am. Without interference.'

The music stopped, and Melbourne released Victoria with a bow.

'And now I must leave you . . . my Lord Leicester,' Victoria said. 'I have promised the Grand Duke that he could take me into supper.'

Melbourne smiled. 'I cannot stand in the way of a Cossack.'

After supper, Victoria danced a polka with Lord Alfred, who was as light on his feet as he was easy to talk to. They came off the floor laughing and breathless, and before she knew what she was doing Victoria found herself standing in front of a tall figure all in black apart from his white mask. He took the mask away from his face and Victoria saw that it was Conroy.

He stretched his mouth into a smile, and with a courtly flourish he held out his hand and said, 'May I engage you for the next dance, Ma'am?'

Victoria hesitated, but then she put her gloved fingertips in his.

It was not a waltz, for which Victoria was grateful, but a minuet, which meant they did not always have to be in close proximity. When they stood opposite each other at the head of the set, Conroy said, 'I am honoured that you would dance with me, Ma'am.'

Victoria said as they passed each other on the diagonal, 'I thought I should like to understand what my mother sees in you, Sir John.'

Conroy said evenly, 'I believe she values my company. She has long been a widow, and of course, as your mother, she was in no position to remarry.'

Victoria crossed to the other side of the set. 'I see.'

As they came together to go down the line of dancers, Conroy said, 'But for you it is different. The country needs an heir to the throne and you need a husband to check your behaviour.'

They were both facing straight ahead and Victoria said tightly, without looking round, 'Really, Sir John, and who would you recommend to keep me under control?'

They ducked under the outstretched arms of the couple in front of them, and as they straightened up, Conroy said, 'Your mother thinks that you would be happy with your Cousin Albert.'

'And what do you think, Sir John?' Victoria said as she turned away from him.

On her return Conroy answered with, 'I think he is a serious young man, who understands the duties of a modern monarch. He will not be swayed by sentiment or folly. And I am sure he will understand the value of experience.'

Victoria, who had been trying to understand Conroy's motives in recommending a match with Albert, began to discern his plan. 'I see. And I suppose you imagine he will need an advisor.'

Conroy gave a half smile, as he approached her to form an arch. 'Who knows, Ma'am? After all, I have some experience in these matters.'

Victoria put her arms down, and said quietly but distinctly, 'At present I have no intention of marrying, Sir John. But if I did, it would not be to anyone who would choose to be advised by you. You may have my mother in your pocket, but you will never, ever have me.'

To her surprise Conroy smiled. 'As you know, Ma'am, I have spent the last nineteen years serving your mother, but perhaps it is time now for me to return to Ireland. I have an estate there which has been much neglected.'

'That sounds like an excellent plan, Sir John.' She turned her back on him and walked away from the dance floor.

But Conroy was not to be dismissed so easily. 'In order to do that I should need some assurances. It would be altogether more comfortable if I were to return to the land of my birth garlanded with some acknowledgement of the faithful service I have rendered to the Crown.'

Victoria looked at him with distaste. 'Would the sort of garland you require involve a title, Sir John?'

'A barony would, I think, reflect the work I have done on behalf of your mother and yourself. But of course, such a title would have to be accompanied by a stipend that would allow me to maintain myself in a way that would not bring disgrace upon my status.'

Victoria nodded. Although it felt wrong to concede anything to Conroy, the thought of never having to see him again was worth any number of Irish peerages. Why, if she had known that his price was so low, she would have suggested this the day she became Queen.

'I am sure we can come to some arrangement, that is, if you can assure me that your retirement will be . . . permanent.'

Now it was Conroy's turn to nod, but he still had something to say. 'You know, Ma'am, I believe that my departure will be very difficult for the Duchess. I think that without me, she will be lonely. Perhaps if you were to pay her the attention she deserves . . .'

Victoria put up her hand to signal that she had heard quite enough. 'I know how to take care of my mother, Sir John.' She turned her back on him again and walked away into the supper room, scattering nymphs and shepherds as she went.

The Duchess, who had observed this scene from the other side of the ballroom, made her way towards Conroy. 'You were dancing with Drina! I could not believe my eyes, but now she is walking away from you. What is happening, dear Sir John? Is she making you angry? She doesn't know how much you are doing for her.'

Conroy looked down at the Duchess's anxious face and heard the eagerness to placate him in her voice. His departure would be very hard for her, he knew. And there might be times, he thought, when he would miss her, that way she had of looking up at him and fluttering her hands. Yes, he would miss her devotion, but even the sensation of being adored could not compensate for a life without power. Conroy would rather go home to Ireland, ennobled and rich, and become the great man there, than linger here watching the chances that should have been his squandered by that ignorant little chit. He knew now that things would never improve for him here. Even if she married Albert, she would stop him from exerting the kind of influence that could bring so much benefit to the monarchy. She was too stubborn ever to change her mind.

No, he would go back to Ireland and become a man of consequence in a place where those things still mattered. He wondered if he should tell the Duchess of his decision, but as he looked into her liquid blue eyes and felt the butterfly touch of her hand on his arm, he thought that perhaps he would wait. It might be better to be sure that Victoria would fulfill her promises before triggering a painful scene. Yes, he would wait. This ball was so very splendid it seemed foolish not to enjoy it; there would not be many such occasions in Ballymeena.

'There is nothing to worry about, Duchess. The Queen and I had a very useful conversation. I think it has cleared the air between us. And now I would like to ask the most handsome woman in the room if she would do me the very great honour of dancing with me.' He held out his hand to the Duchess, who took it with a smile that made even the rusty hinge of Conroy's heart creak.

Leopold, who had watched Conroy's exchange with Victoria with interest, was disappointed by the expression of surrender on his sister's face as she was steered around the room by Conroy. It was time that Conroy exercised his charms elsewhere. His gaze rested more happily on his niece, who was dancing with Alfred Paget. From what Leopold had seen of Lord Alfred, he did not think that his niece was in any danger of succumbing to the charms of this particular dancing partner. But where was Melbourne? Leopold spotted him leaning against a pillar, dressed as an Elizabethan courtier, a costume which, Leopold noted with some pique, showed his legs to advantage. Slowly, so that Melbourne should not recognise his intent and decide to move away, Leopold made a circuit of the dance floor until he found himself standing behind the Prime Minister.

'Good evening, Lord Melbourne.'

Melbourne turned and tried but did not altogether succeed in disguising his displeasure at being accosted by the King of the Belgians.

'Your Majesty.'

Leopold stepped a little closer and said, 'I believe my niece made an impromptu visit to Brocket Hall.'

Melbourne turned to him. 'You are very well informed, sir.'

Leopold smiled. 'I observed that it seemed to leave her in low spirits. Perhaps something in the climate there did not agree with her.'

Melbourne looked out over the dancers, and said in a colourless voice, 'I could not say, sir.'

'You should know, Lord Melbourne, that I wrote to my nephews Albert and Ernst this morning. They will be here within a week.'

This made Melbourne turn round, finally shaken out of his weary neutrality. 'Without the Queen's permission?'

Leopold shrugged. 'They are her cousins. I do not think that they need an official invitation. And in my opinion the sooner they come, the better.' He put a hand to his head to adjust the laurel wreath. 'Because, as I am sure you know, Lord Melbourne, a young girl's head can be turned so easily.'

Chapter Seven

$\mathcal{V}$ICTORIA WOKE UP NEXT MORNING WITH A FEELING that she could not quite identify. Normally after a ball she would lie in bed until lunch time, but today she almost jumped out of bed. There were so many things to be done. As she walked around her bedroom with Dash at her heels she realised that the cloud that had settled over her since her visit to Brocket Hall had gone. The events of last night had given her a new sense of hope. The conversation with Lord M about Elizabeth and the Earl of Leicester had made her feel that there was some room for her in his heart whatever he might say about his dead wife. Perhaps they could not marry; and, Victoria acknowledged to herself for the first time, perhaps that was not exactly what she wanted. A marriage would be too difficult politically and, in a way that she could not quite explain to herself, too awkward. It was enough, she thought, to know that he cared for her in the way that she cared for him.

He had said that he would be her 'companion', just as Leicester had been to Elizabeth. That had been an arrangement that had suited Britain's only great queen till now, and Victoria saw no reason to do things differently. Leopold and her mother were always telling her that she needed to get married, but it seemed to her that she needed to do nothing of the sort. She would be another Elizabeth, answerable only to herself. She looked in the mirror as she said this and was satisfied with the face she saw there. Resolve was the feeling she had woken up with; today she would do what she wanted. Her first act would be to get rid of Conroy. Whatever she had to give him to make him leave would be worth it if it meant that she would never again be reminded of the misery of her early years in Kensington Palace. And once she had done that, she would tell Leopold that she had no intention of getting married, to Albert or anyone else, and suggest that it was time for him to return to Belgium. Victoria smiled at herself in the mirror.

She rang the bell, and after a minute her dressers came in. Skerrett, the younger one, looked a little flustered. 'I am sorry, Ma'am, that we were not here earlier. To be honest, we did not think you would be up so early after such a late night.'

'No matter. I think I shall wear the green stripe today.'

'Yes, Ma'am.' Skerrett went to fetch the dress as Jenkins brought in the washing things.

When Jenkins put the bowl down in front of her, Victoria noticed that the dresser's eyes were red. She looked as though she had been crying. Jenkins started to pour the hot water over Victoria's hands into the basin, but suddenly the air was filled by a crack of rifle fire and Jenkins dropped the pitcher with a shriek.

Victoria, a little alarmed by the noise and now quite wet, went over to the window to see what had happened, and saw a guardsman being reprimanded by his superior officer in the Palace courtyard.

'Oh, it is just a soldier who has let off his rifle by mistake. Nothing to worry about.' She turned round and saw Jenkins crouched on the floor sobbing, her head in her hands, and

Skerrett with her arm around her trying to comfort her. Victoria looked at her in surprise; Jenkins was hardly the sort of woman she expected to have hysterics at the sound of gunfire.

'Mrs Jenkins, I believe you are indisposed. You have my permission to retire.'

Skerrett cajoled the still sobbing Jenkins out of the room and returned a few minutes later. In answer to Victoria's look of enquiry she said, 'You must excuse her, Ma'am. She is out of sorts on account of the execution of the Newport Chartists, Ma'am. They say they are to die a traitor's death. Mrs Jenkins is from those parts, and I believe she feels it most strongly.'

Victoria looked at the girl in front of her. 'Are there many people who feel as Mrs Jenkins does? About the Newport Chartists?'

Skerrett looked at the floor and hesitated before replying. Then she raised her head and said, 'The punishment for treason, Ma'am, is to be hanged by the neck until you are almost dead and then to be cut open while you are still alive. It's not that Mrs Jenkins supports the Chartists, Ma'am, but she thinks whatever they did, they don't deserve to die like that.' Skerrett twisted her hands together, and continued haltingly, 'Forgive me, Ma'am, but I agree with her. And I don't think I am the only one to do so.'

Victoria waved a hand at her. 'That's all right, Skerrett, I asked you for your opinion, and you gave it me. And you are right, it is a terrible way to die.'

As she stood in her sitting room waiting for Melbourne to arrive for their audience, Victoria thought about the exchange with Skerrett. There was a picture at Windsor Castle of a heretic being disembowelled under the reign of Mary – or was it Elizabeth? – that she used to see on her rare visits to her uncle, King William, when she was a little girl. She had passed it many times without really looking until one day it occurred to her that the string of pale lumpy things were not sausages, as she idly supposed, but the poor martyr's intestines. She remembered feeling pleased that she lived in a less barbaric time.

Now it appeared that her assumption had been wrong. Those men from Newport, who even Lord Melbourne said had been motivated more by hunger than by wickedness, were to meet their end in this particularly horrible way. She felt something pricking at her eyelids, and a sob ran through her. It was not right that anyone should die so horribly. And all the emotion that had roiled about her for the last few days swirled and fixed on the fate of the Welshmen facing their awful death. She felt quite faint with pity and had to hold on to the window-sill for support.

She remembered what Flora Hastings had said to her that awful night as she lay dying: 'To be a Queen you must be more than a little girl with a crown. Your subjects are not dolls to be played with.' At the time Victoria had tried to erase those words from her memory, but now they seemed to have a new significance. Her subjects were her responsibility; she could not accept their cheers and not also listen to their cries of pain. She must do something.

It was in this state that Melbourne found her a few minutes later: white and trembling. He saw it at once and rushed towards her, forgetting in his anxiety to bow.

'What is it, Ma'am? Are you unwell?'

Victoria shook her head, and then said, with an effort, 'When are the Newport Chartists to be executed?'

Melbourne tried to conceal his surprise; he could think of many reasons for Victoria's tears, but the fate of the Chartists was not one of them.

'Next Friday, Ma'am.'

Victoria took a deep breath. 'And they are to be hanged, drawn, and quartered?'

'That is the punishment for treason, Ma'am.' But, seeing her face, Melbourne added, 'I believe there are bishops organising a petition for clemency.'

Victoria lifted her head with a quick, decisive motion. 'Then I should like to sign it!' She took a step towards him. 'Such a punishment is not civilised.'

Melbourne said quietly, 'I fear you don't understand the severity of the crime, Ma'am.'

'Indeed I do,' she retorted, the colour coming to her face in a way that Melbourne could not help but admire. 'But I think you do not understand the severity of the punishment. Such things may have been necessary in the reign of Elizabeth– ' she paused and gathered herself into her most regal attitude, 'but I should like *my* reign to be a merciful one.'

Melbourne thought there was something magnificent about her; he had never seen Victoria so passionate about something that did not directly concern herself. She was wrong, of course; these Chartists must be treated with the utmost and most public severity to deter all those other hungry people who believed that they could fill their bellies with high ideals and splendid slogans, but he could not help but admire her spirit. So he smiled a little as he said, 'Then you must know, Ma'am, that as Queen, you may commute their sentences.'

She hesitated before replying, and Melbourne saw that she needed some clarification.

'Forgive me, Ma'am, I did not make myself clear. The Crown has the right to commute a sentence, to make it less severe. So you might decide that instead of being executed as traitors, these men should be transported to Australia to a penal colony, which some might regard as a lesser punishment.' He could not resist making that final sally, but Victoria did not smile.

Instead she said with great firmness, 'Then I would like to exercise my right. I want their sentences to be commuted –' Victoria rolled this new and pleasing word around in her mouth – 'from execution to transportation.'

'You are sure, Ma'am?' Melbourne said in a token protest, although he already knew the answer.

'Quite sure.' And for the first time since the interview had begun, Victoria smiled.

Melbourne gestured towards the boxes. 'Shall we attend to these, Ma'am?'

Victoria gave a peremptory little shake of her head. 'No. I think those men in prison should know their fate as soon as possible. To lie in a cell and imagine that awful death,' she shuddered, 'I can think of nothing worse.'

'Your compassion does you credit, Ma'am, although I can't help feeling that these men deserve their torment. But if you require me to put your wishes into action immediately, I will attend to it at once.' He gave a formal nod of the head to signify that he was acting on orders, not by inclination.

'Before you go, there is one more thing I should like you to do for me. Sir John Conroy has asked me to grant him an Irish title with a pension, and I am minded to give it to him.'

'Really, Ma'am?'

'Yes. He thinks that it is time for him to retire to his estate in Ireland.'

Melbourne looked at her with surprise and respect. Could she really have engineered a way of getting rid of Conroy?

'I think an Irish title with a pension of, say, £1000 a year, would be a very suitable reward for all Sir John's years of service to the Crown,' Melbourne said.

Victoria nodded. 'My thoughts exactly, although I think that it might be safer to make it £2000. I should not want him to run out of money and feel the need to return to court.'

'No, indeed. That would never do.'

Victoria leant forward and smiled. 'I want Sir John Conroy's "transportation" to be permanent.'

When Melbourne had left, Victoria called to Dash and went out into the gardens. As she was walking down the steps, Lehzen caught up with her and held out a shawl. 'It is cold today, Majesty; you should not go out without this. If you wait one moment, I will get my bonnet and accompany you.'

'No, thank you, Lehzen, I prefer to walk alone this morning. I wish to speak to my mother.'

Lehzen nodded reluctantly. 'As you wish, Majesty. I believe I saw the Duchess walking with Sir John Conroy towards the lake about ten minutes ago.'

Victoria smiled. 'Thank you, Lehzen,' and she took the shawl. 'Come on, Dash!' She ran down the path to the lake, the dog at her heels.

She saw her mother and Conroy standing by the summer house on the other side of the lake. Their heads were close together, the Duchess's face tilted towards Conroy like a sunflower facing the sun. The sight of her mother's abjection brought Victoria's resolve to a head, and she almost charged round the path to where they were standing, coming up on them from behind, so that they did not see her coming. 'Good morning, Mama.' The Duchess and Sir John immediately moved apart, startled by her sudden appearance.

Victoria acknowledged Conroy with the briefest nod. 'How fortunate to find you here with Mama, Sir John.'

The Duchess was looking at her daughter with bewildered attention. 'You are looking very well, Victoria.'

'Yes, Mama, I feel well.' She paused, then said, 'I am glad to find you together because I wanted to tell you in person, Sir John, that I have decided to grant your request.'

The Duchess moved her head with agonised slowness from Victoria to Conroy. 'What request?'

A muscle at the corner of Conroy's eye began to twitch, but before he could reply Victoria said with barely concealed glee, 'Didn't he tell you, Mama? I am going to give Sir John an Irish title and a pension of two thousand a year, so that he can retire to his estate in Ireland in comfort.'

The Duchess was very still, the blonde ringlets motionless. At last she said, gazing directly at Conroy, 'You would leave me, for . . .' she hesitated, and then with a cry that made Victoria wince, 'for some money?'

Conroy said nothing, but looked at the ground. Victoria turned to him. 'You have not changed your mind, I trust, Sir John?'

Conroy remained stock still before shaking his head slowly, as if it were made of stone.

'Good. I am glad that is settled.'

Victoria was about to walk away when she saw her mother's stricken face and stopped. 'I have decided to raise your allowance, Mama. It is time you had some new clothes. You should be dressed as befits your status as the Queen Mother.'

The Duchess did not show any sign of having heard her; she was still staring at Conroy as if trying to commit every detail of his face to memory. Victoria, slightly in awe of her own daring, began to move away. 'Come on, Dash.'

When the Queen and her lapdog were out of sight, Conroy spoke, his gaze still fixed upon the ground. 'You must understand that I had no choice. There is nothing for me here.'

The Duchess erupted out of her frozen immobility. 'Nothing? After nineteen years, you call me nothing?'

Conroy raised his head and tried to arrange his face into a smile. 'You know that if I go, she will be kinder to you.'

The Duchess shook her head in disbelief, crying out, 'Do you know how many times Drina asked me to dismiss you? It would have been so easy. But I would not do it. I told her that I could not do without you. But you can just walk away from me as if I do not exist.'

Conroy tried to take the Duchess's hand, but she pulled away from him in fury. This was even more painful than he had imagined. He had expected to be able to break the news to her in his own way, but Victoria, it seemed, was determined to make this as brutal as possible. There were tears in the Duchess's eyes, and he saw the lines that her unhappiness had etched around her eyes and mouth. For a moment he saw the old woman that she would be before very long.

'Believe me, I have no desire to leave you. But your daughter will not be ruled, Ma'am, and I must use my talents somewhere.'

In a gesture that he knew was the only correct response to her pain and his treachery, he slowly and painfully lowered himself to his knees before her. Taking her cold hand in his, he pressed it to his lips, and said in a hoarse cry, 'Please forgive me!'

Rising to his feet, he walked away from her, around the lake and back to the Palace. He did not look round, but he felt the Duchess's gaze on his back with every step.

Chapter Eight

THE GRAND DUKE WAS WAITING FOR VICTORIA AT the Roehampton Gate of Richmond Park. He had sent a note that morning asking if they could ride together somewhere where they could really gallop. 'Your Rotten Row is a place to admire ladies in their fine habits, but today I am not interested in fashion.'

After her meeting with her mother and Conroy, Victoria knew exactly what the Russian meant. She too wanted to gallop so fast that the world receded and nothing mattered except the narrow strip of ground in front of her horse's head. So she suggested Richmond Park, with its ancient trees and herds of deer, where they could let their horses go without the fear of bumping into a carriage or knocking over a nursemaid with her charge.

As the groom helped her mount Monarch, she saw that the Grand Duke's face was set, his mouth harder than she had ever seen it. He clearly was in no mood for conversation, so taking up the reins she said, 'Once round the park?'

The Grand Duke nodded and Victoria dug her heels into Monarch's side. Delighted to be given her head, the horse set off at a clip, the Grand Duke at her heels. They raced around the park, scattering the deer and sending the pheasants nesting in the woods squawking into the air, ducking as they rode under the branches of great oaks and yelping with delight as they careened down the hill leading to the two ponds that bisected the park.

Laughing and breathless, they pulled up their horses in mutual agreement. The Grand Duke jumped off his mount in an easy movement, and before her groom could help her, he was lifting Victoria to the ground. She noticed that the rigidity in his face had gone.

'Thank you for bringing me here, Victoria. I was needing to ride like this very much.'

Victoria smiled. 'My predecessor Elizabeth used to hunt deer in this park.'

'The Queen who never married.'

'But whose reign was long and glorious.'

'I am sure. A great Queen is the superior of any man," and his face was lit up by his smile. Then he turned to his equerry, who was loitering at a respectful distance, and snapped his fingers. The man produced a small package and put it into the Grand Duke's outstretched hand.

'I have something for you, Victoria. A small token of our friendship.'

It was a snuff box enamelled in blue with gold edging. On the lid of the box the letters V and A in diamonds were entwined to form a graceful monogram, almost symmetrical in its peaks and troughs.

Victoria gasped. 'It is so beautiful. And this monogram?' She looked up at him.

The Grand Duke nodded. 'V and A, for Victoria and Alexander. It is not correct perhaps, but I hope you will forgive me.' He put the box in her hand and closed her fingers around it with his own.

'V and A. The letters fit together very well, do they not?'

The Grand Duke nodded and then, releasing her hand, he said, 'The Tsar, my father, has ordered me to return to Petersburg.'

'Is he ill?' asked Victoria.

The Grand Duke shook his head. 'He is in perfect health, but fancies he will die at any moment, so he has decided that I must marry.' He looked at Victoria and sighed.

'My father has chosen a Danish princess. I forget her name. He says that she is very fond of herring.' He gave a shrug and a half smile.

Victoria was touched by his sigh. Although they both knew that any alliance between them could only be a diplomatic one, he was acting the part of a disappointed lover. And while she knew that it was almost certainly an act, she liked him for the conceit.

She put her head on one side and smiled. 'I am sure she will be charming. Fishy, perhaps, but charming.'

The Grand Duke took her hand, and as he looked into her eyes, she echoed the words he had said to her at the ball. 'We cannot marry where we please, you and I,' and this time she sighed too. She heard a rook cawing mournfully behind her and remembered Melbourne holding her hand at Brocket Hall.

Alexander gave her a melancholy look through his long lashes. He thought, of course, that she was thinking of him.

'If things were different . . .'

He leant towards her, clearly hoping for a valedictory kiss, but Victoria evaded him and said brightly, 'I am sure that you and the herring eater will be very happy.'

Alexander threw his arms wide. 'I will do my duty, marry her, have many sons, and one day I will choose their brides.'

Victoria laughed. 'I hope you choose wisely.'

'Perhaps you will have a daughter who will come and rule Russia with my son.'

'You forget that I have decided not to marry.'

The Grand Duke shook his head. 'No, I do not forget, but I do not believe that a woman such as you would live without a husband. I am sorry he will not be a Russian one.' He raised Victoria's hand to his lips and kissed it.

The Duchess did not come down to dinner that evening, and when Victoria sent Lehzen to enquire after her health, the Baroness was sent away without a message. Victoria felt a lump form in the pit of her stomach. She knew quite well that she should have gone to her mother's apartments herself, but had been unable to summon the courage. Much as Victoria loathed Conroy, she knew how much he meant to her mother. While she could never condone her mother's attachment, since that day at Brocket Hall, she thought she could perhaps understand that strength of feeling.

The next morning she asked Skerrett to show her what lace she had. Skerret brought out a cabinet with drawers that filled the air with the scent of cedar when they were opened. Victoria went through the delicate collars, and gossamer veils until she came to a shawl piece so finely embroidered that as she shook it out it glittered like hoar frost. She heard Skerrett gasp.

'It's beautiful, isn't it?'

'It's the most beautiful thing I have ever seen, Ma'am.'

Victoria put the shawl under her arm, and before her resolve could weaken set off towards the north wing.

She found her mother sitting on a sofa staring at nothing. She was dressed, as usual, in black, but her blonde ringlets hung limp and neglected. Seeing her mother's desolation, Victoria felt the knot in her stomach tighten.

As she sat down on the sofa beside her mother, the Duchess did not acknowledge her presence but maintained that terrible glassy stare. Victoria wondered if she had done the right thing in coming, but much as she wanted to leave, she knew that she must do something to put this right.

Leaning over, she placed the lace shawl in her mother's inert hands. The Duchess did not move. Victoria unfolded the shawl, and spread it out over her mother's lap.

'This is for you, Mama. The lace is made in a convent in Bruges. Look how delicate it is.' She held it up in front of her mother's frozen face and shook it so that it trembled like a cobweb in a breeze.

A minute passed, but to Victoria it felt like an hour, and then her mother turned her head at last. Fixing her daughter with that hollow stare she spoke in a low voice stripped of all emotion. 'You sent him away, Drina.'

Victoria let the lace drop onto her mother's lap. 'No, Mama,' she said softly, 'he wanted to go.' Taking her mother's hand, she continued, 'But I know you feel his loss and believe me, Mama, I understand.'

She looked down at her mother's hand and saw the gold wedding band beneath the swollen knuckle of the ring finger.

'How can you possibly understand? You are just a child; how can you know what a woman feels?' The Duchess's voice broke on the word 'woman' and her eyes, which had been dry, filled with tears.

Victoria felt the knot in the pit of her stomach unravel and the words came out before she could check them.

'No, Mama. You are wrong. I do know how hard it is to lose someone you care for.'

Her mother heard the note of despair in her daughter's voice and saw beyond her own misery. Looking into her daughter's pale blue eyes, the same colour as her own, she understood. And, checking her own tears, she put her hand to Victoria's flushed cheek and stroked it with infinite tenderness. 'No man would give you up, Drina, unless he knew that it was his duty.'

At this unexpected kindness, Victoria's resolve finally broke and she threw herself into her mother's arms in a storm of sobbing. 'Oh, Mama . . . I think I will never be happy.'

The Duchess wrapped her arms around her daughter's shaking body and held her tight. 'You are still young, *Liebes*. You will find a place to put your heart, I promise you.'

As Victoria's sobs began to subside into the occasional hiccup, the Duchess lifted her daughter's chin so that it faced her own. 'We have both lost something, Drina. But,' and her eyes were warm with love, 'today I have found something too.' Victoria looked at her in watery bewilderment. 'I have found your *Schockoladenseite*. Your chocolate side. And I thought I had lost it for ever.'

Victoria heard the plea for forgiveness in her mother's voice and laid her head on the Duchess's lap. As her mother's hand stroked her hair, she closed her eyes and inhaled the scent of lavender.

Leopold, who had come to the Duchess's apartments to tell her that Albert and Ernst were already on their way to England, saw this tableau from the door and tiptoed away. He knew, of course, that Conroy had been banished and was thankful for it, but he had worried that a permanent rift between mother and daughter might threaten Albert's chances with Victoria. The sight of his niece lying on her mother's lap like a modern Pietà was most encouraging, most encouraging indeed. If Victoria could be reconciled with her mother, then Albert would not be rejected as a suitor simply because he was a Coburg.

As for the Duchess, she would miss Conroy, but if she regained her daughter's affection then his loss might be a price worth paying, he supposed. And in time his sister would come to see that Conroy had only stayed by her side for the promise of power; once he saw that he was never going to be more than Comptroller of the Duchess of Kent's household, he had given her up. It was unfortunate that the Duchess could not find another man to amuse her, but the Queen's mother, like Caesar's wife, must be above reproach. He thought of his own *chère amie*, tucked away in a villa in St John's Wood, and thought how much better these things could be arranged if you were a man. As he walked down the long corridor back to his own apartments he caught a glimpse of himself in the mirror and was pleased to see that his toupee was sitting at precisely the correct angle.

Chapter Nine

O N THE JETTY AT OSTEND TWO YOUNG MEN WERE shivering in the brisk November wind. They were both tall and fair and there was a clear family resemblance in their wide foreheads and delicately formed lips, but while one had the broad back and swaggering movements of a soldier, the other though a fraction taller had none of his brother's careless freedom; he moved carefully as if calculating how much effort each step would cost him. He looked out over the choppy sea apprehensively and turned to his brother and said in heavily accented English, 'It looks as though the sea will be too rough for us to be sailing today.'

His brother clapped him on the shoulder. 'Nonsense, Albert, the packets to England sail in much worse conditions than these.' Then he looked more closely at his brother's white face and said, 'You will feel better when you are there, you know. What are those lines from Shakespeare that you are always quoting to me, "There is a tide in the affairs of men, which taken at the flood. . ."'

'Lead on to fortune.' Albert finished the quotation, as his brother knew he would. 'But Ernst, I do not know if this is the right destiny for me. Victoria is not serious. She only cares for dancing and ices. I doubt that we are suited.'

Ernst smiled. 'So she is a young girl who likes to enjoy herself. I think that is a good thing. The giddy ones are always the most fun. And besides, Victoria is charming, small, and . . .' he outlined a curvaceous sweep with his arms.

Albert looked at him. 'Perhaps you should marry her then, Ernst.'

'I don't think Uncle Leopold would like that at all.' Ernst pursed his lips in a tolerable imitation of the King of the Belgians. '"It is Albert's destiny to marry Victoria".'

'But suppose she does not think it is her destiny to marry me? She did not seem to care for me so much the last time we met.'

Ernst looked his brother up and down in a parody of appraisal, taking in Albert's dark blue eyes, his noble profile, the long legs in their red-topped boots.

'You have changed a great deal in the last three years, Albert. You don't notice them, but the girls in Coburg are looking at you now in a way that, if I didn't know you to be the most serious man in Christendom, would make me quite jealous. She may be a Queen, but she is also a young woman, and I think she will be quite happy when she sees you.'

'But I do not care to be exhibited for her approval like a waxwork, Ernst!'

'Oh, don't be so sensitive. Do you want to spend the rest of your life in Coburg watching me behave badly, or do you want to be the King of England?'

Albert shook his head. 'Even if I marry her, I would only be the Queen of England's husband.'

Ernst shrugged. 'Well, if you arrive with a face like that you won't be marrying anyone. Remember, Albert, women like to be charmed, not lectured. When you see her you must smile and pay her little compliments. There will be plenty of time to tell about the glories of Italian architecture and the wonders of Babylonian drainage when you are on your honeymoon.'

Albert shook his head again. 'But I cannot be someone I am not, Ernst. I cannot pretend.'

Ernst threw up his hands in mock despair. 'Then, my dear little brother, I suggest we go back to Coburg and you can marry Frau Muller, the mayor's widow, who has an excellent library and a well-stocked carp pond. Reading and fishing, what more could a man want? I know she likes you, and widows, well . . .'

Albert looked out over the grey sea. 'You find everything so easy, Ernst. But for me this is difficult.'

Ernst put a hand on his brother's shoulder and said in a different tone, 'My dear brother, you are a man of great worth. That is why Victoria will be lucky to have you as a husband. It cannot be easy to be so young and to have so much responsibility. She needs someone like you to help her..'

Albert looked at his brother and smiled for the first time. Ernst thought surely Victoria, however wilful she had become, would not be able to resist one of his brother's smiles. As rare as they were, Albert's smiles transformed his face with a child-like radiance that made the recipient feel as if the sun had come out. If only Albert could smile at Victoria, all would be well.

A huge swell broke over the jetty, and the spray landed on their faces. Albert wiped it off as he looked over the ferry boats bobbing precariously on the stormy sea. 'But first we must get there,' he said.

In Buckingham Palace Victoria was amusing herself, as she waited for Melbourne's morning visit, by copying one of the portraits of Elizabeth that hung in the Picture Gallery. Elizabeth looked a little younger in this painting than she did in the miniature that Lehzen had given her, younger and more vulnerable. If she were Elizabeth, Victoria thought, she would not have put this picture on display: it showed her not as Gloriana the painted Queen but as the woman beneath. Was it possible, she wondered, as she painted Elizabeth's russet curls, to be both? Could one be a monarch and a woman? None of the Queens who had come before her on the throne had been blessed with a family. Mary Tudor had married too late and had a pregnancy but no child. Elizabeth, of course, had not taken a husband, and the Stuart Queens – Mary and Anne – had both married, but neither had managed to produce a child that survived them. Mary Queen of Scots had married three times and had a child, but her reign could not have ended more disastrously. Victoria's knowledge of history was not exhaustive, but it seemed to her that only Isabella of Castile had managed to be a successful Queen and a wife and mother; and of course she had married the King next door. Even if Victoria had been tempted to encourage the advances of the Grand Duke, the idea of jointly ruling England and Russia was geographically impossible.

No, if she looked at the Queens of the past, only Elizabeth was truly admired, and she had reigned alone. Of course Charlotte, the dead cousin whose death had engendered her very existence, had been married to Uncle Leopold, but it was the marriage that had killed her. Marriage was a dangerous business.

Victoria started to paint in the pearls on Elizabeth's bodice.

She was putting off the ruff, which, with its intricate lace pattern, looked rather difficult to copy.

She heard a cough and, turning round, saw Melbourne standing behind her. 'I thought you would like to know that the Newport Chartists are on their way to Australia, Ma'am.'

'I am so glad, Lord M.'

Melbourne hovered over a chair behind her, and she gestured to him to sit. 'Although whether the wretched men will feel grateful when they get there is anyone's guess.'

'Their families will be pleased, I think,' said Victoria.

'Perhaps,' and then realising that he was being unduly cynical, Melbourne stood up and inspected Victoria's sketch. 'Elizabeth has become something of a favourite of yours, Ma'am.'

Victoria turned to face him. 'I have decided to follow her example and reign alone.' She tilted her head a little. 'With companions, perhaps,' and she smiled. If Elizabeth could have Leicester, then surely she could have Melbourne.

But Melbourne did not return her smile. 'Really, Ma'am? Have you told your Coburg cousins? I hear they are due to arrive at any moment.'

Victoria stood up, brandishing her paintbrush like a sword. 'My Coburg cousins, Albert and Ernst? But I have not asked them.'

Melbourne avoided the paintbrush. 'Nevertheless, Ma'am, they are coming.'

Victoria began to pace up and down under the pictures. 'Uncle Leopold must have sent for them, against my wishes. Why doesn't he understand that I am quite happy as I am?'

She looked at Melbourne for confirmation, but he slid his eyes away from her. 'I will not be your Prime Minister for ever, Ma'am.'

Victoria stopped in front of him, forcing him to look at her. 'Don't say that, Lord M.'

Reluctantly Melbourne met her indignant blue gaze. 'But I must. If the Tories don't do me in, my infirmities will.'

Victoria laughed, relieved that he was joking after all. 'Infirmities! You always say that illness is for people with nothing better to do.'

Melbourne did not join in her laughter. He shook his head, then said with urgency, 'Let the Coburgs come, Ma'am. Perhaps Prince Albert will surprise you.'

Victoria looked at him, aghast. This was not the answer she was expecting. 'But you told me that the public would not approve of a German bridegroom.'

A muscle quivered next to Melbourne's mouth. 'I am sure they make admirable husbands.'

Victoria sat down very suddenly and in a small voice said, 'But I don't want things to change.'

Melbourne looked at her with an expression that was almost stern. 'I know, Ma'am. But I believe you will not be happy alone,' he touched her very lightly on the shoulder, 'even with companions. You need a husband to love and cherish you.'

Victoria shuddered as his hand rested on her shoulder. 'But there is no one I care for,' she cried, her eyes saying something quite different.

Melbourne gave her a wry smile. 'Forgive me, Ma'am, but I think you have not really looked.'

Victoria put her hands to her eyes as if she did not want to see what was in front of her. Then she gave a great sigh and said, through her hand, 'I was so happy . . . before.'

'I find that happiness can always be recollected in tranquillity, Ma'am,' said Melbourne.

Victoria put her hands down and looked up at him, her pale blue eyes searching his face. 'You were happy too?'

When Melbourne spoke, it was in the voice not of the urbane Prime Minister, but of a man of advancing years who is facing the loss of the only thing that is still capable of bringing him joy. 'You know I was, Ma'am.'

The silence that followed was thick with the weight of all the unspoken feeling. Melbourne saw that Victoria's lip was trembling, and had to clasp his hands together so that he would not reach out and take her in his arms. He thought that if she were to cry now he would not be able to resist the temptation to kiss away those tears. He dug his nails into his palms, and told himself that the only way that he could serve his Queen was to find her a husband who would make her happy.

With a brave smile that almost broke Melbourne's heart, Victoria lifted her chin and said, 'But I am not going to get married just to please you, Lord M.'

Melbourne tried to match her smile with his own. 'No indeed, Ma'am, you must please yourself.'

And then he took her hand, her small white hand, and kissed it.

Book Four

Chapter One

ALBERT COULD HEAR THE MUSIC COMING DOWN THE corridor. Beethoven's Sonata in A flat, played a little too fast. He glanced at his reflection in one of the mirrors lining the walls. Ernst had insisted that they both wear their uniforms.

When Albert had objected, saying that he was not a soldier, his brother had asked, 'But don't you feel as if you are going into battle?' Albert had been forced to admit that he did, though it was hardly a glorious military exploit to walk into a drawing room and be inspected by a young woman. Still, he was glad of the uniform; there was nothing more magnificent than a Hussar's gold-braided jacket, worn with skintight white breeches and boots with gold tassels.

Albert remembered the last time he had been to London, and how tired he had been all the time. Victoria had laughed at him and called him a dormouse. He had not been familiar with the word at the time, but discovered its meaning later and even now felt its sting. This was not going to work. He would be humiliated again by a girl who thought that waltzing was the highest form of human endeavour.

When they reached the double doors of the State Drawing

Room, Albert paused. Ernst put a reassuring hand on his shoulder and said, 'To the victor, the spoils. And Albert–' He squeezed his brother's arm, hard. 'Remember to smile.'

The footmen pushed back the double doors. Albert saw a room full of people sitting and standing in front of the piano, where a girl he thought must be Victoria was playing. He glanced at the Major Domo to see if he would announce their arrival, but the man nodded at the piano, indicating that formalities would have to wait until the Queen stopped playing.

The brothers walked around the edge of the room, where they were noticed at once by Leopold and the Duchess, who blew them a kiss, and there was a flurry of interest behind the fans of the ladies of the household. Albert noticed that a tall man, his blond hair streaked with grey, looked at him with assessing green eyes. Only Victoria – and he could see now that it must be Victoria – seemed unaware of their arrival, continuing to play the slow movement just a little too fast.

Albert moved to the outside of the circle, so that he was standing just behind the piano. The music was on the stand in front of her, and Albert could see that she was about to come to the end of the passage. Instinctively, he stepped forward and at just the right moment turned the page. At first Victoria carried on playing, but then her fingers stopped moving and she turned her head to see him for the first time.

'Albert?' It was not quite a question, more an expression of wonder. She looked very young; her eyes were bluer than he remembered, her mouth softer, and he wondered that he should have been frightened of his cousin, who even if she was a Queen was still only a girl.

Bowing, he said, 'Victoria.'

There was a moment of silence, a pause in which everything

else was set aside. For that brief instant it was as if they were alone in the room.

But then there was a scratching and pattering across the parquet floor. Albert saw a dog with long hairy ears clatter to a stop at his feet, barking furiously, as if he were an intruder.

'Dashy, stop that.' Laughing, Victoria scooped the dog up into her arms. 'You mustn't bark at Cousin Albert, even if he does look quite different to the last time we saw him.'

Albert stiffened; there was a teasing note in her voice that he recognised from their last meeting. He looked at the dog with distaste; his own dog, Eos, was a greyhound, noble and fast. The furry ball that Victoria was holding in her arms did not seem to belong to the same species.

Victoria kissed Dash extravagantly on the nose and gave him to Harriet Sutherland to hold. 'I don't want him to bark at Albert again. He is so protective.'

Albert kissed the hand she held out to him, his lips barely touching her skin. As he stood up he said, 'I am sorry your dog does not recognise me. I, on the other hand, have no difficulty in recognising you, Cousin Victoria. Although I think that now you are playing the piano with fewer mistakes.'

Victoria took a small step backwards and lifted her chin. There was a note in his voice which made Melbourne look up, and caused Ernst to walk quickly across the room. He stopped in front of Victoria and made an elegant bow. 'How magnificent you look, Cousin Victoria. Monarchy clearly agrees with you.'

Victoria smiled and held out her hand to him, which he kissed with a great flourish. Albert did not move, but watched his brother impassively.

The Duchess, who had been on the far side of the room

with Leopold, now came rushing over to the brothers. After kissing them effusively on both cheeks, she started to exclaim over them in German. '*Mein lieber Junge. So gutaussehend!*'

Albert submitted to her embrace gracefully and said, '*Danke, Tante*. But I think we must talk in English. I am needing to practise.'

The Duchess was beaming with pleasure as she stood between her two nephews and put an arm through each of theirs. 'Oh, Drina, are your cousins not handsome? Such fine Coburg specimens.'

Victoria looked embarrassed. 'Please, Mama, they are not racehorses!' Turning to Lehzen, she said in her best hostess voice, 'Baroness, I expect the Princes are tired after their journey. Will you escort them to their rooms?'

Lehzen, who had been watching the exchange between Albert and Victoria with great attention, curtseyed to the Princes and started to walk towards the door. Instead of following her, however, Albert said with some clarity, 'Actually I am not so fatigued.'

Victoria replied with equal distinctness, 'Oh? I remember that on your last visit your eyelids were drooping by nine o'clock.'

Before Albert could reply, Ernst broke in. 'But my little brother is quite the night owl now. He can stay up till midnight without a single yawn.'

Leopold interrupted the proceedings with some impatience. He said, 'I think, Victoria, that you should hold a ball. Now that you have suitable partners.'

Two red spots began to form on Victoria's cheeks. 'I thank you for the suggestion, Uncle, but I believe my people would think me flighty if I am always holding balls.' She turned to Melbourne for reassurance. 'Don't you agree, Lord M?'

Melbourne smiled and shrugged. 'You know your people, Ma'am.'

He looked enquiringly at the Princes. Realising she must now introduce them, Victoria turned to her cousins, 'Albert, Ernst, my Prime Minister, Lord Melbourne.'

Melbourne gave the Princes a modest formal bow. 'Welcome to England, Your Serene Highnesses.'

There was another pause, until Ernst said with deliberate brightness, 'It is so good to be here in London. I have such fond memories of our last visit. Cousin Victoria, we were hoping that tomorrow you might show us the pictures in your collection. I have heard that it is magnificent, and Albert has just come back from Italy and talks of nothing but Old Masters.'

At a look from his brother, Albert said stiffly, 'I believe that there are some works by Leonardo da Vinci.'

Victoria looked at him blankly, and Albert wondered if it could be possible that she had never heard of the greatest painter the world had ever seen.

'Perhaps there are. I really don't know.'

Albert's disapproval must have shown on his face, because she said defensively, 'If you are so interested. I will send for the Keeper of the Queen's Pictures, Mr Seguier. He will know if we have one of these Leonardos or not.' When Albert said nothing, Victoria continued in her most regal manner, 'And as to tomorrow, I shall have to see. We have a great deal of business to attend to, don't we, Lord M?'

The faintest smile touched Melbourne's lips as he nodded his assent. 'The dispatches from Afghanistan will undoubtedly require your full attention, Ma'am.'

Leopold broke in, shaking his head. 'All work and no play, Victoria. It's not good for you. Why don't you take the Princes riding tomorrow in the Park? You can show them the delights of London Society.'

Before Victoria could reply, Albert said, 'I would not like to distract Cousin Victoria from matters of state. I think I should like to visit your National Gallery tomorrow, if that is permitted?' He looked from Leopold to Victoria.

'You must do as you please, Albert. Lehzen will make all the necessary arrangements.' Victoria stared at him before walking over to Melbourne and talking with great earnestness but not much sense about his views on the engagement in Kabul.

Lehzen walked down the corridor, the Princes following in her wake. Albert was so lost in his own thoughts and Ernst so preoccupied with his brother that neither of them noticed Skerrett and Jenkins watching them through the servants' door.

Jenkins said, 'The taller one on the right, that's Prince Albert.'

Skerrett craned her head to get a better look. 'Blimey. He looks like a Prince out of a fairy story. I wonder if he will like the Queen.'

Jenkins looked at her in reproof. 'It doesn't matter what the Prince thinks. It is the Queen who must decide.'

As they started up the staircase to their apartments, Albert finally burst out, 'Imagine not knowing if you own a Leonardo! I should never have come.'

Ernst smiled. 'But Albert, if she knew everything, then you would have nothing to instruct her in.'

Albert continued to shake his head. 'I believe this is what the English call a fool's errand.'

Ernst put his finger to his lips, indicating the governess ahead, and the brothers marched ahead in silence.

Lehzen ushered them into their rooms, a suite in the north wing next to the Duchess of Kent's, but did not linger. She looked as if each moment spent in the company of the Princes was painful to her.

When the door closed behind her, Ernst immediately took off his jacket and flung himself on the chaise longue in front of the fire. 'I think I need a brandy after this evening. And then I am going to go out and see what London has to offer by way of entertainment.'

At that moment the brothers' valet, a shy young Coburger named Lohlein, came in. Picking up the jacket, he nodded earnestly as Ernst asked him to fetch him a brandy before he died of thirst.

Albert did not sit down, but walked up and down as if he were guarding the door of the sitting room.

Ernst watched him for a while and finally could bear it no longer. 'Oh, stop pacing, Albert. Does it really matter if Victoria isn't a connoisseur of Renaissance painting? After all, you didn't know a Leonardo from a Holbein until you went to Florence. It's not her fault that she hasn't had your education. So can't you stop frowning at her all the time and be a bit more gallant?'

When Albert did not reply, Ernst jumped from the chaise longue and seized his brother's hand. 'When you take her hand to kiss it, you should look into her eyes as if you want to drown in them, like this.' He bent over Albert's hand while gazing at him with adoration.

Albert snatched his hand away, but Ernst was rewarded with the beginning of a smile. It was the first time that Albert had smiled since his first sight of Victoria.

'You know I will never be able to match your skill in this area, Ernst. I still think you should marry her instead of me.'

Ernst laughed. 'Well, she *is* exactly my type, small but perfectly formed.' As he described a lascivious silhouette with his hand, he heard a cough behind them.

Standing in the doorway, their Uncle Leopold said crisply, 'Every woman is your type, Ernst. But you will have to find someone else. It is Albert's destiny to marry Victoria.'

Albert's smile vanished. He said in a stiff voice that made his brother wince, 'I am not sure Victoria agrees. And she is the one who must propose.'

Waving this objection away, Leopold said, 'Oh, she will. But Ernst is right. She likes men who are gallant like her Lord Melbourne.'

Albert looked at the floor. 'If my manners are not suitable, then I think I should return to Germany.'

With a snort of impatience, Leopold snapped his fingers under Albert's nose. 'That is not a Coburg talking. Do you think I was like this with Charlotte? No, I went in and took the prize.' His hand reflexively checked his hairpiece. 'If you go home now, people will say she rejected you. But if you stay you could be King of England.'

Albert shied away from him. 'No, Uncle, that is not correct. I should be the Queen of England's husband.'

'For a man of character, Albert, a true Coburg,' Leopold took his arm and looked deep into the eyes that were so like his own, 'it would be the same thing.'

Albert turned away, and, shrugging off his nephew's surliness, Leopold left the room.

There was a moment of silence before Ernst leapt to his

feet. In a whirl of energy he clapped his brother on the shoulder. 'What you need, Albert, is to see London by night. I am sure you will find it most instructive.'

But Albert shook his head. 'I don't want to go out, Ernst.' He gave his brother a wry smile. 'Victoria was right after all. I am tired after my journey.'

In the south wing, Victoria was getting ready for bed. Skerrett was unpinning her hair, while Lehzen stood patiently in the background as she always did. She liked to be the last person to speak to the Queen at night and the first to greet her in the morning.

As Skerrett unravelled the plaits that circled her ears, Victoria said to Lehzen in the mirror, 'Did you see the way Albert looked at me this evening? As if I were a child who hadn't done her lessons?'

The Baroness's nostrils flared. 'He is a younger son from nowhere, and you, Majesty, are a Queen.'

Victoria smiled at the Baroness's indignation, then leant forward to look at herself critically in the mirror. 'Do you know, tomorrow I think I should like to do my hair differently.' She picked up a copy of *La Mode Illustrée* that lay open on her dressing table, and pointed to a hairstyle with tumbling ringlets fanning out over the woman's shoulders. 'Do you think you could copy this, Skerrett?'

'Oh yes, Ma'am.'

Victoria put her head on one side. 'And do you think it will suit me?'

'I think so, Ma'am,' and then, with a little smile at her mistress in the mirror, 'I believe it is called the Temptress.'

Victoria smiled in return, then asked as casually as she could, 'Do you think the Prince handsome, Skerrett?'

Seeing Lehzen's set face in the mirror, Skerrett shook her head. 'It's not for me to say, Ma'am.'

Victoria turned round and said with a touch of impatience, 'But I am asking you.'

'Then yes, Ma'am, I think the Prince is very handsome.'

Lehzen made a noise that was just shy of a snort, but Victoria ignored her and continued to gaze absently into the mirror. 'But he never smiles. I wonder if he can?'

On the other side of the Palace, Albert was in his bedroom looking at a miniature of a young woman. The blonde hair was done in an old-fashioned style with ringlets on either side of her head. Her blue eyes were wide, her mouth smiling. Albert held the candle up so that he could examine it properly, and noticed a speck of dust. He rubbed it away with his shirt sleeve and then, because he was alone and there was no one to chide him for his foolishness, he raised the portrait to his lips.

Chapter Two

O N Mondays, Victoria had made it a rule to hold audiences with those interesting members of the public who did not have the right credentials to attend the formal Drawing Rooms. This morning she was meeting Rowland Hill, an official from the postal service who had come up with an ingenious idea that Melbourne had thought worth her attention. She stood with her ladies and equerry Lord Alfred, with Dash at her heels, examining a sheet printed with a hundred or so minute profiles of herself. Hill had provided a magnifying glass, and one by one Victoria and her ladies examined the tiny images.

Emma Portman said carefully, 'It is really most ingenious, don't you think, Ma'am? And a good likeness.'

Victoria scrutinised the image through the lens. 'It is better than the one on the coins, certainly.' She patted the ringlets that curled at the base of her neck in the new Temptress style.

Rowland Hill stood shifting his considerable weight from one side to the other. He had been told that he should not speak unless spoken to, but he was bursting to tell the Queen of his marvellous invention. When Victoria put the stamps down and said, 'How small they are,' Hill could wait no longer.

'They may be small, Ma'am, but just one of these is sufficient to carry a letter to Brighton or to the Isle of Bute, to Guildford or to Gretna Green.' He paused for effect, something he had rehearsed at home in the mirror as Mrs Hill looked on. 'Or, if I may so, to Windsor Castle or to Wolverhampton.'

Victoria interrupted him. 'It doesn't seem right somehow. After all, Wolverhampton is a lot further away than Windsor.'

Hill smiled; this was an objection to which he had prepared an answer. He was about to launch into it when the door opened and the footman announced, 'Their Serene Highnesses, Prince Ernst and Prince Albert.'

The brothers walked into the room. Victoria's hand went to pat her ringlets. Ernst gave a smiling acknowledgement of the new style, Albert a brief nod. As if affronted by Albert's lack of gallantry, Dash started to bark at him so loudly that Victoria had to pick him up.

She nodded to her cousins and, turning back to the postal official, said, 'Pray continue, Mr Hill.'

Hill took a deep breath. 'In answer to your question, Ma'am, as to why the postage should cost the same no matter the distance travelled, I say this: should a girl in Edinburgh writing to her sweetheart in London pay more than the one who lives in Ealing? Should the merchant in Manchester pay more to write to his broker in the City than the merchant in Marylebone? These stamps, Ma'am, will bring true equality to every part of this island. Distance will no longer be a barrier to commerce or –' Hill put his hand on his heart, in a gesture that Mrs Hill had found particularly affecting – 'to romance.'

Hill's allusion to romance did not meet the reception he

hoped for. Victoria did not soften, but said crisply, 'And my likeness will be on every letter?'

'Yes, Ma'am. This is the Royal Mail, after all.' He made a little bow, in recognition of the stamp's status.

Victoria looked at the sheet. 'But how will the little pictures stay affixed?'

Hill took a step forward and turned the sheet over. 'As you see, Ma'am, the stamps have a layer of gum arabic on the back.'

Victoria lifted her head and said gravely, 'So everybody who wants to send a letter will have to lick my face?'

Hill hesitated. This was not a question that he had anticipated, but then he said tentatively, 'Precisely so, Ma'am, although more genteel users may use a little brush.'

The room fell silent. Victoria's ladies waited to see how she would take this statement; Hill took a step back as he saw the look on Victoria's face. He wondered how he could face his wife if he had offended the Queen.

But before he could fall to his knees and beg forgiveness for his *lèse-majesté*, he saw that the Queen was showing dimples in her cheeks and shaking with what seemed to be irrepressible laughter. The Queen's mirth spread like wildfire to her ladies, to the elegant Lord Alfred, and finally to Prince Ernst, who almost exploded with the laugh that had been building up inside him.

The only people in the room who were not laughing were the footmen, the bewildered Mr Hill, and Albert, who looked at the general hilarity with incomprehension. When Victoria had recovered her composure and noticed the stern look in Albert's eyes, she put her face close to the dog she was cradling in her arms and said, 'Do you think Cousin Albert disapproves of us, Dash?'

Albert said nothing, so she lifted her head and looked at him directly. He frowned and said, meeting her gaze, 'Forgive me, Cousin Victoria, I thought you were addressing your dog.' He looked over at Hill. 'I think that this gentleman has produced a remarkable invention, one that will bring great advantages to your subjects, so yes, I find nothing to laugh at, only to admire.' With this last sentence, he turned back to Victoria.

Hill, who did not know who this extremely intelligent man was, except that he was a Prince, made a lavish bow in his direction. 'I am honoured that you think so, sir.'

Victoria felt her cheeks becoming hot. 'Thank you very much, Mr Hill, for showing me your most ingenious device. And now, if you will excuse me, I have an audience with Lord Melbourne.' With a rapid angry step she walked out of the room without glancing at Albert. The ladies and Lord Alfred followed in her wake.

When they had gone, Ernst looked at Albert and shook his head before saying in German, 'What is the matter with you?'

His brother replied in the same language. 'I cannot pretend to be something I am not. She has courtiers to laugh at everything she laughs at, but I am not one of them.'

He turned to Hill, who was standing in the middle of the room, uncertain as to whether he had been dismissed. He had been told to walk backwards out of the room when the Queen indicated the audience was over. But as the Queen had left the room before him, he wondered whether it was still necessary. Would the Princes expect it of him? In truth, it was the thing that Hill dreaded most; the thought of walking backwards out of a room with the very real possibility that he might bump into something had given him nightmares ever since he had been told that it was a necessary part of court protocol. Perhaps, as they were only Princes, it would not be necessary to walk backwards all the way. He stood fixed to the spot, shifting from foot to foot.

Finally, to his great surprise and pleasure, the Prince who had praised his invention, came over to him and picked up the sheet of stamps. 'Can you tell me, please, how you are able to make the image so exact?'

Melbourne was waiting for Victoria in her private sitting room. He did not even have to look at her to know that she was in a temper; he could tell from the staccato footsteps and her impatient exhalation as she walked into the room.

'I am so vexed I could scream!' she said, circling the room until she was in front of Melbourne. Looking down at her, he thought that there could only be one cause for the Queen's heightened colour, the way that her chest rose and fell.

He had observed with interest the meeting between the Queen and her cousin the night before. Albert was an awkward young man who clearly had no idea how to make himself charming to a woman, but with the heightened senses of one who loves, Melbourne saw the look that had passed between the Queen and her cousin when he had leant over the piano to turn the page of music. It was a look he had experienced a few times in his life, and knew he never would again.

Understanding all this, he said with his normal air of amused detachment, 'Really, Ma'am? But the latest reports say that our forces have defeated Dost Mohammed. They will be in Kabul in a matter of weeks.'

Victoria stopped pacing and collected herself with an effort. 'That is good news, I must write to General Elphinstone and congratulate him.' Then she spread out her hands in front of her. Looking at them, she said, 'Just now, I was talking about my cousin.'

Melbourne said lightly, 'And which cousin would that be? His Serene Highness Prince Ernst of Saxe-Coburg-Gotha, or his brother, His Serene Highness Prince Albert?'

Victoria looked up at him. 'Albert, of course. He is such a . . .' she paused, searching for the right word, before finishing with great emphasis, 'such a prig.'

'Indeed? From my brief glimpse, I thought him rather elegant, for a German.'

'He is always so . . . disapproving!'

Melbourne smiled. 'I think you mistake his natural reserve for disapproval, Ma'am.'

Victoria shook her head vehemently. 'No, I don't think so.'

Melbourne turned to the boxes on the table, and said almost as if it were an afterthought, 'You do not view him as a possible husband, then?'

'I would rather marry Robert Peel!'

Melbourne raised an eyebrow. 'I wonder what Lady Peel would say to that?'

And they both laughed, enjoying the moment of easy intimacy between them and remembering how many jokes they had shared in the past. To Melbourne it felt all the more precious because it gave him back the glimmer of hope. Perhaps he had been mistaken in what he had seen at the piano. Perhaps Victoria would not after all lose her heart to Albert, and they might continue with this happy understanding between them for a little while longer.

It was a frail hope, he realised, and one that was not worthy of him. He knew, more than anyone, that what the Queen needed was a husband on whom she could pour all the passion that was brimming inside her. He reminded himself that the time had come when he must follow his duty rather than his inclination, but even so, as the Queen smiled at him, showing her small white teeth, he hoped that the hour of sacrifice was not quite yet.

'By the way, Ma'am, may I compliment you on your new hairstyle. It is really most becoming.' The curls at the nape of her neck gave her face a voluptuous softness.

'I thought I would try something new.'

Melbourne nodded, unable just at that moment to speak.

Albert and Ernst walked down the steps of the National Gallery in Trafalgar Square, where one brother had spent an absorbing couple of hours admiring the fine specimens in the collection, while the other had been equally engrossed in admiring the fine array of London's fairer sex. They walked out into the Square attended only by Lohlein.

Lehzen had put a carriage at their disposal, and Alfred Paget had asked them if they would like him to show them the sights, but Albert had refused both offers. He wanted to see London for himself, not as the Queen's cousin, or worse still her suitor. Ernst had protested; he had an idea that Lord Alfred might be able to show him some of the attractions he would find most interesting, and as a cavalry man he could not understand Albert's passion for walking everywhere. But he knew better than to protest when his brother had made up his mind.

They walked past a large building project in the middle of the square. It looked as if a giant finger was pointing upwards from a cluster of scaffolding. They stood and watched as a huge piece of granite was hauled up by a series of cranes and pulleys till it rested on top of the finger, bringing it even closer to the sky.

Turning into Regent Street, Albert stopped in front of a window that held a display of the new daguerreotypes. The small glass plates mounted against a length of red velvet were mostly portraits of men, although there was one picture of an old lady where it was possible to see all the lines and wrinkles on her face.

Albert gazed at the daguerreotypes intently, and turned to his brother. 'It's remarkable. A way of reproducing nature quite faithfully.'

Ernst tore himself away from admiring the fetching redhead on the other side of the street to glance at the crone that his brother was poring over. 'Look at the wart on her face. I am not sure I want to be reproduced that faithfully.'

'But don't you want to see yourself as you appear to others?'

'I'm not sure; it depends on how much I have had to drink the night before!'

The sharp-faced young proprietor of the shop appeared in the doorway. 'If you would like to step inside, sirs, I would be happy to make daguerreotypes of you both. And you don't need to worry about having to stand still for a long period. The exposure time is now only ten minutes, and I promise you will find no more artistic photographer anywhere in the city.'

'Is that what you call yourself, a photographer?'

'Yes, sir, from the Greek – *photos* meaning light and *graphos* meaning to draw. I like to think of myself as painting with light.'

Albert's eyes gleamed. He had heard about daguerreotypes, of course, and had even seen one or two, but he had never before met someone who was a practitioner. He was about to step into the shop when he saw that Ernst had struck up a conversation with a lady on the other side of the street. He hesitated; surely he was not always to be his brother's keeper. Then he remembered how Ernst had left his beloved regiment to accompany him on the trip to London, and with a regretful glance at the photographer and a promise to return another time, he crossed the street to take his brother's arm and lead him into safety.

'Ooh, this must be your brother,' said the redhead. 'The likeness is unmistakable. Seeing as you are foreigners, would you two gentlemen like me to show you some of the sights? I can assure you that I know my way around.' She gave Ernst a lascivious wink.

'Thank you, Miss, but that won't be necessary. We have business to attend to,' Albert said firmly, and pulled his brother by the arm. In his eagerness to get away from the temptress, Albert turned into a narrow side street that could not have presented a greater contrast to the wide avenue of Regent Street, with its handsome shop fronts and prosperous-looking people. Here everything was darker; the light was almost blocked out by the buildings on either side, and there was a strong smell that worsened as they walked further towards a courtyard where there appeared to be some sort of pump. Children dressed in little more than rags, with nothing on their feet, chased each other round a line of women who were waiting with buckets and pails. Albert looked about him with horror; this foetid courtyard seemed to be the negative imprint of the bright prosperity he had just left. Here there were no green parasols or advertisement hoardings proclaiming the latest performance of *La Sonnambula* at the Italian Opera House; here there was only sooty washing hung out to dry and the rhythmic clank of the pump.

Albert felt a touch at his arm. It was Lohlein, who said in German, his face anxious, 'I think we should return to the Palace, Highness; this is not a good place to be.'

The unfamiliar sound of German made one of the women look up and stare at them. Her gaze made Albert uncomfortable. He had seen poverty at home, of course, but nothing had been quite so dirty; and the peasants at home had not looked so without hope. He was about to turn around, when he felt something touch his knee. He shuddered, thinking it was some stray dog, and saw a little girl no more than four years old holding up a single match.

'Buy a match, sir?'

Albert looked at the little girl's weary face and saw her thin arms. He reached into the pocket of his coat and found a coin, a half crown, which he pressed into the child's palm. He turned away and began to walk towards the light, but before he could take three steps he felt another touch at his knee.

He looked down and saw the little girl holding up his match. Smiling, he bent down to take it from her.

As the brothers strolled back towards the Palace, Albert said, 'We do not have such things as photographers in Coburg, but we at least do not have children begging on our streets.'

Ernst was tipping his hat to a pretty blonde in a blue pelisse riding past in a yellow phaeton. 'There are lots of things here that we don't have in Coburg.'

'How can Victoria sit in the Palace with her lapdog when

all around her there is such poverty? I think London is not an honest city.'

'Oh, I don't know, Albert.' Ernst watched the blonde disappear into the Park. 'If this is dishonesty then I think there is something to be said for it.'

Dinner that night was *en famille*, which meant that besides Leopold, the Duchess of Kent and the two Princes, it included only the immediate members of the household, Lord Melbourne, and Dash, who liked to linger at Victoria's feet waiting for scraps.

The conversation around the table was fitful, as the household and Leopold tried to finish their courses before the Queen. Only Ernst, who did not know that the *timbale de saumon* in front of him was about to be whisked away before he had even had a forkful, ventured to make conversation.

'May I compliment you on your dress, Cousin Victoria? I have seen so many fashionably dressed women today, but I think you are the finest of them all.'

Victoria looked pleased. It was a new dress made of a shot silk that shimmered like a peacock's tail from blue to green as she moved. The neckline was just off the shoulder, revealing the length of her white neck, and the thin lines of her collarbones were traced by a diamond necklace that glittered in the candlelight. She looked like a hummingbird, iridescent and sparkling, bending down constantly to pop the choicest morsels into the mouth of the waiting Dash. She was in high spirits tonight, fizzing with the excitement, or perhaps tension, of sitting between her two cousins.

She turned to Ernst. 'I am glad that you were able to enjoy yourself today. Lord M and I have been so busy with the army lists. Now that we are in Afghanistan there are so many military matters to attend to.' Melbourne, who had Emma Portman between him and Albert, noticed that the Queen's eyes slid over to Albert as she said this, but the Prince was looking at his plate.

Ernst continued in the same affable tone, 'It was a most educational day. Albert and I visited the National Gallery. We are quite the tourists.'

Having eaten as much of the timbale as she cared to, Victoria put down her cutlery. Like a flight of herons, the footmen swooped and took away the food. Leopold gave a deep sigh, but Albert looked up surprised as his plate was spirited away. He protested to the footman, 'I have not finished!'

The footman glanced over at Victoria. 'But the Queen has, Your Highness.'

Albert shook his head and looked over at Victoria, who was just at that moment dangling a tidbit she had saved for the slavering Dash. When she noticed Albert, she asked, 'Did you see my portrait at the gallery? The one of me in my Coronation robes. It always reminds me of that day, and how nervous I felt.' She gave a little smile, and Emma Portman murmured that although the Queen may have felt nervous, it was not visible to the audience.

Albert waited for Emma to finish and then said in his accented English, 'We did not see the portrait. We went to look at the Old Masters. There is a very fine Rubens there, among many other most interesting paintings. I think it is a wonderful thing that so much beauty should be available to all for free. I believe it will create a nation of aesthetes.'

Victoria, who was cutting up her veal farci with small precise movements, said, 'I don't care for Rubens at all. All that wobbling flesh.'

The table fell silent. Melbourne, who could not help the smile playing at his lips, addressed Prince Albert. 'The National Gallery is most certainly of great benefit to the nation, but I doubt that it will do much to change the national taste. Although I believe it has become a favourite refuge for tramps, so perhaps we will have the most cultivated vagabonds in Europe.' The room echoed with the silvery peal of Victoria's laughter.

Albert put his fork down and said, 'I believe even vagabonds, as you call them, deserve to glimpse the sublime.'

Melbourne smiled in reply, but before Albert could say anything further, Ernst broke in. 'Well, if the ladies I saw in the gallery today were vagabonds, then their taste clearly needs no education.'

Victoria caught her mother's eye and stood up. The entire room rose to its feet, and the gentlemen escorted the ladies to the door, Albert putting out his arm for Victoria, which she brushed with the tips of her fingers without so much as looking at him.

After the ladies had withdrawn and the footmen had come in with the port, the men moved towards the end of the table where Leopold was sitting. Melbourne placed himself next to Alfred Paget and was enquiring after the health of his many siblings, when to his surprise Albert came to sit on his other side.

Without preamble, the Prince said, 'You know, Lord Melbourne, that I should very much like to visit your Parliament. We have nothing like this at home.'

Albert looked so serious that Melbourne wondered whether he was capable of smiling. He could not see Victoria ever being happy with a man who had no sense of humour.

'It would be my pleasure to show you, sir. But I hope you won't be disappointed. The peril of representative government is that it can often end up resembling a bear garden. And you might want to go incognito.'

Albert looked surprised and wary. 'Why is that?'

'There are some MPs, Tories mostly,' Melbourne dismissed them with a wave of his hand, 'who might not care to feel that they were being inspected by a German prince.'

As he said this, he saw the colour rise in Albert's cheeks. 'I see. And what do you think, Lord Melbourne?'

Melbourne rose from his chair. 'I think,' and he gave his most polished smile, 'that we should join the ladies. The Queen does not care to be left waiting.'

In the State Drawing Room, Victoria was playing cards with Harriet, Emma and Lehzen. The Duchess was sitting by the fire with her embroidery. The men walked in according to precedence, first Leopold, who went to sit next to his sister, then the Princes, and finally Melbourne and Alfred Paget.

Victoria looked up at their arrival and reached out an imploring hand to Melbourne. 'Oh, Lord M, you must come and play with me. I feel sure you will bring me luck.'

'With pleasure, Ma'am.' Melbourne looked over at Albert and Ernst. 'Perhaps we could set up another table so that the Princes can play too.'

Albert looked at him with what Melbourne thought was a

faint trace of hostility. 'Please don't bother. I do not care to play cards.'

Again the moment of discord was broken by Ernst, who said with a determined smile, 'But *I* do. May I join the game, Cousin Victoria? I warn you I am very unlucky with cards, but you know what they say,' and he directed his most flirtatious gaze at the beautiful Harriet Sutherland, who lowered her eyelids in acknowledgement.

Victoria gestured to the footmen, who brought chairs for Ernst, Melbourne, and Alfred Paget, and they began a game of whist.

Albert walked over to the pianoforte and, after a brief hesitation, sat down and began to play, quietly at first and then with increasing confidence.

The Duchess looked at Albert with a happy smile about her lips. 'Dear Albert, he looks so like you at that age, Leopold.'

Leopold glanced sideways at his sister, but it was clear that she meant nothing more by the remark than an innocent observation. 'Yes, I believe there is a certain resemblance.'

The music from the pianoforte grew louder, but Victoria may have been the only person in the room to notice that Albert was playing the Beethoven Sonata in A flat minor that she had been playing the night before as he and Ernst arrived. There was a particularly difficult passage coming up, which she always struggled with, but Albert played it effortlessly.

Victoria looked at him, impressed despite herself. Ernst noticed the look and said with a look of supplication, 'Cousin Victoria, would you do me the very great honour of playing for me?'

Victoria glanced at the other end of the room. 'The piano is in use.'

'But I feel the evening can only be complete with a Schubert duet.' He turned to Harriet Sutherland with a wolfish smile. 'Don't you think, Duchess?'

Harriet stretched her long white neck. 'I adore Schubert, and the Queen and her cousin both play so well.'

Rather to her own surprise, Victoria found herself standing up and walking to the piano. At her approach Albert immediately stopped playing and got to his feet. 'Apologies. I did not know you wanted to play.' His tone was studiedly formal.

He began to move away, but Victoria put out a hand to stop him, and said with equal stiffness, 'Ernst has requested a duet. Schubert. I believe there is some music here.'

She pointed to the sheet music lying on top of the piano. Albert looked at it and nodded. 'Yes, I know this. Which part do you prefer? I believe the primo part is more difficult.'

'I have never had a problem with it,' Victoria said, taking her seat at the upper end of the keyboard.

'No? But it has so many chords and you have such small hands.' They both looked at Victoria's hands, which were resting on the keyboard, poised to play. Victoria tried to keep them still as he sat down next to her on the piano stool. Although he was careful not to touch her body with his, she was aware of the heat from him and the sweet faint scent of his skin. When she looked down at the keyboard, she could see that his hands too were shaking.

Without looking at his face, Victoria lifted her chin and said, 'Ready?' and before he could reply, 'One, two, three.'

She struck the first chord and Albert echoed it in the base, but as they reached the melody it was clear while Victoria was playing with attack, Albert was keeping to an altogether more contemplative tempo.

As the difference in their tempi became a jangling discord, Victoria stopped playing and turned her head. 'Am I going too fast for you, Albert?'

Albert looked back at her with his clear blue eyes, which were, she realised, so like her own. 'I think you are going too fast for Schubert. But if that is the pace you want . . .' With a softening of his mouth that might in another man have been mistaken for a smile, he laid his fingers on the keys waiting for her to begin.

This time they played not against each other but together. He followed her tempo, and she resisted the temptation to rush through the difficult bits in the hope that the speed would disguise her mistakes. As they arrived at the end of the page, Albert reached up to turn it. For a moment their eyes met and there was an echo of the moment when Victoria had first seen him the night before. The second movement of the duet required the players to cross into each other's register and as Albert's hand crossed over Victoria's she felt a flash of heat. A few bars later it was her turn to play a chord in the lower octaves and this time she could not lift her wrist high enough to clear his so that they could not help but touch. His skin felt warm and the suggestion of a hair tickled the underside of her palm. Her fingers found the notes by themselves; all her conscious attention was on the tiny patch of skin on her wrist that was touching Albert's. She dared not glance at his face and felt something like relief when the movement came to an end and their hands moved apart.

In the third movement, the legato passage called for the sostenuto pedal. Victoria automatically reached for the pedal with her foot, only to find she was pressing down not on the cold brass pedal but on Albert's leather-shod instep, her ankle in its cloud of skirts rubbing against his calf. This time it was Albert who shuddered as her foot touched his. Victoria felt the pressure of his thigh through her petticoats and thought that underneath the torrent of notes she heard him give a sigh.

As the piece drew to its conclusion, they found that they were exactly in time, and when they struck the final chord at the same moment, they looked at each other in triumph. Victoria could not help but smile, and for a moment she thought she saw a glimpse of white teeth beneath the golden moustache. They sat looking at each other, quite still, listening to the sound of each other's breathing until the moment was lost in a clattering of applause from the card table.

Albert immediately got to his feet and gave Victoria a formal little bow of the head. Still slightly breathless, he said in a low voice, 'You play very well, Victoria.'

Victoria looked up at him. 'As do you, Albert'

Leopold, who could contain himself no longer, turned to Melbourne with a smile of triumph. 'The Coburgs are such a musical family, don't you think? To see the two cousins playing together as if they were one is most pleasing.'

Melbourne gave him a polished smile that did not reach his eyes. 'It was a most enjoyable performance.'

Victoria laughed and said playfully, 'At least we were making so much noise that you could not fall asleep as you usually do when you think I am not looking, Lord M.'

Melbourne held out his hands in surrender.

After watching this exchange, Albert turned to his cousin, and said in a clipped tone, 'But you will forgive me, Victoria, if I observe that, you do not practise enough. It is necessary to play every day for at least one hour.'

Now it was Victoria's turn to stand up, stung by the reproof, and also by the return to his cold stiff manner. Holding herself very straight, she said with regal hauteur, 'Indeed. But I must remind you that a Queen does not have time for scales every day.'

Albert dipped his head as if to acknowledge her remark, then said, his blue eyes as wide and as antagonistic as Victoria's own, 'No. Only for card games, I think.'

Victoria looked at him blankly, and then with a sharp turn of her head she walked over to the card table and sat down. Only after she had made a great show of looking at her cards did she glance at Albert. He was staring at her as if he might be trying to map her face, but the moment their eyes met he flinched and looked away.

That night Victoria and Albert both looked at miniatures before they went to sleep. Victoria picked up the likeness of Queen Elizabeth that had been her inspiration, and wondered whether the earlier Queen had ever felt the surge of excitement she had experienced when Albert's hand had touched hers. How was it possible that her body should react so violently to someone she found so difficult?

She put the miniature down and lay back on her bed and looked at the ceiling. How long would her cousins stay, she wondered? Surely they could not be here for much more than a week; then they would go back to Coburg and life would return to the way it had been. But even as she told herself this, her hand still tingled in the place where his wrist had touched hers.

Albert was looking at the portrait of the young woman with the blonde ringlets. He stared at it intently and then put it away in the drawer of his nightstand and threw himself face down onto the bed.

Chapter Three

G FLAT MINOR WAS THE HARDEST SCALE, THOUGHT
Victoria, as she tried for the third time to make her
fingers get to the third octave without stumbling. She knew
that she ought now to try playing the scale contrapuntally with
both hands going in the opposite direction, but just the idea
of it was daunting. Then she thought of Albert's face as he
had taunted her about card games, and plunged in, trying to
obliterate the image from her mind's eye. She had reached the
opposite ends of the keyboard and was making her painful,
chromatic way back when Leopold walked in, carrying a cup
of coffee.

Victoria stopped playing and looked at him in irritation.
Why couldn't he understand she was busy? Leopold ignored
her frown and, taking a sip of his coffee, said enquiringly, 'So,
Victoria?' He raised an eyebrow.

She knew exactly what the eyebrow meant but kept her face
blank. 'Uncle Leopold?'

Taking another sip of coffee, Leopold observed her. 'Normally
it is the man who must declare his love.' He gave her a little
nod of the head. 'But in your case you will have to overcome
your maidenly modesty and propose to Albert.'

Victoria did not move. 'Or not.'

'No?' asked Leopold. 'But the duet yesterday was so charming.'

Victoria brought the lid of the keyboard down with a crash. 'I'm sorry, Uncle, but Albert and I are not suited. He has no manners; yesterday he was playing my keyboard as if he owned it!'

Leopold raised his cup to his lips. When he put it down on the saucer, Victoria could see that he was smiling broadly, as if her vehemence only served to confirm his assumptions.

'I must congratulate you, Victoria,'

Victoria stood up, and answered reluctantly, 'On what?'

'On the excellent coffee at the Palace. When I was married to poor Charlotte it was undrinkable, but now it is almost as good as the coffee in Coburg. Yes, I think Albert will be very happy here.' Before Victoria could reply, he walked out of the room.

Victoria wished she had something to throw at him as he walked jauntily away. Catching sight of herself in the looking glass over the chimney piece, she decided that her hair, which was still dressed in the temptress style, was all wrong. She walked quickly back to her dressing room and told the footman to fetch her dresser.

A few minutes later, Skerrett arrived, looking a little flustered. 'I am so sorry, Ma'am; I went down to breakfast.'

Victoria waved a hand to dismiss her apology and sat down in front of the mirror, looking at herself critically. 'I want you to redo my hair. I think that it looks too . . .' she paused, trying to find the right word, 'too frivolous.'

Skerrett met her eyes in the mirror and looked puzzled briefly, then nodded with sudden understanding. 'I suggest something very close to the head, with the accent at the back.'

Victoria looked back at her earnestly. 'I want to look substantial, you see.'

'Of course, Ma'am.'

Skerrett began the tedious work of unpinning Victoria's hair and redoing it, but her mistress kept fidgeting. At one point Victoria moved her head just as Skerrett was pinning a false braid to the crown of her head, and a hairpin almost pierced the scalp.

Victoria gave a little yelp of surprise and pain, and Skerrett made a grimace of apology. 'If you could try and keep your head still, Ma'am.'

Victoria quivered with impatience. 'Yes, yes, I know. But everything takes so long, and I told Harriet that I would meet her for a walk around the Palace gardens at eleven.'

Skerrett tried to distract her squirming subject. 'Are you not going riding this morning, Ma'am?'

'Not today. Harriet Sutherland suggested last night that the Princes might like to see the gardens here, and I remembered that I have not been to see the summer house since it was repainted. I think that the Princes will be most favourably impressed by the gardens. I don't suppose they have anything on such a scale in Coburg.'

'No, Ma'am,' said Skerrett, concentrating on the task in front of her. Ever since Prince Albert had arrived, the Queen had been a good deal more particular about her appearance. Skerrett remembered the wager in the servants' hall concerning Victoria's marital prospects and thought that Mr Francatelli might be onto a winner with his sixpence on the Coburg sausage.

At another mirror, on the other side of the Palace, Albert was being shaved by Lohlein. Normally he shaved himself, but that morning his hand kept slipping, for some reason, and he had asked Lohlein to take over before his chin resembled a battlefield. Ernst came in just as Lohlein began to pull the cutthroat razor against Albert's skin. Although Ernst was smiling, Albert could see that he was pale from lack of sleep. He looked at his brother in the mirror but dared not speak with the blade so close to this throat.

Ernst leant against the door jamb. 'I went to a most interesting establishment last night, called a nunnery – but I saw no nuns there.' He gave a leer that Albert knew was a reference to their father, who was notorious for his carnal appetites.

'Among the lower orders they are using an ingenious code: *titfertat* means *hat*, *whistle and flute* for *suit*, and *trouble and strife* for *wife*. Quite poetic, don't you think?'

Albert found his brother's eyes in the mirror, and repeated slowly with a mischievous glint, 'Trouble and strife.' Then his face clouded over. 'I wish you would be more prudent, Ernst. It is bad enough with Papa; if you were to go the same way I don't think I could bear it. Without you I have no one.'

Ernst heard the appeal in Albert's voice and, coming forward, put a hand on his shoulder. With sudden seriousness, he said, 'Don't worry, Albert. I will not be like Papa.' Then his expression lightened. 'But the girls here are too delicious. The sooner you marry Victoria, the faster I can go back to Coburg, where there are no distractions.'

Albert shook his head. 'But Victoria is impossible. She spends more time talking to her lapdog than to her mother.'

His brother shrugged. 'Oh, what does that matter?' He leant down and faced Albert directly in the mirror. 'I saw you at the piano; it seemed to me that you played together rather well.'

He winked at Albert, who pretended not to notice. 'She has some facility, I suppose.'

Ernst poked his brother in the ribs. 'But did you have to touch her quite so often?'

'It was a complicated piece.'

Ernst raised his eyebrows and stared with such knowingness that finally Albert had to smile.

It was so mild for November that Victoria and Harriet went out into the gardens without bonnets or shawls.

'Another new hairstyle, Ma'am? I hardly recognised you,' said Harriet as Victoria came down the steps.

'I worried that the ringlets were too frivolous.'

'Well, the chignon is both elegant and serious.'

'And becoming, Harriet?'

'Most becoming, Ma'am.'

Reassured, Victoria led the way through the parterres to the path that led to the lake. Distracted, her eyes flicked from left to right until she finally said, 'I think, Harriet, that I must do more to entertain the Princes.'

'Indeed, Ma'am?'

'Yes, I think perhaps a small dance after dinner, with perhaps a few of the household – nothing elaborate.'

'An excellent plan. Would you like me to ask Alfred Paget to arrange matters?'

'Yes, do ask him.' Victoria was still looking around, but then she stopped walking. Harriet saw the Princes coming round the corner of a beech hedge.

Ernst smiled at them warmly. 'Good morning, Cousin

Victoria.' He turned to Harriet. 'Duchess, I have just seen a most unusual shrub. I am thinking that perhaps you would be able to tell me its name.'

Harriet caught the hint. 'With pleasure, sir. Strange shrubs are my speciality.' When Ernst offered her his arm, they went down the avenue of beech hedges, leaving Victoria alone with Albert.

They were silent with each other. Victoria noticed that Albert was wearing a frock coat of an unusual cut and white cashmere breeches that showed the muscles of his thighs. Feeling self-conscious, she cast around for something to say. 'Do you like gardens, Albert?'

Albert looked out across the box-trimmed parterres, the neat clipped hedges of russet beech, and shook his head. 'No. I prefer forests.'

Beginning to wonder if Albert would find anything that he liked, Victoria said tartly, 'I must tell you that this is the largest private garden in London.'

'But it is still a garden, a man-made creation.' Albert began to walk towards the lake, Victoria following. Gesturing up towards a clump of elms on the other side, he said, 'A forest is part of nature. To be among the trees when the wind is blowing is to feel the sublime.'

As he lifted his head to look over to the trees, Victoria saw the muscles of his jaw and the strong column of his neck. He had changed so much from the thin, rather hunched boy he had been on his last visit.

'Well, if you like trees so much, you should go to Windsor. There are plenty of trees there; the Great Park has some which are over a thousand years old.'

Albert turned to her. 'But I can only go there if you invite me, Cousin Victoria.' Was there reproach or supplication in his tone? She could not be sure.

Victoria thought about her reply as they walked around the side of the lake. She was just about to invite him to Windsor, but as they came round the corner she saw her mother. The Duchess was standing at her easel, painting the summer house in watercolours. Victoria could hear her humming, and she stopped on the path and turned to go back to the house, assuming Albert would follow. But Albert had seen the Duchess too and was already walking over to her. To Victoria's amazement he smiled at her mother as he examined her sketch. 'I had no idea you had such talent, Aunt. The shading is superb.'

Pleased, the Duchess tilted her face towards him. 'I am doing my best. Of course I was never properly trained, unlike Victoria, who always had the best masters.'

Albert leant in to examine the sketch more closely. 'But talent such as yours cannot be taught, Aunt.' He pointed to the sketch. 'If you will permit me to suggest a little shadow here to balance the composition.'

The Duchess continued to gaze at him. 'Thank you. You know, Albert, I am so happy you and Ernst are here.' Her voice was thick with emotion. 'You remind me so much of my beloved Coburg. Even though I have lived here for so long, I am still missing my native land.'

Victoria, who had not moved from the path, saw Albert pick up her mother's hand and kiss it.

When Albert rejoined her on the path, Victoria was no longer thinking about Windsor. 'Did you really like Mama's sketch?' she said, walking away from the summer house as fast as she could.

Albert nodded. 'As a matter of fact, I did,' he looked down

at Victoria, 'but I think I would have admired it anyway.'

Still walking at a brisker pace than normal, Victoria said, 'I am surprised. I didn't take you for a flatterer.'

Albert considered this remark. 'I try not to say things I don't mean, but I also try to be kind where possible.'

The reproof in his voice made Victoria stop. Turning to him, she said, 'And you think Mama needs kindness?'

Albert looked back at her steadily. 'Don't you?'

His certainty gave Victoria pause. She had blamed her mother for so much for so long, it felt peculiar to have the Duchess framed not as the criminal but as the victim. Victoria found that she had to look away from Albert's candid blue stare. Finally, she said in a rush, 'When I was growing up, she and Sir John Conroy – you remember him?' Albert nodded. 'When we lived at Kensington they kept me under constant supervision. I was allowed no friends, no society, no life of my own. I even had to sleep in Mama's room.'

Albert looked thoughtful rather than sympathetic. 'Perhaps she was trying to protect you, Victoria. It can't have been easy for her, a widow in a strange country trying to bring up the heir to the throne.'

'That's what Mama says. But I know what it felt like.' She burst out, 'I was a prisoner, and she and Sir John Conroy were my gaolers!'

She shuddered slightly, but still Albert did not relent. He looked back at the Duchess and then to Victoria. 'Maybe that is how you felt, but I have seen how she looks at you, Victoria. She loves you very much.'

Victoria stamped her foot in frustration. 'You don't know anything about it.'

Albert shook his head. 'No. That's true.' He looked down

at the ground and said quietly, 'I only know what it is like not to have a mother.'

Before Victoria could reply, Ernst and Harriet appeared from the other side of the lake, laughing about a swan that had hissed at them, and the moment passed.

As she walked back into the Palace, Victoria felt ashamed. She had forgotten that Albert's mother was dead. She was still thinking about this as she sat with her boxes waiting for Melbourne. The portrait of her father hung on the wall in front of her, and as she looked up at his bewhiskered face, Victoria thought she could not miss someone she had never known. It would have been so much harder to bear if she had a memory of him. She wondered how old Albert had been when his mother died, and an image came into her head of a small boy weeping by a bed.

Victoria was lost in this reverie when Melbourne came in full of news from Afghanistan. It took her a moment to understand what he was saying; Afghanistan seemed more distant than ever. But she forced herself to concentrate and, when his meaning dawned on her, said in astonishment, 'You mean the Russians are paying the Afghans to fight against our troops?'

Melbourne nodded. 'They want control of the Khyber Pass, Ma'am.' He walked over to the globe that stood in the corner of the study. 'If you look at the position of the Pass, you can see that it is the gateway to India. Alexander the Great tried to do the same thing.'

Glad to have something else to focus on, Victoria said, 'I shall write to the Grand Duke and tell him I think it's wicked.'

Melbourne's lips twitched. 'Perhaps we should keep that in reserve, Ma'am. In case the military strategy fails.' He picked up the Macnaghten Dispatch. 'Now, if you will excuse me, Ma'am, I should go back to the House.'

He started to back out of the room, but Victoria called him back. 'I will expect you for dinner tonight, Lord M, and,' she hesitated, 'there will be dancing afterwards. Nothing elaborate, just a few couples.'

Melbourne looked at her. 'I thought you weren't going to have any more balls?'

Evading his gaze, Victoria said as carelessly as she could, 'Oh, this isn't a ball, just a very small dance. I must do something to entertain the Princes, after all.'

'Even though you told me that Prince Albert does not care for dancing?'

Victoria felt Melbourne's eyes on her face and hoped she was not blushing. 'Oh, I wouldn't want to dance with him, anyway. It would be like dancing with a poker!'

Melbourne was silent, and then he said, 'Perhaps he will surprise you, Ma'am,' and there was something in his tone that made her look up.

'The Baroness asked me to lay out the white muslin, but I thought you might prefer the blue silk, Ma'am?' Skerrett was pulling the laces of Victoria's corset tight.

'The blue silk definitely.' Victoria looked at herself critically in the mirror. 'Can you make it a little tighter?'

Skerrett shook her head. 'Any more, Ma'am, and you won't be able to breathe.'

'I suppose you are right. I want to be able to dance.'

Skerrett lowered the blue moiré silk over Victoria's head and started to hook it up at the back. 'Will you wear the diamonds tonight or the pearls, Ma'am?'

'Oh, the pearls, I think. They look so pretty in the candle-light.'

Skerrett went to answer a knock at the door. Brodie held a silver salver on which lay a spray of gardenias. He handed it to Skerrett, who said, 'Melbourne?'

Brodie nodded. 'All the way from Brocket Hall.'

Skerrett closed the door and put the flowers down in front of Victoria. 'From Lord Melbourne, Ma'am.'

Victoria brought the flowers close to her face. 'The scent is heavenly. What are they called?'

'Gardenias, Ma'am.'

'Lord Melbourne always remembers.'

'Yes, Ma'am.'

Victoria pinned the spray of gardenias to the bodice of her dress, and leaning forward towards the mirror she bit her lips and pinched her cheeks. Her nose, she decided, looked a little shiny, and she was just dabbing it with a *papier poudré* when Lehzen came in through the interconnecting door.

'Are you ready, Majesty?'

Victoria spun around in her blue dress, the candlelight catching the patterns on the watered silk.

'Quite ready.'

Although Victoria had said she only wanted a small dance, Lord Alfred decreed that a pianoforte would not be sufficient and they needed a full complement of musicians.

'Prince Albert is so very musical,' said Alfred. 'I think he will expect nothing less.'

'But I wonder if he dances?' said Harriet. 'The Queen says that the last time he was here he did not care to.'

'It is unthinkable that a young man can reach the age of twenty without being taught how to dance, even in Germany.'

Harriet laughed. 'I am sure Prince Ernst is a very accomplished waltzer, but Prince Albert, who knows?'

The eyes of the household were all on Prince Albert when he entered the ballroom after dinner with his brother. Would he join the dancing?

Lord Alfred had instructed the small orchestra to play some Highland dances to start off the evening's entertainment, and Ernst immediately approached his cousin and begged her to instruct him. Victoria took his hand, and they were soon dancing an eightsome reel.

But Albert did not join in. He stood at the edge of the room looking at the dancers intently as if he was trying to understand how they could be enjoying themselves. He looked uncomfortable in his skin, and indeed in his clothes; he kept pulling at his cravat as if he was trying to loosen his bonds.

On the other side of the room, Melbourne watched the proceedings with Emma Portman. As Victoria and Ernst executed their reel, he said, 'It appears that Prince Ernst, at least, enjoys the company of women.'

'Yes, indeed. He has been flirting outrageously with Harriet Sutherland ever since he arrived. And charming too, so unlike his brother, who though handsome enough is stiff and awkward.'

Melbourne's eyes flickered over to where Albert stood alone and aloof on the other side of the room. 'The Clockwork Prince.'

This pointed remark made Emma look at Melbourne. It was most uncharacteristic for him to say anything so unkind. She saw that underneath his outward composure, he was struggling to contain his emotions. To renounce Victoria had been his duty, but she reflected that knowing one had done the noble thing did not make it any easier to watch another man take his place. Of course the Prince might not succeed in winning the Queen's heart, but if not, Emma felt certain it would be someone else. Victoria was the sort of woman who flowered in male company, and it was inevitable that she would marry sooner rather than later. Emma knew William had accepted this in his head, but seeing the muscles in his jaw clench as he regarded Albert, she was afraid that his heart did not agree.

Gently she tested him. 'But look at how he is gazing at the Queen, William. I think he is a man of real sensibility.'

'Yes, but what is he looking at?' said Melbourne with asperity. 'A woman? Or the most eligible match in Europe?'

Emma pretended not to hear the bitterness in his tone. 'Surely the Queen is both? If he is to marry her, then he must care for the woman and acknowledge her position. She is not some ordinary girl.'

Melbourne's gaze shifted to Victoria, who was laughing with Ernst. 'No, indeed she is not.'

There was such bleakness in his voice that Emma did not have the heart to say any more.

In the centre of the room, Victoria was out of breath from being whirled around in a figure of eight by Ernst. 'You have learnt the dance very quickly. I can hardly believe this was your first time.'

Ernst smiled. 'That is because I have an excellent teacher. I like your Gay Gordons very much, what a vigorous dance.' Then he said in a lower voice, 'But nothing compares to a waltz. Should they play a waltz you must dance with Albert.

He would benefit greatly from a lesson from someone as graceful as you!'

Victoria looked doubtful. 'I can't imagine Albert waltzing.'

'No? That is because you do not know him as I do,' Ernst said, and smiled at her, showing his teeth. 'I think all Albert needs to waltz is the right partner.'

When the reel finished, Ernst sought out Alfred Paget, who was standing by the musicians acting as master of the revels. 'I think, Lord Alfred, that it is time for something a little more . . . *intime.*'

Alfred did not have the blood of eighteen generations of courtiers in his veins for nothing. 'A waltz, perhaps?'

'Precisely so.'

As Alfred conferred with the musicians, Ernst circled the room to stand next to his brother, who was still on his own with his gaze fixed on Victoria. 'It's time you stopped loitering on the sidelines, Albert. The next one is a waltz. And there is nothing like it if you want to get to know a woman.'

Albert tugged at his cravat and looked down at the floor. 'I think she would much rather dance with you.' He paused. 'Or with Lord Melbourne.'

Ernst shook his head. 'Nonsense, Albert. Look at her!'

Lifting his head slowly, Albert saw that Victoria was smiling at him across the ballroom. Still he hesitated, but Ernst persisted. 'She is waiting for you, Albert.' Ernst put his hand on his shoulder and turned him to face the Queen.

On the other side of the room, Melbourne saw the Queen without a partner and decided to take advantage of her solitude. He stepped in front of her and had the pleasure of seeing her eyes light up. 'Lord M! Thank you for the flowers. They are as beautiful as ever . . .'

Melbourne bowed. 'The glasshouses of Brocket Hall are at your service, Ma'am. Perhaps I could have the pleasure of –' he said, but as he straightened up, he saw that Victoria was no longer listening to him. Without turning round, he knew she was looking at Albert. 'Of seeing you wear them, Ma'am,' he said in a lower voice, then moved to one side so that Albert could reach Victoria unimpeded.

Albert stood in front of Victoria, magnificent in his gold frogged jacket, white breeches, and red-topped boots. His eyes met hers, and with a stiff nod he said, 'May I have the pleasure?'

Victoria held out her hand. Taking it, he moved towards her and put his hand lightly on her waist. Lord Alfred, who had been waiting for this moment, gave the conductor the signal to start playing.

For a moment Victoria thought that Albert would not move, and then to her relief his hand tightened round her waist and together they moved off in time to the music. She realised that he had been waiting for the beat.

For a minute they danced in silence. To her surprise, Victoria found that Albert was an excellent dancer; it was she who had to keep herself from stumbling. Finally, after they had completed a circuit of the room, Victoria dared to look up and say, 'But you dance beautifully, Albert!'

'I think before that I was afraid.'

'Afraid?'

Albert glanced down at her. 'Of appearing ridiculous. It is hard to find the rhythm.' Victoria thought he pressed her hand a little harder. 'But not with you, Victoria.'

Victoria smiled up at him, and as the music swelled around them, Albert smiled back. It was as if a light were shining down on the two of them. Everything else in the room receded, and it was as if they were alone, waltzing together for the first time; but as they circled around to the triangular beat it felt as though they had been dancing together for ever.

The music changed key, and Albert touched the corsage on Victoria's bodice.

'Those flowers . . .' he stopped, and Victoria could see that he was struggling with emotion. 'That scent. It reminds me . . .'

He stopped again and Victoria prompted him gently. 'Reminds you?'

Albert's words came out in a torrent, quite different from his usual careful speech, and she could feel the pressure of his hand gripping her waist. 'My mother used to come in and kiss me goodnight before she went to parties. She would always wear those flowers in her hair.' He blinked, and Victoria could see that there were tears forming in the corner of his eyes.

The waltz came to an end. Victoria reached for her corsage and unpinned it from her bodice. 'Then I give you these, to remind you of your mother.' And still standing as close to him as when they were waltzing, she pressed the gardenias into his unresisting hand.

He inhaled their scent and looked down at the intricate gold embroidery of his jacket. 'But I have no place . . .' He hesitated before bending down and taking what Victoria saw was a knife out of his boot. With a swift movement he cut a rip in his golden jacket, revealing a glimpse of the white flesh beneath, and with great tenderness tucked the gardenias in the hole he had created. 'I will put them here, next to my heart.'

Across the room, Melbourne watched as Albert pressed his gardenias, the ones he had grown at Brocket Hall, in the hope that one day Victoria might wear them, into the hole in his jacket. He felt a strange kind of relief. It had begun, the dance between Victoria and Albert, and that faint flicker of hope that even now he could not quite extinguish must be quenched entirely. Feeling a touch on his arm, he looked up and saw Emma. Somehow he managed to greet her with something like a smile.

Gesturing to Victoria and Albert, he said, 'It seems I was too hasty. It appears that the Prince is quite the Apollo of the ballroom.'

Emma did not move her hand. 'The Queen seems to like dancing with him.'

'Yes.'

'I am glad, as the Queen does love to dance.' Melbourne did not reply. 'It was rather marvellous, the way he cut open his jacket like that. He must have a romantic soul after all.'

Melbourne tried to keep his voice light. 'Yes, I daresay he does.'

Emma squeezed his hand. 'Of course, he doesn't know where the flowers came from.'

Melbourne looked at her and saw the sympathy in her eyes. 'You don't think she told him?'

Emma shook her head. 'There are some things that a woman always keeps to herself.' She smiled at Melbourne. 'I never told Portman, for example, that I only accepted him because the man I really loved could never be my husband.'

'Emma!' He felt tears coming to his eyes, unbidden and unwelcome. 'I had no idea.'

'It was a long time ago, William, and I am not that girl any longer. But I remember how she felt.' She smiled at him. 'And that is how I know that, for Victoria, they will always be your flowers.'

Later that night, Albert sat by the window in his bedroom looking out over the gardens, the dark skeletons of the trees lit by a waning moon. He took the flowers that Victoria had given him and buried his face in their sweet waxy scent. The door opened, and Ernst came in, his face lit up by the candle he was carrying. He walked in and put his hand on his brother's shoulder and squeezed it.

Then he laughed and said, 'Lohlein says that you aren't allowed to rip open any more jackets, Albert. You don't have enough to squander them so recklessly.'

'I am not such a reckless person.'

'Maybe you are changing, Albert.' Ernst sat down on the bed and noticed the miniature that lay on the nightstand. He picked it up and looked at it by the light of the candle.

'I didn't know you had this, Albert. I thought Papa had got rid of everything.'

'I found it in a bureau in the library at Rosenau.'

'You look so like her,' Ernst said.

Albert got up and took the miniature from his brother. 'You know, I can't remember her face. But tonight when I was dancing with Victoria, she was wearing these flowers, and suddenly I remembered Mama coming to kiss us goodnight. She had these flowers in her hair, but I was not allowed to touch them.' He put the picture down. 'How can you miss someone you barely remember, so much?'

Ernst put his arms round his brother. 'It will be different when you and Victoria are married.'

Albert returned his brother's embrace. 'She has to ask me first.'

'Oh, I think she will, don't you?'

'Perhaps. But it is not so simple. Tonight, yes, I felt that we could understand each other, but she is so . . . so fickle, as the English say. I am not the only person she likes.'

Ernst held his brother at arm's length and said with uncharacteristic seriousness, 'You have nothing to fear, Albert. Victoria is not like Mama.'

Albert turned away. 'I hope you are right.'

Chapter Four

THE NOVEMBER SUN SHONE THROUGH THE WINDOW onto Victoria's face as the maid pulled back the curtains. She stretched out her arms like a cat and was smiling broadly when Lehzen came in through the interconnecting door.

'Good morning, Majesty. I see that you slept well.'

Victoria beamed at her. 'Very well.'

She swung her legs to the floor and danced over to Lehzen. Humming the waltz she had danced to last night, she twirled around her governess, Lehzen laughing in protest as Victoria took her hand and made her join in.

'I have decided to go to Windsor,' Victoria said.

Lehzen stopped in mid-twirl and said in surprise, 'Windsor? But you don't like Windsor.'

Victoria did a pirouette and spun round to face Lehzen. 'Of course I like Windsor!'

Lehzen could not hide her consternation. 'When do you want to go?'

Victoria danced over to the window and looked out. 'Immediately. Please make all the arrangements.'

Lehzen frowned and then said slowly, 'Is everyone to come, Majesty? Even the Princes?'

Victoria turned around and laughed. 'Are you suggesting that we leave them behind?'

Lehzen looked at the floor. 'No, Majesty, of course not. If you will excuse me, I must inform the servants.'

Victoria waved her away, and continued to dance round the room, humming to herself, until Skerrett came in to do her hair.

Victoria was walking down the staircase wearing her bonnet and pelisse when she saw Melbourne coming the other way. He looked up at her, surprised by the travelling clothes.

Victoria felt herself blushing for no reason that she could explain. 'Lord M!'

Melbourne bowed, and produced a letter from his pocket. 'I have brought the latest dispatch from Macnaghten in Kabul. I knew you would be anxious to read it.'

Victoria stopped. 'I do want to read it, very much.' She hesitated, and then blurted out, 'But, you see, I have decided to go to Windsor.'

'On a Wednesday, Ma'am?' Melbourne looked at her closely, and Victoria found she could not meet his eyes.

'Yes. I would like some . . . some fresh air.'

'Really?' Melbourne's eyebrows hovered quizzically.

'You know how fond I am of trees.'

'Trees, Ma'am?'

Victoria lifted her chin defiantly. 'Yes. There are some very fine specimens in the Park there.'

'Indeed there are.' Melbourne then added lightly, 'Will Their Serene Highnesses be going too?'

'Yes, of course. Everybody is going.' She took another step down the stairs, and then stopped and looked back at Melbourne. 'We will expect you for dinner.'

Melbourne shook his head. 'I think that might be difficult, Ma'am. You see, I must go to the House to give a statement about Afghanistan.' He paused. 'You will have much to distract you at the Castle. There are the trees,' he smiled, 'and I am sure Prince Albert will want to see the Windsor collection.'

Now it was Victoria's turn to shake her head. 'But I won't be . . . comfortable, unless you are there, Lord M. You always make things so easy.'

Melbourne said gently, 'You know, Ma'am, I believe you might be surprised at how comfortable you will feel. You seemed to be enjoying yourself very much with the Princes last night.'

'But *you* were there last night!' Victoria's face took on its most regal cast. 'You would come for dinner if we were staying here. I don't see why Windsor should be any different. I shall expect you.'

Melbourne bowed, and said with a smile that did not reach his eyes, 'Is that a command, Ma'am?'

Victoria looked up at him. 'Not a command, but a request for your company. Please, Lord M?'

'In that case, Ma'am, I can hardly refuse.'

The line of carriages stretched along the turnpike, flanked by outriders with their plumed helmets. It could have been a small army on the move, but it was only the Queen's immediate household, the Duchess of Kent, King Leopold, and of course the Princes. In the first carriage, Victoria sat holding Dash, with Lehzen at her side and Harriet and Emma sitting across from her. Lehzen, who did not approve of this spontaneous desire to visit Windsor, said for the umpteenth time, 'I expect we won't get there before dark.'

Victoria said, 'Oh, stop grumbling, Lehzen. Think how splendid it will be to walk in the forest.'

Lehzen looked puzzled. 'The forest, Majesty? But we never walk in the forest.'

'Then it is time we did!'

Emma caught Harriet's eye, and they spent the next ten minutes trying to stifle their giggles. They had no difficulty in interpreting Victoria's enthusiasm for all things arboreal, but there was something inexpressibly comic about Lehzen's failure to understand the Queen's behaviour.

Fortunately, they were able to laugh unobserved when the carriage had to stop outside London for a few moments to change horses. Emma said to Harriet, 'The Baroness chooses not to see what is in front of her eyes. The Queen is very taken with the Prince, I think.'

Harriet's face went suddenly serious as she replied, 'But can you blame Lehzen? When the Queen has a husband she will not need the Baroness any more.' Emma remembered Melbourne's face yesterday as the Queen was dancing with Prince Albert, and she too stopped laughing.

In the carriage belonging to the King of the Belgians, Leopold looked at his nephew with approval. 'Victoria is always so reluctant to leave London.' He smiled at Albert. 'I wonder if this sudden enthusiasm for Windsor has anything to do with you?'

Albert looked out of the window. 'I wouldn't know, Uncle.'

Ernst nudged him and laughed. 'Poor Albert. He can't see that this whole excursion has been arranged because he told Victoria that he likes to wander among trees.'

Albert turned to his brother. 'I don't think Victoria would go to such trouble simply to amuse me, Ernst.'

Ernst nudged him again. 'That shows how little you know about young ladies, Albert.'

Albert pushed his brother back. 'How lucky I am that I have you to remind me, Ernst. Otherwise I might begin to think of myself as a ladies' man.'

Ernst said with mock solemnity, 'My dear brother, you may be popular with the ladies, but I feel sure that you will never be a ladies' man.'

'Yes. There are quite enough of those in the family!' said Albert.

Before she left London, Victoria had sent word to Mr Seguier, the Keeper of the Queen's Pictures, asking him to meet her at the Castle. This summons had caused great upheaval in the Seguier household, Seguier wondering if perhaps it was connected to the knighthood that he felt was long overdue, and his wife trying to remember what she had done with her husband's best silk stockings. Fortunately, the stockings had been found, so that Seguier was able to reach the Castle only an hour after the Queen herself. To his surprise, he was ushered into the Presence immediately upon arrival.

Victoria was waiting for him in the Blue Drawing Room, surrounded by her ladies. A corpulent man, Seguier found as he kneeled in front of the Queen to kiss her hands that his breeches were unaccountably tight. He got up rather gingerly and said in the courtly manner that seemed to work with all his aristocratic clients, 'Your Majesty. Such an honour to be summoned to the Castle. It is such a long time since I was here last. Your Uncle George was good enough to ask me down to catalogue his acquisitions; what a connoisseur he was. But since the accession of your Uncle William, I have only been here once – he asked me to find him a picture of a frigate.' Seguier gave a little shudder, and his jowls wobbled. 'So I am delighted to be here again and to offer any assistance it is in my power to give.'

He looked at Victoria expectantly. Could this be the moment when he could at last tell his wife that she was to be Lady Seguier?

But Victoria had another reason for summoning him to the Castle. 'I have discovered, Mr Seguier, that I do not know as much about my collection as I would like. There are so many fine pictures here at the Castle. I was hoping you might be able to tell me a little of their history,' she hesitated, 'in case I should be asked about them.'

Seguier concealed his disappointment with his most knowledgeable smile. Although a knighthood was the pinnacle of his ambitions, he was not unhappy to be asked to take charge of the artistic education of the monarch. If he could guide her taste, then no doubt he would be able to help her expand the collection. There was no better tonic to an art dealer than a royal patron.

'Of course, Ma'am. May I suggest that we start with the Raphael over here? It is a very fine example of his early work. I particularly commend you to look at the brush work around the mouth. Such exquisite command of line and tone. And then, of course, you have the Rembrandt on the opposite wall that I acquired for King George. His Majesty told me he thought it to be one of the finest pieces in the collection.'

As Victoria moved around the room listening attentively to Seguier's discourses on the paintings, Emma and Harriet exchanged glances.

'I never knew that the Queen was so interested in art.,' said Harriet.

'I don't think she has ever even noticed the pictures before,' said Emma.

Both women began to laugh, not noticing Baroness Lehzen, who found herself feeling slightly faint and had to hold onto the edge of a sofa to steady herself.

Windsor Castle felt appreciably colder than Buckingham Palace, and the Princes were grateful for the blazing fires that had been lit in their apartments. Albert was standing in front of the hearth in their sitting room warming his hands, as Ernst wandered about the room trying to get the blood circulating after the long carriage ride.

'Of course I don't consider this a real castle,' said Ernst. 'It's more like what someone thinks a castle ought to be than the real thing. It's too airy and clean. Where are the dungeons? And the cobwebs? When you are married you should bring Victoria to the Rosenau and then she can see what a real castle is like.'

Albert shrugged. 'I think, Ernst, that you are, as the English have it, counting your chickens before they are being hatched. There is no certainty of marriage between myself and Victoria.'

'No, and there is no certainty of spring coming after winter. She likes you, Albert, I can see it in her eyes. I don't think you will have to wait very long.'

Albert looked moodily at the fire. 'But I wish that *I* did not have to wait, as if I were the maiden waiting for a proposal. It is not . . . correct to be so much in another person's power. I would like to make the decision for myself.'

'You could always refuse her,' said Ernst, laughing. 'Of course it feels strange that she is the one who must propose, but I think the rewards are worth it, don't you?'

'I don't know, Ernst, if she likes me or not, or if she will propose, or even if I want to marry her. It is too complicated. Even if I become her husband I will never be the master.'

Ernst was about to reply when the door opened and Penge, the Queen's steward, came in, followed by two footmen carrying tailor's forms, each clothed in a jacket dazzling with gold braid. Penge bowed and with great solemnity said, 'For your Serene Highnesses, with the Queen's compliments.'

Ernst surveyed the navy blue jackets thick with gold and silver embroidery with a quizzical eye. 'Fancy dress?'

Penge said in a tone stiff with reproof, 'The Windsor uniform, Your Serene Highness, was designed by His Majesty King George III for members of,' he paused and then said with emphasis, 'the English court.' With another bow he left the room, followed by the footmen.

Ernst took off his jacket, tried on one of the Windsor jackets, and looked at himself in the mirror. 'Well, no one will miss me in the dark wearing this. I wonder if King George designed it before or after he went mad?' He picked up the other jacket and held it out to Albert. 'Here, put yours on.'

Albert donned the heavy jacket reluctantly. Ernst looked

him up and down. 'I think King George would be very proud to see you in his uniform. Not to mention his granddaughter.'

Albert looked at himself in the mirror and frowned.

'Why the long face, Albert? I think it suits you very well.'

Albert shook his head. 'You will say that I am being ridiculous, but it seems that I am now able to choose nothing for myself, not even my clothes.'

'I don't think you are being ridiculous, just ungrateful. Why, there is enough gold braid on this jacket to buy most of Coburg.'

To Ernst's relief, Albert's lips twitched. 'Are you suggesting that we melt them down and make off with the proceeds?'

'Well, if she doesn't propose, at least you won't come away empty-handed!'

Albert laughed and lunged for his brother, who stepped aside so that Albert fell onto the sofa. Ernst sat down next to him.

'I am so glad you are here,' said Albert, putting his hand on his brother's arm. 'I don't think I could do this on my own.'

Ernst covered Albert's hand with his own. 'I will always be here if you need me.' And then, standing up with a laugh, 'Besides, there are compensations for being your nursemaid. The Duchess of Sutherland, for example. What a profile.'

'I hope you will remember, Ernst, that she is a Duchess and not a serving maid from Coburg.'

Ernst spun around, glittering in his golden jacket. 'Duchess or serving maid, they are not so very different, although the Duchess, I think, has cleaner fingernails.'

Leopold admired himself in the looking glass above the chimney piece in the Blue Drawing Room, where the guests were assembling before dinner. He had not worn the Windsor uniform for many years and was pleased by how well it still fitted him. Catching Emma Portman looking at him from across the room, he was encouraged that he was still the subject of admiring glances from the fairer sex. He did not know, of course, that Emma Portman was smiling not at the man, but at his evident pleasure in his own appearance.

Leopold's happy self-congratulations were punctured by the steward announcing the arrival of Viscount Melbourne. Leopold turned in annoyance; he had not expected the fellow to be at Windsor, and his chagrin was increased by the fact that Melbourne, who was also wearing the Windsor uniform, managed to look very well in it. He gave the Prime Minister a curt nod. 'I did not know you were at the Castle, Lord Melbourne.'

Melbourne shook his head. 'Indeed, I should be at the House. The situation in Afghanistan requires it, but the Queen was most insistent.'

'And you do not care to refuse her?' Leopold's tone was mocking, but Melbourne looked back at him unsmiling, and said simply, 'She is the Queen, sir.'

Leopold did not miss a beat. 'Then you will welcome her marriage.' He smiled. 'It will make your duties less . . . onerous.'

Before Melbourne could answer, the doors opened and the steward announced,

'Their Serene Highnesses, Prince Ernst and Prince Albert.'

Leopold and Melbourne both turned to see Albert and Ernst walk in, resplendent in their gold braid. Leopold's smile grew even broader. 'There are my nephews, and in the Windsor uniform. How very pleasing. Such a mark of favour.'

He turned again to Melbourne, the smile never faltering.

'As I was saying, Lord Melbourne, your life will soon be much easier.' He walked over to greet his nephews.

After glancing at the Princes, Melbourne moved to join Emma Portman on the other side of the room, when the steward announced, 'Her Majesty the Queen.' Victoria entered, followed by Lehzen and the Duchess of Kent.

To his surprise, and secret pleasure, Victoria made straight for Melbourne, smiling happily. 'Oh, Lord M, I am so glad that you were able to come.'

Melbourne inclined his head. 'I should be waiting for dispatches from Kabul,' he smiled at her, 'but I decided that I would rather observe the skirmishes at Windsor.' He glanced over at the Princes, and Victoria laughed delightedly.

'Do you think Windsor is a battlefield, Lord M?'

'Well, there are quite enough men in uniform, Ma'am.'

Melbourne had the satisfaction of hearing Victoria laugh again. But her reaction did not please everyone in the room. Albert, who felt unaccountably piqued by the way that Victoria had greeted Melbourne before anyone else, moved over to the Duchess of Kent, Ernst at his side.

'How charming you look tonight, Aunt. I think the air here must agree with you.'

The Duchess smiled up at him like a wilting flower that has just been watered. 'I am so happy to be here with both of you. How nice it would be if you were here always.'

Seeing Albert talking to her mother made Victoria turn to her cousins and say brightly, 'Albert, Ernst, how well you look in the uniform. I am so glad that we were able to find ones to fit.'

Ernst gave a theatrical bow. 'They are certainly most splendid. Your grandfather clearly spared no expense.'

Victoria looked over at Albert, who did not meet her eyes. 'And you, Albert?'

'I find the gold braid rather heavy.'

Victoria heard the reproach in Albert's voice, but could see no reason for it. So she smiled and said, 'Perhaps you would care to see the pictures here, Albert. I know how fond you are of art.' She went to stand in front of the Rembrandt, a portrait of a Dutch burgher's wife all in black apart from her intricate lace collar.

Victoria began to regurgitate her new-found knowledge. '*Agatha Bas* by Rembrandt, who is generally considered the finest of the Dutch masters. My Uncle George bought this in 1827.'

Albert peered at the painting closely. 'He had excellent taste. The brushwork is exquisite. Look at the lace.'

But Victoria looked at the warts that covered the woman's face and wrinkled her nose. 'It is not very flattering, though.'

Albert looked back at her, and said seriously, 'Perhaps. But it is truthful. What would you prefer? Flattery or truth?' As he said this, his glance flickered over to Lord Melbourne, who was watching them from the other side of the room.

'Do I have to choose?' Smiling warmly at Albert, she said, 'I think I would like the truth presented in the most flattering light possible.'

Albert frowned at her flippant answer, but on the other side of the room Melbourne had to stop himself from smiling.

At dinner Victoria sat between Leopold and Ernst, Albert next to the Duchess, and Melbourne with Emma Portman. 'How strange it is to see you and Prince Albert both wearing the Windsor uniform,' said Emma.

'Are you trying to say that you think it looks better on the

Princes?' said Melbourne, laughing. 'Don't worry, Emma, I know my limitations. The Princes look like demigods and I am a mere mortal.'

'I meant no such thing, William, and false modesty does not become you at all. No one looks more splendid than you do in the uniform. I believe Prince Albert agrees with me; he keeps looking at you.'

'Not with admiration, I think.'

'No. I think his look has something of the green-eyed monster.'

'I think, Emma, that as a lover of intrigue you are trying to create a drama where there is none.'

'Perhaps, but there he is looking at you again.' Melbourne looked over to the other end of the table and saw that Albert's eyes were indeed upon him. Melbourne recognised that the frisson of pleasure the Queen's greeting had given him must have occasioned an equal sense of displeasure in the young Prince. Could Emma be right? Had Albert's perfect nose been put out of joint? Melbourne allowed himself a moment of ignoble satisfaction, or what the Germans called *Schadenfreude*. It made his current predicament just a touch more bearable to know that he was not the only person to feel what Emma called the 'green-eyed monster'.

The men did not linger at their port after dinner, but headed to the drawing room at the first possible opportunity. Albert went straight over to look at the Raphael, and Melbourne, seeing that the Queen was surprised to be ignored in this way, went over to talk to her. They chatted in a desultory way about this and that, but Melbourne saw that Victoria kept glancing at the back that Albert kept so firmly turned on her.

At last she said in a rather louder voice, hoping perhaps to attract Albert's attention, 'Have you read the new novel by Mr Dickens, Lord M? *Oliver Twist?* I have just started and find it uncommonly fascinating.'

Melbourne shrugged. 'As I have no desire to consort with coffin makers, tavern wenches, pickpockets and the like, why, pray, would I want to read about them?'

Victoria smiled. 'But Mr Dickens is so entertaining, Lord M. I think you would enjoy the book very much, although I daresay you would never admit to it.'

Melbourne was about to reply when Albert turned round. Looking at Melbourne with his clear blue eyes, he said, 'I believe that this Mr Dickens writes most accurately about conditions among the poor in London.' He paused and did not bother to disguise the challenge in his voice. 'Don't you wish to know the truth about the country that you govern, Lord Melbourne?'

Victoria gasped, and looked at Melbourne anxiously, but to her relief he smiled and replied in his most aristocratic drawl, 'It may have escaped your notice, Your Serene Highness, but I have been in government for ten years, first as Home Secretary and then as Prime Minister. So I believe I am tolerably well-informed.'

He spoke a little louder than normal, and those around him turned to listen. Seeing the expression on his brother's face, Ernst moved forward and said lightly, 'Albert, our aunt has been asking to hear some of the Coburg folk songs. As your voice is so much better than mine, I thought that if I were to play, you could sing. That is, if Cousin Victoria will indulge us?'

Victoria turned to him with relief spreading across her face. 'I would like nothing more. Mama always talks so fondly about the music of her youth.' She addressed Melbourne eagerly.

'Don't you think that it would be delightful to hear some simple German folk tunes, Lord M?'

'I'm afraid that my appreciation of German music stops with Herr Mozart, Ma'am.' Seeing the tremble in Victoria's lip, he added, 'But as the Princes are so musical, I am sure my education will be greatly enhanced.'

He was rewarded by a smile from the Queen, but his self-sacrifice did not extend to keeping his eyes open for the whole of the recital that followed.

Before retiring for the night, Victoria had engaged her cousins to ride with her in the Great Park the following morning. But when she came down to the stables, Dash at her heels, she found only Ernst chatting easily to Alfred Paget.

When he saw Victoria he said, 'Good morning, my dear cousin. I must apologise for Albert. He woke up very early and thought he would go for a gallop before joining us. I hope you do not object.'

Victoria smiled. 'Not at all. But I hope he doesn't see all the trees I was hoping to show him.'

'Albert can never have enough trees, I find.'

They rode through the ancient woods, their horses' hooves crunching through the gathering leaves, Dash darting about looking for rabbits. The air was still misty, and the hoar frost still clung to the bare twigs. Victoria looked about her and said, 'Albert must have got up really very early.'

Ernst laughed. 'Sometimes I find it hard to believe we are brothers. He is always up at dawn, whereas I have only got out of bed for the honour of riding with you.'

'You do seem to be very different. You are so easy, and Albert is . . . well, he is not easy at all.'

Ernst pulled his horse up and turned to face Victoria, his face uncharacteristically serious. 'I know that sometimes he can be awkward, but you must know, Victoria, that Albert is worth ten of me.'

Victoria was so struck by the expression on his face that she said, 'You care for him very much.'

'Since we lost our mother we have been everything to each other. And although I am the older one, Albert has always looked after me.'

They were interrupted by frantic barking from Dash. A moment later Albert rode into view. He was hatless, with his hair tousled from the ride; his cheeks were flushed, and there was mud on his boots. Victoria was struck by how different he looked to the stiff, gold-braided figure she had seen the night before. As he came up to them, she wondered whether he would smile, and was relieved when she saw the corners of his mouth going up. It was not quite a smile, but it was not the mask of disapproval she dreaded.

'Good morning, Albert, I hope you find the park here more to your taste than the gardens at the Palace.'

Albert pulled up his horse in front of her. 'There is a word we have in German. *Waldeinsamkeit*. A feeling of being at one with the forest.' He gestured to the trees around him. 'I have it here.'

Victoria repeated, '*Waldeinsamkeit*, what a lovely word. I feel I know exactly what it means.'

Albert looked at her, and the softening of his lips became more pronounced. Seeing this, Ernst wheeled his horse's head around and said, 'I had completely forgotten that I arranged to meet Uncle Leopold this morning. Will you excuse me, Victoria, if I go back? You know how punctilious he can be.'

Victoria nodded her assent. Ernst turned to Alfred Paget and, looking back at the long straight ride that led to the Castle whose turrets were clearly visible, said with a wink, 'Lord Alfred, will you be good enough to show me the way?'

Alfred gave him a complicit smile. 'With pleasure, sir.'

'And a guinea on the first to get there to make it interesting?'

'You're on!' The two men set off at a gallop towards the Castle.

Albert and Victoria rode on in silence, apart from the breathy exhalations of the horses, the occasional yelps from Dash, and the screeching of the rooks nesting in the bare branches of the trees. For a moment Victoria thought of Melbourne and the last time she had been alone with a man in a wood. Deciding she must speak, she pointed to a thicket in front of them. 'I believe there is an oak over there that's been here since the Norman Conquest. Would you like to see it?'

'Very much.'

'I think it might be easier on foot.'

Albert jumped off his horse and came over to help Victoria. As he put his hands around her waist to help her down, Victoria felt herself shudder. For a moment their eyes were level, and it felt as if they were looking at each other for the first time. Then, gently, Albert set Victoria on her feet. Tying their horses to a tree, they started to walk towards the wood. But Dash picked up a scent and raced between them after some imaginary rabbit. Victoria hesitated before picking up the skirts of her habit and running after the dog, not checking if Albert was following, but knowing somehow that he would be. They ran through the copse, jumping over branches and dodging the brambles that sprang across their path.

Victoria was running so fast that she did not notice the branch that whipped off her riding hat and the twigs that pulled her hair out of its neat coils, so that it hung loose around her shoulders. As she felt her hair fall, Victoria stopped; it made her feel vulnerable to have it hanging loose. As she began to twist it into a chignon, Albert picked up her hat and handed it to her. Before Victoria could use the hat to cover her hastily rearranged hair, he put up a hand to stop her.

'No, I like to see you like this, unbound. With your hair down, you are not so much a Queen.'

Victoria narrowed her eyes at him. 'I think that might be treason, Albert.'

Albert stared at her in consternation, and then, at last, his face cracked into a smile which transformed his face, wiping away the look he sometimes had of a little boy trying to remember his twelve times table.

'Oh, I see you are teasing me! Ernst is always telling me that I am too serious.'

Victoria looked back at him, and said with just a little bite in her voice, 'And you always tell me I am not serious enough.'

Albert's smile did not falter. 'For a Queen perhaps. But now without your hat, and your hair like this, I think you are just right.'

He leant towards her and put his hand to her face, delicately removed a strand of hair that had fallen across her mouth. She looked up at him and for a breathtaking moment thought that he was about to kiss her, but then he pulled away and they started to walk again through the woods, Victoria agonisingly conscious of his body next to hers.

Albert looked up at the canopy of trees above them. 'When I was a little boy I was imagining that the trees were my friends.'

'How funny. I used to talk to my dolls.'

Albert looked down at her. 'We were not such happy children, I think.'

Victoria heard the sadness in his voice. 'Albert?'

'Yes?'

Victoria said in a rush, 'What happened to your mother? I only know that she died when you were young.'

Albert was silent. Victoria saw the shadows coming back to his face and wished she hadn't mentioned it, but then he continued, 'She ran away from my father, just before my fifth birthday. With her equerry. She died a few years later, but I never saw her again.'

Albert turned his face away from her, but Victoria put her hand on his arm. 'How awful. You were so young, and you must have missed her so much.'

Albert slowly turned to look at Victoria. 'You know, when I see Aunt Victoire looking at you with so much love in her eyes, I feel jealous. No one is there to look at me so.'

Victoria felt for his hand and squeezed it. 'That is not true, Albert. You have Ernst, and now, well, now you have . . .' But at that moment the leafy ruminations of the forest were pierced by an agonised yelp of an animal in pain.

Victoria froze. 'Did you hear that? It sounds like Dash.'

Albert was already running in the direction of the noise. Victoria picked up her skirts and hurried after him. She saw him kneeling on the ground, but without turning round he said, 'Stay there, Victoria! You should not see this.'

But Victoria could not ignore her pet's cries. As she knelt down beside him, she gasped in horror. Dash's leg had been caught in the steel jaws of a poacher's trap; the paw was limp and there was blood on the ground.

'Oh, how wicked!' she said and cradled Dash in her arms as Albert pried the trap apart with a stick and gently took out Dash's injured paw.

Victoria looked at the mangled limb and started to cry. 'Oh, my poor little Dashy!' She felt her dog's rough tongue licking her hand. 'He will never walk again.'

'No, no. I think it is broken, but it is possible for it to mend,' said Albert. 'I will make a – how do you call it in English – a frame for the leg to mend.'

Shrugging off his jacket, he spread it out on the ground and gestured for Victoria to sit on it. 'Now you must hold him tight while I am making the . . .'

'Splint.'

'*Jawohl*, the splint.'

'But we have no bandages.'

Albert took his knife out of his boot and with a quick movement cut a rent in his shirtsleeve and ripped it off. Victoria saw his sinewy arm, the white skin covered in fine gold, the suggestion of dark hair in the armpit. Dash whimpered as Albert ripped the linen in half, and Victoria had to hold the trembling animal as Albert wrapped the linen round two sticks to keep the broken leg in place. He worked quickly, and Victoria could see that he was trying as hard as he could not to cause Dash any more pain. At last it was done. The broken leg was held tight and Dash was already licking the linen bandage trying to worry it off. Albert sat back on his heels and announced, 'I think this will be sufficient for now.'

Victoria kissed Dash on the nose, and then looked up at Albert with wet eyes. 'I am so grateful to you. Dash means so much to me. When I was growing up at Kensington, he was my only real friend. Whatever happened, I knew that Dash would always be there.'

Albert put a hand out and pushed a lock of hair away from her tear-stained cheek. 'But now it is different, I think?'

Victoria felt her cheek burn under the touch of his hand. She looked down to hide her confusion. 'Oh yes, I have Lord M now . . . and my ladies, of course.'

As she said Melbourne's name, Albert stood up and the tender look on his face vanished. Looking down at her, he said in a voice that she had not heard before, 'I wish, Victoria, that you had not been so much with Lord Melbourne. He is not serious.'

Victoria felt the blood rushing to her face. Still clutching Dash, she struggled to her feet so that she could answer him with dignity. 'Lord Melbourne does not choose to appear serious. It is the English manner. But he is a man of great feeling.'

Albert picked up his jacket and put it on, before turning to Victoria and saying, 'Then perhaps you should marry him.'

Dash whimpered as Victoria tightened her grip on him. She stared back at Albert. 'That is not possible.'

Albert turned away from her as if he was about to go, but turned back, his words tumbling out in an impassioned torrent. 'Do you know what I saw the other day near that fine thoroughfare called Regent Street? A child, maybe three or four years old, selling matches, one at a time. Your Lord Melbourne chooses not to look at these things, but I must. That is the question, Victoria. Do you want to see things as they are, or as you would like them to be?'

If she had not been holding Dash in her arms, Victoria felt that she would have slapped Albert's self-righteous face. Her voice trembling with fury, she said, 'How dare you! Do you imagine that I am a doll waiting to be turned this way or that? May I remind you that while you were looking at paintings in Italy, I was ruling this country. And yet you have been here a few days and assume you know my people better than I do. I am the Queen of England and I don't need you to tell me what to think!' Hearing the emotion in his mistress's voice, Dash gave a bark of sympathy.

Albert looked back at her, his blue eyes icy now. 'No, that is Lord Melbourne's job.'

Chapter Five

THE CARRIAGE HIT A POTHOLE, AND LEOPOLD narrowed his eyes at Albert, as if he were personally to blame for every rut in the turnpike from Windsor to London. He had had such hopes of the impromptu visit to Windsor, and had been delighted when Ernst told him that he had left Victoria and Albert riding alone in the Great Park. Surely they would return from their ride an engaged couple?

But when Albert and Victoria returned to the Castle a good hour later, Albert leading the horses as Victoria held her lapdog, not only were they not engaged; they were barely on speaking terms. Victoria went straight inside, carrying Dash, and Albert got back on his horse and rode off into the Park. An hour later the order was given that the royal party would be returning to Buckingham Palace that very afternoon.

There was another massive jolt to the carriage, and Leopold could not hold his tongue any longer. 'I don't understand what you and Victoria were doing this morning. You were gone for hours and then you returned with nothing. Nothing! I can hardly believe you are a Coburg. Why, Ernst would have taken her to bed by now.'

Sitting next to Albert, Ernst frowned at his uncle. He could see his brother's unhappiness and did not want him to make it worse. 'You forget, Uncle, that it is Victoria who must decide whether they are to be married, not Albert. It is not an easy position for him.'

'Nonsense! You know as well as I do that women are like thoroughbreds; they must be handled with care, but once you know how to stroke them in the right way they will do anything you want.'

'But a Queen is not an ordinary woman,' said Ernst.

'All women are the same, in my experience. When I met Charlotte, she was not a Queen, it is true, but she was heir to the throne, and she proposed to me after only three days. Of course, I was a very fine-looking young man, but so is Albert. Perhaps I was more charming, but Albert could be that too, if only he would set his mind to it.'

There was a thwack as Albert slammed his hand against the carriage window. 'Enough!' He turned to Leopold, his eyes blazing. 'This is my future, not yours, and I have decided to go back to Coburg.'

Leopold was about to reply, but a look from Ernst stopped him. Perhaps it would be better to let his brother reason with Albert; they were so close, after all. So he settled back into his seat, pulled his hat over his eyes, and tried to make the interminable journey go faster by going to sleep.

Victoria's coach was the first to arrive at the Palace. Still carrying Dash, Victoria went straight up to her bedroom and let it be known that she would not be coming down for dinner.

She lay on the bed with Dash beside her, running her hands

over the spaniel's silky ears. 'Oh Dash, why is everything so difficult?' Her injured dog licked her hand in reply.

She stared at the gilded cartouches on the ceiling. That morning in the woods she had felt so close to Albert; when he had told her about his mother, she had wanted to embrace him and tell him that she would make that hurt disappear. But then – she squirmed with the injustice of it – he had made that unreasonable attack upon Lord M, a man he hardly knew. She could not bear it. How could she offer her heart to Albert if he could not understand how much Melbourne meant to her? She twisted Dash's ear in frustration, and the little dog yelped.

'Oh, sorry, my darling Dashy. I didn't mean to hurt you.' She saw the improvised splint made from Albert's shirt and remembered his white skin gleaming in the pale November light.

The door opened, and Lehzen walked in, her eyes wide with drama. 'I am sorry to disturb you, Majesty, but the Princes' valet has been asking about the sailings from Dover. I thought I should tell you that they were leaving. But perhaps you already knew?'

Victoria shook her head. Albert was leaving? She put her hand over her eyes.

Lehzen sat down on the bed beside her and put her arm around her. 'It is for the best, Majesty. I think that Prince Albert does not show you enough respect.'

Victoria pulled away from her. 'You know nothing about it, Lehzen. And now I should like to be left alone. I have a headache.'

'A headache, Majesty? Shall I fetch Sir James?'

'Stop fussing! Can't you see I just want to be left in peace!'

Lehzen picked up her skirts and fled.

In the Princes' sitting room in the north wing, Albert was throwing his books into a trunk, relishing the thud as they hit the bottom. Ernst came in and, seeing what his brother was doing, threw up his hands in exasperation, 'You are being childish, Albert. You can't just leave because you and Victoria had a squabble.'

Albert threw an English dictionary into his trunk with particular vehemence. He looked up at his brother. 'Victoria and I are not suited. This marriage is convenient to everyone except us.'

Ernst came to stand between his brother and the trunk so that Albert was forced to look at him. He put a hand on his brother's shoulder. 'You say that, but you like her, Albert, I know you do, and she likes you. She blushes when she looks at you.'

Albert threw off his brother's hand. 'I think Victoria likes many people. Lord Melbourne, for example.'

Ernst shook his head and said slowly, 'You are jealous of Lord Melbourne? He is old enough to be her father.'

'But she smiles at him in a way that is not correct. Perhaps she cannot marry him, but I will not be second best.'

Ernst sighed and gripped Albert by both shoulders. 'Believe me Albert, I have seen the way Victoria looks at you. You will never be second best. Perhaps there was a little girl who liked her Lord Melbourne, but Victoria is a woman now, and she likes you, not some old man.'

Albert looked at him, then went to the bed and picked up his coat. 'Where are you going now?' Ernst asked.

Albert turned round. 'To have my daguerreotype taken. I should like to have one souvenir of my visit.'

'Then I shall come with you. I too would like a souvenir,

and I believe there are a few young ladies who would not be sorry to have my likeness.'

'Women! That is all you think about.'

'They are not the enemy, Albert,' Ernst said, laughing. Catching sight of Albert's face, he continued in a different tone: 'You know, I saw her once, after she left.'

Albert looked at him. 'Mama?'

'Yes. We were playing in the park in Coburg. It had been snowing, I remember, and we were throwing snowballs at each other. When I was running after you, I looked up and saw her on the terrace that overlooks the gardens on the town side. She was all bundled up and wearing a veil, but I knew at once it was her. I ran up to the terrace, but you can't get to the town side from the Palace, so all I could do was stand there and wave. She waved back, not a big wave but a little one like this,' he raised his hand in a small sad gesture, 'and then she lifted her veil.' Ernst stopped and swallowed before continuing. 'Her face was wet, Albert. I have never forgotten those tears.' He put his fingers to his nose, trying to hold back his own emotion.

'Why did you never tell me before?'

'I don't know. I thought it would be easier for you to forget her if you didn't know. And I wanted to protect you. But now I see that I was wrong. She didn't want to leave us, Albert, but she had no choice. You know what Papa is like. This was her only chance of life. And I know she would have taken us with her if she could.' Albert stared at the ground, biting his lip. 'She loved us, Albert, so much. And it broke her heart to leave us. If you had seen her face that day.'

Albert looked up. 'Why did she never write?'

'I am sure she did, but do you think Papa would allow us to read those letters?'

Albert was trembling. Ernst put his arms around him and held him tightly. 'Not all women leave, Albert.'

He felt his brother's chest heave with emotion, and then in panting breaths, 'I . . . wish . . . I . . . could . . . be . . . sure.'

Ernst relaxed his grip and held his brother at arm's length so that he could see his face. 'You know so much more than me about everything, but on women I am the authority. I can tell you that Victoria loves you, Albert. If you marry her, and I hope so much that you will, she will never ever leave you. Perhaps you will find diversions,' he saw Albert's face, 'or maybe not; you are not like me. But Victoria will not waver. You have the chance to be happy, little brother, and for my sake alone, you must take it.'

When Alfred Paget told him that he had left the Queen with Prince Albert in the Great Park, Melbourne had ordered his carriage. He knew that he should stay to hear them announce their engagement, but he found he could not bear to. He had gone straight to the House and from there to his club. He had lost a good deal of money at whist, a loss he found mordantly pleasing as it disproved the adage about being unlucky at cards, lucky in love. He was, it seemed, unlucky in everything. He was half-cut when he finally got back to Dover House.

His valet found him in the morning stretched on the sofa in the library, surrounded by papers and texts written in Ancient Greek, a language that the valet had come to recognise in his ten years of working for Lord Melbourne. The valet slid the coffee under his master's nose, knowing from experience that its smell was the way of waking him that had the least violent results.

Melbourne stirred and blearily reached for the coffee. 'Has anything come from the Queen?'

The valet shook his head. 'But I understand that the royal household came back to London last night, my Lord.'

Melbourne put his cup down in surprise. 'The Queen is at the Palace?'

'Yes, my Lord.'

'But there has been no letter from her.'

'No, my Lord.'

Melbourne was silent. He had expected Victoria to write to him at once to announce her engagement. She was not someone who liked, or was indeed capable of, keeping things to herself. But perhaps she was waiting to tell him in person.

He drained the last of the coffee and forced his creaking limbs to stand up. His head throbbed, and he felt a wave of nausea, perhaps the result of the excesses of the night before, but was also dread at what was to come. Still, if nothing else, he knew his duty.

'I must go to the Palace. Do what you can to make me look presentable.'

The valet bowed his head in sympathy; no man could keep a secret from this particular valet. 'I will do my utmost, my Lord.'

An hour later, Melbourne, clean-shaven and bedecked in linen so fiercely starched it dug into the flesh of his neck, was walking up the grand staircase of Buckingham Palace. He saw Lehzen coming towards him and looked at her face for some clue as to the engagement, but the Baroness's face was demure as usual, her eyes cast down, her lips faintly pursed.

'Good morning, Baroness.' Lezhzen gave him a modest curtsey. 'I must say I was surprised to find the Queen at the

Palace today. I rather thought that she would stay at the Castle a while longer.' He raised an eyebrow. 'To indulge her new passion for trees.'

The Baroness gave him a humourless smile. 'I do not think that she found anything very agreeable in the forest, Lord Melbourne.'

'I see. Thank you, Baroness,' and Melbourne found himself almost running to the top of the stairs. He saw at once from the set of Victoria's shoulders that Lehzen had been right. Whatever had happened between the Queen and her cousin in the Great Park, it had not been a proposal of marriage.

'Good morning, Ma'am.' As he bent over her outstretched head he said brightly, 'I have good news. The army has reached Kabul without opposition.'

'That is splendid,' Victoria said without a trace of enthusiasm. Melbourne saw with a pang that her eyes were red and swollen from weeping. But he carried on in the same bright tone, hoping she might respond to him, 'At least the army will have somewhere to spend the winter. I confess that I have been most uneasy. The Khyber Pass is uncommon cold, I hear, and while every army must bear its losses, they should not be vanquished by the weather.'

Victoria's eyes remained dull; she was looking at him but he knew that she did not see him. Taking a deep breath, he said in a gentler voice, 'Forgive me, Ma'am, but is there something wrong?'

She turned away from him and said in a clipped voice, 'The Princes are going back to Coburg.'

Melbourne clasped his hands in front of him. 'I see. And you would rather they stayed?'

Victoria whirled round, her face animated at last. 'No! Well, maybe.' She was looking directly at Melbourne now, and he could see the confusion in her eyes as well as the desire. 'Albert is so difficult!'

He hesitated before replying. This was the decisive moment. He could push just a little, and the Clockwork Prince would scuttle back to his tinpot kingdom. He and Victoria could resume their easy relationship. She would have her Lord M by her side, and he, well, he would be as content as he had ever been.

As this vision of the future shimmered before him, he said cautiously, 'You have very different temperaments. The Prince strikes me as a man who enjoys his own company, and indeed his own opinions.'

He saw at once that she was not listening to his words, and the vision of them walking arm in arm through the Palace gardens vanished.

Victoria blurted it out. 'He thinks I am too friendly with you.'

He felt it like a blow to his chest, and it was a moment before he could reply. 'And what do you think?'

Victoria turned her head this way and that, as if she was trying to shake off a fly. At last she looked at him and said, 'I don't know. Albert always looks at me as if I have done something wrong.' Melbourne waited for her next words, his heart hammering in his chest. 'But even so . . .' Her eyes were imploring. 'I would like him to smile at me.'

Melbourne knew what she was asking for. Willing himself to speak as lightly as he had always done, he said, 'The Prince does not smile very often.' He forced himself to continue.

'But if you want him to smile at you, Ma'am . . . then I don't see how he can resist.'

The smile erupted across her face. 'Do you really think so, Lord M?'

'I do, Ma'am.' Her eyes were shining and before Melbourne could stop himself he said, 'Only a fool would turn you away, after all.'

With a small rapid gesture, she took his hand and squeezed it. They looked at each other for a long moment, the air between them full of all the things that could never be said, and then she dropped his hand and ran out of the room.

As he stood on the Palace steps waiting for his carriage to be brought round, Melbourne saw the unmistakable figures of the Princes with their new-fangled frock coats walking through the Marble Arch.

The carriage pulled up; the footman was already lifting down the steps. Melbourne was about to step in and avoid an encounter with the Princes, until he thought of what Albert had said to Victoria and knew where his duty lay.

'Good morning, Your Serene Highnesses.' Albert's nod of acknowledgment could not have been stiffer if he had really been made of clockwork, thought Melbourne, but he perse-vered. 'I am just on my way to the House, and I remember, sir,' he looked at Albert, 'that you expressed your desire to see it.'

Albert tried to hide his surprise. 'That is correct. It is a British institution that I admire greatly. But I think you told me, Lord Melbourne, that I would have to go – how did you put it' – he glared at Melbourne – 'incognito?'

Melbourne did not flinch, but smiled back. 'I think, sir, that under my protection you will be safe even from the most uncouth Tories.'

As Albert hesitated, Melbourne looked at Ernst. 'Won't you

persuade your brother to come, sir? I think he would find it most enlightening.'

He caught Ernst's eye and saw, to his relief, a flicker of comprehension. Really, these brothers could not be more different.

'We shall certainly come. You are always talking, Albert, about the place where tyranny was banished. I would like to see it even if you don't.'

Albert shifted from foot to foot, torn between his hostility to Melbourne and his desire to see the Mother of Parliaments. 'But we have so much to do if we are to leave tomorrow.'

'Nonsense,' said Ernst. 'It is not as if we have a pressing appointment in Coburg. I think they will manage without us quite well for another day or even two.'

Albert's eyes slid over to Melbourne, who gave his blandest smile. 'It is true that I wish very much to see your Parliament. If it would not be too great an inconvenience, Lord Melbourne, then I shall accept your kind offer.' This little speech came out painfully, as if squeezed out of him by a giant hand, but Melbourne pretended not to notice and gestured affably towards his carriage.

'Please join me, and I will tell you something of the history along the way.'

Victoria had spent the hours since her interview with Melbourne trying to avoid her mother. She very much did not want to talk to her about Albert. She thought the Picture Gallery would be the safest place, as the Duchess had no reason to go there, but to her dismay she heard her mother's voice coming from the staircase. She turned to go the other way and saw that Leopold was coming towards her. Trapped between two Coburgs, she resigned herself to the inevitable lecture.

'Oh, Drina, there you are.' The Duchess waved her hands so that her ringlets fluttered in the breeze of her own making, 'Albert and Ernst are going back to Coburg.' She put her head on one side, and said plaintively, 'I was so happy with them here.'

Leopold came to stand in front of Victoria. 'And they are leaving with no engagement.'

Victoria lifted her chin and caught a glimpse of Elizabeth I over her uncle's shoulder. 'Albert is not a British subject. I could not stop him going even if I wanted to.'

Leopold shrugged and his hand wandered to his toupee as if to check that at least one thing was in its rightful place. 'Of course you can stop him. All you have to do is propose.'

'Oh, is that all? I am afraid, Uncle, that it is not so easy.' To her horror she found her voice was not steady.

Leopold looked at her in surprise. 'But why not?'

Victoria looked at the floor and then back at her uncle, holding his gaze until the Duchess broke in. 'Yes, why not, Victoria? I know it is not the custom for ordinary women to propose, but you are a Queen and it must come from you. Why do you hesitate?'

The sound of her mother's voice made Victoria snap, so that she spoke without thinking. 'Because I am not sure he will say yes.'

To her surprise, Leopold took her hand, and in a voice stripped of his usual pomposity said quietly, 'No, you cannot be sure. But at least you know that if Albert says yes, it will be with his heart.'

Victoria realised that her uncle, for once, was right. He continued, 'But you will never know unless you ask him, Victoria.'

Victoria looked at him and then walked back to her apartments. She sat down at her dressing table and examined her face. There were dark shadows under her eyes, and she could feel an ominous bump on her chin. If she asked anyone, they would say she looked lovely, but Victoria knew that today she did not look her best.

'Can I get you anything, Ma'am?' Seeing that her voice had made the Queen start. Skerrett began to apologise. 'Oh, I am sorry, Ma'am. I didn't mean to startle you.'

'No, that's all right.' Victoria touched the plaits that circled her ears. 'I don't think my hair is quite right today. It is too . . . too . . .' she trailed off.

Hearing the confusion in the Queen's voice, and guessing its origins – everyone was talking about the imminent departure of the Princes – Skerrett said, 'Perhaps a low chignon at the back of the head. For a softer silhouette?'

Victoria caught Skerrett's eye in the mirror. 'Softer? Yes, why not.'

'With perhaps some flowers at the back?'

'Flowers?' Victoria smiled. 'I should like to wear gardenias in my hair.'

'And this, gentlemen, is Westminster Hall, the oldest part of the Palace that remains. It has been used as a court of law since medieval times.' Melbourne ushered the Princes into the great vaulted chamber. 'But now as you see, it is being used for record keeping. We are pushed for space at the moment.

There was a great fire a few years ago and until the Palace is rebuilt we must make do.' He gestured at the army of clerks beneath them.

Albert was looking up at the massive wooden hammerbeams. 'I believe that is the place where King Charles was tried by his people?'

'That is correct, sir. He was sentenced to death as a tyrant and a traitor.'

'A great moment. The victory of the people.' Albert gestured out into the hall.

'Indeed.' Melbourne smiled. 'But I am not altogether comfortable with regicide.'

Ernst said quickly, 'Neither am I! I want my people to love me.'

'A responsible monarch has nothing to fear,' said Albert. 'But he –' he hesitated – 'or she must know that they rule on behalf of their people.'

Melbourne nodded a trifle wearily. After listening to Albert's views on the conduct of government for an hour, he was beginning to lose patience. Still, he reminded himself, he had not come here for his own amusement. He had a duty to perform. He turned to Albert with a smile.

'Very neatly put, sir. The hard-won balance between Crown and Parliament is the great glory of the British constitution. And to serve as Prime Minister has been the greatest privilege of my life.' He paused, feeling his way. 'I wish that the Queen shared your feelings. I fear sometimes that she finds the un-ruliness of our parliamentary system distasteful.'

Albert looked at him closely. 'I thought she followed you in everything, Lord Melbourne.'

Melbourne shrugged. 'Once perhaps, but now that she has

settled in to being Queen, I find she ignores me more and more.'

Out of the corner of his eye he saw Albert's brother glance at him. 'I sympathise with you, Lord Melbourne,' Ernst said with a look that showed that he understood the direction of travel. 'I am most fond of my cousin, but I understand that she only listens when there is something she wants to hear.'

Melbourne nodded, and sighed. 'I have done my best, but my Ministry cannot last for ever, and then I will return thankfully to Brocket Hall. I must finish my life of St Chrysostom. In the end, to add to the sum of human knowledge is the only thing a man can be truly proud of.'

Both brothers were looking at him, but it was Ernst who spoke, his voice sympathetic. 'It will be hard for the Queen, I think, when you go.'

Melbourne swallowed before turning to Albert. 'Perhaps. But in truth it is time for me to retire.'

Albert stared back at Melbourne, and after a second gave him an imperceptible nod.

'And now if you will excuse me, gentlemen, I must return to the House.' Melbourne bowed to each of the Princes in turn, and walked away. Albert continued to gaze at the ceiling, but Ernst saw the Prime Minister take a handkerchief from his pocket and blow his nose with extreme violence as he left the hall.

'Which dress will you wear, Ma'am? The blue silk or the pink organdie?'

Victoria stood in her corset and petticoats, looking at the two dresses that Skerrett was holding out. She had worn the blue silk on the night she had danced with Albert. It was most becoming, but she had never worn the pink, and at this moment she wanted to look different.

She pointed to the pink dress, and put her arms in the air so that Skerrett could lower it over her head. As the dresser fastened the hooks of the bodice, Victoria felt the waxy blooms that flanked the chignon at the back of her head. 'So clever of you to find gardenias.'

Skerrett permitted herself a little laugh that hinted at the desperate lengths she had been to that day to procure hothouse flowers in the middle of winter. 'It wasn't easy, Ma'am.'

'I suppose not. Lord Melbourne grows them at Brocket Hall, of course.' She paused. 'But I could not ask him.'

Skerrett said nothing. She understood, of course, why the Queen could not call on Lord Melbourne's hothouses, but she also knew she must never by a flicker reveal that understanding. She drew the laces of the skirt tight and tied them in a bow, tucking them under the hem of the bodice, and stepped back. 'There. Are you happy with your choice, Ma'am?'

Victoria walked over to the cheval mirror and looked at her reflection. The gauzy dress seemed to hover about her, the pink reflecting a rosy light over her skin. She could smell the lush velvety scent of the gardenias. She bit her lips. The image in front of her was not a Queen, but a woman.

'Yes, Skerrett. I believe I am.'

Brodie knew that running was forbidden in the Palace, but thought in this instance he would break the rules. To walk from the Queen's private apartments to the north wing took a good ten minutes, and in his opinion, he did not have ten minutes to spare.

He sprinted along the corridor to the Princes' apartments and, knocking lightly, opened the door. Prince Ernst was lying on the chaise longue smoking a cigar, while Prince Albert sat at the writing desk.

'I have a message for Prince Albert from the Queen.' Brodie stopped. Although Skerrett had sworn him to secrecy, like every servant in the Palace, he knew the significance of what he was about to say. 'She is waiting for you in the Picture Gallery, sir.'

Albert did not run as he made his way to the other side of the Palace. Indeed, when he got to the grand staircase he hesitated for so long that Ernst, who had been following him at a discreet distance, was forced to reveal himself.

'You don't want to keep her waiting, little brother.'

'No. She is the Queen, after all.'

Ernst put his hand on his brother's arm. 'Victoria is also a woman, Albert.'

Albert pushed a lock of hair out of his eyes. 'Maybe she wants to say goodbye.'

Ernst laughed. 'Yes, I am sure that is why she has sent for you.' He added, 'I know you are scared, Albert, but remember she will be too.' He gave his brother a little push towards the staircase. 'Now off you go.'

Although it was only five o clock, it was already dark outside and all the candles had been lit. As Albert walked through the hall towards the Picture Gallery, he caught sight of his reflection in the looking glass glowing in the light from the candelabra. He pushed the errant lock back from his forehead again and walked into the gallery.

She was standing with her back to him, in front of a picture of Elizabeth, Dash at her feet. The floor creaked as he walked towards her, and she gave a little shriek and Dash started to growl. She whirled around in a flurry of pink and looked as if she had never seen him before. Albert took another step towards her. 'Forgive me for surprising you, Victoria.'

Victoria continued to stare at him, her lip quivering.

Albert took yet another step towards her. 'I was told that you wanted to see me.'

Dash growled again, which seemed to rouse Victoria from her trance. She looked up at Albert, and frowning with effort, she said, 'I want to ask you something, Albert, but before I do, I must be sure that you will not mind me asking.'

Albert heard the trembling in her voice and took one more step towards her. At once he was overwhelmed by that scent which reminded him of all he had loved and lost.

'You are wearing those flowers again.'

'Yes, they are called gardenias.'

'Gardenias.' Albert rolled the word around his mouth. He was so close now that he could now see the tiny bump on her chin. 'May I?' Victoria shuddered her assent as he leant forward to smell the flowers. He drank in the waxy, voluptuous perfume and said with a sigh, 'That scent, it makes me feel safe.'

Victoria opened her eyes wide. 'Really?'

Albert nodded, unable to speak. Victoria swallowed. 'Shall I ask my question now?'

'I wish you would.'

Victoria bit her lip and then, as if she had learnt the words by heart, 'Albert, will you do me the honour?' She stopped and shook her head. 'No, that sounds wrong.' She looked away and back at him and then in her clear voice said, 'Albert, will you marry me?'

Albert felt the smile spreading across his face. 'That depends.'
'On what?'

He could hear the surprise and pique in her voice, and for a second he enjoyed his moment. 'On whether you will let me kiss you.'

Victoria's eyes widened and now she smiled. 'If I do, will you say yes?'

Albert shook his head. 'I must kiss you first.'

Victoria's lips parted and she said in a whisper, 'Very well.' Closing her eyes, she raised her face to his.

The smell of the flowers, the weight of Victoria against him, the flickering candlelight – Albert felt his heart give way. As he pressed his lips to hers and felt them respond with such eagerness, he knew he had found the piece that had always been missing. He put his hands around her waist and pulled her to him, and they kissed until they had to stop to breathe.

Victoria caught his hand and said, laughing with excitement, her lips swollen with desire, 'So. Are you going to accept my proposal? I do not intend to go down on one knee, you know.'

Albert took his face in her hands. 'My heart is yours, Victoria.' He kissed her again, harder and longer than before. 'For me this is not a marriage of convenience.'

Victoria leant back to look at him. With a flash of queenliness, she said, 'No, I think it will be a marriage of inconvenience.'

She leant in so that her lips were next to his. 'But I have no choice.'

Albert picked her up by the waist so that she was looking down at him, and said with joy, 'Neither do I.'

Dash began to bark at the man manhandling his mistress, but for once in his life, he was ignored.

Acknowledgments

This novel was written as I was writing the television series *Victoria*, so I must thank all the cast, particularly Jenna Coleman, Rufus Sewell and Tom Hughes for bringing my characters to glorious life, and to Damien Timmer and Rebecca Keane for teaching me how to tell a story on screen. The inimitable Hope Dellon and Imogen Taylor, my US and UK editors, have reminded me how to tell a story on the page, and my agents, the glorious Caroline Michel and Michael McCoy have mopped up many tears along the way.

Thanks to Professor David Cannadine who introduced me to Victoria's diaries when I was a student at Cambridge and to Andrew Wilson and Helen Rappaport for their support with all things Victorian. Undying gratitude to Rachel Street for support with the twenty-first century.

I am lucky to have a father, Richard Goodwin, who is also my most enthusiastic reader, and a best friend Emma Fearnhamm who kept her lecture notes from university.

Thanks to my daughters: Ottilie who kept me sane and was always right, Lydia who provided all the source material I could ever need for a teenage queen and to Marcus who has taken me to the Isle of Wight, twice.